Bronwyn Parry's manuscript for *As Darkness Falls*, then titled *Falling into Darkness*, was awarded the 2007 Golden Heart Award by the Romance Writers of America. She holds an honours degree in History and English and for twelve years she worked in senior professional development positions, writing a wide range of educational materials. Bronwyn is currently undertaking a PhD, researching online communities of romance readers and writers. She is a member of the Romance Writers of Australia and the Romance Writers of America. *As Darkness Falls* is the first in a proposed series of three loosely linked novels; the second, *Dark Country*, will be coming soon from Piatkus. Bronwyn lives in New South Wales.

Visit the author's website at www.bronwynparry.com

As Darkness Falls
BRONWYN
PARRY

An Hachette UK Company
www.hachette.co.uk

www.piatkus.co.uk

piatkus

PIATKUS

First published in Australia and New Zealand in 2008 by Hachette Australia
(An imprint of Hachette Australia Pty Limited)
First published in Great Britain in 2009 by Piatkus

A CIP catalogue record for this book
is available from the British Library

ISBN 978-0-7499-4292-2

Printed and bound in Great Britain by Clays Ltd, St Ives plc

Papers used by Piatkus are natural, renewable and recyclable
products sourced from well-managed forests and certified
in accordance with the rules of the Forest Stewardship Council.

Mixed Sources
Product group from well-managed
forests and other controlled sources
www.fsc.org Cert no. SGS-COC-004081
© 1996 Forest Stewardship Council
FSC

Piatkus
An imprint of
Little, Brown Book Group
100 Victoria Embankment
London EC4Y 0DY

For my parents

My father, who has demonstrated every day of his life what true courage and heroism are; and

My mother, who has a beautiful, giving spirit, and the grace to look beyond the surface of people to their hearts.

PROLOGUE

No, not this.

Detective Sergeant Isabelle O'Connell dragged up every ounce of self-discipline to halt the cry of denial, and it lodged, unsounded, in her throat. She closed her eyes against the sight as tears that couldn't be shed scalded her eyelids.

Nearby, her colleagues cleared their throats, muttered curses, avoided looking at each other.

The heavy mantle of failure kept them all quiet. Seven days, the child had been missing. Seven long, hellish days and nights of searching and hoping and feverishly following any prospect of a lead, no matter how weak, desperately trying to find some trace of her.

And now this.

The fact of the girl's small body, dumped in a hollow in front of them, was horrific enough. But the single gunshot to the head that had killed her was clearly less than twenty-four hours old. She'd been alive for at least six of those days, and they'd failed to find her. They'd failed *her*.

Superintendent Barrington pulled himself together first. 'I'd better go and inform the parents,' he said, his voice gruff and constrained. 'Detective Fraser, get Forensics up here, now. You two,' he indicated two of the uniformed police, 'secure the scene. Nobody, but nobody, is to touch a thing until they get here. O'Connell, you'll come with me.'

Isabelle stifled the instinct to run and nodded mutely. As senior female officer on the case, of course she had to accompany him for the nightmare task. Ten years on the job, and each time it became worse, not easier. This time, she knew the parents, had grown up beside them in this small town. Somehow she had to find the courage to face them and deliver this news. Somehow tell Sara, whom she'd sat beside in fifth grade, that her only child was dead.

Cope with it. You have to do this.

Despite the orders, no one moved.

Steve Fraser, his face flushed, burst out angrily, 'Sir, shouldn't we haul in that bastard Chalmers again? This is just like that other kid. There's got to be something we can hold him on.'

Barrington fixed the sergeant with a cold stare. 'Evidence, Fraser. If you find me one shred of evidence that connects him with this murder, we'll arrest and charge him. But to date all you've given me is innuendo, gossip, and the fact that he was tried and acquitted on a similar case two years ago. That is not evidence. And I have so far seen absolutely no reason why Chalmers should be under any more suspicion than anyone else in this town.'

'But he's so weird, sir,' Fraser persisted, reckless in his challenge. 'Everyone thinks he did it.'

Isabelle braced for Barrington's explosion, but the superintendent just sighed wearily. 'Being weird is not a crime, Fraser, and the prejudices of a town are not the basis for thorough police investigation.'

Barrington sat, tense and silent, in the passenger seat as Isabelle drove the short distance back into town. Only as she pulled up in front of the modest home where the girl's parents lived did he speak.

'When we've finished here, O'Connell, you should go and warn Chalmers. Fraser's partly right – half the town does think he did it, and they'll be baying for his blood.'

'Protection arrangements, sir?' she asked, dragging her mind to practical needs to keep away the dread of the task to come.

'If he wants it. Use your judgment.'

She switched off the engine, and her fingers fumbled as she unbuckled her seat belt. Barrington made no move, his face white.

'I'm a week from retirement, O'Connell,' he muttered. 'This isn't the way I wanted to finish.'

She saw a curtain flick in the window, knew she had to move frozen limbs out of the car and do the unthinkable. Mitch and Sara had to come first. Later – much later, when duty had been done and whoever had committed this crime arrested – she'd maybe have the luxury of time to give in, to weep and grieve. Not now.

'No, sir. We have to go, sir.'

The door jerked open as they mounted the steps, and there could be no escaping the terrible, inevitable moment when all hope and light drained from Sara's eyes, in that instant when she knew, before the words were spoken, before Mitch howled like no man should have to, before Sara folded in on herself and crumpled to the floor.

Because she'd failed them.

Isabelle barely managed to hold herself together, focusing on their needs, doing her job. If she allowed herself to feel, the fragile shell of self-control would crack into a million useless pieces.

Cope with it.

After they finally left the house, she drove the superintendent back to the tiny police station and forced herself to continue to her next duty. An eerie, uncomfortable quiet hung over the town. In the main street, people stood in groups, shaking heads, dabbing at tears, sniffing in handkerchiefs.

They stared at her as she drove past, their eyes critical, accusing, and neither heart nor intellect could begrudge them that judgment. A child lay dead, and she and her colleagues had not been able to prevent it.

Once, long ago, Isabelle had been a part of this small, isolated community. They'd welcomed her back a week ago, trusting her as one of their own amongst the strangers in the rest of the police team – the very reason the superintendent had brought her in on this case. Yet after this terrible failure, any friendliness, any welcome they might have had for her, would be gone.

Just do your job, O'Connell, she ordered herself, crushing back the emotion that choked her throat. There's a killer out there to find.

During the twenty-minute drive to Dan Chalmers' secluded shack, she kept a bare grip on her sanity by methodically reviewing the facts of the case in her mind, seeking a clue, a lead, anything they might have missed. Like the superintendent, she believed in Chalmers' innocence. The man was certainly strange, a true eccentric, but he had consistently and quietly denied any knowledge of the child's disappearance, and she sensed his honesty. This was the second time that human nature's distrust of difference had singled him out, yet he'd been resigned to the questions, cooperating with their enquiries fully.

As the car rounded a bend in the rough track and the shack came into view amongst the trees, a groan escaped her lips and her pulse skittered unevenly. There were vehicles there already, and a small crowd had gathered. Their angry yells disturbed the bush landscape, and in a glance she recognised that the emotional temperature was rising, fast. Someone picked up a rock and hurled it through the window, to the cheers of the others.

She radioed for backup before leaving the car, aware even as she did so that it would take too long to arrive. Apprehension roiled in her stomach. This would be one hell of a situation to defuse, and she'd have to do it herself.

ONE

One year later

Alec Goddard drove down the dirt road as fast as the conditions allowed, determined not to waste time. He swore as he had to stop, yet again, to open another gate. Damn the woman. Couldn't she have chosen somewhere more accessible to hide away? This isolated area, tucked into the mountains north of Sydney, was far from anywhere.

With no cattle or sheep visible, he defied the country conventions and left the gate open, knowing he'd be back this way shortly, whatever the outcome of this visit.

He still wasn't sure if he was doing the right thing. Just because Bob Barrington had agreed with his initial idea, it didn't mean it was necessarily a good one. He'd always trusted

Bob's judgment, but the retired superintendent, laden with guilt and regret, hadn't been the same this last twelve months.

Well, he'd find out soon enough if it was a mistake.

She emerged from the back garden as he brought the car to a stop in front of the old timber cottage. For an instant, he wondered if some of the wilder rumours he'd heard were true, after all. With a scarf wrapped untidily around her head, and a dusty, loose shirt over a pair of equally baggy, grubby jeans, she indeed looked more like a mad recluse than a highly regarded police detective. The pitchfork in one hand and the huge German shepherd standing beside her only added to the impression. Her scowl wasn't exactly welcoming either.

She made no attempt to greet him or come closer as he got out of the car.

'Isabelle O'Connell, I presume? I'm Detective Chief Inspector Alec Goddard, from State Crime Command in Sydney.'

He held out his identity card for her inspection. He'd have taken a few steps towards her if the dog hadn't growled in warning.

She barely glanced at his ID.

'What do you want, DCI Goddard?'

Her voice sounded clear, firm, but the grey eyes that met and held his made a chill wind up his spine. They were like some ancient, black hole in space, holding every sorrow known.

Yet her steady gaze showed no sign of insanity, and he perceived immediately the sharp intelligence that had earned her a formidable reputation.

'I want your help, Detective O'Connell.'

Her scowl deepened. 'Drop the "Detective" stuff. I've resigned from the police force.'

'Your resignation isn't effective until the end of your leave, which is still two weeks away.'

He saw her bristle and mentally rebuked himself for taking the wrong approach. He needed to talk her into this, not bully her.

'Yes, and I'm officially on leave, not on duty,' she reminded him coldly. 'So I'll give you just three minutes to ask your questions and then you can go.'

'It isn't that simple.'

Her eyes narrowed. 'Go on.'

He came straight to the point. 'I want you to work with me on a case.'

She gave him her answer just as straight, 'No.'

She turned abruptly and began to walk away.

If it had been a normal case, he'd have let her go. But for this one, he'd use whatever resources he could gather – even a traumatised, almost ex-detective who'd removed herself from the world.

'Another child's gone missing,' he said. 'From Dungirri.'

At the mention of her home town she stopped.

Long seconds passed before she slowly turned around, and those grey, ghostly eyes stared at him as if he were a messenger from hell.

'When?'

'Yesterday afternoon. On her way home from school, just like Jess Sutherland a year ago.'

She closed her eyes briefly, took in a ragged breath.

'Who? Which kid?'

He didn't need to consult his notebook.

'Tanya Wilson. Her parents are –'

'Beth and Ryan.'

She said the names clearly enough, but all the colour drained from her face and she wavered, leaned heavily for a moment on the pitchfork. He took a step towards her, hand outstretched to catch her, stopping when the dog growled again.

He saw the effort it took to draw herself back under control.

'You want me to go with you to Dungirri, now?'

'Yes.' He felt like a messenger from hell indeed, asking her return to her nightmares. 'I appreciate what I'm asking is hard for you. But you know the town, and you were involved in the investigation last time. We need to find her, before it's too late.'

Biting her lip, she moved to rake her hand through her hair, dislodging the scarf instead. She pulled it off in frustration, a mop of rich brown curls falling loose around her shoulders. With her fine features, the tangle of hair gave an impression of youth, of vulnerability, yet that keening pain in her eyes wasn't in the least childlike.

'We failed a year ago. Jess died. Dan Chalmers died.' Her voice echoed with bitter hollowness. 'Whether he was guilty or innocent, we failed. Are you sure you want me working with you?'

Was that how she saw herself – as a failure? Hell, from what he'd heard, she had no reason to carry any guilt. She'd been the one to continue searching for other evidence when virtually everyone else had focused on Dan Chalmers. The one who'd stepped in to protect him from the townsfolk's angry accusations. And when she'd recovered enough to be told the investigation had finished with Chalmers' death, she'd argued from her hospital bed to have the case re-opened.

'Barrington speaks highly of you, says you were the best on the team. I'll trust his judgment.' And my own, he thought. He was too familiar with the weight all the 'what-ifs' carried after a failed case. No matter how much you rationalised things, the questions always came back...and the regrets. The more conscientious the cop, the harder it was. Isabelle O'Connell seemed to have taken it very hard indeed.

Abruptly she moved, thrusting the pitchfork at him as she strode past him towards the house. 'Put this away in the shed and shut the garden gates while I grab some clothes.'

Alec let go a breath that he hadn't realised he'd been holding. She'd agreed to come. If asking her proved to be a mistake, he'd deal with that later. But two little girls had already died, and he was absolutely determined that this time the outcome would be different. Failing was not an option.

He didn't for a moment doubt his own skills, but a crime like this – possibly the work of a serial killer – needed the best team possible and, by all accounts, O'Connell was damned good. Sharply intelligent and perceptive, and dedicated with it. He hoped to hell that she still was.

According to Barrington, she'd hidden herself away these past months, shunning contact with anyone. Although she'd physically recovered from her injuries, the police force had been willing to accommodate her request for extended leave, and apparently no one had been surprised when her letter of resignation arrived.

Yet Alec hated to see the loss of a good officer.

He cast his eyes around, trying to gain an insight into the woman from the place she'd chosen as a refuge.

The closest he'd ever come to gardening was killing potted plants in his apartment, but even to his uneducated eyes, her garden was impressive. Surrounded by a high wire fence, the array of vegetables, berries and fruit trees appeared healthy and productive, an oasis of green in the midst of dry bushland.

The fence initially puzzled him. Why did she need to feel safe in the garden when the house wasn't secured in the same way? But the sight of a kangaroo grazing on the other side of the wire made him realise that it had nothing to do with personal security and everything to do with protecting the plants from the hungry wildlife.

He felt foolish for his mistake. He was Sydney born and bred, and the gap between city and country loomed larger now than it ever had. All the more reason to have O'Connell on the team. Dungirri was way out in the north-west of the state, on the edge of the outback, and her knowledge of the place, the people and the culture would be invaluable.

He found the shed and stowed the pitchfork amongst a variety of other tools. Conscientiously he closed the garden gates, making sure they were properly fastened, before he returned to the front of the house to wait for her.

When she emerged with a duffle bag just a few minutes later, the difference in her appearance had him catching his breath. The navy trousers and short-sleeved white shirt revealed a slim figure that her gardening clothes had entirely disguised. She'd washed the garden dirt from her face and hands, and brushed her hair back into a soft knot. The absence of make-up enhanced rather than detracted from the impression of professionalism, of trustworthiness. Her fine, almost gaunt features held no artifice or pretence, but rather a stark, natural beauty.

Yet her tightly controlled expression and rigid spine brought to mind a queen walking to her execution.

Isabelle clenched her teeth hard as she approached the car and the man who stood waiting. She'd always feared this day would come – another child taken, at risk because she and the others on the police team had botched the job last year. Her stomach coiled so tight that her breath grew shallow.

Dan Chalmers had been innocent, after all. And all these months that she'd been trying to convince herself otherwise, to believe the evidence the others believed, the malevolence they'd left unchecked had not vanished.

Malevolence like that did not simply evaporate, sated. It could never be sated. The twisted specimen of humanity that had taken Jess had undoubtedly been simply biding time; waiting, watching, planning, anticipating.

Cope. The mantra she'd repeated to herself ever since the car had driven up echoed again in her mind. *Don't think about the possibilities.*

She called to Finn, her voice managing to sound almost normal, and he bounded over to her obediently. She caught the man's glance at the dog and at the harness in her hand, saw him about to object as he realised her intention.

'Finn goes with me,' she told him in a tone that brooked no argument. 'I'll put a towel on the seat to protect your car, if you like, but I'm going nowhere without him.'

After a fraction of hesitation, he nodded. 'Will he handle flying okay? We're only driving as far as Richmond – the police helicopter will pick us up from there. There's a briefing in Dungirri at noon.'

So soon. She'd assumed they'd drive out to the town, that she'd have six or seven hours to prepare herself. Now she'd have to face it all again in less than two hours.

She had to fight the tightness in her throat again. 'He's an ex-Air Force guard dog. He's used to aircraft.'

14

A small, wry smile softened the hard lines of the man's face. 'I hope you fed him this morning. He's looking at me like I'd make a good breakfast.'

She refused to let his attempt at humour affect her. 'He won't attack you unless I order it.'

He seemed to recognise the warning and just nodded, the softness of the smile evaporating. He stowed her bag in the boot, watched while she buckled in the dog, and in a few moments they were driving away.

Trying desperately to keep her mind away from thoughts that could crack her control, she clinically assessed the man beside her.

He was concentrating on his driving, which was just as well, for he drove faster than she'd ever dare to on this rough road. His strong, muscular hand gripped the gear stick between them, and he deftly changed gear in response to the terrain. If nothing else, she had to give him credit for being an excellent driver.

Alec Goddard. She pulled the name from her memory of his brief introduction. Bob Barrington had mentioned him a few times in passing – wasn't there some sort of family connection? – and she had a vague recollection that she'd seen his name in media reports once or twice, but State Crime Command in Sydney had little in common with the country towns where she'd served.

He was tall, six one or six two, she estimated, and the broad shoulders under the sports jacket suggested that he kept in shape. His hands and face were tanned, and his light brown hair seemed naturally sun-bleached. An outdoors type of man then. Frown lines carved into his forehead hinted at a serious nature, yet the crow's-feet at the edge of his direct blue eyes had crinkled when he'd smiled.

Maybe around his late thirties, he was young for chief inspector ranking. The air of self-confidence, of authority, sat comfortably on him. She guessed he'd be used to getting his own way.

In the past, she might have trusted him, might even have thought him handsome. Now, all illusions she'd had about the innate goodness of people were well and truly shattered, and she didn't trust anyone, not even herself.

She turned away from him, stared out the window. What did Barrington's – what did anyone's – judgment matter when Jess had died? She'd failed Jess, and now...

She closed her eyes, forcing back burning tears. Of all the children in her old home town, why did it have to be Beth's daughter? Beth, who'd made the effort to keep in touch all these years, sending photos of her girls as they grew, samples of their childish artwork. Tanya's kindergarten drawing of a brightly coloured fish had hung on Isabelle's fridge for a year.

Now the child needed her help, and she had no idea if she had the strength, or the ability, to give it.

The chopper put them down in a dry paddock on the edge of town, and the local constable, an Aboriginal man, picked them up in a dusty police vehicle.

So, this is Dungirri, Alec thought, as they drove the short distance to the police station.

The place looked like a ghost town, except the ghosts were out on the streets and they weren't dead. They stood in front of shops which had seen better days, shoulders slumped, turning empty faces and resigned gazes to the police vehicle as it passed.

He risked a glance at the woman in the back seat. She stared straight ahead. The brief discussion they'd had on the flight had been totally focused on the facts of the case, and he'd been impressed by the concise briefing she'd given him of the previous investigation and the sharp questions she'd asked about the search for the missing girl. Yet it had all been delivered in a cold, impersonal manner.

He figured that the veneer was her way of protecting herself, but for the first time he doubted the wisdom of bringing her here. It would be damned hard for her to face those who'd been involved in the attack on Chalmers last year, and he didn't have the time or resources to deal with her if she cracked under the pressure. Barrington had assured him she wouldn't, and for now he'd just have to hope that the former superintendent's assessment was correct.

Still, he'd keep a close eye on her.

He got out of the car, into the hot, parching wind, and looked back along the main street. It wasn't beautiful. A few plants struggled to exist in the garden beds in the middle of the wide road, but most were dead or dying. The buildings – half of them empty – needed painting, and a sign hung crookedly, squeaking inexorably as it swung in the wind. A few dusty utilities and trucks were parked haphazardly in front of the old double-storeyed hotel, the wrought iron bordering its wide upstairs verandas the only hint of long-gone splendour.

He knew most small towns were struggling, but there was more than that here. This place wasn't just dying of hopelessness and neglect. It was eerie, haunted, and he wondered what secrets still lay festering in the lives of its three hundred inhabitants.

'We're setting up the operations room in the memorial hall, sir.' The constable indicated the dilapidated weatherboard building beside the police cottage. 'The team from Regional Command in Dubbo arrived an hour ago. They'll have computers and communications up and running shortly.'

Alec felt a flash of sympathy for the guy. The New South Wales Police Force covered a huge state. Most of the time, the uniformed officers in these tiny outposts worked in isolation, with even the 'local' commander often hundreds of kilometres away. And then when something like this happened, they were invaded by detectives from larger towns and from Headquarters in Sydney and expected to take a back seat in the investigation, despite their knowledge of the area.

He glanced at the man's name tag – Adam Donahue – and made a mental note to ensure that the local officers didn't just get stuck with the menial jobs this time around.

Isabelle, the dog on a short lead at her side, was already heading into the hall. Behind her, he witnessed the sudden stiffening of her shoulders, heard the slight intake of breath.

A dark-haired man in his mid-thirties stood up from plugging in a computer as he saw them, eyebrows raised.

'Hello, Isabelle,' he said warily. 'I didn't expect to see you here.'

She nodded acknowledgment, with no hint of pleasure at seeing him.

Well, there's a history of some sort between the two of them, Alec thought. As long as it didn't get in the way of them working together on the case, he didn't care.

The man came forward to introduce himself with the air of someone who planned to make himself noticed by his seniors. That immediately set Alec on guard.

'I'm Steve Fraser...'

'DCI Goddard.' He briefly shook Fraser's outstretched hand, deliberately giving only his rank and surname to stress his authority.

In their phone discussion late the previous night, Bob Barrington had mentioned that Fraser had been on the team last year. He hadn't said anything particularly critical about him, but then he hadn't said anything complimentary, either.

'We'll start the briefing in three minutes. Gather everyone together, please.'

A uniformed female sergeant strode into the hall and did a visible double-take. 'Bella! What on earth... I didn't realise you were coming.'

The two women embraced – or rather, Alec observed, the sergeant embraced Isabelle, who didn't pull away.

Isabelle introduced them. 'This is Kris Matthews. She's been here a few years.'

The sergeant's handshake was firm and added to the impression of down-to-earth capability and practicality. Good – someone he could rely on. He wasn't yet sure if he could rely on Fraser.

'We've got eight uniformed officers pulled from towns in the region, and Moree may be able to send us a couple more if we need them,' Matthews told him. 'Steve Fraser's come from Moree. There are two detective positions at Birraga, but Jim Holt's in hospital with a burst appendix. Phil Katsinis is on his way back from leave in Cape York, but still at least a day away. He'll be here as soon as he can. Dubbo has sent two comms technicians, and can send their media liaison officer if she's needed.'

He cast a considering eye over them – not a whole lot of resources for an investigation of this nature. He knew all the usual arguments – competing priorities, budget constraints, staff shortages. And out here, police resources were already stretched over vast, sparsely populated distances. He might be granted a few more people if the child wasn't found straightaway, but for now he'd have to work with what he had available, and somehow pull this diverse group into a disciplined, cohesive team.

'Okay, folks,' he called out to the room in general. 'Let's get this briefing underway.'

He gave his name and rank and held up his ID card as procedure required. 'I'm from State Crime Command in Sydney, and I'm in charge of this investigation. Tanya Wilson, an eight-year-old girl, is missing, and as of now this is officially a suspected abduction.'

He pulled some papers from the folder he'd set on the table in front of him, aware, in the periphery of his vision, of Isabelle watching him from where she leaned against the wall.

'Some of you were here just over twelve months ago, when another girl of the same age, Jess Sutherland, went missing in similar circumstances.' He pinned up Jess's photo beside Tanya's as he spoke. 'She was held by her abductor for seven days before being murdered. Two years ago, Kasey Tomasi was abducted near her home, at Jerran Creek, two hours' drive from here.' He pinned the third photograph up. 'Kasey was also held for some days before she was murdered. We will regard these three cases as being possibly connected.'

A murmur rippled through the room, and he caught tones and expressions of surprise, agreement and disagreement. Isabelle remained silent, her face impassive.

Fraser stood. 'This case can't be related. The man who killed Jess and Kasey is dead. One of Jess's shoes was found in his house. And he had the same sedatives that she and Kasey were drugged with.'

Alec fixed him with a steady eye. 'I have been over the case notes, Fraser. The fact that the shoe was found in the ruins of Daniel Chalmers' house following his murder,' he stressed the word, 'is not conclusive. It may well have been planted. And diazepam is a common sedative that many people have access to.'

He'd deliberately addressed the man by his surname. With his own team, back in Sydney, he used a more informal, even casual, leadership style. In these circumstances, however, he'd decided formality was better, so that Fraser could be in no doubt who was in charge.

The detective opened his mouth again, about to argue, then wisely decided not to. Just as well, Alec thought. There wasn't time to waste in arguments, and he had no desire to be any more heavy-handed than he'd been so far. He turned back to the local officer.

'Sergeant Matthews? Would you bring us up to speed on what's occurred so far?'

The sergeant came up to the front and Alec stepped aside, moving to stand next to Isabelle.

Matthews taped up a simple map, hand-drawn on a large piece of butcher's paper: a standard small-town grid of straight intersecting streets, only disrupted by the curve of the creek.

'Tanya left school at three fifteen yesterday afternoon.' She pointed to the school on the map in the south-west corner of town. 'She bought a few sweets at the Truck Stop Cafe at the west end of Bridge Street at approximately three-twenty. Her normal route home is north along the road past the showground, and then east across the top of town. She usually takes a shortcut through the TSR to get to her home, just out of town on Scrub Road.'

'TSR?' queried Alec sharply.

'Travelling stock reserve. The distance from school to home is just over a kilometre, and Tanya is normally home well before four o'clock. She's not the sort of kid who wanders off alone. Her mother reported her missing at five o'clock.'

'You've searched the route for evidence?' he asked.

'As best we could,' Matthews replied. 'Unfortunately, a mob of five hundred cattle moved into the stock reserve around 4.30 pm, pretty much obliterating any chance of finding tyre marks, scents, or anything useful.'

Yep, I'm definitely in the country, Alec thought wryly. Having a mob of cattle destroy his evidence had never happened in Sydney.

'We've questioned Tanya's friends and everyone who lives along her normal route,' Matthews continued. 'I called in the volunteers of the State Emergency Service last night, and they've searched along the creek banks and dragged the swimming hole and the dam in the reserve. There's a team searching the scrubland north of town as we speak. So far we have nothing.'

'I suppose this Truck Stop Cafe doesn't have video surveillance?'

'Don't need that sort of thing out here.' The sergeant gave him a grim half-smile. 'We're hardly on a major highway. Most of the drivers are well known – regular district runs of stock, agricultural supplies, that sort of thing. Jeanie at the cafe knew everyone who stopped yesterday.'

'Thanks, Matthews.' Alec walked back to the front of the room. 'Folks, if the person responsible for this is the same person who abducted Jess and Kasey, then the chances are that Tanya is still alive and is being hidden somewhere. But we have a limited time to find her. Fraser, get a list of everyone who stopped at the cafe yesterday and have a team start checking them out. Donahue, keep the SES crew searching – any place you think the girl could have gone. Matthews, see if any of the kids at the school saw anything. O'Connell, you and I will start interviewing people in town.'

He thought he saw a hint of alarm beneath the expressionless mask. He knew he was throwing her in the deep end, making her face the townsfolk straightaway. Except, in reality, his purpose in getting her out there was exactly the reverse – making the townsfolk face her. Making them face the consequences of last year's incident in the hope that it would force them into confronting the truth and revealing the menace within their community.

The sense of guilt he felt in using Isabelle this way was only mitigated by the knowledge that it might save a little girl's life.

Isabelle took a deep, slow breath, pushing down a wave of panic. Concentrate on the job, just concentrate on what needs doing, she lectured inwardly, gradually feeling the iron determination moderate the screaming emotions. As if sensing her unease, Finn leaned against her leg and she touched his head lightly, the connection helping to steady her.

With Finn trotting between them, she and Alec worked

their way down Bridge Street, stopping at the store, the council depot, the hotel, the agricultural and hardware store.

No one had expected to see her. Fists clutched tightly at her sides, she ignored the surprised expressions. Some tried to be friendly, some were guarded, others so uncomfortable that they couldn't meet her eyes. She held Tanya's image in her mind as a shield against the dark memories that would otherwise claw at her, and didn't let herself respond as anything other than Detective O'Connell.

Always beside her, Alec's natural authority and official courtesy compelled attention from those they questioned, yet he showed no need to throw his weight around aggressively. He let her take the lead, working as a team with her, his probing questions complementing hers.

A year ago, he might have earned her respect for his professionalism.

She shut that thought out too, just as she tried to block out the disturbing awareness of his constant presence near her. He never touched her, never came between her and Finn, just stayed within an arm's reach of her, all the time. She clung to the logic that her awareness of him stemmed only from the fact that she'd lived in isolation for months now, hardly seeing anyone.

At Ward's Rural Supplies, Joe Ward's nervous gaze kept slipping from her face as he told them no, he'd not seen Tanya yesterday, and except for one delivery run he'd been out the back stacking feed most of the afternoon. His daughter, who helped run the store, was also unable to help.

Alec was thanking them both when the bell at the door jingled, and almost before she could turn around Isabelle found herself enveloped in a strong hug.

'Bella, my dear!' Jeanie Menotti from the cafe down the road let her go eventually, just enough to hold her by the shoulders and look her over. 'How are you?' she asked earnestly. 'You've recovered okay?'

Isabelle briefly closed her eyes, battling to maintain her composure. How like Jeanie to talk about the subject that everyone else had studiously avoided. But then Jeanie, with her sane, sensible personality, had never been one to avoid difficult topics when she cared about people.

'I'm fine.' Isabelle tried to brush off the elderly woman's concern, all the while fighting the urge to throw herself into Jeanie's arms and weep, as she had done sometimes as a motherless teenager. But she wasn't that naïve, trusting kid any more, and she never would be again.

By the time they arrived back at the hall an hour later, Alec's respect for Isabelle had grown.

She'd handled herself well, cool when faced with some people's obvious surprise at seeing her. She'd remained polite but distant with them all, not responding to their reactions, focused only on seeking information.

Yet what had the cost been to her? He'd seen the hurt look on Jeanie Menotti's face when Isabelle had pulled away from her. It was as though she was denying, even to herself, any trace of the woman behind the detective – the woman who had spent her childhood as part of this town.

While they compared notes with Fraser and Matthews, she leaned on the edge of a table, Finn at her feet, her concentration on the whiteboard where Fraser scrawled anything that might be relevant. The mask was firmly in place, yet strain etched fine lines around her eyes.

The crack of a gunshot and the simultaneous fracturing of the window behind Isabelle jolted Alec out of his thoughts and into instinctive action. He threw himself at her, pushing her down onto the floor, as everyone else in the room also dropped down.

In the few seconds that followed, while they waited to see if more gunshots were coming, he became aware of three disparate things in rapid succession: he liked the soft warmth of the woman lying beneath him; her dog had its teeth clenched around his ankle; and the white shirt Isabelle wore was turning red with blood.

TWO

The shock of the breaking glass became a rush of panic as Alec's body pinned her to the floor, crowding too close, and she instinctively fought to push him away. Finn's instant muffled growl – and Alec's 'Shit' – conveyed the situation to her.

'Finn, release,' she gasped.

Immediately, Alec's weight rolled off her, and he knelt beside her. Still with the haze of terror in her mind, she tried to move away from him. She needed space, didn't want anyone touching her.

'Hold still, Isabelle. You've been shot.'

Shot? The pain in her shoulder pushed through the panic and she twisted her head, stunned to see the bloodied rip in her shirt.

'I have to see how bad it is,' Alec said, and while the irrational, frightened part of her wanted to scream and hide, she made herself hold still while he pushed back the neckline of her shirt with one hand and easily flicked the buttons open with the other.

'Someone get me a first aid kit, and call a doctor,' he ordered in a controlled but direct tone. 'Fraser, find out where that shot came from. Everyone else, keep down and close to the wall.'

A first aid box thumped on the floor and Kris crouched down on her other side. 'The nearest doctor is at Birraga, sixty kilometres away,' she said quietly. 'Let's hope we don't need her.'

'It's not bad. It must be just a graze,' Isabelle insisted through clenched teeth.

'We have to make sure, Bella.' This time Alec's deep, authoritative voice held a softer note.

It's *O'Connell*, she wanted to scream at him. Not Isabelle, and definitely not Bella. Especially not in that gentle tone.

Biting her lip, she averted her face from his and stared at the floor as his deft fingers swabbed the blood and investigated the injury.

'You're right – the bullet just grazed you. There's a fair bit of bleeding, but it doesn't look like anything major's been hit.'

He continued to work in silence, Kris helping him.

'I thought you said your dog wouldn't attack unless ordered,' he commented at last.

'He must have thought you were attacking me.'

With her good hand she reached out for Finn, and he crept forward until she could sink her fingers into his fur, grateful for his constant presence and guardianship. She didn't miss Alec's wary glance at him.

'Is your ankle okay?' Kris asked the DCI.

Isabelle waited for the criticism, for anger at what had happened, but he just continued his task, his closed expression unreadable. 'It's fine. Mostly slobber I'd say – he didn't close his teeth tight.'

When he slid her bra strap from her shoulder to better clean the wound, she couldn't help flinching.

'Why don't I take over here, sir?' Kris's timely suggestion sent a wave of relief through her.

Alec frowned, hesitated, and seemed about to refuse, but Steve Fraser interrupted them.

'The sniper must have fired from the trees by the creek – it's the only cover in that direction,' he reported. 'I don't see any sign of movement there now.'

'Let's go and check it out.' Alec rose to his feet, nodded to Kris to take over, and moved away.

Kris grinned at Isabelle as she took his place. 'I wouldn't mind a gorgeous guy playing with my bra straps,' she whispered with a wink, 'but I got the impression you weren't feeling quite the same way.'

'Thanks,' Isabelle murmured.

While Kris worked, Isabelle was aware of Alec briskly giving instructions and stationing officers at the doors and windows. Her stomach tightened as he and Steve left the hall, weapons held ready.

'Okay, that looks clean. Now hold still while I bandage it up,' Kris commanded.

It might have been just a surface wound on top of her shoulder, but it hurt when she moved her head and pulled the skin and muscles of her neck. They were both silent while Kris efficiently covered the injury with a dressing and taped it, each listening intently for any indication of what might be happening outside.

Alec held his uneasiness in check with difficulty.

Even as he and Fraser scouted the area around the hall for any sign of the gunman, images he couldn't shake hovered before his eyes – the blood staining Isabelle's shirt, the soft swell of her breast under lace, the faint white traces of scars on her smooth shoulder, disappearing down her back. It took conscious effort to push his swirling thoughts to the back of his mind and concentrate on the search.

The creek ran in a curve around the east and north of the hall, its dry, sandy bed lined on both sides with dense eucalypts, native pines and a few weeping willows. It all seemed quiet.

Alec indicated to Fraser to check behind the hall, while he took the east side. He approached the trees with caution, gun raised, alert for any sound that might give away the shooter's presence.

Silence, except for the call of birds and the wind in the leaves. No one was lurking there now. Whoever had been there had fired the single shot and disappeared.

Alec walked out onto the old timber bridge, looking up and downstream, and along the road in both directions. There were no vehicles on the road, in sight or in hearing. A curtain moved at the window of one house, a shadow behind the screen door of another, the residents probably too wary to emerge from their relative safety.

He rejoined Fraser and signalled an all clear to those watching from the hall.

'That's the beginning of the Dungirri scrub on the other side of the creek,' Fraser commented. 'The majority of it's State Forest, but there's some private land. My bet is he's gone off into there, maybe hidden his vehicle some distance away, where we wouldn't hear it.'

Alec acknowledged the suggestion with a vague nod, and surveyed the dry forest. Scrub was a good term for it. Few of the mix of eucalypts and native pines were full grown, and the ground was thickly littered with fallen timber and dead branches and leaves. He couldn't see more than twenty metres amongst the trees.

Clamping down his rising unease, he holstered his weapon and strode back inside, Fraser following. Isabelle stood in the middle of the room, deep in discussion with Matthews, and he was relieved to see that other than a pale face she seemed okay. Her torn, blood-wet shirt covered the bulky dressing on her shoulder, a graphic reminder of how close the sniper had come to causing tragedy. He briefly considered instructing Matthews to take her to the doctor in Birraga, but until he knew enough to assess the risk, she'd probably be safer here than on a long, lonely road with only one officer for protection.

'We found the bullet, ricocheted off the wall.' Kris pointed to the bullet lying under one of the tables near the west wall. 'Probably from a .22 rifle, which are as common as dirt around here. Just about every household will have one.'

'Get it down to ballistics in Sydney,' Alec replied. 'Call in a crime scene team to go over the creek area straightaway.' He stopped as Kris shook her head.

'Sorry, regional specialists aren't available – I already asked for them. There was a double murder up near the Queensland border last night and we can't have them until tomorrow at the earliest.'

He stared at her in disbelief. How could they be expected to conduct an investigation without the resources they should be able to count on – resources he took for granted in Sydney?

'Welcome to bush policing,' Isabelle commented dryly.

'Don't worry.' Kris gave him a grin. 'We're used to do-it-yourself out here. Adam is as good as any forensic team at finding evidence, even without all the high-tech gear.'

Fraser snorted. 'Oh, sure, having Koori blood gives him magical powers that are better than years of scientific training.'

'Murri,' Isabelle corrected him, her eyes cold. 'The Aboriginal people in this region call themselves Murris, not Kooris. And learning to read the environment is a survival skill that takes years of observation and practice, irrespective of one's genetic inheritance.'

Isabelle, one, Fraser, zero. Alec stifled the urge to cheer, at the same time hoping she'd never turn that look on him.

'Adam is a skilled tracker,' Kris explained. 'He works with the local elders here to teach the old skills. And Bella is damn near as good.'

A flush crept up Isabelle's face but she met Alec's enquiring look with a defiant tilt of her jaw. 'My father taught me what I know. He lived most of his life in the bush, and learned from the local Murri people and the old stockmen.'

Intrigued, Alec almost wished it was the time and place to ask more questions about her life. Instead he nodded.

'Good. We'll need to use all the skills and knowledge we can. But I'm not sending you out in the open just now, O'Connell.' He held up his hand as she took a step forward in protest. 'Not until we find out whether whoever fired that shot was aiming deliberately at you. We'll get Donahue to go to the creek and see if the gunman left us any clues.'

He caught Fraser's cynical expression out of the corner of his eye. The man was beginning to irritate him. Deciding that the best way to stop Fraser going off in his own direction was to make sure he had specific duties, Alec told him to arrange interviews with nearby residents to see if they had witnessed the sniper.

As Fraser and Donahue left to their tasks, Alec mentally sifted through the other things to be done. An officer had been shot and he was required to report it immediately. His superiors would not be amused if they heard it on the news first.

'Matthews, I need to use your office.'

'Sure,' Kris said. 'Bella, you want to come across to the station to change? Your luggage must be somewhere around here.'

They found her bag stowed beside Alec's in the foyer and all three went next door to the police cottage, Finn shadowing his mistress as usual.

Kris showed Alec into her office, then disappeared with Bella into the residence at the rear. It didn't take him long to phone in his initial notification, and by the time he'd finished, Kris was back. She slammed a file drawer shut before she came to the door of the office, her mouth drawn tight.

Alec looked up. 'Say what's on your mind, Matthews.'

'Fine, I will,' she responded without hesitation. 'What were you thinking of, bringing Bella back here? Don't you know what she went through?'

'She agreed to come. I didn't force her.' No, just asked her to come, guessing that her conscience wouldn't let her refuse. He didn't need Kris to tell him that it was pretty much the same thing.

He stood up, moved to the window and gazed out, the reality of what he'd done sitting uncomfortably on his own conscience. Of course he'd known what had happened to her. He'd heard the news at the time, been aware of the discussions afterwards on the police grapevine, and he'd read the official reports. He'd even spent more than one evening talking sense into the guilt-stricken Barrington.

But all that was only abstract knowledge. It wasn't until he'd bared her shoulder and seen some of the scars that he'd actually begun to comprehend, deep in his gut, the frightening enormity of what she'd experienced.

His imagination could see, as if through her eyes, the crowd converging, becoming a mob, grief and anger transforming into a blind, hate-filled madness that sheared all links with reason. Saw them descend on the hapless Chalmers, and Isabelle's desperate struggle to protect him. They'd killed Chalmers with rocks and sticks and their bare hands, and they'd damn near killed her too.

'Some of them are still out there, aren't they?' he asked.

'It was a mob. How can anyone – even those who were there – really know who was in the thick of it? Two men came and volunteered confessions, and from what they said we charged a third. They all pleaded guilty and are in prison now.'

'What about the others? There must have been a dozen of them – probably more.'

Kris sighed, and he turned to face her.

'We've had three definite and two probable suicides in the last twelve months. Several families have left town. Maybe we could have gone out and tried to charge more people. I don't know.'

She thrust her hands in her pockets, shoulders hunched. 'This town was already in a bad way, well before Jess was abducted last year. It's lost half its population in the past ten years, and with the timber mill closed and most of the graziers shedding staff there's chronic unemployment. What happened last year – Jess's abduction and murder, Chalmers' death – can you imagine what that does to a community like this? The place is so traumatised it's barely functioning.'

Yes, he'd seen that today. Seen it in the people who couldn't look each other in the eye. Wives looking sideways at husbands, friends doubting friends, and no one daring to speak of the unspeakable.

'If it turns out Chalmers was innocent after all, it's only going to get worse,' he reflected.

'Dan Chalmers had nothing to do with the murders.' Isabelle spoke from the doorway, her voice low and sure.

Alec spun to face her. Her grey eyes burned into his, serious, unwavering in belief.

'What makes you so certain?' He suspected it himself, but he needed to know the reasons for her conviction. Instinct alone wasn't enough.

She came into the room and sat on the edge of a chair. 'The evidence pointing to him was only ever circumstantial. But the man hid from the world because he couldn't bear the suffering that he saw. He abhorred violence in any form. He would never have harmed anyone, let alone a little girl.'

'Yet he was charged with Kasey's murder.'

'And acquitted,' she reminded him sharply. 'The case should never even have made it to court.'

She was right about that, Alec acknowledged. He'd read the case notes, and the flimsiness of the prosecution case had astounded him. Chalmers had been the last person to see Kasey alive, but he'd come forward to police straight-away to tell them of his sighting. Illogical distrust and prejudice against anyone different had meant suspicion had fallen on him, and when several days later the police had found drawings of the girl in his house, they'd arrested him.

'How do you explain the pictures?' he asked.

'He was an artist, for heaven's sake. The National Gallery has some of his work. He gave up the art world years ago, but drawing was his way of dealing with the things that his mind saw. He drew when Jess was missing too, because his imagination wouldn't let him rest, thinking about what might be happening to her.'

'You have to admit, though, there must be a connection of some sort,' he insisted. 'Chalmers was living in Jerran Creek when Kasey went missing from there. Two years later he's living in Dungirri, and Jess is abducted and killed in exactly the same manner.'

'I know...' Isabelle paused, thinking. 'I've always believed the killer took advantage of that fact, knew he was setting him up, at least in Jess's case.' She leaned forward. 'Look, the person who's taken Tanya *has* to be the same one who took Jess and Kasey. Three blonde girls, all around the same age, all disappearing on their way home from school, no ransom demands and no clues. Neither Jess nor Kasey was sexually assaulted, and there were no injuries other than the single shot to the head that killed them. That's not the average child abduction pattern.'

Alec followed her logic. 'So, no sexual factor, no violence

or use of physical power other than the disposal of the girls. What are your thoughts?'

'We've been saying "he", but it could be a woman, I guess. Perhaps a bit confused, unstable, maybe thinking that the girls are someone else – perhaps a child she lost – and then kills them when she realises they're not?'

He tried to work it through in his mind.

She watched him, his narrowed eyes reading thoughts that were more instinct than fully formed. 'You're not convinced.'

'We won't rule anything out at this stage. Matthews, we need to know everyone who's lost a child – died, adopted, whatever. Get someone onto the registry people –'

'Don't bother with that,' Isabelle said. 'Jeanie Menotti will know.'

'We're not after town gossip –'

'Jeanie doesn't gossip. People tell her things because she can be trusted not to gossip. She's lived here all her life, knows everyone, and we can trust her discretion.'

'I'll ask her to come up,' Kris offered, heading straight out to the phone in the other office.

Isabelle stared into space, thinking, and Alec sat on the edge of the desk.

'What if it isn't about the girls at all?' she asked suddenly, focusing on him again.

'Then what? Revenge for something?'

'Perhaps. Or some sort of…game?' He could almost see the analytical processes going on in her mind. 'Each abduction carefully planned to leave no clues, to leave us floundering.'

'Challenging us, wanting to prove how clever he is.' Yes, it made a degree of sense. 'The police in general, do you think? Or one of us?' The question still gnawed at him: had the sniper hitting Isabelle been pure chance or intentional? The possibility that she might have been targeted more than worried him.

Her frown deepened as she considered the question. 'It would have to be me, wouldn't it? If it was anyone. Except…' her teeth nipped at her bottom lip, 'except I can't see why. I mean, I wasn't involved with Kasey's investigation, and I've got no connection with her town. If it is some sort of game, then it *must* have started out as just challenging the police.'

'You think there's more to it now?' He watched her closely, gut feeling telling him to trust her judgment.

'I honestly don't know.' She turned to Kris, who had just returned to the room. 'The Wilsons…they're still in the old weatherboard place just north of the stock reserve, aren't they?'

Kris nodded.

'What about it?' Alec demanded.

Isabelle's gaze met his, concern clouding her eyes. 'I thought it was just coincidence at first. I hope that's all it is. But Tanya's house – it's the house that I grew up in.'

THREE

From the grim set of Alec's mouth, Isabelle knew her revelation worried him as much as it did her. Kris looked scared, which didn't do much for her own peace of mind. Maybe it was coincidence – there were only about a hundred houses in the town, after all. A one in one hundred chance wasn't impossible. Just damn long odds.

Still, sitting around brooding wasn't going to find a killer. She stood abruptly, anxious to get on with the investigation, needing to keep busy.

'Let's just concentrate on finding Tanya. Which way are the cattle moving?' she asked Kris.

'East. Came in down the Birraga road yesterday. Take the patrol car if you like.'

Isabelle caught the set of keys Kris tossed to her. Alec frowned, but she didn't care. Too bad if he was used to being in charge.

'We need to talk with the drovers,' she said.

'Why?'

'Bridge Street goes west out of town and becomes the road to Birraga. The cattle – and the drovers – came in from that way yesterday, past the cafe, turning north to go past the showground and into the stock reserve.'

He nodded, understanding. 'Exactly the way Tanya went.'

'Five hundred cattle don't move very fast. The drovers may well have seen something.'

At the car, she went automatically to the driver's side.

His hand on the passenger door handle, Alec hesitated. 'Sure you're okay to drive?' He nodded at her shoulder.

'Yes. It's not far.' She spoke more confidently than she felt, caution overridden by stubbornness and the need to have some control in the situation, something to do other than sit passively beside him.

To her relief, Alec didn't argue, folding his tall frame into the front passenger seat while she clipped the back seatbelt into Finn's harness. At least the guy wasn't so macho that he insisted on driving, she grudgingly admitted to herself.

They caught up with the cattle a couple of kilometres east of town. Spread out over the road and the verge on either side, the large mob moved slowly, grazing as they went, and she kept the car to a crawl as she made her way through them.

Three horses were tied up under a tree, the stockmen sitting on a log nearby in the shade, enjoying a break. She pulled up on the verge and, without stopping to see if Alec followed, walked over to them.

Memories edged out from behind her tight concentration. Memories of being on the road with her father, of droving cattle for weeks on end around the back roads and stock routes of the state during times of drought. The scent of cattle, of horses, of sunshine, dust and dry grasses brought an unexpected wave of nostalgia for a life left behind, long ago.

The stockmen were watching her, expressions guarded but not hostile. She knew they were aware of the missing girl, for they'd been in town last night and had already been questioned briefly.

She didn't know any of these men, but she felt a connection with them, a level of comfort that she hadn't felt in town. Some of the barriers that she'd constructed around herself melted away, and she didn't, for the moment, fight to hold them in place.

She greeted them in the informal manner of the bush, showing her ID in an offhand way as she hunkered down beside them.

'How long have you been on the road?' she asked out of interest.

''Bout ten weeks,' one of them replied. 'We've come from out Walgett way. There's not a scrap of feed left out there.'

She nodded, understanding. Even around here the drought was bad, but on the plains further west the paddocks would just be dust. You didn't take cattle out on the roads for months – 'grazing the long paddock', they used to call it – unless you really had to.

'I need your help to track down Tanya's abductor,' she told them. 'We need to know where everyone was yesterday afternoon. What can you remember about who you saw, either on the Birraga road or while you were coming into town?'

She gave them time to think, and gradually they remembered.

'Joe Ward – he went out and back, in the delivery truck, might have been, oh I dunno, a half-hour or so he was away from town. And that weird old bat from the farm a few miles out, she was presumably going home.'

Isabelle stifled a wry smile. She knew exactly who they meant, and 'weird old bat' was an apt description.

'The mobile library van,' one of the men added. 'Can't really be sure of the time then – maybe three thirty-ish.'

'Yeah, it was just after the school bus with the primary kids from Dungirri,' another remembered.

'Oh, and there was the noxious weeds guy in his truck – what's his name? Oldham? He stopped and yarned for a bit,' the oldest of them said. 'The bus bringing the high school kids from Birraga must have come in about four fifteen or so. Apart from that, there was a white truck I didn't recognise, could have been a Toyota or a Holden. Can't think of anyone else.'

'Any vehicles on the showground road while you were moving the cattle up?'

'Nah,' came the decisive reply. 'We were lucky – we had a clear run up there, nothing to upset the stock.'

It was just as she'd expected, but she couldn't help feeling a pang of disappointment. She jotted down in a notebook what they'd told her, to compare later with the statements they'd already collected. The truck they hadn't recognised could be anyone: white trucks were as much a part of country life as Akubra hats and blue work shirts.

'Seen anyone on the road this afternoon?' she asked.

'This arvo? Not much. Oldham stopped and yarned for a while again, then he went and sprayed some weeds in the paddock over there. He only left about fifteen minutes ago. Other than that, it's been dead quiet.'

She thanked them for their help, and walked back to where Alec waited, leaning against the car. She was glad he'd had the confidence to let her handle it. In his well-tailored city clothes he looked out of place on the bush road, and he'd probably have had a hard time earning the drovers' trust.

'Anything of use?'

'Not a lot. We can wipe Darren Oldham off our list of suspects for the shooting – he was here when the shot was fired.'

'Do you know Oldham?' he asked as they got back into the car.

'He was in my year at school.'

She made a careful U-turn, grateful that the caution needed to avoid the cattle also reduced the strain on her shoulder. He must have misinterpreted her silence for his next question surprised her.

'Did you ever go out with him?'

'Darren?' she scoffed. 'God, no.' She cast him a quick glance as she drove slowly through the herd. 'Besides, in a town this small, kids don't really "go out" together. There was nowhere to go out to, other than the swimming hole and the occasional dance at the hall, and everyone went to those. Definitely not much chance for romance.'

'Not even pashing off behind the hall?'

She felt the blush rise, and when she risked another quick look, his deep blue eyes, usually so serious, twinkled at her. The blush heightened further, yet why she was embarrassed she wasn't sure. Maybe just memories of the awkwardness of being discovered by her dad. Well, DCI Alec Goddard probably wasn't much of a stranger to passionate explorations in dark corners himself.

'So, who kissed you behind the hall, Isabelle?' he asked softly, a grin quirking his mouth.

Free of the cattle, she thrust the vehicle into top gear and picked up speed before answering. She was tempted to tell him it was none of his business, but maybe he'd misconstrue that.

'Mark Strelitz,' she said matter-of-factly. 'But we were caught by my father.'

'Mark Strelitz? Not the politician?'

'Yes, he's a Dungirri boy.' She couldn't help the slight smile that curved her lips as she recalled the night, the thrill of teenage excitement. 'Better at politics than he was at kissing, though.'

Alec's laugh filled the car, the sound drawing another glance from her. She had to drag her eyes back to the road, scarcely seeing it, distracted by the image of his smile crinkling the corners of his eyes and curving his mouth, transforming the hard lines and angles of his face to reveal another side of his character. Her sudden, unexpected awareness of him as a man – an *attractive* man – caught her off-guard and brought the panic she'd experienced earlier slamming back again, tightening around her chest to stifle her breath.

Don't even think about liking him, she berated herself silently, struggling to get a grip on herself.

'Strelitz is chairing that conference in Canberra at present, so we can cross him off the suspect list too,' Alec commented, back to business after that one relaxed moment. 'Anyone else we should look into? Ex-boyfriends who might still be upset?'

Despite the logic of the question in the circumstances, her frayed nerves resented the intrusion into her private life.

'No,' she snapped, not caring if he thought her rude. 'I left here when I was sixteen.'

Out of the corner of her eye she saw his quizzical gaze, but he didn't ask any more questions and she didn't volunteer anything else.

Isabelle used the excuse of getting water for Finn to avoid going straight into the hall with Alec. She needed a few quiet minutes away from him, away from everyone. It was only that she'd been so long by herself, she rationalised. She'd seen more people already today than she had in the past ten months.

She found a relatively clean bucket beside the rainwater tank at the side of the hall and filled it. While Finn lapped gratefully at the water, she crouched beside him, making herself draw slow, deep breaths. This side of the hall was in the shade, but the wall she leaned against still carried some warmth from earlier in the day and the tight muscles of her back found it soothing. Right now she didn't really care that she was in clear view of the creek where the sniper had been only a short while ago. Crime scene tape bounded an area amongst the trees, but a pair of brightly coloured rosellas were pecking their way along the creek bank, a sure sign that nothing was there to frighten them away.

Despite her bravado in front of Alec, driving had increased the pain in her shoulder, and, as if that wasn't enough, the stress and tensions of the day were building into a headache. She massaged her temples with her fingers. She needed to be on the ball, not battling against pain to think.

'I'm glad you're here,' she murmured, rubbing her hand through Finn's mane.

He lifted his head from the bucket and, as if sensing her mood, rasped his slobbery tongue on her cheek.

'No, Finn!' She pushed him away and stood up, delving for the handkerchief in her pocket to wipe her face. 'Don't give me that cute dog look,' she scolded, as he sat back on his haunches, head appealingly tilted to one side. 'You know you're not supposed to lick faces.'

'Does he ever answer back?'

Her head whipped around. Steve Fraser stood about a metre away, leaning against the wall, arms folded casually over his chest.

Great. Steve was the last person she wanted to deal with right now. Years ago, stationed in the same town, they'd gone out together for a few months. That was before she discovered that his boyish charm with women didn't make up for his need for recognition – a need that drove him to show off, and to belittle others when he felt threatened. Yet she'd never managed to completely convince him that she wasn't interested.

'What do you want, Steve?'

'Just wanted to make sure you're all right.'

She stifled a sharp retort. He sounded genuine. It wasn't as though he had no good qualities – just not enough of them.

'I'm fine.' Not the whole truth, but he didn't have to know that. Fine as long as nobody came too close. Fine as long as she stayed away from crowds. Fine as long as nobody raised their voice or moved too quickly.

He took a step towards her, hesitated, and looked at the ground, stuffing his hands in his pockets.

'I'm real sorry about...you know...last year.'

Yes, he probably did feel sorry she'd been hurt. But not about anything else.

'Maybe if you and your cronies hadn't been so damn quick to jump to conclusions, we would have found the real murderer and Jess Sutherland might still be alive.'

'It could have been Chalmers,' he insisted. 'This one might just be a copycat.'

'Sure, and Santa Claus lives in the Dungirri scrub.'

The hurt in his eyes reproached her. 'Shit, Bella, what do you want me to do? We don't even know yet if it was a mistake, but you seem to want me to grovel and beg forgiveness anyway.'

'No, I don't want that.' Letting anger and resentment take over wouldn't help them work together to find Tanya. 'I'm sorry – I'm just a bit...edgy, I guess.'

To her amazement, he didn't pursue it further. He seemed less arrogant, less cocky. Could it be that he'd changed in the past year?

He smiled wanly, as though accepting her apology. 'What's your opinion of Goddard?'

Definitely a change in him. Twelve months ago he'd rarely asked for others' opinions.

What could she say? That Alec was everything Steve wasn't? That he worked well in a team, irrespective of the difference in rank. That he didn't have to push himself forward, be the expert.

'I only met him this morning.' She brushed off the question, every sense warning her that contemplating Alec any more than necessary led to dangerous ground. 'He seems okay so far.'

Steve raised an eyebrow. 'I assumed you'd known him for a while. You seem to be pretty pally with him.'

The edge in his tone made her swear silently.

'I'm not "pally", or whatever else you might want to imply, with Alec Goddard. Or with anyone else, for that matter.'

She signalled to Finn and walked past Steve, biting her lip to keep her temper from exploding.

FOUR

Inside the hall, everyone worked quietly, the underlying tension evident in the fact that no one laughed or joked. Alec, deep in conversation with Adam Donahue, glanced across as she entered, as if he'd been keeping an eye out for her, but he just nodded to acknowledge her presence and turned his attention back to the constable.

In a partially screened-off area, Kris sat at a table with Jeanie Menotti. The older woman's kind face creased into a drawn smile as Isabelle joined them.

'I was just saying, Bella, that I can't think of anyone likely who's lost a child. Most of the cases I can think of, the people are long gone from town. Mick Barrett's still here, but he's been propping up the bar at the pub for the last seventeen years since Paula was killed, and incapable of anything. His wife gave up on him and left years ago. Other than Mick, there's only Joe Ward – he and Mary lost a little boy twenty years or so ago. He had a severe asthma attack and they couldn't get him to Birraga in time.'

Isabelle nodded. 'I remember.' She also remembered Joe's unease earlier today in his hardware store. But that didn't mean a lot. Joe had at least one other good reason to feel embarrassed around her – not that she intended to share that with anyone.

'I really can't see Joe being involved, though,' Jeanie said. 'I mean, he was devastated, of course, when they lost the boy, but his daughter was just a baby then, and they've always been close, especially since Mary died.'

'And he's not the brightest of guys,' Kris added. 'I don't believe he'd be able to plan something like this.'

No, Isabelle couldn't imagine Joe committing this crime. Other crimes perhaps, but not this one.

Her chest tightened as she asked, hating every word, 'It's been a year, and Tanya is the same age now that Jess was. I know they've left town, but can we verify where Mitch and Sara were yesterday?'

Jeanie jerked in surprise. 'You don't seriously think…No, they couldn't have, Bella.'

Kris rested a hand on the older woman's arm. 'It's okay, Jeanie. I phoned Sara last night. I thought they needed to know, before they saw it on the news.'

Isabelle exhaled in relief. 'We can rule them out?'

'Yes. Sara's working on a research project for State Forests in Victoria. She's been down there for seven months. Mitch…

well, he's been doing casual stock work up in Queensland, on some of the Kidman and Co properties. Sara told me he was at Durrie Station just a few days ago, and I got hold of him there this morning.'

'They've split up?' Isabelle asked.

Jeanie nodded. 'Many marriages don't survive the death of a child. And theirs was struggling well before that.'

Sorrow and guilt replaced Isabelle's brief sense of relief. If they'd saved Jess last year... She swallowed hard. She had to focus on here and now, on Tanya.

'What about anyone who's maybe lost custody of a child? Or had to give a baby up for adoption?'

Jeanie thought for a long moment. 'Once again, no one who's still around, that I'm aware of. Barbara Russell had a baby, the year after she finished school. A little girl, I think, but she was adopted out.'

'I didn't hear about that,' Isabelle said. 'We're the same age, and went through school together, but I didn't see her or anyone else much after I left.'

'Oh, her parents are dreadfully old-fashioned, didn't want anyone to know. They sent her away to have the baby, and pressured her to give it up.'

'Do you know where Barbara is now?' Kris asked.

'She lived in Sydney, but she died a year or two back. Some form of cancer apparently – it was very quick.'

'What about her parents?' Kris tapped her pen against her notebook. 'They're still in town. Could they...? I mean, they've lost a daughter and grandchild now – guilt and regret might have tipped them over the edge.'

Instinctively Isabelle knew that didn't fit, but it took a moment to work out why. 'Barbara was dark-haired. The girls who've been abducted are all blondes. If you were trying to replace a kid, surely you'd go for at least some resemblance?'

'That makes sense,' Kris commented. 'And the Russells – well, I just can't see either of them doing something like this. Neither of them are very mobile, for a start.'

'It's highly unlikely to be either of them,' Isabelle agreed. 'Any other thoughts, Jeanie?'

'I can't think of anyone. I'm sorry that I haven't been much help –' Jeanie stopped suddenly, her hand flying to her mouth.

'What is it?' Isabelle demanded.

'I just remembered…someone who had a baby – it was years and years ago, when there were homes for girls who got into trouble, and the babies were always adopted out.'

'Who?'

'She wouldn't…no, I'm sure she couldn't…'

'Who, Jeanie?' Isabelle leaned forward. 'It could be important.'

Jeanie met her gaze briefly, and dropped her eyes away, clasping her work-worn hands tightly on the table. 'It was Delphi.'

Isabelle stared at her as though she'd said the sky was green, shock reverberating all the way to her stomach. '*Delphi*? Delphi had a baby?'

'You've got to be kidding!' Kris added in equal astonishment.

'No. It was way before you were born, Bella. Fifty years or more ago. She was maybe eighteen, nineteen.'

'Hell.' Isabelle shook her head, trying to clear the confusing fog enough to come to grips with the revelation. No wonder Jeanie had been hesitant – and if it had been anyone but Jeanie saying it, she would never have believed it.

She pushed back her chair and crossed the room to Alec.

'There's someone you need to interview,' Bella said, and Alec looked up from his conversation with Donahue. 'She was out on the Birraga road yesterday coming from town around the time Tanya was taken. The drovers saw her. And she had to give up a baby for adoption years ago.'

She heard Kris beside her, felt a gentle hand on her arm. 'It probably isn't Delphi, Bella. I mean, I know she can be a bit strange at times, but…'

'But we all know that she's a loner, holds grudges, and doesn't like men or people in authority – or anyone else much, for that matter,' Isabelle maintained, conscience calling for the truth while her instinct screamed denial.

'So, who is this Delphi?' Alec asked.

'Philadelphia O'Connell. She's…she's my father's sister.'

For all her aunt's strange ways, Isabelle held a fondness for her which unbalanced her normal professional instincts. But if it turned out to be Delphi, she'd never, ever forgive herself for missing it last year.

'Are you close to her?' He watched her, eyes narrowed.

'No one is close to Delphi.' That was the honest truth. Her aunt had never gone in for playing happy families and they kept in touch only sporadically. 'But I'm her only relative and we get along okay.'

'Good. We'll go see her together then. I'd like to know who else she saw on the road yesterday.'

'It's not correct procedure for a relative –'

He waved a hand and cut her off. 'It won't be a formal interview. I presume, if your aunt doesn't like men or people in authority, she's hardly likely to be very open with me or Fraser, is she?'

'Consider yourself privileged if Delphi even speaks to you,' Kris told Alec. 'I rarely get more than a grunt.'

'But you don't believe she could be involved?'

His question to Kris was open, genuinely seeking her view, as he'd asked for and listened to others' views during the day. Another point in his favour, Isabelle noted. If she was counting. Which she definitely wasn't.

'I doubt it,' Kris answered. 'The thing about Delphi is that she's got a pretty solid code of ethics, and most people don't live up to them, in her opinion. You can always rely on her to help out in a crisis, but the rest of the time… well, she's an independent soul and goes her own way.'

And that, thought Isabelle, was a very tactful way of putting it.

'Before we talk to Delphi, I need to go and see Tanya's parents.' Once again, Alec's eyes settled on Isabelle. 'How well do you know them, Isabelle? Should you come too?'

She closed her eyes briefly, the headache that had been lurking in the background tightening its pressure around her head. She appreciated that he was leaving it to her judgment whether she went as well, but in reality she had no choice. Beth and Ryan Wilson would be torn by their anxiety and fear for their daughter. The more human and personal the police presence was, the better for them.

She would have to steel herself to face them. The memory of the terrible, agonising pain in Sara Sutherland's eyes last year was burned in her heart, and she had prayed silently that she would never, ever have to face anyone else with the same news.

'I'll come,' she answered.

'Good. Tell me about them as we drive up there.'

'It's not far – we can walk.'

'Not until we find out who shot at you.'

And that, she recognised from his stony face, was not a decision there was any point arguing with.

They went out into the heat again, the three of them, Finn insinuating himself between her and Alec. He acted of his own accord, but she couldn't help feeling relieved that he did. At least it meant that Alec's disturbing presence was not too close. Of course, once they got into the car, his broad shoulders would fill the confined space and she'd have to fight the panicky feeling she got whenever someone came close. She'd already learned today that months of avoiding people hadn't cured her of that legacy from last year.

Breathe in, hold, breathe out…

She pulled open the back door for Finn, the movement setting off the pain again in her shoulder and causing her to catch in a sharp breath instead of the next slow one. And, trust her luck, Alec had seen her wince. She dug in her pocket for the keys and reluctantly tossed them to him before he had the chance to make some smart 'I told you so' comment. But he just went to the driver's side without a word, adjusting the seat to accommodate his height while she got in beside him.

'Beth is a local,' she started explaining before he'd even reversed out, trying to keep her mind on anything other than the panic pressing around her. 'She's a couple of years younger than me. Ryan's from Birraga originally. I only know him slightly – he was at Birraga High School when I was there.'

'Any chance either of them could be involved in this?'

It was a legitimate question, but she shook her head decisively. 'Beth wouldn't hurt a fly. Her nickname as a kid was Mouse. And I don't see how Ryan could be – his spine was injured in a rugby game a couple of years ago, and he's a paraplegic now.'

A grimace of sympathy flashed across his face. Real sympathy, as though he cared about a person he'd never even met. Yet another point in his favour – except she wasn't counting, of course.

She gritted her teeth to suppress all the thoughts that could blast away her shaky self-control, and pulled the memory of Tanya's photograph back into her mind. That's why she was here. To save a pretty, blonde, laughing little girl who

should be playing with her friends right now, instead of...
No, don't think about that either.

Fingers clenched so tight in her palms that they hurt, she stared at the scene out the window, grappling for control. They passed the park and the swimming hole, quiet and deserted. Normally, on a hot day, once school was out the place would be teeming with kids, but today parents were obviously keeping their children very close to home.

The emptiness of the scene tensed her muscles even further. The surface of the water lay undisturbed, and the ancient swing hanging from the branch of a gum tree rocked in the wind, as though some invisible, ghostly child played on it, all alone.

FIVE

The car was hot from sitting in the intense sun, and the air conditioner hadn't had time to make any difference. Alec sweltered in his sports jacket, but he planned to keep it on, conscious of the need to show the Wilsons the respect of a professional appearance.

Isabelle sat silent beside him. She must be dreading this as much as he was. God, how he hated cases like this – and he hated putting her through it.

His fingers itched to reach out to her, to close around her hand and reassure her that it would be all right, but for a zillion and one reasons that was impossible. Including the fact that, no matter how hard they tried, it might not turn out all right.

Within a short distance they reached the edge of town, the Wilsons' home separated from those in the street by vacant blocks and the stock reserve. He parked the car on the verge and waited beside it while Isabelle released Finn from the back.

On the east side of the road, the scrubland echoed with the song of small birds, yet in spite of the pleasing sounds a sensation of menace prickled Alec's skin.

'Do you get the feeling we're being watched?' he asked quietly, turning to scan the trees.

She stopped, cocked her head slightly to one side, listening while she surveyed the forest. After a few moments she shook her head.

'I doubt there's anyone there.'

'How can you tell?'

'The only birds giving alarm calls are the ones near us.'

He believed her, yet the uneasiness remained and he cast another wary glance at the forest. Seeing nothing in its denseness, he turned back to the house and followed Isabelle through the gate.

The old weatherboard house Isabelle had grown up in had seen better days, but someone had made an effort to look after it. A couple of rose bushes bloomed red in the front garden, in defiance of the extreme summer heat, and a garden bed of low-growing native plants appeared well-tended. A plastic wading pool awaited happier times, and he caught a glimpse of a swing set in the backyard.

Isabelle commanded Finn to stay and he obeyed, stretching out in the shade of the house.

The door swung open before Alec could knock. Instantly, he remembered what Isabelle had said about Beth Wilson's nickname. The woman before him was just like a mouse – petite, with large brown eyes, red-rimmed, in a dainty face. She wore a neat blue sundress, and over it, a cotton apron, clean but for a few small spots of flour. Her glance flickered from him to Isabelle, apprehension draining her face of colour.

'Bella! Is there any news?'

Isabelle swiftly shook her head and, to Alec's surprise, touched the other woman lightly on the arm. Her normally closed expression softened. 'Nothing yet, Beth. Just a courtesy call. This is Detective Chief Inspector Alec Goddard. He's come from Sydney to be in charge of the police team.'

'I'm sorry that we're meeting in these circumstances, Mrs Wilson,' Alec said, in place of the standard 'How do you do?' It was obvious how she was – exhausted by worry and a sleepless night, terrified for her daughter's safety.

'Please, come in,' Beth invited, her gentle, restrained dignity a contrast to the initial mouse-like impression.

In the living room, with its comfortable clutter of toys, books and knick-knacks, Ryan Wilson waited in his wheelchair, a small girl of about five years old curled asleep on his lap. Another child, a toddler, lay asleep on the sofa, thumb in mouth and clutching a well-worn soft toy in the other hand.

Alec's throat constricted. Small touches in the room told him this was a loving family. Photos of each of the girls stood proudly on the mantelpiece, carefully framed childish artwork hung on the walls, and a blue ribbon and first prize certificate from the Birraga Show decorated the shelf of a cabinet.

Some bastard was putting them through this worst of ordeals, and Alec fought to suppress the anger that burned in his gut.

Isabelle greeted Ryan, then introduced Alec to him as she had to Beth, using his full title.

'Kris Matthews told us someone was being sent from Sydney. It's good of you to come and see us.'

Ryan's handshake was firm, his courteous welcome delivered in a voice that held more than a trace of strain. Alec admired his composure, not sure he could have been the same in the circumstances.

Ryan was a big man, probably equalling him in height if he'd been able to stand. His broad, muscular shoulders and chest would have made him a good pick for a rugby team. The day's growth of beard and crooked nose which had likely seen a fist at close quarters gave the impression of a man who'd not always led a quiet life, yet his left arm held his daughter gently and protectively.

Alec dismissed instantly any thought that the man could be involved in the abduction of his daughter. Some fathers were capable of it, but not this one. And he wasn't just thinking about physical ability when he made that assessment.

'Can I get you a cool drink, Detect... Inspect... I'm sorry,

I don't know the right...what to call you.' Beth blushed in embarrassment, too distressed by such a little thing.

'Just Alec, please. And yes, thank you, a cool drink would be wonderful, if it's not too much trouble.'

'No...We were just going to have one too.'

'I'll come and help,' Isabelle offered immediately, touching Beth's arm once more in silent sympathy.

Ryan's tender gaze followed his wife as the two women walked into the kitchen.

'Bella always used to look after Beth at school,' he said softly. 'I'm glad she's here for her.' He indicated an old armchair, its worn upholstery visible under the corner of a brightly coloured crocheted blanket. 'Please, take a seat. Is there any news?'

'Nothing of substance yet, I'm sorry.' Alec considered his words carefully. 'Mr Wilson, there's still a chance that Tanya has just wandered away and got lost, and we'll keep the SES crews searching. But because we haven't found her yet, and she doesn't usually wander, I need to advise you that I'm treating the situation as a suspected abduction.'

'You think it's the same person who took Jessie?' It was a harsh whisper, and Alec saw the tightening of the man's arm around his younger daughter, as if he wouldn't ever let her go again.

'That is one of our lines of enquiry, yes.' The cautious words he had to use sounded so damned inadequate. Alec's throat contracted again; he wished there was something he could say that would give this family back their lives, yet he knew the only thing that could do that was finding their daughter.

He cleared his throat, the sound loud in the quiet room. 'Mr Wilson – Ryan – is there anyone – anyone at all – you can think of who might want to hurt you like this?'

Ryan shook his head wearily. 'Kris already asked us that, and I can't think of anyone.'

'You work for the Shire Council?'

'Yes. Before the accident, I supervised the road maintenance crew. Now I do three days a week at the Council office, taking rates payments, that sort of thing. They've been good to me, found me a job I can do.'

Just as they should, Alec thought, with an edge of anger towards the Council, figuring that three days a week was scarcely enough to support a young family. Surely they could have found something full-time for him?

Ryan turned away and brushed at his eyes with the heel of his hand. 'It's about all I can do now,' he muttered, biting his lip. 'I used to be in the SES, and captain of the local fire brigade. What kind of man is it who can't go and search for his own daughter?'

It could so easily have been me, Alec realised, remembering all the games of rugby he'd played, all the action sports he'd tried over the years, all the physical encounters with criminals. One slip, one foot in the wrong place, and he too might have been locked in a wheelchair for life. He struggled for something meaningful to say, and only managed, 'That's not your fault.'

Ryan made a bitter, disbelieving sound. 'Isn't it? You know, Beth sat here all last night with her rosary beads, and all I could think was maybe I was being punished. I wasn't a saint as a youth. I don't know why a woman like Beth even looked twice at me – I don't deserve her. And now I keep thinking that maybe, if I'd done more last year, I could have stopped what happened, and that this is God's retribution for that.'

'What do you mean, about last year?' Alec asked sharply.

Ryan's heavy sigh seemed to come from deep inside. 'I was in the pub that day Jess was found. Everyone was upset about it. We knew Dan Chalmers had been questioned by the police, and some of the guys talked about going and roughing him up a bit. I didn't think they meant anything – the drink and anger talking, you know? I had to go back to work, but a little later I saw the cars leaving, all at the same time. The more I thought about it the more worried I got, so I called up the police. If I'd tried to talk them out of it, or rung the cops earlier, maybe...' His voice drained away.

Alec filed that information away in his memory for further consideration.

'You did more than others did, Ryan. You can't hold yourself accountable for their choices.'

'Can't I?' He was silent for a moment, then asked abruptly, 'Are you a father, Alec?'

'No. An uncle, that's all.'

'Well, I don't know if you can understand this, but if the bastard who took Tanya was in front of me now, I can't help but wonder whether I wouldn't do the same thing they did, even in this damned wheelchair.'

What could Alec say to that, in all honesty? If one of Jill's, his sister's, kids went missing and he had to sit helpless, he'd probably feel the same way. Even now, although he'd never met Tanya, he was conscious of the rage burning under the surface of his own control. How much more intense that would be as a father, he could only imagine.

Ryan watched him, mutely, waiting for some response, as the detective sought for words that might make sense.

'I won't insult you by saying I understand,' Alec said slowly, 'because I'm not a parent and I don't. I can't tell you what I'd do, what I'd feel, in the circumstances. But I hope I'd remember that revenge like that – and I've seen it a few times – doesn't help. It doesn't bring anyone back, it doesn't change what's happened, it doesn't make the pain go away.'

And people get hurt, he added to himself. People like Bella, who, alone, had faced the angry mob and tried to protect Dan Chalmers. No wonder that terrible pain haunted her eyes and she shut out the world. Her physical injuries had healed, but how long would it be before she had faith in humanity again?

Isabelle wished she was anywhere but here, in the kitchen she'd once known so well, with Beth's huge brown eyes begging her for hope and reassurance. Little Beth, little Mouse, who'd suffered under the teasing of the other kids at school without it warping her generous nature, now needed something from her she no longer knew that she could give.

How could she comfort Beth when she'd had to close her own heart off? She'd seen the violence that people were capable of, knew there were no guarantees that Tanya would be found alive. Her own pain and apprehension were hard enough to bear without taking on Beth's as well.

The homely smell of fresh baking in the kitchen contrasted with the grimness she felt. The wood-fired stove still sat in the fireplace, radiating heat to add to the oppressiveness of the temperature outside.

Time faded, and her memory saw the old rocking chair in front of that same stove, and herself curled on her father's lap, the two of them rocking away the long nights of grief after her mother's death.

We'll make it through, little one, she heard his whisper in her memory. *We'll give each other strength to keep going.* She could almost feel his arms around her, the sense of safety, of love and protection.

I can't do this, Dad, her heart cried, and swift and sure the response he'd always made in his encouraging way slipped into her mind: *Yes, you can, love.*

A tear trickled down Beth's cheek. Somehow Isabelle found the strength she needed and held out her arms to her friend.

'I'm sorry,' Beth sobbed into her shoulder, letting her tears flow. 'I shouldn't...'

'It's okay – you're allowed,' Isabelle murmured.

Tears seared her own eyelids. This shouldn't be happening – not to Beth, gentle Beth who'd never raised her voice, never held a grudge. She was the exception to the rule, a person who would never lose control in anger. The old protectiveness that she'd always felt for the younger girl brought a wave of caring and affection surging from the small corner of her heart she'd unlocked.

'You should have someone with you. Can I call one of your friends?' she asked when Beth's sobs eased, struggling to focus on the practical to keep her doubts and fears from overwhelming her.

Beth pulled a handful of tissues from a box on the bench and wiped her eyes. 'Jeanie stayed last night and this morning. She's been wonderful. My parents are on their first trip overseas, and our other close friends are in the SES, so they're out searching. Some of the older ladies have been by and offered to stay, but I didn't really want them, you know? It's all been so uneasy this past year, and now...now they're scared, and I couldn't cope with that. Jeanie's different, and you. I don't have to be...polite with either of you.'

Her small, brave smile sliced into Isabelle's heart. 'Of course you don't.' She'd tried to make her voice light, but emotion clogged her throat and it came out cracked and strangled.

Beth wiped her eyes again. 'I was getting drinks, wasn't I? I made some biscuits too – we'll have some of those.'

She busied herself finding a tray, pouring glasses of cold juice, and sliding still-warm biscuits from a baking tray onto a plate.

The rich, fresh-baked aroma woke Isabelle's stomach and reminded her she'd not had lunch – not eaten anything, in fact, since early that morning. No wonder that headache still pressed at her temples.

She carried the tray of glasses into the living room while Beth followed with the biscuits. Alec met her eyes as they entered, concern etched in the tight lines of his face. Concern for Beth? For her? She averted her eyes quickly, conscious that her own might betray traces of tears. She could handle this, damn it. She didn't need Alec looking at her with that expression, worrying about her. Beth and Ryan were the ones who needed him, but she didn't.

The child on the sofa woke and looked shyly around, thumb still in her mouth. Her lips trembled at the sight of strangers and Beth went quickly to her, sitting and taking her onto her lap in a reassuring cuddle.

Isabelle handed the glasses of juice around – to Beth, to Ryan, to Alec. She kept her eyes on the tray, not Alec's face, noticing only the long, strong fingers that closed around the glass as he took it. Capable hands. *Sensual hands,* whispered a voice, buried, long forgotten.

She turned away, unsteady, almost spilling the remaining glass on the tray.

'Would you pass the biscuits around, please, Bella?' Beth asked, her youngest daughter still clinging to her. 'They're choc chip – Tanya's favourites,' she added, a shake in her voice, another tear escaping.

Isabelle bit her lip so hard she tasted blood, but she took the plate from the coffee table and offered it around.

'Then I'll just take one, Mrs Wilson, so there's plenty left for Tanya,' Alec said.

The gentleness, the quiet certainty, with which he spoke of Tanya's return contradicted, challenged, the fear in Isabelle's mind. She took a slow, deep breath as she sat down on the sofa beside Beth.

'Do you really believe it – that Tanya will come home?' Ryan stared at Alec, all the terrible, raw pain in his face demanding an honest answer.

Isabelle heard Beth's sharp intake of breath beside her, and felt fingers curl tightly around her own.

Alec met Ryan's gaze without flinching.

'I have to believe it, Ryan. And I promise you – you and Beth – that Isabelle and I will do everything humanly possible to bring Tanya home to you. We'll search for her as though she was our own daughter. Won't we, Isabelle?'

His choice of words startled her. Then rationality returned and she interpreted it as he'd surely meant – that they would both give all that a parent would give to bring Tanya home.

'Yes.' Without hesitation, she made the commitment to Beth and Ryan, and to Tanya: *As though she was our own daughter.*

SIX

They found Delphi out in a paddock on her property, and she watched them, unmoving, as they walked across the dusty, parched earth towards her.

The slight impression of eccentricity Alec had experienced when he'd first met Isabelle paled to nothing beside the picture her aunt presented. Surrounded by goats of all sizes and colours, Delphi O'Connell looked like some bizarre cross between the wicked witch of the west and a scarecrow. Her too-large faded jeans were belted around her waist with a piece of rope, and an old checked shirt flapped open in the wind revealing an equally ancient, patched T-shirt. To top it all, her wiry grey hair stuck out in all directions around a face that had surely never been beautiful, with its square jaw, heavy brows and weather-beaten skin. It seemed that Isabelle's fine features didn't come from her O'Connell genes.

Yet the cool, grey eyes that met his held a very familiar guardedness.

'Who's he?' she asked Isabelle straight out, without any word of greeting.

'Alec Goddard,' Isabelle replied, as though she was well-used to her aunt's unconventional ways. He noticed she made no mention of his rank, as she'd been so careful to do with the Wilsons. Doubtless because it wouldn't go down too well here.

Delphi's eyes swept over him, blatantly assessing, before coming back to meet his in a challenge that he was more accustomed to receiving from tough guys in back alleys. He held eye contact with her, letting her take her time, not backing down.

'Boyfriend?'

The question wasn't directed at him. She was testing him, trying to rile him.

'Colleague,' Isabelle said hastily, and he thought he saw a faint hint of pink rise on her cheeks. 'We're here on police business.'

Surprise flickered across Delphi's face. 'What's happened that needs you back in town? I thought you were giving up the plods?'

'I am. But I'm here because young Tanya Wilson went missing yesterday afternoon.'

Either Delphi was an actress worthy of multiple Academy Awards, which Alec doubted, or this was genuinely the first she'd heard about the abduction. She frowned, rubbed her hand over her temple, shook her head in disbelief.

'Wilson? The family up at your old place?'

'Yes.' Isabelle explained what little they knew so far. 'You came into town yesterday – did you see anyone, anything, at all suspicious?'

'Whole damn town's suspicious, if you ask me,' Delphi muttered. 'Wouldn't trust a single one of them.'

'Who did you see yesterday?'

'Went to Joe Ward's store for some fencing wire. He tried to overcharge me as usual. Got some fuel and bread at the Truck Stop, then came straight home.'

Alec let Isabelle ask the questions. No sense in getting Delphi offside by appearing pushy, not when Isabelle was perfectly capable of dealing with her.

Unfortunately, Delphi had nothing new for them. The only vehicles she'd seen corresponded with the information the drovers had given them. The times she recalled fitted what they already knew and gave her a reasonable alibi – although as far as Alec was concerned, she didn't need it. Delphi O'Connell might not be best of friends with the world, but she had no involvement with Tanya's disappearance, of that he was convinced.

A little to his surprise, Delphi walked back across the paddock with them, her solid, masculine strides a stark contrast to Isabelle's light grace.

'Your dog needs water,' Delphi chastised when they reached Finn, waiting patiently in the shade of a tree where Isabelle had ordered him to stay. 'There's a water dish by the house.'

Finn didn't look that thirsty to Alec – he was scarcely even panting – and he half-suspected that Delphi was doing a little manoeuvring to get Isabelle out of earshot. A suspicion confirmed when Isabelle and Finn headed across to the old farmhouse and Delphi turned her sharp eyes on him.

'You're some big-shot cop they've sent from Sydney?'

Not exactly how he would have described himself, but he nodded anyway.

'Then you'd better find the fiend who's doing this.'

'I intend to.'

'Good. And look out for Bella while you're at it. She crawled away like a wounded animal last year. Blamed herself for that kiddy's murder, but it was more than that. What those idiots did to her... She might not show it much, but she's afraid.'

He watched Isabelle pour water from a tap for Finn and stand beside him as he drank. All day she'd held herself together with a strength and determination few people could have mustered. Not letting fear show, not balking at coming back to face a nightmare in her dedication to find Tanya. And yes, he'd sensed that fear in her. Fear that she held just in check by keeping herself distant from everyone but Finn. Who could blame her? Yet she was here in spite of it.

'She's a very courageous woman,' he said.

And beautiful, a voice from somewhere deep within pointed out, and the small part of him that wasn't detective chief inspector saw the sunshine dancing bronze and gold glints in the rich chestnut of her hair, noticed how the fine cotton fabric of her shirt skimmed the subtle curves of shoulder, waist, breast...

'You're interested, aren't you?'

Delphi's candid observation jerked him back to reality and a flood of guilt. Isabelle's sharp-eyed aunt had read what he'd obviously not hidden well enough – yes, he was interested. Interested in Bella as a woman, not only as a colleague. It had been so long since he'd noticed a woman in that way, he wasn't used to reading the signs. He didn't get involved with female colleagues – heck, not with anyone much, these days. He'd buried himself in his work and allowed himself only brief, casual relationships when time permitted.

So it didn't matter one bit that he could picture Bella's face even with his eyes closed, that just the sight of her did strange things to his pulse rate, and that his protective instincts – and his imagination – had clicked into overdrive since this morning. He'd keep an eye on Isabelle during this investigation because he'd brought her here, but after that he'd go back to Sydney, and she'd get on with her life, and they'd probably never see each other again. That's the way it would be.

'We're just colleagues, Ms O'Connell.'

She snorted and glared at him. 'Sure. But I warn you, although I've never been much good at the aunt stuff, if you hurt her, I'll personally take great pleasure in cutting off your balls and feeding them to her dog.'

He didn't take offence at her candour, just felt pleased that Isabelle had someone who cared enough about her to warn him off. He smiled wryly. 'Don't worry, you won't need to. Besides, if I gave him even the slightest cause, I'm sure Finn would be more than happy to help himself.'

Isabelle saw Delphi's grin and wondered, with an inward groan, what mischief her aunt was up to now. But the two faces that turned towards her as she joined them were carefully innocent and unreadable. Something had just happened, but she had no idea what.

She stole another quick glance at Alec, wondering if Delphi had said something outrageous. There were no clues in his expression, just his unsmiling, professional veneer as he thanked Delphi with his usual courtesy, then headed towards the car, tactfully leaving her alone with her aunt.

'I'll try and stop by again –'

'You concentrate on finding that kid,' Delphi interrupted. 'That's more important than visiting an old hermit like me.'

How come it was so hard to leave? She should just go straight to the car, let Alec drive them away. Delphi had never been one for hugs or expressions of fondness, never been the sort to offer a shoulder to cry on. Life had carved Delphi's character with hard work, loneliness and disappointments. And yet a gentleness, glimpsed only occasionally, lurked behind that solitary, stubborn pride. When she'd first woken in the hospital last year, it had been Delphi sitting beside her – and her calloused hands had been as gentle as any mother's.

Until Jeanie had dropped her bombshell this afternoon, Isabelle had never quite understood why Delphi kept her distance from the world. Now she recognised that behind the stubborn pride lay a pain and betrayal that was still too raw, even fifty years later, to be laid open.

She could identify with that hurt and betrayal, understood in her own heart why Delphi had wanted to shut out any feelings, shut out the world. She'd done the same thing herself. You couldn't be hurt if you didn't let yourself care.

Except it didn't quite work that way. Shutting off your heart didn't make the pain go away, and she saw that in Delphi's eyes now, even as she recognised that her own heart had to respond to those around her – first Beth, now Delphi.

So much for trying not to care.

But what could she do? *You should have had your chance to be a mother,* she wanted to say, and couldn't. Not now, not when it would take a whole lot of explaining about how she knew, not when it needed time, not when she didn't feel strong enough to deal with Delphi's hurt, not when Tanya was still out there and another mother needed the little she could give.

Instead, Isabelle surprised them both by brushing a quick kiss on her aunt's leathery cheek and murmuring a promise to return. She noticed, as she got into the car, that Delphi didn't wipe that kiss away as she'd half-expected.

Alec drove with his eyes fixed on the road, grim-faced and uncommunicative. Had Delphi said something to offend him? Or did he suspect that she was involved in Tanya's abduction?

'I didn't ask her about the baby,' Isabelle said after a few kilometres had passed in silence. 'Do you think I should have?'

He raised an eyebrow. 'Not from the point of view of the investigation.'

'You don't think she did it?'

'I'm certain she didn't.'

'How can you be so sure?'

He glanced across at her. 'It doesn't fit.'

'But she can be so...difficult...'

The corner of his mouth twitched. 'I can be difficult too. That doesn't make me – or Delphi – a murderer.'

Alec – difficult? She wouldn't have applied that word to him. At least, not in the same way it applied to Delphi. She could well imagine that he would hold fast and argue a point if he believed he was right, even to his superiors; that he'd expect the highest levels of performance from his staff, not tolerating slack work. She had no doubt he could, at times, get angry, critical, even harsh. Yet she suspected it would take a lot to make him lose his temper. Everything he'd done so far had been controlled. Controlled, but not cold. The compassion and sensitivity he'd shown the Wilsons revealed that underneath his composed, professional exterior his emotions were alive and active. So many cops shut them down, became pessimistic and cynical in the face of the daily exposure to the worst elements of humanity. Somehow Alec had kept his intact, although shielded behind the proficient DCI persona.

'I like your aunt,' he continued. 'She's upfront and honest about what she thinks. She's also lost none of her marbles. She's not going to mistake another person's child for her own daughter.'

Isabelle didn't answer, but a deep breath of relief caught in her throat, halfway between a sigh and a sob. She hadn't realised how scared she'd been that maybe she'd read her own aunt so wrong all these years. Twelve months ago, before she'd been called in on Jess's case, she would never have doubted Delphi for a moment. But now she doubted herself and her own judgment almost as much as she distrusted humanity in general.

'So, we're back at square one. What next?' She spoke her thought aloud.

'The more I think about it, the more I doubt we're looking for a woman.' He changed down a gear as they approached the outskirts of town. 'Both Kasey and Jess were found in the clothes they'd been wearing when they were taken. Their hair was untidy, probably not brushed or combed for days. They'd been sedated, probably for most of the time they were held.'

She understood his meaning. 'If a woman abducts a child, there's usually an element of caring, of nurturing, involved. New clothes, toys or other gifts. Attempts to establish a relationship. But with Jess and Kasey there was…nothing.'

'Exactly.' Alec slowed as they approached the Truck Stop Cafe. 'I want to go over the route Tanya took. This is the road here, isn't it?'

He turned right and drove down past the school, then did a U-turn and drove slowly along the length of the showground road. Past the cafe, past the empty pavilions in the dilapidated showground, past the deserted timber mill buildings, until he stopped again at the gate that led to the stock reserve.

Isabelle knew that Kris and the others had thoroughly searched the route, including the showground and timber mill, last night. Had Tanya even made it as far as this?

Alec let the car idle, studying the area around them, while Isabelle looked at the stock reserve. She'd walked through it herself almost every afternoon through all the years of primary school.

The little grass that grew in spite of the drought was closely cropped by stock and wildlife, leaving the ground mostly dust. Dust and cowpats, Isabelle observed. Five hundred cattle naturally left considerable evidence of their overnight stay.

She glanced at the few houses facing the reserve along Mill Road. A couple were boarded up, and outside another a faded 'For Sale' sign leaned crookedly. Next door, house stumps were all that was left on the block – probably yet another house relocated to Birraga or elsewhere since the timber mill had closed and Dungirri's population had begun its rapid decline.

All in all, it meant there were few eyes around that might have been watching a small girl walk into the stock reserve yesterday afternoon.

She unclipped her seatbelt and wrenched the car door open before Alec stopped her with a firm hand on her arm.

'You're not going out in the open, O'Connell.'

The warmth of his hand on her bare forearm prickled along her skin. He moved it quickly, back to the steering wheel, but she could still feel its impression.

'I need to look over the reserve.'

'Matthews said they'd searched yesterday, and found nothing.'

'Yes, but they probably only searched along the direct line from the gate to the house. I don't think she went that way.'

His eyes narrowed, questioning, and she ploughed on in explanation. 'I walked home this way when I was a child. Kids often don't go in straight lines.'

'I still don't want you standing out there in the paddock – it would be a clear shot for anyone.'

She waved an exasperated hand back along the road. 'No one is following us. No one knows we're here. Besides, I may not have been the target earlier – it might have been random. And I know this area better than anyone.'

He hesitated a long moment before slowly nodding. 'Okay – but just for a few minutes. And stay close to me.'

Once inside the reserve, she allowed Finn the luxury of a free run, knowing he wouldn't go too far from her. His tail wagged in excitement as he dashed round like a puppy, trying to sniff the interesting manure piles and other smells all at the same time. If there *was* anyone around, Finn would alert them.

'So you came this way when you were eight?' Alec asked her.

'Yes – when the grass was short. Too much risk of snakes if it was long, but that wasn't often.'

She stood inside the gate and looked around, casting her mind back twenty-seven years. The reserve took up fifteen hectares, the land rising gently to a pile of huge granite boulders on the northern boundary. Ancient eucalypts scattered around the paddock provided some shade from the relentless sun. It had been her playground, her adventure land. Who needed theme parks when you had open space, a few props and an imagination?

'I used to watch for frogs and tadpoles over there.' She pointed towards the small dam not far from the gate. 'But the cattle will have churned up the ground too much to leave any traces there, if Tanya did the same thing.'

'Where else did you play?'

She turned and nodded at the boulders. 'Up there. You can see for miles.'

A fort, a castle, a spaceship, a sailing ship – the pile of boulders had held a zillion possibilities for her youthful imagination, and she'd spent hours there, by herself, making up stories. Would Tanya have found it as interesting as she had? Maybe the kid was too afraid of spiders and bugs to clamber over the rocks.

They walked together up the rise in silence. She glanced across at Alec; his brow was furrowed in thought. He'd taken off his jacket and carried it slung over his shoulder. The rolled-back cuffs of his white shirt contrasted with his tanned wrists and forearms. His shoulder holster pressed the thin fabric against the muscular broadness of his upper body.

Even when she looked away, the awareness remained. He carried both his physical and emotional strengths lightly, self-contained, and she envied him his balance, his self-reliance. She'd never been able to keep the emotional distance needed to survive the demands of the job. Years of sleep broken by nightmares had proved that to her.

She made herself breathe slowly, desperately trying to fend off the memories of the nightmares of the past year. The ones that still woke her screaming in terror and despair night after night.

She'd echoed Alec's promise to the Wilsons without hesitation, because she'd known from the moment he'd told her another child was missing that she would give everything to solve this case. She couldn't be more personally involved than if Tanya were indeed her own child.

Alec stopped abruptly and turned to survey the way they'd come.

They were still about twenty metres from the rocks. Up here, on the sloping ground, there was less evidence of cattle, for the majority had stayed closer to the water on the flatter ground. Which meant that if Tanya *had* come up here, they might find some evidence of it.

'It's out of the way,' he commented. 'Would she really come this far off the direct route home? Up a hill on a hot afternoon after school?'

'Didn't you ever have a secret place of your own?' Isabelle countered.

'Not like this.' The touch of a rueful grin softened his features again. 'I grew up in the suburbs. Hardly even any decent trees to climb.'

'There's a path.' She pointed to the faint, trodden line in the grass leading towards the rocks.

Alec studied where she indicated and nodded in recognition.

'Not heavy feet, the grass is just thinner, the ground's not broken up,' she continued, glancing back and forth along the path. 'It could be a wallaby track, but it's a straight line from the dam to the rocks, as though she comes up here regularly.'

The boulders towered above them, covering a reasonable area of ground; the tallest, in the middle of the group, was a good six metres high. The land dropped away more steeply on the other side of the rise, gradually levelling out to the flat western plains in the far distance.

A curse escaped Isabelle's lips as she saw for the first time what had been staring her in the face since they'd parked in front of the reserve.

'The boulders and the slope effectively screen the other side from the town. The abductor could have waited there and no one would have noticed.' Her chest tightened so much she had to drag in breaths to keep talking. 'He knew, damn it. He planned this whole thing. He knew she came here, knew the cattle were coming yesterday to throw us off.'

'Someone local then. Not some stranger from out of town.'

He sounded like she felt: the small hope that it wasn't one of the town's own people ground into the dust around them.

She scrambled up the boulders, recalling the path she used to take, the steps up no more than an eight year old could manage. There was a high, flat rock, four metres from the ground, which had a commanding view.

Alec followed her up, and they stood there side by side, the hot northerly wind whipping around them. The long summer day was drawing to a close, and with the sun shining towards them from low in the sky they could see little to the west. Not that there was much to see, Isabelle knew. Dungirri stood at the edge of the scrub. Behind them lay the vast forest wilderness; to the west spread mostly paddock after paddock of dry brown grass, a farmhouse and outbuildings tiny spots in the distance, scatterings of eucalypts here and there. The harsh beauty of the plains and the distant horizon folding over the edge of the earth had always appealed to her wandering spirit. Now it all seemed menacing, vast, hiding its secrets and Tanya's whereabouts.

She turned to survey the other rocks and a flash of colour caught her eye, between the flat rock and the next one. A bright pink plastic backpack wedged deep in the crack, not obvious unless one looked straight down the crevice from the rock she stood on. Despite the heat radiating from the granite, a chill shook her body.

She dropped to her knees and then lay flat on the rock, trying to reach down into the crevice, but her grasp fell short. Alec stretched out beside her and scooped up the bag by its strap. Kneeling again, she took it from him, the name 'Tanya Wilson' written across the top of the bag in large black letters sending another shiver through her.

'There's something else there,' Alec said sharply, and he wriggled forward to reach the item, almost beyond his fingertips. He grasped it carefully to preserve any finger-prints and lifted it out, turning to show it to her as he stood up. A single small shoe – an Adidas or Nike or one of those other fancy brands she never paid much attention to. A new shoe, hardly worn.

The pounding of her heartbeat, loud in her head, seemed to drown out all other sound.

'It's not Tanya's shoe,' she said, her voice barely audible even to herself. 'It's Jess's.'

SEVEN

Suspended from Alec's fingers by its lace, the shoe swung lazily, mocking her.

'Are you sure?' Alec asked.

'Of course I'm sure.' She had to stop to swallow back the rising nausea. He'd left it, the abductor, to taunt them. She knew it in the pit of her violently churning stomach. 'Jess got new shoes for her birthday, three days before she went missing. And Beth and Ryan can't afford shoes like that.'

Alec frowned. 'But Jess didn't go missing from here – she lived on the other side of town.'

'It's clean – it hasn't been out here all year. He put it there yesterday.'

'Why? If he figured the cattle were coming in to destroy the trail, and we wouldn't get this far?'

'In case we did. Maybe he assumed I'd come back if he took Tanya, and I'd look here. He wants us to know – *me* to know – beyond doubt that we failed last year.'

Alec nodded slowly. 'So he put the other shoe in Dan Chalmers' house, to pin the blame for Jess's murder on him and get the investigation closed, and now he's letting us know how clever he is.'

They both stared at the swinging shoe in silence, the implications frightening. Isabelle felt so sick she could scarcely breathe.

'Great way to stop us getting cocky,' Alec rasped at last, with an uncharacteristic edge of bitterness. He reached into an inside pocket of his jacket and drew out an evidence bag, dropped the shoe inside.

Isabelle's head pounded, the pressure in her ears making the world rock alarmingly around her. Unsteady, her stomach rolling, she slipped down from the rock, staggered a few yards away, and threw up the juice and biscuit she'd had at the Wilsons'.

She was still crouched, her head hanging down, when a large white handkerchief appeared in view.

'I've got my own,' she muttered, digging it from her pocket and wiping her mouth. It didn't get rid of the bitter taste. She straightened up gradually, not altogether sure she could stay that way.

Alec stood a couple of feet away, watching her intently. 'I feel like doing the same thing myself,' he commented. 'Let's sit in the shade for a minute.'

He didn't touch her or come closer, just moved to the shade of a large tree and lowered himself to the ground. She followed, immediately relieved to be out of the blazing sun and off her feet. Finn bounded over and, with a warning glare at Alec, crowded himself between them, his body hot yet comforting against her leg.

The tangle of incoherence inside her head gradually unknotted into separate strands of thought as the dizziness and nausea eased.

Alec rested his forearms on his knees and stared out across the next paddock. Underneath the tan, his face did look paler. Perhaps he'd been telling the truth, not just being polite, when he'd said he felt like throwing up too.

'I wanted to be wrong,' she said flatly, unsure why she was telling him that. 'You've no idea how much I wanted someone to turn up real proof that Dan Chalmers was guilty, after all. Something I could believe.'

He turned to face her. 'I wanted you to be wrong too. But you weren't. Chalmers was innocent and we're dealing with a serial killer – one whose aim, it seems, is to prove his superiority over us.'

The wind gusted, stirring up the dust and forming a willy-willy in the next paddock. They watched the swirl rise twenty metres into the air, catching up dirt, leaves and twigs as it made its erratic way across the ground. It died after twenty seconds or so, scattering debris on the ground, but another rose just as quickly, scouring the paddock in its short wake.

'What's the bet there won't be any identifiable tyre marks?' It was a rhetorical question only. Isabelle already knew the answer.

'Probably not. I'd say the abductor's covered his steps very carefully. The backpack and the shoe will come up clean of prints as well. He wouldn't have left them otherwise.'

'So, we're left with no physical evidence, just like in the other two abductions, and the only thing we have to go on is that it's likely he knows me.'

'Yes. Not many people would have thought to look amongst those rocks. It could be coincidence, but I doubt it.'

'Well, that narrows it down to about two hundred and fifty people,' she said bitterly. 'More, if you count the surrounding properties and people in Birraga.'

'Then we'll go through them all,' he responded, grim determination carved into every feature. 'We'll eliminate those with a cast-iron alibi, and see what we have left. If we have to hold everyone in this damn town under suspicion, then we will.'

Faces of the people she'd known for as long as she could remember paraded through her mind. Faces that she'd once trusted, that she knew now were capable of blind and extreme violence. But which one among them had taken Tanya? Which one had so little humanity that they thought this calculated, evil crime was a game?

Worry gnawed at Alec. He shouldn't have let her come out into such an open space where a sniper would have an easy shot. Until they'd found the shoe, he'd almost convinced himself that Isabelle mightn't have been the shooter's specific target. Now that seemed a whole lot less likely.

He scanned the area, keeping a watch for any hint of movement, for anything that might be a threat to her. As soon as they'd had a few minutes' rest, he'd take her back to the comparative safety of the hall. And he'd make sure she had some food and something more to drink as soon as possible. Himself too – one choc-chip biscuit wasn't enough to keep him going for long, and there were a lot more hours to get through before the day would be over.

He cast an occasional glance at Isabelle. That frozen look had returned and the child she'd once been, playing in this paddock, seemed impossibly far away. A little colour had returned to her pale cheeks, but her fingers dug tightly into Finn's fur and her unnatural stillness, like a bowstring drawn taut, deepened his worry for her.

The dry heat and the wind blowing dust into his face added external discomfort to the internal turmoil of emotions. Everything about this case shook him. He'd always been empathetic to the victims of the crimes he investigated, but he'd never before become as emotionally involved.

Sometime during the course of the day, he'd lost the ability to hold a private corner of himself separate from the madness of his job. The commitment he'd given to Ryan and Beth Wilson went beyond his professional responsibility, but he would keep his promise, whatever the cost. He'd break rules, give his own life, do whatever it took to get Tanya back to her family.

They walked down the slope in silence, and were almost back at the car when Isabelle asked the question he'd been trying to avoid in his own mind.

'Do you think she's dead already?'

'It wouldn't follow the pattern of the last two abductions,' he replied cautiously, knowing he couldn't leave it unanswered. 'He kept the other two girls alive for almost a week.'

'Maybe he just wants us to think that way – keep our hopes up while he's laughing at us.'

He felt the same fear – a sick, dead weight in his gut. But for Tanya's sake, for Bella's sake, he refused to give in to it.

He paused with his hand on the doorframe and met her apprehensive gaze across the top of the car. 'It's a possibility, but I doubt it. There's an element of risk for him in keeping Tanya alive, and I suspect he gets his kicks from outwitting us in spite of that risk. If he killed her straightaway, it would be too easy, not enough of a challenge.'

She stared at him for a long moment, considering, and finally gave a fraction of a nod. 'I hope to God you're right.'

Neither of them spoke as he drove back to the hall. Her last words beat in his head again and again. He desperately hoped he was right too. The alternative was far too terrifying to consider.

He glanced again at her tightly drawn face as he parked and understood, with sudden, startling clarity, that if they failed to find Tanya alive, then Bella, too, would be lost. She held herself responsible, and had carried the ghosts of Jess and Chalmers for the past year. If Tanya's was added to that burden, it would shatter her soul beyond bearing.

Everything that defined the man he was meant that he could not – would not – allow that to happen.

EIGHT

Midnight came and went, and Isabelle steadfastly remained working at her makeshift desk. Alec's attention kept straying to her, despite his determination to concentrate on his own work. Screen after screen flickered on her computer as she searched databases for information, and the pile of notes beside her grew. Systematically and methodically she was checking out every person who didn't have a solid alibi – and even some who did. On the floor beside her, Finn lay sleeping, his nose resting contentedly on his paws.

She stifled another yawn, all the signs suggesting that she was almost at the end of physical endurance – eyes blinking frequently, the droop in her shoulders, the occasional shake of her head as she stared at the screen. She didn't notice when Alec left his desk and came to stand behind her, until Finn lifted his head and nudged her leg.

'Time to get some rest, O'Connell.'

Frowning, she shook her head.

'A few hours of sleep and you'll work better. The others have gone to get some rest.'

'I'm fine.' She stared resolutely at the screen.

'No, you're not. You've had a damned hard day and you need to put your head down for a while.'

Now she looked up at him, a flare of anger and something deeper flashing in her eyes. 'I can't. Not while Tanya...'

Not while Tanya is still out there. She felt it too deeply, couldn't stand back for even a moment. She was overtired, stretched to the limit. Hard as it was on the rest of them, Alec knew it had to be worse for her. He'd brought her into this, and therefore the responsibility lay on him to look after her.

He hunkered down beside her chair, resting his hand for balance on the back of it. Finn sat up, brown eyes glaring at him across her lap.

'Exhausting yourself won't help Tanya. You know that, Bella.'

Strange how that name rolled off his tongue so easily. He'd diligently kept to 'Isabelle' or 'O'Connell' in front of the others all night, yet ever since Kris Matthews and others had called her 'Bella', it was the name he used in his mind.

'I'll nap here if I need to.' Her teeth clenched tightly, she faced the screen again.

'I need you at your best in the morning. Your knowledge and expertise are critical. These guys can do this routine checking overnight.' He waved his hand towards the couple of uniformed officers who had volunteered for the night shift, to watch over the equipment and files. 'Kris has booked rooms for us at the hotel and sent our gear across. I have the room keys.'

The battle between dedication and common sense flickered across her face. Would he have to order her to rest? No. She nodded, the chair scraping along the wooden floor as she rose.

Outside, the town lay still, the wind that had buffeted it all day now silent. The air was fresher here than in the stuffy hall, and Alec took in deep breaths of it. Despite all his worry, a peacefulness seemed to settle around him, the darkness strangely soothing. Moving away from the dull light of the hall, he paused in the street, looking up in awe.

No moon lit the sky, only thousands and thousands of stars, brighter and more numerous than city dwellers would ever see. Not isolated diamonds, but a dense, brilliant tapestry of light and mystery.

Isabelle stopped too, her face raised to the sky. They both stood, unmoving, in the middle of the deserted street. In the faint light he thought he saw some of the creases on her brow disappear. She, too, took a slow breath of the cooler night air, and as she exhaled gradually it seemed as though the tense line of her shoulders dropped a fraction.

'So beautiful,' he murmured. He wasn't sure if he meant the stars or Isabelle. Both were beautiful. Incredibly, wonderfully beautiful. Soft wisps of hair escaped from her knot and fell in waves around her face. His fingers itched to brush those locks back, to trace the graceful curve of her cheek.

' "Blessed is the night, when souls unfold with dreams and whispers." ' She spoke softly, words that were familiar, although the origin of the quote hovered outside the edge of his awareness.

In the perfection of the moment they stayed silent, still, like the night wrapped around them. The soul unfolding – was that what was happening to him? It fitted these strange sensations, the lightness inside him. As though a part of him, too long denied, was stretching out, filling the empty places he hadn't known existed.

He didn't have to look at Isabelle to see her in his mind. Beautiful, enigmatic Bella. The words she'd just spoken, so unlike her usual sparse, factual style, hinted at the depths he had sensed but had not yet been allowed to see.

A memory fell into his thoughts, and he knew now where the quote had come from. The collection of short stories, by one of his favourite Australian writers, sat on his bookshelf, with the three novels the man had written.

'Patrick O'Connell.' He quietly offered the author's name into the stillness.

Slowly turning away from the sky, she met the enquiry in his eyes. For the first time he sensed that she really saw him, as a person, not a detective, her silent appraisal not giving away the thoughts behind her shadowed eyes.

'My father,' she said, after a moment.

He nodded, another piece of the puzzle falling into place. O'Connell's unique insight into human nature set him apart as a writer, his very individual characters drawn compassionately and realistically from his own experiences in the Australian bush.

Knowing her relationship to O'Connell brought Alec a step closer to understanding Bella's complexities. When she let down the guard that protected her, she had the same depth of feeling, the emotional connection and natural understanding of people that shone through in her father's writing. Yet somewhere along the way, she'd lost the quiet joy and optimism that also characterised his work.

'He really existed, the old man who said that,' she volunteered, her hushed voice scarcely disturbing the quiet darkness. 'Each night, like a prayer...a benediction. We met him when we were out camping one summer. I would have been nine or ten years old. People said he'd lost his mind, but he was saner than most people I know. I didn't realise my father remembered it too, until he wrote that story, years later.'

A hundred questions hovered. He held his breath and asked none of them, scared of breaking the fragile new connection between them. Those few sentences were the most she'd revealed about herself since he'd met her.

She gave a tiny, crooked smile. 'Crazy isn't it? Remembering something like that for all these years.'

He shook his head. 'Not crazy at all.'

A car approached along the Birraga road, the rumble of its engine and the sweeping headlights an intrusion of reality into their stolen moment.

Well-trained, Finn headed for the footpath and they followed. As they moved off the road, Bella stumbled up the high, uneven gutter. Losing her balance, she fell towards him and he caught her with an arm around her waist. The fresh scent of her hair and the press of her body against his caused an avalanche of sensation to blast away the serenity he'd been experiencing just a moment before.

His breath stalled in his lungs as the urgent craving to pull her fully into his arms flooded his awareness. He almost did. Almost lost his self-control and gave in to the longing his subconscious had been pounding him with all day.

Something nudged his leg as the car swept past, and Finn's eyes glowered at him, wolf-like, in the reflection of the headlights.

The dog's disapproval reactivated his own conscience. Hell, he was DCI in charge of a case and he had no business thinking such thoughts about one of his colleagues. Especially not when he'd brought her into a situation so stressful for her. He'd seen enough times during the day that she didn't like to be touched. The way she'd stiffened when Kris and Jeanie Menotti had hugged her, and the way she'd held herself apart from everyone, spoke volumes about her discomfort when others came too close. The last thing she needed was her superior officer engaging in unprofessional behaviour.

The moment she was steady on her feet again he dropped his arm and stepped away from her, almost tripping over himself in his haste. Ashamed of himself, he didn't dare to look at her, strangely apprehensive of what he might see. Hands thrust into his pockets, he walked on, not needing Finn's presence to keep him a good metre away from her.

Comfort. Warmth. Strength. Isabelle hardly had time to recognise the sensations before he pulled away quickly, sharply, as though perhaps she'd acted inappropriately by leaning against him longer than necessary. Had she? She couldn't be sure, her thoughts swinging crazily between wanting the moment back and relief that he was now a safe distance away.

You're here for one reason only, she reminded herself. Alec Goddard was just a colleague. She wasn't here to make friends, to get involved, to care about anything other than finding Tanya and returning her to her parents. All going well, in a few days she'd be back in her mountain refuge, and she'd probably never see him again.

A few police vehicles were parked outside the hotel, and a light burned in the hallway as they entered through the unlocked main door. Both the front and back bars were dark, the place quiet and empty.

'The hotel has eight rooms upstairs,' Isabelle explained quietly to Alec. 'Some of the police who've come from Birraga and beyond will be staying here. If more come, then they'll have to camp out with the SES crews in the showground.'

Alec dug in his pocket and pulled out a couple of keys, scrutinised the plastic tags under the light. 'Rooms four and five. Do you know the way?'

She led him upstairs, where a night light illuminated the corridor. Alec opened the door of room four and flicked the light switch, revealing a small room with an ancient double bed, wardrobe, an armchair and small table. The décor hadn't changed since last year, Isabelle noticed, and probably not for a few decades before that. French doors led to the veranda, and an open window let some breeze in. Alec's bag had been placed beside the bed.

He unlocked room five and stood aside to let Isabelle in. The furnishings were identical, although the chenille bedspread in this room was a faded blue, not red. Clean and basic was the best that could be said. Like the other room, French doors opened on to the veranda.

'There are shared bathrooms off the veranda,' she told him. 'Women's round the corner to the left, and the men's round to the right.'

'Colonial original, by the sounds of it.' His voice, rich with a restrained chuckle, resonated somewhere deep inside her and, before she recognised it, a vestige of the old Bella surfaced and responded.

'Early Federation style, actually. With a few modifications circa 1950. But you'll probably find there's a chamber pot still under the bed, if you'd prefer that.'

Now he did chuckle, light and low. 'I'll take my chances with the bathroom.'

His eyes sparkled warmly at her and her stomach did a slow-motion somersault. Her emotional armour seemed to melt and she was helpless to stop her traitorous imagination picturing him naked in the shower, all hard muscle and male strength. A hunger she'd almost forgotten woke sharply, deep in her abdomen, and grew quick, strong.

God, had he seen it in her eyes? His narrowed slightly, grew intense, the laughter leaving as swiftly as it had come.

Heat infused her face and she dropped her eyes from his and stared instead at chest level, hearing the sudden unevenness in his breathing.

'Bella?'

The strange, almost harsh tone didn't belong to the confident man she'd seen during the day. But no way, no way at all, could she dare to answer that unasked question.

She turned away with a hastily mumbled 'good night' and, ushering Finn before her, fled into her room. Heart thumping so loudly she thought it must wake everyone, she closed the door and leaned her forehead against it. Anger with herself fumed. Damn it, she was supposed to be concentrating on finding Tanya, not wasting time and energy behaving like a weak-kneed teenager. How absolutely, positively stupid. One thing was for sure – she would keep her distance from him from now on. Tomorrow, she'd get herself partnered with Kris, or even Steve, if needs be. At least the constant irritation that Steve provoked in her would be better than the distracting and unsettling presence of Alec Goddard.

Her mind made up, she lifted her bag on to the bed and pulled out the things she'd need for the night, while Finn investigated the smells of the room. He found a spot he liked beside the bed, and with a canine 'hrmph' settled himself down, watching her with his nose resting on his paws.

She bent down and rubbed his neck. 'You're probably not supposed to be in here, boy, but we'll deal with the publican in the morning, okay? At least there's no carpet for you to shed hairs on.'

The night had cooled off only a little from the heat of the day, and the room was stuffy and hot. The breeze from the window didn't do a lot to change that, and neither did stripping off her clothes and pulling on cotton pyjama trousers and a singlet top. She slipped a light cotton robe over them and found her toothbrush and a towel.

Leaving Finn in the room, she stepped on to the wide veranda, closing the door behind her. A light on the corner, essential in the dark night, guided her way to the bathroom around the side. A few minutes later, she emerged, flicking off the bathroom light as she did. Immediately she was plunged into darkness. The veranda light had been switched off, and the light from her own room didn't reach around here. She hesitated, reaching her hand out for the wall beside her.

The muffled footstep behind her didn't give her time to react before thick cloth was pulled down over her head and a hand closed across her mouth and nose, stifling her scream.

She clawed frantically at the hand, feeling the cloth tightening around her neck. Her assailant held her close from behind, one hand smothering, the other twisting the cloth and choking any remaining breath out of her.

She fought, kicking, struggling, slamming her elbows back into the hard muscle of his chest, terror increasing her strength as she desperately tried to dislodge his iron grip. It was a losing fight. Her lungs screamed for air and blackness pressed inside her head while his hand stayed clamped, unyielding, on her face. Dimly she heard Finn's barking as her legs collapsed beneath her.

NINE

The worn texture of the veranda floorboards under her fingers was real. Strange how she knew that, when everything else floated so indistinctly. Her fingertips anchored her to the smooth, cool surface, the only part of her body still belonging to her. Even the burning in her lungs had faded now she was no longer trying to breathe.

'Bella!'

The voice pushed through the thick darkness enveloping her. She tried to reach for it, to tell the voice it was okay, it didn't hurt now, but the slight scrape of her fingernails against the wood was all she could manage. Not enough. She was falling, falling through the floor, and any moment now nothing would matter any more.

The floor began to fight her, vibrations jarring through her fingers, arms, ears. Someone running. Knees thudded against the floor beside her.

'Oh, God, Bella, be okay…please…'

Fingers fumbled at her neck, releasing the choking pressure, and instinctively she drew a shuddering gasp. The cloth lifted from her face and light blinded her. Strong, gentle arms held her as she coughed and retched, struggling to fill empty lungs through her rasping, painful throat.

'That's it, Bella, breathe… I've got you…you're safe now…'

She hauled in breath after breath, each one a little easier, each one reverberating through the fog of physical pain and confusion in her head. Alec's deep voice continued its comforting encouragement, even as she felt his fingers feeling for her pulse, then lifting her hair and checking her neck.

The violent shaking started as reality sank in. Someone had tried to kill her – had very nearly succeeded. She struggled to sit up, resisting Alec's attempts to help her. She leaned back against the railing and pulled her knees up to her chest, but the shivering wouldn't stop.

Comfort…warmth…strength… It was all there in the man kneeling beside her. Need to escape the nightmare carved through her, and the longing to bury her face in his shoulder and let his arms hold her, safe, very nearly demolished all the cautions of the past year. Except she wouldn't be safe. Physically, yes; he'd use his strength to defend her, or anyone else in need, to his last breath. But emotionally…emotionally the need to keep far, far away from him made her pull back further, clutching her knees even tighter.

He saw her movement, raised a hand as though to touch her, then dropped it, sitting back on his heels. Emotions flashed underneath the grim stillness of his face – pain, fear, fury, and others she didn't dare name – and his pulse drummed visibly at the base of his neck, yet he kept his voice steady.

'It's okay, Bella. You're safe now.'

No, I'm not, her heart cried out, and she buried her head on her knees so that she couldn't see him. If she let herself give in, succumbed to the aching need not to face this alone, he could tear apart the little left of her soul as effectively as the person trying to kill her could snuff out her life.

Doors opened, other footsteps came running, voices called out. She didn't move, keeping her head down and trying desperately to subdue panic and reconstruct at least some small degree of self-command.

'What the fuck?' She recognised Steve's voice.

'Bella's been attacked,' Alec said, still close to her. 'I didn't see him, but I heard him go down the back stairs. Find him, Fraser.'

'I'll bloody kill him.'

The veranda railing she leaned against shook, and so did the floor, as Steve sprinted off, taking the stairs at least two at a time judging by the sounds. Typical Steve, she managed to think. Always wanting to be the action hero. At least one other person followed him.

'Shall I call an ambulance?' A woman's voice, timid.

No, let me stay here for just a bit longer. I'm not ready yet...

'Yes, Constable,' Alec answered.

Then she had to raise her head, face reality, the movement

causing the world to rock alarmingly. Her tongue rasped in her dry mouth as she croaked a protest.

The young constable looked uncertainly between her and Alec. Behind the woman, a couple of male officers watched in concern while they dragged police overalls up over their T-shirts.

'You need to be checked over, O'Connell. You stopped breathing – and there could be a neck injury.'

Alec had gone all formal again, that determined, man-in-charge expression chiselled into his features.

'I'll be fine.' She tried to sound convincing, even though it hurt to talk, her body shook no matter how much she tried to hold it still, and the walls and floor seemed to be moving in a surreal slow-motion dance. 'The ambulance is in Birraga. You'd have to wake up the on-call people and the doctor, and it's the middle of the night, and they'd take ages to get here and...there's no need.'

Had that made sense? She couldn't tell, couldn't even quite remember what she'd just said. He watched her closely, eyes narrowed. 'I'll be fine,' she repeated, hoping he wouldn't insist on making a fuss. More than enough people had been dragged out of bed already for one night. And she hated hospitals. With sheer force of will she stopped her body shaking.

He checked her pulse again, looked into her eyes, made her follow his fingers as he moved them from one side of her vision to the other. Then he placed one hand on either side of her neck and, with gentle pressure, felt along her throat.

His tender touch sent a whole new shiver coursing through her. He knelt close, too close, so that his breath brushed against her forehead and every sense registered his proximity. She should have wanted to run away from that intensity; instead, she had to fight the urge to lean into his hands, lean into *him*. She held herself still, willing her heartbeat to slow, while he assured himself that she wasn't injured.

He dropped his hands and sat back on his heels.

'If you're sure you feel okay, we'll skip the ambulance for now, since it's so far away. But in the morning you should go into Birraga for a check-up and X-rays.'

She leaned back against the railing and closed her eyes. In the morning she'd talk him out of that plan. She'd have herself right back under control and be able to convince him that, other than a bruise or two, she'd escaped unhurt. Another shiver jarred through her. Unhurt, but only just. A few seconds longer...

She shut her mind to that thought.

Alec knew she'd argue in the morning, but he'd deal with that then. He'd given in for the moment, only because his inspection had shown that most of the pressure had been to the front and side of her neck, not her spine. It might not be the right decision, but he'd seen the flash of panic in her eyes at the mention of the ambulance, and he'd take the risk for now rather than put her through more stress and wake up half the town. But he'd keep a damn close eye on her, and if there was even the slightest hint of anything wrong he'd call the ambulance straightaway.

The three other officers were still watching, and Alec ordered them to search the hotel and grounds. 'Make sure no one's still here and secure any evidence. Then check with the neighbours to see if anyone heard or saw anything.'

They left, and it was just the two of them again, Bella still sitting hugging her knees, so alone and vulnerable he wanted to kill the bastard who had almost killed her. Wanted to close his own hands around the man's throat and squeeze hard…

The insistent sound of Finn whining and scratching at the door of her room brought him back to reality.

'I'll carry you back to your room,' he said.

'I can walk,' she protested with an echo of her usual stubborn independence, and pulled herself to her feet. The sudden movement had her reaching to the railing to steady herself.

'Let me…' His voice caught in his throat, making it sound more like a plea than an instruction. Maybe it was.

He expected more resistance, but instead she nodded slightly, biting her lip. He lifted her carefully, smoothly, trying not to jar her, carrying her slight weight with ease against his body. She looped an arm around his neck, making the balance easier for him. With her free hand she pulled the edge of her robe, dishevelled in the struggle with her attacker, back across her thin top.

He kept his eyes forward, trying to be as impersonal as possible. He wished he was still wearing his business clothes, but he'd changed into a T-shirt and cotton sweat pants before he'd heard the muffled sounds of a struggle followed by Finn's barks. Now the knowledge that only thin layers of fabric separated their skin seemed to be fusing the circuits in his brain.

Yet the way she'd cringed away from him out there on the veranda reminded him forcibly how little she trusted anyone – even him. Especially him. No matter that he wanted to pull her into his arms and kiss away the dark shadows in her eyes – hell, he wanted things that his imagination shouldn't have even come up with. But the simple, undeniable fact remained that she didn't want him. Given that he had no intention of starting anything with her, that fact should have sat easier with him than it did.

He elbowed the door handle and carried her into the room, sidling with difficulty past Finn, who leapt up repeatedly, trying to lick her face.

'Down, Finn,' she ordered several times, to no avail.

'He seems to have forgotten his training,' Alec commented as he lowered her to the bed, and immediately cursed himself for being insensitive and criticising her dog. The words had just slipped out from his spinning mind.

Finn stood on his hind legs to inspect her, whimpering and licking in a frenzy. She pulled herself up, drawing the sheet over her knees, and pushed Finn's head away from her face with a firm command to 'leave it'. She scratched behind his ears in reward when he gradually calmed.

Alec stood uncertainly by the bed, feeling out of place as he saw the closeness between the two of them. No simpering, no gushing, but affection, companionship and respect.

Isabelle's small, rueful smile didn't reach her eyes. 'I'm sorry. Finn was "let go" from the Air Force because he gets a bit... over-protective sometimes.'

That made two of them that felt over-protective. Yet neither he nor the dog had been able to stop her being attacked just metres away from them. The sense of inadequacy, of failure, almost shredded his composure.

'Don't apologise. If he hadn't barked, I might not have heard...' The rest of the sentence froze in his throat.

He glanced around the room, closed the door they'd come through, then pulled the worn armchair closer to the bed and sat down.

'Are you feeling up to a few questions?' He made himself move into his normal investigation mode: sympathetic but thorough. It should be familiar territory, for he'd asked questions like this a thousand times before. He'd just never had to ask them when his own pulse still hadn't resumed its regular rhythm, and emotions he couldn't make sense of threatened to cloud his judgment.

'I'm okay. Just a bit shaky,' she admitted.

'Have you any idea who it was?'

She shook her head, and winced. 'No. Male, maybe a few

inches taller than me, not much more. He came from behind – I didn't see him.'

'Can you tell me exactly what happened?'

She tightened her arms around her knees and stared ahead. When she spoke, her voice was flat, lifeless, as though the telling could only be done by disconnecting it from herself. Her police training was evident in the way she stuck to the facts, reciting what had occurred in a linear way, from the time she'd walked out of the room until he'd released the cloth from her neck. And all the while she stared ahead, her knuckles white in her tightly closed fists.

God, he hated doing this to her.

'Did he say anything?'

She closed her eyes, drew a shaky breath. 'No, he didn't talk…but he…he laughed.'

'Laughed?'

'A sort of chuckle.'

She gave an imitation of the noise – a harsh, cruel snigger, devoid of pity. Every muscle in Alec's body contracted in reaction. Rage burned red before his eyes.

He shoved back the chair and went to the window, gripping the window frame. Only the knowledge that his anger wouldn't help Bella allowed him to pull together some semblance of self-control.

He turned to see her watching him, warily. Too pale, except for the vivid red marks across her throat. Too pale, yet her amazing inner strength kept her going despite the horrors of the day just past.

But the day wasn't over yet, and he still had more to put her through.

Alec swallowed, once, twice, his Adam's apple moving above the neckline of his T-shirt. Isabelle found his hesitation and discomfort strangely reassuring. If he was shaken up by what had happened, then maybe it was okay for her to be, too.

'Can you think of anyone who might believe they have reason to harm you?' The uneven edge to his voice softened the formality of the words. 'Anyone who might hold a grudge against you or your family?'

'Enough to want to kill me? I wouldn't have thought so.'

She dropped her head onto her knees, closing her eyes for just a moment to draw some strength. She had to go through this, had to search through memories, share them, dissect them, try to find the one that might unravel a reason, a cause.

The chair creaked as he sat down again. 'Tell me about your family, your relationships with the town.'

Sure. Start with the easy stuff, she thought wryly. How could she summarise the complexities of community attitudes built up over generations? Especially to a man who, she guessed, had spent most if not all of his life in the relative anonymity of a city. Things that were forgotten in the fluid populations of the suburbs were hung on to in a town where generation after generation grew up together and everyone knew each other's history, good and bad. And those histories shaped the growing up, the person you became, because there was no escaping them as long as you stayed.

Yet if there were something in her background that might reveal who had attacked her, she had no business letting her reserve stand in the way of finding it. *This is for Tanya.*

She took a fortifying breath and met his steady gaze. 'The O'Connells have always been sort of outsiders in town, but it's never translated into anything overt before.'

'Outsiders? Why's that?'

'My great-grandfather owned one of the largest properties in the district. He bought out a few places during the Depression, properties that had been in families for fifty years or more. He was a hard man, a loner with few friends and no desire to make them.'

'Not a popular person in town then?'

'No. He was respected in a way, because he was always straight down the line, but there were also hard feelings because he didn't see himself as part of the community. Out here...well, community is important.'

Alec nodded, and she continued.

'He died just after the Second World War began. My grandfather stayed to run the property, although he helped his two younger brothers evade the reserved occupation status and join the army. Both of them were killed in the war, and my grandfather never forgave himself. He became a recluse. His wife died when my father was a baby, and a few years later my grandfather had a disabling stroke. Delphi sold off some of the land, worked what was left, raised my father and looked after their father pretty much single-handed.'

Alec raised an eyebrow. 'That can't have been easy for her.'

No, and maybe it went a long way to explaining why Delphi had had to give her baby away. But that was a question for some time in the future, when she had the time to talk with her aunt.

'Delphi takes after her grandfather and father – tough, stubborn and reclusive. My father was different. Delphi recognised that, let him go his own way. He worked around various places, earned a lot of respect as a cattle man around the region. People admired him, trusted him, even if they didn't always agree with him, but…'

She cast her eyes around the room, as if seeking in the air for the words she needed to explain. How could she make Alec understand how it had been when she didn't really understand it herself?

'But something set him apart?' Alec prompted.

'Yes, I guess so. Dad's world was large, wide – he was a voracious reader, a deep thinker. He had to leave school early, but he educated himself. In this town, many people's reading consists only of the sports pages of the newspaper, so, no, he didn't really fit in. Then he became active in the campaign to stop logging in the old-growth areas of the forest. Virtually all the town opposed it, because Dungirri relied on the timber industry. Around the same time, his first book was published and…'

She turned her head, meeting those steady eyes watching her. 'You know what they say about the tall poppy syndrome?'

'Of course,' he said tightly, and she realised that there'd be some in the old guard of the police service who would be resentful of competent younger men, would seek to cut them down. 'I take it his success didn't go down well?'

'On the surface, everyone said the right things. But underneath, it just emphasised the differences.' She picked at a loose thread in the sheet covering her knees. 'Dungirri has been dying for a long time. Even before we left, it was changing, struggling. Many of the properties around had already been bought up by the big pastoral companies after the drought in the 1980s. Men who'd owned their land were working as managers if they were lucky, or casual stockmen if they weren't. The big companies buy in bulk and truck supplies in, so shops in town were hard hit and began to close. People with other options – training, skills, money to start again elsewhere – left town. In that kind of environment, Dad's campaign to stop logging was seen by many as a betrayal, even though he actively argued for eco-tourism as a more viable industry.'

'Was that why you left?' Alec tilted his head, all his attention on her, and it occurred to her that she'd talked more about herself in the last few minutes, prompted by his questions, than she'd said to anyone in a long time.

'I suppose it was part of it. We saw the place on the mountain for sale when we were on holiday, and we both loved it. There was a good school not too far away, with subjects Birraga couldn't offer, and there wasn't a lot to keep us here, so we moved.'

'What about you, Bella? How did you get on with your contemporaries?'

'Me?' She gave a rueful smile. 'I guess I inherited the O'Connell recluse gene. I was always something of a loner. I spent most summers droving with my father. I got along okay with the others my age, but I was just as happy by myself.'

'Anybody you didn't get along with? Perhaps someone who resented your father's stance on the logging issue?'

And that was the crux of all these questions. She stopped, thought, tried to put herself back into the teenage mindset.

'Not really. Mark wielded a fair amount of influence in our age group, and he was right behind Dad's conservation ideas – and I guess we were all at that age where idealism appeals. None of the kids around my age were from logging families anyway. Mark, Mitch and Sara were all on the land; Beth's father is a vet involved in large-animal research programs. The Barretts have been agricultural workers for years.' And damn, she wished she could come up with something, anything, but nothing in her memories rang any warning bells. 'There was the usual good-natured teasing, but I honestly can't think of anyone I might have upset, who might have a grudge against me.'

'Perhaps it's not so much you,' Alec said slowly, 'but something that you represent in his mind.'

'Envy, you mean? We were as poor as the proverbial church mice. Dad's work was mostly casual, seasonal, and even when he was published he didn't exactly rake in the dollars. Australian authors rarely earn even a bare living.'

'What about your mother? Was she local?'

Her mother...it always seemed harder speaking of her mother than of her father, although the grief of losing him was fresher, the images and memories of her mother blurred by time.

'No, she came from down near the Victorian border, was transferred here as a teacher. My parents were...very close. She died when I was young, and Dad never remarried.'

Never even went out with another woman, and boy, the attack must have left her off-balance, because thinking of that brought tears to her eyes and she turned her head away from Alec to wipe them with the heel of her hand.

Footsteps outside and a light tap on the door stopped Alec from reaching out to touch her. Hell, he'd been battling the whole time not to touch her, hold her, reassure her and soothe her instead of grilling her with questions she could clearly do without.

He crossed the small room, putting his body between her and the door, wishing he had his gun handy, and opened the door a crack to find Steve Fraser, breathing heavily and with sweat dripping from his forehead.

'Did you find him?'

Fraser shook his head. 'Sorry. He went east out of town. I chased him, but he had too much of a start. Then he headed into the scrub and I lost him. I tried to find him again, but you can't see a thing in there with no light. I could leave a couple of uniforms patrolling the road, but fact is, he could come out anywhere.'

And wasn't likely to walk straight into the arms of the waiting cops, Alec thought bitterly. He'd got away into an area he probably knew well and their chances of capturing him tonight rated below zilch. Leaving Bella vulnerable, at risk.

Fraser tried to peer past him into the room. 'How's she doing?'

'"She" will live,' Isabelle answered for herself.

Reluctantly, Alec opened the door wider and let Fraser in. The man sat down on the end of the bed with a familiarity that Alec found disturbing. At least he didn't hug her or touch her.

'You sure?' Fraser asked.

'Yes,' she said, with a touch of exasperation edging her voice. 'See...breathe in...breathe out...all working.'

'You want me to stay with you? You shouldn't be alone.'

'I'll be watching over her,' Alec interrupted. He held the man's stare for a long moment.

'Bella? You okay with that?'

Fraser looked away only to check with her. As Alec should have done himself, he thought, before that damn surge of testosterone. She had every right to throw him out. She might well prefer to have someone with her who she'd known for longer than a day. Even if that someone was Fraser. While they mightn't be best buddies, it seemed there was some sort of friendship between the two of them. Fraser's 'I'll bloody kill him' as he'd gone after the attacker hadn't been the cry of a disinterested acquaintance, and Alec experienced an unsettling shaft of envy.

'It's okay,' Isabelle said to Fraser with an attempt at a nonchalant shrug that didn't quite work. 'He gets paid more than us – let him sleep for what's left of the night in an uncomfortable chair.'

Despite that glimpse of humour, Alec couldn't glean from either her tone or her expression the real reason she'd agreed to let him stay.

TEN

Even with exhaustion clawing at her, Isabelle had trouble getting to sleep. She didn't bother trying to decide whether it was because of the after-effects of the attack or because of Alec's silent presence in the room. Not quite silent – the old chair made small creaking noises each time he moved, and she found herself waiting for the next one, knowing he couldn't be comfortable and yet guiltily, selfishly glad he'd insisted on standing guard.

The attack had shaken her more than she wanted to admit. She'd never have consented to having Alec stay in her room if she could have blotted the sickening horror of the night's events from her thoughts. Her neck ached, the wound on her shoulder burned, and every muscle quivered tight in primeval readiness to either flee or fight. Somewhere out there in the darkness her attacker hid, most likely waiting for another opportunity. At least with both Alec and Finn nearby, nobody would get to her without a colossal struggle – and surely three against one made good odds.

Her eyelids were grainy against her eyes but she couldn't make herself relax enough to slip into the sleep she desperately needed. She turned on to her side and pulled the sheet up to her chin, more for the consolation of snuggling into something than for warmth. She could see Alec in the light that spilled from the veranda through the thin curtains: feet stretched out in front of him, head leaning back against the wall. A shadow from the window frame fell across his face and she couldn't tell if his eyes were open or not. His black T-shirt stretched across the pronounced muscles of shoulder and chest, the dark colour and closer fit giving a rougher edge to his appearance, an impression of raw masculine energy no longer civilised by business clothes.

The knowledge she fought uncoiled deep within her. No need to ask herself why she'd let him stay rather than Steve. Steve had been genuine in his offer and his concern, but he was shifting sand compared to Alec's rock-like dependability; a hot-tempered more-boy-than-man compared to Alec's unwavering determination.

If she could trust anyone, she could trust Alec. But she didn't want to trust anyone, couldn't bear to let her heart crack open, melt the ice. Especially not with a man who stirred feelings and emotions and desires that she'd thought were long dead within her.

'Are you okay?'

He moved his face into the light and she realised he'd been awake the whole time she'd been studying him.

Heat flamed in her cheeks. 'I can't settle,' she muttered, and punched the lumpy pillow as if it were the cause of her discomfort.

'Can I get you anything?'

She shook her head. He said nothing more, and she gradually let her eyelids close. The small sounds of Finn shifting position on the floor and settling back down reassured her in their ordinariness. Finn would rest peacefully, his doggy brain dreaming only about the simple basics of food, play, sleep and attention. He probably couldn't imagine the future, or remember his dreams once he woke, and she envied his uncomplicated consciousness.

She shifted her head on the pillow, trying to find a place where lumps didn't press into her head.

Alec's voice drifted across the semi-darkness, low and gentle.

'We'll find Tanya, Bella. And I won't let anything happen to you. I promise you that.'

He sat in the uncomfortable chair at the foot of the bed and watched her sleep. How was it that just yesterday morning she'd been a stranger to him, and now... Well, now he couldn't tell what the hell was happening to him.

She'd tilted his world off its steady axis, and past experience gave him no clue how to respond. If it had just been lust, he could have dealt with that. Lust was straightforward, uncomplicated, easy to either accede to or ignore. Lust didn't call on every protective instinct to hold her and reassure her until the heartache and fear disappeared from her eyes. Lust didn't admire and respect her strength and courage, and fear for her vulnerability. Lust didn't produce the choking, consuming terror he'd experienced when he'd seen her slumped on the veranda.

All these years he'd kept relationships – when he had time for them – deliberately casual. Undemanding, uncomplicated interludes of fun and mutual pleasure with a short span that left neither party heartbroken or wanting more. And he'd been careful – always careful – not to let anyone become, or even appear to be, close to him. No way would he let any woman become a possible target for those wanting to get to him.

The reek of blood and the sound of his partner's last gurgling sobs echoing in the warehouse still haunted him, even after fifteen years. A drug boss, desperate to get hold of evidence against him, had kidnapped Rick's wife to get what he needed – and two people Alec cared for had died as a result. So what if Eddie Jones was locked away for life now for what he'd done to Rick and Shani? There were others out there just as brutal.

Yet here, in the silent darkness, he had to accept the fact that in less than twenty-four hours he'd come to care more for Isabelle O'Connell than for all of the past women in his life put together. But no chance existed for any sort of relationship between them beyond this temporary working partnership.

Although she was a cop, and better equipped to handle threats than Shani had been, he knew in his heart that this was Bella's last case. Even assuming they found Tanya unharmed, Bella would not come back to that world – his world – again, despite all her undoubted skill as a detective. Jess's death and its aftermath had carved too heavily into her soul. Her strength would enable her to heal, but she would not return.

Once they found Tanya, Bella would be free to discover her new path in life, and he would walk away. He'd go back to what he did best, to the work he'd dedicated his life to, the work that left no room for attachments.

Memories of his own childhood remained vivid in his mind, unforgettable, inescapable. Night after night, his mother waiting, never knowing whether her inner-city detective husband would walk through the door or whether he'd become another headline. Until the day – Alec's twelfth birthday – when he hadn't come home. Four days later, a man at twelve, Alec had half-carried his grieving, broken mother up the aisle in the church to face the coffin that contained what a gun-toting drug runner had left of his father.

Rick's and Shani's deaths had cemented his belief that a serious relationship was entirely incompatible with the type of detective work he'd dedicated his life to. But until this moment, he'd never really understood what that dedication to his career could cost him. He would never hold Bella close, never share quiet joys and intimate moments, never know her in the thousand and one ways of friends and lovers. The wave of loss caught him unawares and he locked his teeth against the groan that rose from deep in his gut.

The few hours left until dawn ticked past slowly. He sat rigidly in the chair and watched over Bella while Finn watched him, his dark canine eyes glittering in the half-light. Just the two of them, on guard in the dark, protecting her.

The dreams came, and, as they had since those first days in hospital, her subconscious mixed real memories with imagined fears so that she no longer knew what was recollection and what was fear. People crowded in around her, terror rising as she tried to use her body to protect her charge from the rain of fists, sticks and rocks. She needed to protect his head, and she closed her arms tighter, desperate to make the two dozen paces to the car. They hit her, tore at her arms, pulled her head by her hair to get to him. Agony erupted in her shoulder, along her arm, and she heard the crack of breaking bones and her own cry of pain. The struggling, the panic rising, the heart-rending realisation that they'd succeed in dragging her away from him and she'd be helpless to save him...

Then arms wrapped gently around her, protected her from the mob just as she'd tried to do for Chalmers, and the soothing rumble of a familiar voice convinced her she was safe from harm.

ELEVEN

The warmth of sunshine on her face woke her. Still half in the grip of sleep, she took a moment to register that it must be well past dawn for the sun to be high enough to shine through the window. No sign of Alec, but outside the open door she could hear Kris and Jeanie talking in low voices, and the not so subtle sounds of Finn wolfing down crunchy food, his dog tag rattling against what must be a metal bowl. Sometime while she'd been sleeping Kris must have taken over guard duties. She checked her watch – just after seven. Much later than she'd intended to sleep.

Reluctant to move immediately, she stayed where she'd woken, lying across the bed, the sheet half across her. She felt strangely rested despite the short amount of sleep. It must have been at least two in the morning before she'd drifted off, maybe later.

She'd had nightmares again. Nothing new in that. Every night she'd wake up at the worst point, sweating and thrashing and silently screaming, then she'd get up, drink some water, wake herself fully to clear the nightmare, and lie down and try to sleep again.

Except she couldn't remember waking up last night. The nightmare – yes, she had a hazy memory of that. Oddly disconcerted by the variation from normal, she closed her eyes again, trying to catch the fleeting remnants of the dream.

Small details drifted back. She'd dreamed someone had intervened – helped her. Someone? No, not a faceless anyone – Alec. Her imagination had replayed that moment on the veranda in a different context, and her subconscious had allowed her, in the dream, the comfort she'd denied herself in reality.

Now her conscious self fumed against that lapse. She didn't need, didn't want, anyone. Okay, so she'd had to have a bodyguard last night because she'd been exhausted and shaken and her police training knew it made sense, but a guard was a hell of a lot different from…from dreaming of his arms encircling her, skin touching her own bare arms, gathering her into the shelter of him, the stronghold of him.

She scrunched her eyes tightly shut as if that might blank out the vividness her imagination had conjured, but it didn't help erase memories imprinted as physical sensations rather than images. And that was so unlike her normal reserve that she felt lost, uncertain, confused by the betrayal of her internal self in wanting to rely on another, even just in a dream. She'd never been one for playing the weak female, the victim; she'd grown up independent, capable and resourceful, and ten years in the police service had only reinforced her self-sufficiency.

Well, she'd just have to put it down to the fright of the recent attacks on her and assume it was a one-off occurrence. She definitely didn't want to add dreams about Alec Goddard to the already large catalogue of disturbing imaginings her subconscious taunted her with.

The conversation outside finished and she hurriedly sat up, swinging her legs over the edge of the bed as Kris entered.

When Isabelle first met Kris at a training course in Sydney a few years back, she'd warmed to her honest approach to life and good-natured sense of humour. She could be tough, uncompromising and blunt when needed, but she could also be perceptive and curious, and right now Isabelle didn't want Kris noticing anything amiss.

'How are you feeling?' Kris asked, watching her closely as she sat in the chair Alec had spent the night in.

'I've been worse,' Isabelle replied, rubbing the stiffness in her shoulders and neck. 'Was that Jeanie just now?'

'Yes. She brought some food for Finn.'

'That was kind of her.'

Just like Jeanie to see what needed doing and do it. Kids, adults, animals – she looked after waifs and strays of all sorts, not letting anyone go hungry or uncared for. Late yesterday she'd mobilised the ladies of the Country Women's Association to feed the police contingent a nutritious evening meal

– a better option than the limited takeaway the cafe and pub could provide.

The latest beneficiary of Jeanie's thoughtfulness finished his breakfast and trotted in to give Isabelle an exuberant morning greeting. So many times in the last year, the responsibility of feeding Finn and exercising him had been about the only reason she'd dragged herself from bed to face another day. And every day, his unconditional adoration and delight in the simple pleasures of life gave her reason to keep going.

She stood up and pulled her robe around her. 'I should take him for a walk.'

'The boss went for a run with him earlier on,' Kris said.

Damn the man for being so...so *human*. It was hard enough trying not to like him without him being considerate. She averted her face from Kris's and rubbed Finn's mane. 'Have you become friends with him now, boy?'

Kris chuckled. 'I wouldn't say that. Looked more to me like a challenge for supremacy rather than a friendly jog. But Finn didn't bite him, so I suppose that's a good sign.' She tilted her head slightly and asked with a teasing smile, 'So, are you friends with him?'

Isabelle turned her back to rummage in her bag, although she wasn't sure what she was looking for. 'We're all just doing a job,' she managed through the tightness in her throat. Her hand closed on her toiletries bag and she transferred it to the bed as though that was what she'd been after all along. *Underwear. Clean shirt.* She rummaged again. 'It doesn't matter what I think of him.' Armed with clothes and toiletries, she turned back, ignoring Kris's raised eyebrow. 'I'm going for a shower.'

She washed and dressed quickly after Kris had checked out the bathroom for hidden threats. Isabelle put up with that, and Kris standing guard outside, but protested when her friend insisted on driving her the two blocks to the police station.

'No one's going to attack me in broad daylight in the main street!'

'Boss's orders,' Kris said calmly. 'And I happen to agree with him on this one, so don't waste your breath trying to talk me out of it, okay?'

A station wagon with the area health service logo on it pulled up as they parked in front of the station, and the driver, a woman dressed in jeans and a shirt, greeted Kris.

'Where's my patient?'

'Right here,' Kris replied. 'Bella, this is Doc Morag Cameron. She's on her way out to do a clinic at Friday Hill, so I asked her to detour via here and make sure you're okay.'

'Boss's orders, I suppose?' Isabelle asked dryly.

Kris grinned. 'It was Morag or the hospital. I figured you'd prefer this. You can use my place.'

Down to earth and practical, Morag Cameron quizzed Isabelle about her injuries and examined her as thoroughly as the limited facilities of Kris's kitchen allowed.

'You've been lucky,' the doctor commented as she packed away her stethoscope. 'Physically, you're okay. But you've experienced two attacks in less than twenty-four hours. If you need a few days to deal with the trauma, and maybe talk to a counsellor, I'm happy to give you a medical certificate for some time off. It would probably be wise, in fact.'

'No,' Isabelle said hastily. Too hastily, she thought. She finished buttoning her shirt and spoke more calmly. 'Thanks, but I don't need time off. I need to be here.'

'Given the circumstances, I understand. But if you experience any dizziness, any increased pain, or have any difficulty talking or swallowing, you're to get into Birraga straightaway.'

Assuring the doctor that she would, Isabelle walked her back to her vehicle.

She found Kris and Alec in Kris's office in the police station, discussing resources. Alec waved Isabelle inside, and she pulled up one of the 1970s vinyl chairs.

'There are ten more general duties officers on their way from various stations in the region,' Kris was saying. 'Another SES unit arrived this morning, and we can have more if we need them. And just about every adult in the district who's not in the SES wants to volunteer to help somehow.'

Alec rubbed the back of his neck. 'I don't want too many volunteers around until we know more about what we're dealing with. So, other than the two SES units, tell them thanks, but not yet. Unless,' he added as an afterthought, 'the SES need feeding.'

'Birraga Rotary Club has that in hand at the showground. Jeanie and the CWA will continue to look after us.'

'Good. Now, since we've door-knocked everyone in town already, I want you, Kris, to work with Fraser and coordinate visits to all the surrounding properties. Ask landholders for permission for the SES to search outbuildings – machinery sheds, woolsheds, especially any that are a fair way from houses. But I want at least two armed police officers with each SES unit all the time they're out there.'

Isabelle leaned forward in her chair. 'We need to liaise with State Forests, too. There are a few camping areas and also work huts in the scrub that should be searched. I'll contact them.'

'No.' Alec's objection was quiet but unarguable. 'Kris and Adam can deal with that. You and I need to talk.'

Isabelle's stomach tightened, but she didn't argue. Of course he'd want to discuss last night's attack, decide on follow-up strategies. That was appropriate procedure, whether she liked it or not.

'I'll organise some coffee,' Kris offered, and headed out the door, leaving them alone.

Alec rose restlessly from his chair and leaned against the window sill, almost as if to block the view of anyone looking in, although the office looked on to the hall. The tan trousers and white shirt he wore emphasised his long, lean muscularity.

His eyes, twilight-dark, studied her, reading her.

'How are you feeling?'

Question of the day, probably. News of last night's attack

136

had no doubt spread all over town by now, and just about everyone was going to be asking her the same thing.

'Minor aches, that's all. Nothing to stop me working. The doctor gave me the all clear.'

He folded his arms over his chest. 'I want you to go to a police safe house,' he said abruptly. 'You should stay under protection until we catch your attacker.'

'No.' She held his gaze steadily, firmly. She was a police sergeant – she could do immovable.

'Damn it, Bella, some madman has tried to kill you, twice!'

'I can't leave this case.' She stated the simple truth without heat, despite the unease flickering in her stomach.

A full thirty seconds went by before he nodded. 'Yes, I know,' he said quietly. 'I didn't think you'd go.'

He raked his hand through his hair and she noticed, almost against her will, the heavy shadows under his eyes and the worry lines carved deeper into his brow. He could scarcely have had any sleep. That selflessness, the refusal to take his responsibilities lightly, couldn't be denied her respect. She wished she could find something she didn't like about him.

'If I let you stay, it has to be under my conditions,' he told her, concern softening his own immovability only slightly. 'You have an armed officer with you at all times. You don't step away from this building and the hall unless I give authority. And you carry a weapon wherever you go. Did you bring yours with you?'

'No. It was returned to Tamworth when I was in hospital. I haven't been back so it hasn't been reissued.'

'I'll have one brought out from Birraga for you this morning.'

His eyes drilled into hers and she recognised it as an order, not a request. Although detectives were technically supposed to carry arms, in practice they sometimes didn't.

Her heart pounded. 'I... I'm not sure I should...'

He came closer, sat on the edge of the desk near her. 'I was told your medical review agreed that you were cleared to return to duty. Have you got any reason to doubt your fitness to carry a weapon?'

'I don't think... I don't trust myself.' Words jumbled about in her head and she struggled to find coherent sense in her doubt. 'If I was startled... I'm not used to being around people lately.'

On the edge of her vision, she saw his hand close around the edge of the desk where it rested, but his voice sounded as even as ever when he spoke.

'How many times have you pulled out your gun, Bella?'

'What do you mean?'

'Do you go straight for your weapon when there's a threat?'

'N-no... I didn't always carry one as a detective.'

'So what makes you think you'd reach for it instinctively?'

She bit her lip, eyes downcast, tracing the edge of the chair's armrest with her thumb. How had he known that her instinct had never been to strike out? Even before last year, she'd rarely pulled a gun, preferring to rely on other techniques for difficult situations, and she'd never used a weapon in anger or fear. Not yet, anyway. But it was the 'yet' that chilled her.

'I trust you, Bella. And I ... *we* need you to be safe.'

The gentleness in his voice in those last few words unsettled her, just as it had yesterday. It didn't mean anything, she hastily told herself. It was just a part of his way of working, the same way he treated everybody. She had to be professional too, and see through these last days in the police force without compromising her own standards of performance.

'All right,' she conceded, reluctantly.

'Good. I'll get Kris to arrange it.'

'As for your other conditions, I don't want to just be sitting on the sidelines pushing paper.'

'You won't be pushing paper. You know most of the people in this town. The killer knows you. I need you to analyse every piece of information that we have – find the connections, find what doesn't fit. You'll tell us who to haul in for questioning, and you'll do the interviews with me.'

She nodded, accepting that she had to be satisfied with that – for now.

Adam Donahue knocked on the door, delivered two mugs of coffee and left again, closing the door behind him. Finn watched warily from the position he'd taken under the desk, then stretched out again on his side.

Wishing she could relax as easily, Isabelle took a sip from her coffee; the acrid taste of cheap instant gunk hit her empty stomach hard. Alec wasn't drinking his, just staring down into the mug as though he somehow hoped answers might magically appear on the surface of the liquid.

Any moment now he'd start asking more questions, the kind that would of necessity pry further into her life, her privacy, to try to ascertain who might have cause to attack her. And he'd enjoy it as little as she would.

He exhaled, took a sip of the coffee, grimaced and set the mug down on the desk in disgust. He dragged Kris's chair out from behind the desk, sat down opposite her.

'O'Connell, I need to –'

'Ask more questions. I know.' She did her best to sound reasonable, although she couldn't help her fingers tightening around the mug.

'Okay, you know the drill. Is there anyone in your past who might have done this? Crims you've put away? Ex-boyfriends with a grievance?'

Safer, much safer, to deal with the first rather than the second.

'I'm a country detective. The case load is mostly burglaries, stock thefts, assaults and domestic violence. I can't think of anyone I've seen convicted who has connections with Dungirri, and most wouldn't fit the profile for this anyway.'

'Most?' he queried sharply. 'What about the ones who might?'

'There's one, maybe...' She paused, reluctant even to think about that case. She rose from her seat, thrust her hands in her pockets and paced the length of the small room. 'He bashed his wife and his kids – killed one, just a baby...'

She felt a tear bead at the corner of her eye and turned her back on him abruptly, brushing it away with her hand. When she didn't have nightmares about Dan Chalmers and Jess, she had them about two tiny, broken, bleeding children, one of whom she'd been unable to save. As a female officer, she'd seen more than her share of domestic violence over the years, but that case had been the worst, and the monster masquerading as a man who had done it a vicious, vindictive bastard. She stared, unseeing, at the file shelves in front of her and forced logic to prevail.

'It can't be him though. He's been in Goulburn jail for eighteen months, has a life sentence.'

'We'll check it out, just in case,' Alec said, and his voice – gentle, suffused with understanding – almost undermined her shaky composure.

She fiddled with the edge of a folder on the shelf, kept her face averted. 'As for the other, there aren't many ex-boyfriends.' Plenty of fingers left over after counting them, but she wasn't about to say that. Not to a man who could undo buttons with one hand and probably had women perpetually falling at his feet. 'And none that would be a threat like this.'

'Was Steve Fraser one of them?'

The quietly spoken question caught her unawares and she barely managed to hide the sharp catch of her breath.

'Why do you ask?' she countered.

'It's obvious there's some history between the two of you.'

Best to stick with the straight-out truth. The man didn't miss much, and, after all, what did it matter to her what Alec Goddard thought? She turned and faced him, shrugged her shoulders casually. 'It was a long time ago. We went through the academy in the same group, got posted to the same town as probationary constables. Accommodation was short and we shared a flat for a while. The relationship part was short-lived.'

Nothing in his expression gave away his thoughts. 'How did he take the break-up?'

'It took a week to convince his dented pride that it was over, and the next week he found someone new.' And the week after that someone else new, and so on through the female population of the town, revelling in his playboy reputation. Whereas she'd spent the majority of the ensuing ten years single, not short of offers but not tempted by many. 'The Ice Princess' some of her male colleagues called her, not always behind her back.

'How would you describe your relationship with him now?'

A reasonable question, she reminded herself, given that the majority of murders and assaults were committed by people known to their victims.

'I hardly ever see him. He's based in Moree now, I was in Tamworth. He thinks I'm too serious and need to lighten up; I think he's impetuous and careless in investigations. We irritate the hell out of each other on the rare occasions we work together.'

Alec gave a bare nod, and looked off into space, his fingers tapping the wooden arm of the chair in unconscious tension.

'I don't see what my relationship with Steve has to do with this case,' she added, when he didn't respond.

'I'm not sure either,' he said slowly. 'I've been going over the communication logs. Ryan Wilson phoned the station at eleven fifty-three on the morning that Jess was found, to report a mob heading out to Chalmers' place. Steve Fraser took the call, and reported to Birraga that he was going to investigate. But it wasn't until twelve thirty-one that he called for an ambulance for you.'

She did the mental calculations quickly. Thirty-eight minutes for a twenty-minute drive at normal speed, maybe fifteen at maximum eighteen at a faster speed. Give or take a few minutes for response time at either end, it still left one hell of a gap.

Her mouth as dry as sawdust, she asked, 'What time was my call for assistance?'

'Twelve eleven.'

Legs shaky, she sank back down into her chair. If Steve – if anyone – had left the station straight after Ryan's call, she'd never have had to face that mob alone. Dan Chalmers would have lived to prove his innocence and Tanya might now be safe at home with her family. If Steve had left straightaway...

'Are you suggesting he delayed on purpose?'

'I'm not suggesting anything, yet.'

But he was sure as hell thinking through a range of possibilities, she could tell. *Stay calm, stay focused on fact*, she lectured herself against her thumping heartbeat. Steve could have had any number of legitimate reasons for his delay.

'Have you asked him about it?' she said.

'No. He's coordinating a search this morning and I can't get through on the radio.'

'He could just be out of transmitter range.' She found herself searching for logical explanations. 'Coverage around here isn't great.'

'Yes.'

The tap, tap, tap of his fingers against the wooden armrest echoed in the silent room.

'What aren't you telling me?' she asked.

He jerked his gaze back to her, considering, deciding.

'Fraser was called back from leave the night before last to work on this case,' he said slowly, as though choosing his words carefully. 'I checked with staff records and the day Jess went missing he was also on leave.'

'He could have been here to take the girls…'

Breath almost deserted her. The chair slammed back against the wall as she rose hastily, but the small office held nowhere to go, nowhere to run from a possibility that sickened her. For all that it was a lifetime ago, she'd slept with a man who might have become a murderer, and there was nothing that she could hold on to to tell her, one way or the other, what the truth might be. Her head was spinning. She leaned against the window frame and hugged her arms around her waist. Finn butted her knee with his nose but she hardly noticed.

The play of light and shadow on the wall beside her shifted as Alec stepped closer. 'Is Steve capable of that, Bella?'

'How the hell would I know?' she cried out, struggling for control, losing it, drowning in despair. She closed her eyes against burning tears, huddled closer into the wall, wanting to disappear through it. Away from hurt and disillusionment. Away from the endless distrust that her life had become. Her will to fight on crumpled under the onslaught of doubt, the fear of another unbearable betrayal.

'I don't know what Steve could do,' she whispered, and all the anguish she'd carried for months spilled out, unstoppable. 'I never thought Dungirri people could do…what they did. They were people I knew… I thought they were good people. Johnno Dawson used to go fishing with my father. Dieter Sauer – he sold me my first bike. And Bert Dingley…'

Tears ran down her cheeks and she no longer had any power to stop them.

'Every year, for the school Christmas party…' A sob caught in her throat, then another, and she forced the last words out in a wave of pain. 'He…he was Santa Claus…'

TWELVE

Alec caught her as she started to slide down the wall, gathered her into him and held her while sobs shuddered through her body.

Only a few hours ago he'd thought that the silent scream that had ripped across her face in her nightmare was the worst torment a person could endure. Now he knew differently, and he was powerless to do anything that could ease her living hell.

His own eyes stung and he could find no words to murmur as he'd murmured assurances of safety in the early dawn. He wanted to weep for her, weep with her, for a loss of faith so profound it would have shattered a lesser person. No matter how bad the atrocities he'd seen, he'd always been able to maintain a belief that there were some things – some people – worth fighting for. He'd seen glimpses of hell in some of the crimes he'd investigated, but he'd never seen those dark, crazed depths in the eyes of friends, people he trusted, as Bella had done. Now he understood why she'd run from the world, isolated herself from all but Finn.

'I'm sorry, Bella. I'm so sorry,' he whispered into her hair, knowing the words were meaningless given her experience, and totally inadequate to make up for his incredible, stupid insensitivity in raising his doubts about Fraser before anything was proved.

He held her close against him, with no code to decipher all the messages, thoughts and sensations tumbling within him, only the sureness that this moment was changing him irrevocably, that he couldn't just pack away how he felt about Bella, how he felt about himself.

One thing he didn't doubt: he wanted her in his arms. And the wanting was much more than physical, although that was there too, underneath it all. Her head nestled into his shoulder, dusky brown hair soft against his neck, her curled fists pressed lightly into his chest, and the toned muscle of her back flexed slightly underneath his hands. Damn logic and sense and propriety and rules – being here and now was *right,* more right than anything he'd ever experienced before.

She gradually stilled, yet didn't move, and he didn't want her to move, because as soon as she pulled away from him reality would intervene, and chances were he'd never be that close to her again, never breathe in the simple, fresh scent of her, never feel as connected to one another as he did right now.

Isabelle drew in a slow, shaky breath, then another, as awareness inched back. Drained, she stayed exactly where she was, needing the arms around her, the tall body to lean against, to support her.

In a minute she'd face the real world. Now, eyes closed, she floated in a strange, in-between space, not letting herself think consciously, just reconnecting through sound and sense and touch to the present.

She could feel every detail of the shape of the hand on her back, five fingers, a large palm, the firm pressure radiating heat directly into her muscles and nerves. Another hand at her waist. Along the length of her body the restrained strength of his body, legs and hips and arms touching, her fisted hands against his chest, her face resting against the meeting place of shoulder and chest. Underneath her cheek, a heartbeat hammered.

Maybe it hammered a touch of reality into her disconnected consciousness, for it occurred to her to wonder that she wasn't fighting him, wasn't panicking at his closeness. Instead, there was a comforting familiarity about it, and the little voice that said to move away sounded only faintly in her mind, easy to ignore.

Wrapped in that haven, she let herself flow back into the empty shell of her body. And along with the Isabelle of the last year it seemed that parts of the Bella she'd once been –

trusting, confident, *content* – came back too. The raw, painful places in her heart still ached and hurt, yet she felt more whole than she had for a long time. Fragile, scared, and worried – but *whole*.

With that came conscious thought and awareness of the moment, of being held by a man who sent her body humming with a slow, spreading heat. She'd been fighting it, trying to deny that attraction to him, but it was no use pretending to herself any longer. Alec Goddard affected her and she, it seemed, affected him.

The dream she'd had that morning drifted back, and the acceptance of the truth trickled into her mind.

She opened out one hand, let her palm rest lightly against his chest. Her fingertips registered the immediate gallop in his heartbeat, answered within an instant by her own.

'It wasn't a dream, in the night, was it?' she asked, her voice scarcely more than a whisper into his shirt.

He swallowed, and she both heard and felt it. 'What wasn't?'

'This.' She shifted her head very slightly against his shoulder, too uncertain to face him.

There was a two-second pause. 'No.'

'I'm sorry. I don't usually…' She faltered, and heat flushed up her neck, over her cheeks. Maybe she should have moved then, but his arms closed just a little tighter.

'It's okay, Bella.' Another pause, and then a murmur she almost didn't catch. 'Don't go just yet.'

She stayed motionless, knowing she shouldn't, knowing it was dangerous to let down her guard, and yet wanting the moment to go on and on.

His breath feathered against her forehead. Against her shoulder blade one thumb moved, and there was nothing sexual in the gentle caressing, yet the intimacy of the small movement almost undid her. And it was the sudden sense of drowning, of being in over her head, that allowed the voice shouting caution to be heard.

Then she did move, took a step back, turned away from him, and he dropped his arms to let her go and she felt bereft by the sudden absence of him, as though she'd torn away a part of herself rather than merely stepped away from a man she had no business being close to.

She scrubbed at her eyes with her handkerchief, blew her nose, and looked out the window instead of at him. Sanity returning, she knew she had to put this in perspective, keep their relationship to officers and colleagues, and pretend that whatever it was that had just happened between them was of no importance.

She took a deep breath, gathered some shreds of dignity.

'I apologise. I don't know what came over me. I don't normally... I don't normally trust anyone enough to let go like that.'

'But you trust me.'

She squeezed the handkerchief into a tight ball. The temptation to say, *no, you scare me*, thundered in her head, but she recognised that it wasn't Alec who scared her. It was herself and her own *lack* of fear of him that terrified her.

'Yes.' It came out as little more than a whisper. 'Yes, I trust you.'

A car pulled up outside, tyres crunching on gravel; a door slammed, voices drifted in. The silence inside hung between them. Isabelle stared out the window, avoiding his eyes, and for all that she'd just admitted to trusting him, Alec sensed her withdrawing from him again.

She broke the silence with a small, self-conscious laugh. 'The first rule of female cops is don't cry on the boss's shoulder. I guess I just blew that one big-time, huh?'

He let himself grin to lighten the mood. 'I'm sure you don't really think of me as the boss. I get the distinct impression you'll only do what I say if you agree with it.'

He must have struck the right note for she did meet his gaze then, and despite her reddened eyes a half-smile twitched, once, twice.

'Call it a courtesy title,' she retorted.

She was back in control again, proud and independent. Tension still showed in stiffness of her shoulders, but she seemed more at ease with him and for that he was grateful.

A knock on the door interrupted them. Instinctively he moved in front of Isabelle as Kris showed in a man wearing the traditional neat moleskins and blue shirt of the bush.

'DCI Goddard? I'm Mark Strelitz, local MP.'

Alec recognised him instantly, of course, and quickly squelched the adolescent spike of testosterone as he shook hands with the man who'd kissed Bella, long ago. The detective in him noted the man's easy manner and quiet self-confidence. Strelitz had been elected to the federal parliament very young and had risen quickly through the ranks, but he had a reputation for honesty and integrity unusual in politicians, and Alec had the distinct impression that representing his constituents rated higher on Strelitz's priorities than climbing the political ladder.

It wasn't just the detective part of him that watched the greeting between Isabelle and Strelitz. Strelitz must have seen, but didn't comment on, her reddened eyes. He kissed her affectionately on the cheek and Bella didn't seem to mind. Alec did.

Even Finn, Alec noticed wryly, wagged his tail and waited for a pat from the newcomer. However, the moment the greetings finished, the politician moved straight down to business.

'I won't keep you from your work. But I wanted to let you know that if there's anything you need that a little political pressure might help get, then just ask. Officially I don't have any influence in state affairs, but I do have a fair few connections.'

'I need this case given top priority,' Alec answered. 'I'd appreciate any pressure you can exert to ensure we get the resources we need.'

'I'll make a few phone calls. Anything else?'

'Encourage the townsfolk to talk to us,' Isabelle said. 'People are being very reticent, but we need every bit of information, every idea, we can get. You know most people around here – they'll listen to you.'

Strelitz nodded. 'I'll do what I can. They're all feeling guilty and suspicious about last year. No one talks about it, because if they were there they don't want anyone to know, and those that weren't there don't know who was. Facing the truth that Chalmers was innocent is going to be damned hard for this whole community.'

Alec came to a decision, one he was sure Isabelle wouldn't like at all, and which might damage the fragile friendship between them. But finding Tanya was more important than anything else, even Isabelle.

'Off the record, if it helps to get people talking, you could mention that you think it's unlikely any further charges will be laid over Chalmers' death.'

Beside him, Bella drew in a sharp breath, but she said nothing.

'No guarantees?' Strelitz queried.

The man was sharp, Alec acknowledged. 'No. It's not my decision to make. But given that the major players have been prosecuted, I would think it unlikely in the circumstances that further prosecutions will be sought, unless there is someone who actively instigated the attack.'

'Thanks. I'll be circumspect and offer it only as my opinion.' He pulled out a business card and scribbled some numbers on the back before handing it to Alec. 'I've cancelled my appointments in Canberra for the next few days, so I'm at your disposal for whatever you need. That's my home number and personal mobile. Please call me if I can do anything else.'

When Alec returned from escorting Strelitz out, Bella had left the office and was sitting beside the water cooler in the tiny reception area, a plastic cup in her hand. With all the police action happening in the hall next door, the station was empty except for them. Finn lay near her on the floor, head on his paws, watching.

Alec sat down in the hard plastic chair beside hers. 'You have every right to be angry with me for suggesting that some of your attackers might go free.' Hell, in many ways he was angry about it himself. 'I should have talked with you first before saying that to Strelitz.'

'One of them has Tanya,' she replied, her voice flat and toneless.

She drained the cup, tossed it into the bin and leaned back in the chair, letting her head rest against the wall. It worried him that she seemed too soul-weary even to be angry with him.

'No.'

She jerked her eyes round to meet his at his quietly spoken contradiction. He closed his hand over her much smaller one. The part of him that was DCI Goddard told him he shouldn't. The man, Alec, cared only that he'd brought her into this and had to see her through it.

'Bella, I don't believe that the person who has Tanya is one of them. He's plotted this for ages – planned and schemed and prepared, just like he did with the other two girls. And he's taking pride in it. But what happened to Chalmers, to you, was an aberration. There was a pressure cooker of anger and grief that found an outlet and burst. It happened because they were human enough to care about Jess.'

She stared at their hands for a long moment, and her pulse flickered against his thumb, but she didn't move her hand away, and neither did he.

'You don't think he was there?'

Could the guy have been there? He let his instinct curl around the question, feel out amongst the few pieces of knowledge they had so far. The man likely treated this as a game – enjoying the control he held over others, his power.

'Yes, I think he might have been,' he thought aloud. 'But probably in the background, watching, maybe encouraging.'

A shudder rippled through her body, echoing the anger and disgust curdling his own stomach. Only a sick bastard could have stood by and watched her being beaten – sick and dangerous, and Bella would remain at risk until he could be locked away for good. Not just Bella, either. The man still held Tanya, and if he was so pitiless that he could shoot small girls then there would be no limit to what he might do to anyone who stood in his way.

'Bella, I know you were too badly injured at the time to give much of a statement, but can you remember who was there? If we could narrow down the suspect list –'

'But I don't *know*,' she protested, biting her lip.

The clock on the wall above them ticked away several seconds before she let out a heavy sigh.

'There were about a dozen people when I got there. I knew most of them. I talked to them, persuaded them that I cared as much as they did about capturing Jess's killer, and to leave it to the police. They started heading towards their cars, and I went inside to talk to Dan. Some vehicles left, and I heard others arriving. We heard the splash of petrol against the wall and next thing the shack was going up in flames around us. We got out and they were waiting. I was trying to protect Dan, get him to the car, and I didn't see who they were. I don't know who left and who stayed.'

'Not even some of them?'

Bella leaned her head back against the wall again with a weary shake. 'I'm sorry. I'm not a reliable witness anyway. I keep dreaming about it, and it's always different people I see – even people who couldn't possibly have been there. I can't be sure of anything any more.'

Alec curled his fingers tighter around hers, the only response he was capable of at that point, short of pounding his fist through a wall or through someone's head. But if he did that, he'd be no better than the people who had pounded their fists and sticks and rocks into Dan Chalmers' head – and into Bella.

'You asked about Steve,' she said eventually, and she disengaged her fingers from his and stood, poured herself another drink from the water cooler. 'He's not a patient man.

And I think I agree with you – this crime, it's taken patience. To plan, to carry out. I don't see how it could be him.'

Her words stifled the slight flicker of hope he'd had that morning. If she was right – and he trusted her instinct and her knowledge of Steve – then it meant another dead end. Tanya had been gone for more than thirty-six hours, someone had tried to kill Bella twice, and all they had was dead ends.

THIRTEEN

Alec confronted Steve Fraser as soon as he returned from the search site. He directed him into the interview room in the police station – away from where Isabelle worked in the hall – and pulled the door shut behind them.

'You must have waited fifteen or twenty minutes before you responded to Ryan Wilson's call last year. Why?'

At least the man had the decency to fidget uncomfortably, although he shot a glare back at Alec like a guilty teenager and didn't give a direct answer.

'Is this official?'

'Should it be?' Alec countered. He waved a hand at the recorder. 'I can turn that on if you want, but I was hoping you had a simple explanation.'

Fraser dragged a chair out and sat in it sideways, leaning back against the wall.

'I had to find someone to go with me – there was no one else here. Barrington had locked himself in the office and the others were all out.'

Alec also pulled out a chair and sat down, but he did it slowly, deliberately sitting ramrod straight, his eyes never leaving Fraser's face.

'It took you fifteen minutes to find another officer?' Alec challenged him.

He saw the cocky defensiveness rise even further, the muscle twitching in his jaw, the lie in his eyes about to be spoken – and then, for some reason he couldn't tell, the man deflated in front of him. The brashness vanished and he sighed with a deep-set weariness.

'Okay, maybe I could have moved quicker. But the truth is I believed Chalmers was guilty as hell and I figured if he had a bit of a scare before I got there it was only a fraction of what he deserved.'

Anger surged red-hot, and Alec just managed to keep it under control. 'You left Isabelle alone with a mob –'

Fraser's fist slammed against the table. 'Christ, Goddard, do you think I'd have hesitated for even an instant if I'd known she was there? What sort of bastard do you think I am?'

A swirl of relief cooled some of Alec's anger. The raw pain in the man's eyes couldn't be a lie. But he wasn't ready to let him entirely off the hook.

'I don't know,' he replied, letting his doubt of Fraser show in the coldness of his voice. 'You acted as judge without enough evidence and your hesitation meant a man died. What sort of bastard would you say that makes you?'

Fraser flushed and slumped back into the chair. 'Yeah, well, maybe I'm not some great hot-shot never-screw-up detective like you, but I didn't think they'd go that far. When I got there and saw Bella… Christ, there was blood everywhere and I thought at first she was dead.' He looked over at one corner of the table, then another, before he lifted his chin with a wary defiance. 'Look, you're way, way wrong if you think I'd ever do anything to hurt Bella.'

'Why? What's your relationship with her?' Although he'd asked the same question of Isabelle, he wanted to hear Fraser's version.

'Bella?' Fraser shrugged. 'We were an item once, years back. It didn't last long – we're too different – but we're still mates. A bit of friendly rivalry, you know, but that's all it is. If I could undo last year, I would in an instant.'

Good – the guy felt guilty, as he should.

'You still care for her,' Alec observed.

The man paused, closed his eyes and stayed silent for a few moments. When he opened them again, he met Alec's gaze, the last of his rebellious spirit had drained away. 'Yeah, I care for her. I'm nowhere near good enough for her, though, and I've known that for years. Bella is special, and a half-hearted cop like me is a whole lot less than she deserves.'

The confession surprised Alec, coming as it did without a hint of bitterness, just resignation and acceptance. Maybe there was more to Steve Fraser than he'd given him credit for.

'Why are you a half-hearted cop?'

'Oh, when your father's Assistant Commissioner Fraser, third-generation police officer, an only son doesn't get a whole lot of career choice. Don't get me wrong, there are parts of the job I enjoy, but... Well, maybe recent events are telling me something.'

Alec watched him, reappraising. He knew AC Fraser – a hard, uncompromising man. Growing up in the senior policeman's shadow couldn't have been easy. Perhaps the egotistical arrogance Fraser displayed at times was more of a protective mask than his real self. His honesty just now showed that he had at least some capacity for critical self-reflection – and that he'd done some uncomfortable thinking these last twelve months.

'I could bust you out of the force because of that delay last year, you know that, don't you?'

'Yes, and I'd probably deserve it.'

No excuses, no begging, no calling on his father's influence – Alec's estimation of him moved up a notch or two. He mightn't be the most thorough detective he'd ever worked with, but he had the sense he could trust Fraser to do his best now that they knew where each other stood.

'Well, I'll hold off putting a report in for now. We've got a murderer to find. We'll talk again after this case is over.'

Alec stood up, moved to the door, and Fraser stood too.

'Goddard...' He gulped down a deep breath. 'Thank you. I won't let you down.'

'Don't let Tanya and Isabelle down – that's what counts.'

Later in the morning, Alec saw Fraser follow Isabelle into the kitchen at the end of the hall. The large servery window was open, but he was too far away to hear their voices. Although he tried not to watch, his attention kept shifting to them. It wasn't a comfortable conversation, going by their tense body language. He had to give Fraser credit for facing her. If Fraser had changed in the past year, if he was becoming a better man, maybe it was due in part to his desire to earn her respect.

Isabelle's stony expression didn't change while Fraser said his piece. His earnestness must have impacted on her, however, for she heard him out without interrupting, and after some ten minutes of subdued discussion she seemed to soften a little towards him. Not enough to smile, but enough that when Fraser touched her lightly on the shoulder she made no move away from him.

They'd been lovers once, and that small sign of their familiarity with each other brought to mind intimacies that Alec didn't want to think about. He looked away, staring instead at some papers on his desk. Nine or ten years ago, he forcefully reminded himself, and it wasn't any of his business anyway.

Whether Isabelle understood Fraser's actions, whether she forgave him, didn't matter except to the extent that it affected their working together. And if there were problems, then Fraser would be the one to go. Not reporting him was a judgment call Alec had made predominantly for Isabelle's sake – he figured that the more people there were around who cared about her, the safer she would be.

One of the few civic improvements that had been made since Isabelle had moved away from Dungirri was the installation of bathrooms inside the hall, replacing the ancient outdoor dunnies. Now she was grateful to be able to escape into the ladies' after her encounter with Steve, needing a place away from the curious glances of her colleagues for a few minutes to gather her thoughts together.

She turned the tap on to splash her face with cool water, but the corrugated iron water tank on the sunny side of the building had heated the water way past cool and there was no relief from the heat there. No relief from the heat or the stress anywhere.

Except in Alec's arms, a small voice inside said, and the longing for that sanctuary weakened her knees before she made her common sense stomp on it.

'Absolutely not,' she muttered to her reflection in the mirror. Another kind of heat lurked there; a kind she couldn't risk being vulnerable to. No matter how enticing it might be.

Kris came in and closed the door behind her, leaned against it as if to hold off any intruders.

'Everything all right?' she asked.

'Fine,' Isabelle lied. 'Just hot.' A second possible meaning of that statement sprang to mind, making her hastily add, more for her own benefit than Kris's, 'I'm not used to Dungirri summers any more.' *Or men who scramble my brain.* Not that she could remember any man having done that quite so effectively before.

'Nobody ever gets used to Dungirri summers,' Kris commented. 'Do you want to talk about it?'

'About what?'

'You and the boss.'

'There's nothing to talk about.'

'Are you sure?' Kris asked gently. 'I happened to glance across at my office window earlier on.'

Isabelle stifled a groan. Of course, the office window looked on to the hall, directly into another window with only a few metres between them. Any of the officers could have seen her crying on Alec's shoulder – and Kris obviously had.

Resigned to dealing with her friend's probing, Isabelle leaned back against the wall. 'It didn't mean anything.'

The denial was easy to utter, harder to convince herself of. But she couldn't *allow* whatever it was between herself and Alec to mean anything. Maybe talking about it with Kris – convincing her – would help to keep everything in perspective. They were friends, after all, and Kris had kept in touch this last year, with regular phone calls to check on her and even a couple of weekend visits when she could get away.

'I don't know a lot about him,' Kris said, 'but everything I've heard is good. And he's apparently single *and* straight. You could do a whole lot worse.'

'Oh, heck, Kris, I'm not interested in him like that. I'm having enough trouble just holding myself together. I'm in

no shape even to think about involvement with anyone…
let alone with someone like him.'

'You're doing better than you think, Bella. You're one of
the bravest, strongest people I know.'

A sob and a laugh rose at the same time and tangled in
her throat. 'Brave? Me? I'm hiding in the ladies' toilet!'

Kris smiled faintly. 'If someone had tried to kill me twice,
I'd probably have my head in the toilet. But in a few minutes,
you'll be back out there,' she waved her hand at the hall,
'working to solve a crime that's worse than many officers
ever see.'

A few minutes, if that, and yes, she'd have to go back out
there, because no one was going to wave a magic wand and
make everything better. Yet she wanted to cling for a moment
longer to this short breathing space, to Kris's supportive
company.

'You know I'm leaving the police force after this?'

'Yes, I figured that.' Kris's voice held no judgment or censure,
and Isabelle appreciated that. 'Any idea what you'll do?'

'No. I haven't really thought much beyond keeping away
from all this sort of madness.'

Kris opened her mouth as though to say something, shut
it again, and then decided to say it anyway. 'Bella, hon, I
know you needed to go away by yourself for a while. It's in
your nature to need space to work things out alone. But…
well, it would be a waste if you hid away for ever.'

'I can't go back.'

'None of us can. We're all changed. But that doesn't mean we can't go forward.'

Kris spoke sense – she always did – but the thought of returning to life amongst others still seemed to Isabelle a perilous road. If there was a way forward, away from the darkness, she couldn't see it yet.

'Every time I'm talking to someone out there, I'm asking myself – were they there? I don't know, I can't remember, and I have nightmares all the time where I see people there who couldn't have been – you, Jeanie, even my father. I don't trust my own judgment any more. And I can't tell... I have no idea which of them murdered Jess, or has Tanya. I thought I knew these people – and I don't.'

'I understand, Bella.' Kris sighed and let her head fall back against the door. 'I've worked and lived in this town for almost five years and I don't have a clue either. I wasn't sure about Chalmers, but it was so much easier to believe he killed Jess, that it was all over with his death. And now – now I'm looking at people I see every day and wondering which one has been laughing at me all this time.'

They were silent a while.

'Will you stay? When this is over?' Isabelle asked.

'Probably. If they still want me. I've kind of got attached to the place, and there'll be a lot of healing to do.' Kris cast a sideways glance at her. 'What about you? Will you come back, spend a little time here? There are people here who would like to make things up with you, you know.'

Were there? She hadn't given much thought to how others felt about her injuries; didn't know, right now, whether she had the courage to deal with them. Her focus had to be on Tanya, and too much depended on the next few days.

'Maybe,' she conceded. 'After we find Tanya.'

'Yes. After we find Tanya,' Kris echoed.

Someone knocked on the door, and one of the young constables poked her head around as Kris moved and opened it.

'Oh, there you are, Isabelle. Darren Oldham's here, asking to speak with you.'

'Thanks. I'll be right out.'

Duty called, and Isabelle had to pull on her professional face again and put aside her own issues. Finding a way forward, whatever it might be, remained a task for another time.

Darren waited for her at the table in the area they'd screened off for interviews. She tried to remember if she'd spoken to him last year, other than in passing. She knew he'd been interviewed then – virtually everyone in town had – but one of the other detectives must have handled it, for she had no memory of talking with him.

Darren the Dag some of the other kids had called him, when he'd been a scrawny teenager who always looked as though he'd slept in his clothes and never knew quite the right thing to say. He hadn't seemed to mind – after all, 'dag' didn't carry the nasty connotations other nicknames might have. It was a gentle teasing; in some cases, almost a term of affection. In a small community such as theirs, there weren't enough kids to divide into groups, so the trendies and the dags and the goody-goodies and the nerds and the rough rebels had all mixed together happily enough.

At least these days the legs of his trousers were long enough to conceal his socks, and although his tan uniform showed many creases it was no more than one would expect in the hot weather. He'd been in the army, she recalled someone saying, and it showed in the way he'd filled out over the years, no longer scrawny, except, maybe, in his face.

'Hello, Isabelle.'

He greeted her with a smoothness and confidence he'd not had all those years ago. No, he'd had confidence then – just a misplaced sort; a type of eager over-confidence that had been awkward and, at times, annoying. Yes, he'd certainly matured, and his hand, when she shook it, was no longer clammy as she remembered from the obligatory high school dance classes.

'I was talking to Delphi this morning, and she thought I ought to tell you something I saw the other day,' he went on. 'I didn't think it was important, so it never crossed my mind to mention it to Kris when I talked with her.'

'Tell me – anything might help.'

'I was coming back from Birraga – the main Weeds office is there, you know, although I keep some stuff at the Council depot here so I don't have to always go to Birraga.'

'Yes, go on.'

'Well, it must have been around four, maybe a bit before. Anyway, that old track – the one that comes out on the Birraga road, the short-cut to the Hammersley road – there was a ute coming out of it, turning towards Birraga. It wasn't anyone I recognised.'

That track joined with another that bordered the paddock behind the stock reserve. Isabelle reached for the pen and notepad on the table.

'Can you describe the ute for me? And the driver?'

'Sorry – I didn't really pay much attention. It was white, might have been a dual-cab ute – a Hilux or Navara maybe. Reasonably new. The driver would have been average height probably – didn't see much else though. He was wearing a hat. Standard bush type, you know.'

Yes, she knew, and she pressed the pen so hard against the paper that it stabbed a hole in it. A driver in a hat in a white utility – two-thirds of the men driving around these roads would answer to the same description. Even narrowing it down to a dual-cab ute probably wouldn't help much – and the person might have nothing to do with Tanya's abduction anyway.

She made an effort to give a polite smile. 'Thanks, Darren, we appreciate your help. If you remember anything else…'

'I'll be sure to tell you. Well, the boss has given me the rest of the day off to help with the search, so I should get moving.'

Alec approached them and Darren glanced over at him before turning back to her with a tentative smile.

'Maybe when this is all over, we could have a drink at the pub, catch up on old times?'

She muttered something non-committal, more conscious of Alec's fleeting frown than of Darren's response, but the man sauntered off happily enough, apparently not offended by her lack of immediate enthusiasm.

'That was Oldham, I take it? Do we know where he was on Tuesday afternoon?'

'Driving back from Birraga and then unloading chemicals at the Council depot, according to Kris's notes. He's the noxious weeds ranger for the district. There are witnesses for his whereabouts. But he did see something that could be relevant,' she added, and relayed what Darren had told her. 'The abductor may have used that track – he could have just driven across the paddock to get to the back of the stock reserve. The vehicle Darren saw may have been him.'

'Does anyone live on that road? Anyone who might have seen the vehicle pass?'

'Des Gillespie's place is out that way,' Bella replied. 'Although he's not likely to be very forthcoming even if he did see anything. He's been an alcoholic for as long as I can remember, but not the friendly type.'

'Let's go and ask him anyway.'

They told Kris their intentions and she handed over her car keys, but glanced at Finn and said, 'You'd better leave him here with me. Gillespie's a cranky, mad bastard and he's laid fox baits all over his place.'

Although Finn was trained not to pick up food, Isabelle wasn't prepared to risk it in a strange place. So she told him to 'stay', stoically ignoring his whimper as she walked out the door with Alec.

The patrol car was parked out front and even though the windows had been left open it was stiflingly hot inside. Alec put the keys in the ignition. Still stiff in the shoulders and neck, Isabelle hadn't offered to drive.

They took the Birraga road out of town and, on her instruction, Alec slowed down about three kilometres along, watching out for the road to their right. He'd engaged the clutch, changed down a gear, when she heard a small sound – a hiss and a faint thunk – and he stiffened. She glanced at him, saw him look down, and the colour in his face drained away. Instead of turning the wheel, he kept straight on.

'Okay,' he said softly. 'What do you do when you have a large snake sitting at your feet?'

FOURTEEN

Panic almost overwhelmed her senses, thundering in her head, blurring her vision. A voice screamed from deep inside, *No – not Alec too.*

But if she panicked, she could lose him. Through a throat that felt as though the snake were curled around it, she managed to instruct, '*Don't move.* Did it bite you?'

'No – it hit my boot, not me.'

Calling on every internal resource she possessed, Isabelle forced herself to think logically, rationally. They were travelling about seventy kilometres per hour, and he mustn't move or the snake would likely strike again. At least it was a straight road.

She slid one hand around the emergency brake between them, and eased her other hand onto the steering wheel above his, praying the snake wouldn't notice the movement.

She looked down at his feet, but the snake wasn't near the foot on the accelerator and she couldn't see clearly into the darker space around his other foot without leaning closer, and that she couldn't risk.

'What colour is it?' *Please say 'black'.*

'Brown. They're venomous, aren't they?' His voice was miraculously even.

'Yes.' *Deadly*, her inner voice screamed, and to counteract the new wave of almost paralysing panic she made herself say, 'But I know the correct first aid treatment, if…'

'Let's hope you won't need to practise it.'

Focus on what needs doing.

'We need to stop the car as smoothly as possible. Very, very slowly ease off the accelerator. *Don't* move your other foot.'

He did exactly as she instructed, and as the car slowed to a crawl she pulled the hand brake up so that it stopped with only a minimal jerk as the engine stalled.

'Stay absolutely still,' she ordered, and with slow, even movements she opened her own door and slid out, leaving the door open. Her knees were threatening to give in but she made herself walk around to his side of the vehicle and, standing back behind his door, she carefully, carefully, inched it open.

Please, snake, please leave.

'Keep still,' she said softly. 'It might leave by itself. If we try to move it, chances are it will get aggressive and strike out.'

In the silence, it was harder to subdue the memories. *A classroom full of children, scared, screaming, and a long, slithering brown shape darting in amongst them, whipping around, raising its head to strike. And her mother…*

No, she wouldn't let *that* happen again.

The sun burned down on her head, on her back, but she held his eyes, willing him to have patience, to remain still. Willed herself to stay calm, despite the scream lodged in her throat. The rational knowledge that the modern first aid techniques saved lives did little to drown the terror embedded in her childhood memories.

Neither of them moved. Alec held himself rigid, only the grim line of his mouth and narrowed eyes revealing the strain of maintaining his legs in such an uncomfortable position. She stared into those blue eyes, holding the connection between them, and knew from the dark shadow of pain when the leg cramp hit him.

'Hold on,' she murmured, and he gave the slightest nod, his gaze locked on hers as though he'd gripped her hand.

Out of the corner of her eye she saw a flicker of movement and the brown head appeared, poking over the edge of the door frame. She didn't let herself breathe while it looked around, then finally wriggled down onto the dust of the road and slithered between her feet. She made herself count to five after the tip of the tail passed her boots before she dared to look over her shoulder, in time to see the reptile disappear into the dry grass beside the road.

'It's gone,' she said, and he collapsed forward, head on the steering wheel, hands dropping to grasp his leg and massage the calf muscle.

She sagged against the open door, her knees too fluid to risk walking, and let her eyes stay on him, on the glimpse of tanned skin between collar and hairline, on the strong line of neck and cheek and jaw.

He could have died.

She watched him, wordless, as he got out of the confined space of the car, leaned his hands against the roof and let his head drop down between them, stretching his legs, stretching his neck first one way, then another.

If she went to him, she could knead her fingers into those muscles, straighten the kinks... She stepped away, folded her arms in front of her, hauled in slow breaths and tried to control the visions alternating between inappropriate, dangerous thoughts of Alec and the equally dangerous vision of a snake poised to strike.

He could have died.

A footstep crunched on the gravel behind her but she didn't turn, not even when he placed a hand on her shoulder.

'It's unlikely the snake got into the car by itself,' she said, before he could say anything. Before he could say anything *dangerous*.

'You're suggesting someone put it there deliberately?' His hand on her shoulder drew her to face him, and she hated the way her heart tightened, but she couldn't look away again.

'Yes.' The anger buried deep within her began to stir, tasted bitter in her mouth.

He swore, and his hand tightened on her shoulder, gripping almost painfully.

'You could have been hurt –'

'Or Kris or Adam or someone else,' she interjected. *Or you,* but she couldn't say that out loud. She wrenched herself away from him. 'Any one of the team could have used the car. It just happened to be you and me. But it was aimed at me.'

'But he'd have no way of knowing –'

'It didn't matter to him who the snake bit, it was still aimed to upset me.'

And it had, although just at the moment fury was melding her blood into steely determination, outweighing the distress that might otherwise have crippled her. And the anger wasn't just at the bastard who was playing this dangerous game with their lives. Part of it was at *him*, Alec, for making her care. For giving her more reason to be afraid.

She thumped her fist into the bonnet of the car, and paced several steps away, her back to him.

'What makes you so sure?'

Something about the evenness in his voice made that momentary anger with him begin to dissolve, although the other anger, the real fury, continued its slow burn.

She turned back to face him, drew in a long breath.

'My mother was killed by a brown snake. She taught the kindergarten class, and one got in the classroom, started going for us when we came in after lunch. She was trying to get it away from us, and it struck her several times. They didn't have the treatments then they do now and she died in Birraga hospital.'

He took a step towards her, stopped. 'Oh, God, Bella, I'm sorry.'

'It was thirty years ago,' she said, as if to convince herself that she didn't still feel the raw grief that had bewildered her five-year-old self. Except she did, and the knowledge of what could have happened, what she might have felt if he'd died too, had the power to bewilder her still, if she let it.

She looked at the ground – scared her fear might show in her face if she looked at him – and made herself concentrate on practical issues. 'Everybody in town knows what happened to my mother. It doesn't bring us any closer to a suspect. We need to check the car in case there's any other surprises.'

She snatched up a stick from beside the road and poked under the seats with it, emotion blurring her vision so that she kept poking longer than she needed to, just to be sure. She heard Alec open the car boot, and the sounds of him rummaging amongst the equipment kept there, and then he closed it again, presumably satisfied nothing else lurked, waiting for them.

She slammed the back door, threw the stick to the side of the road, and drew in breaths to keep her temper from boiling over. *Get determined, not angry.* Anger might lead to mistakes, and they had to get the person responsible for this madness before anything worse happened.

Before anything worse happened…

Another worry surfaced, made her grit her teeth as she got back into the front seat. She fiddled with her seatbelt to avoid looking at Alec, but her conscience forced her to voice the concern.

'My presence on this case is endangering others. Do you want me to leave?'

He started the engine, paused with his hand on the gearstick between them. 'Do you want to leave?'

'No. But...you could have died.'

The words sounded worse out loud than in her head, and she stared at her own hands, clasped in her lap, all too aware of his large hand at the edge of her vision. She could make no rational sense of her acute awareness of him, the inexplicable way he affected her senses, her heart, and that confusion threw her way off-balance. She could accept that in the short space of two days she'd come to like and respect him, but anything else...No, she was more reserved, more cautious than that. It *had* to be the tension of the situation affecting her, not Alec.

'I didn't get bitten, Bella, thanks to you.' The deep timbre of his voice should have reassured her, but didn't. 'I probably couldn't have stopped the car, got the snake out, by myself. And I wouldn't have known how to treat it if I'd been bitten. I presume the old tourniquet technique I learned in basic training isn't current.'

'Pressure bandage,' she corrected automatically, because it was far easier to deal with facts than to *feel*. 'Up the entire limb, then a splint and keep still. That slows the venom's spread through the lymph system, if applied immediately.'

'And gives some time to get to hospital?'

'Yes.' Would they have made it to Birraga hospital before the venom hit if he'd been bitten? Maybe, maybe not. The sick dread of what could have been curdled her stomach as if it were the venom itself. 'He's trying to get to me. I'm sorry you were put at risk.'

The words fell between them, and he didn't respond, the engine idling. When she turned to see why he hadn't moved, she found him staring at her, deep in his own thoughts.

Several heartbeats passed before he shook his head slightly, exhaled a breath, and quietly said, 'Every day I go to work, I could die.' There was no bravado or flippancy about it, just the flat, emotionless tone of a man who had made his choice and understood the risks he faced.

She knew his unit worked on some of the worst, most violent cases facing the police, and the thought that one day a knife or a bullet or some other means could end his life made her throat tight again.

He released the brake, turned the wheel to head back to the track, and drove with his eyes straight ahead as though she wasn't there at all.

Nerves stretched to brittle, she could think of nothing to say – nothing *safe* to say – and they travelled in silence.

Des Gillespie's shack had once been a slab hut, now heavily and poorly patched with pieces of roofing iron and rough-sawn timber. Broken machinery, car pieces, boxes of empty bottles and other junk littered the yard around it.

The front door swung open in the breeze, and no one

answered Isabelle's knock. She peered into the dark interior, called out the man's name. Prickles ran the length of her spine.

Alec drew his gun, waved her to one side and entered the shack first, his head almost scraping the low roof.

Heart pounding, Isabelle reached for the Glock Kris had given her and followed him, not prepared to let him out of her sight. Her eyes slowly adjusted to the dim light that filtered through the rags that passed for curtains.

The man they sought wasn't in the squalor of the main room. A rough partition separated off another room, and they rounded that with caution. The sharp smell should have warned her about what they'd see.

Gillespie lay on his bed, curled almost into a foetal position. He cradled a rifle between his hands, the muzzle in his mouth, blood and brains spread over the pillow and the wall behind him.

Gillespie wouldn't be telling them anything.

FIFTEEN

'Suicide? Or murder?' Alec broke the silence to voice the question Isabelle was also contemplating.

'We have to consider murder,' she replied. 'An aggressive, defiant man like Des Gillespie is unlikely to curl up in bed to shoot himself.'

'That's what I wondered. That and the coincidence of timing.' He glanced around the room, checked inside the wardrobe that leaned drunkenly. 'Stay here, Bella. I'll check around outside.'

Being alone in a room with a corpse shouldn't have unnerved her, but her body's reactions didn't seem to be listening to her rational brain. The physical symptoms of unease started the moment Alec stepped out the door: the body's tension in preparedness for flight or fight. If her feet had their way, she'd be on her way out the door to Alec.

Maybe, her inner voice whispered, it wasn't so much the silent company in this room that unsettled her, but the lack of Alec's presence.

Quit thinking stupid things and do your job, O'Connell.

'So, what have you got to tell me, Des?' she murmured to the corpse.

As a kid she'd avoided going near him, and even her father, who'd got along well with virtually everyone, had usually given him only a courteous nod in passing. Now Gillespie looked small, no longer terrifying, his foul temper and quick fists stilled for ever.

She leaned over the body, carefully not touching anything, and studied the dead man. His arms, his hands, his torso, his feet – she scanned all of him, working her way down, seeking anything, however small, that might give a clue to what had happened.

Instinct told her there was a connection between this death and Tanya's abduction, but she needed evidence. Instinct could be wrong, could be more a function of prejudice and blind assumption than fact. She had to keep an open mind.

She finally straightened up from the body and examined the room without moving from where she stood, her eyes flicking over walls, floor, the rough furniture, and a half-empty scotch bottle tipped over on the floor beside the bed. An expensive single-malt whisky. Not what she'd expect on Des's budget.

Footsteps cracked against dead twigs near the house, and although she drew her pistol again, she did so without haste or worry. Her internal Alec-radar functioned just fine, and, sure enough, he called out to her as he came in, letting her know who it was.

'Nothing moving outside.'

She nodded acknowledgment. 'He'll be long gone. I'd say Des died yesterday afternoon, probably later rather than earlier.'

'Based on?'

'Based on the size of the maggots.'

Alec didn't blink. 'I'll take your word for it. Anything else?'

'The soles of his shoes are coated in dust, but the floor has been swept of dust and therefore footprints. I doubt Des did that.'

'Yes, everything else in this place suggests a distinct aversion to housekeeping, doesn't it? Let's radio Kris.'

They'd left the car in the shade of a large gum tree on the track, and while Alec called the murder in to Kris and to Birraga, Isabelle walked around the exterior of the shack, every now and then crouching down to examine something more closely on the ground or in the piles of junk. Small signs – crushed leaves, broken twigs, a few marks in the dust – told her only a little.

She rejoined Alec beside the car as he finished his calls.

'Kris is on her way,' he told her. 'She's heard from the forensic team, and they'll be here within the hour.'

'Good. He hasn't left us much to go on, but I can see where a vehicle was parked, and where he put the sweepings from the house, so maybe they'll be able to get something from that. We'll need the whole place combed – if this is part of the game, then the obvious things like fingerprints are unlikely to be there. He brushed away his footprints in the dust outside the house too.'

'Damn him.' Alec breathed the words out on an exasperated sigh. 'Has Gillespie got family?'

'One son, Morgan. He's around my age.' Isabelle leaned against the vehicle, appreciative of the cooler temperature in the shade and the slight stirring of a breeze. 'I don't know where he is these days. Jeanie might be able to tell us.'

Alec drummed his fingers on the roof of the car, a habit she recognised as accompanying his thinking. 'Morgan Gillespie. There's a publican in Sydney by that name, about the right age. Known to have mixed with some rough company in the past. If that's him, and he knows you, knows the area – could he be our man?'

'Morgan?' She considered the idea, felt around it in her mind. 'I wouldn't have thought so, but I guess we'll have to check him out. He and Des kept pretty much to themselves – I don't think Morgan had it easy at all. He was rather rough around the edges, often in trouble, but…'

She paused, a distant memory taking shape.

'But?'

'Twice he brought injured animals that he'd found out in the bush to my dad, late at night. I remember him standing with an orphaned joey all wrapped up in his old jacket, begging my father to look after it. There was a gentleness about him.'

'Being an animal-lover as a kid doesn't rule out becoming a killer,' Alec commented quietly. 'I wish it did.'

The image of the rough, gentle boy vanished and the disillusionment of the last year slammed a reminder that she had no way of knowing what Morgan Gillespie might have become, what he might be capable of.

'No, you're right,' she acknowledged, through a sudden, acrid taste in her mouth. 'No more than being Santa Claus at kids' Christmas parties does.'

And because the memory of sharing that with him this morning tempted her to take two steps closer to him, she did the reverse, putting distance between herself and the danger he threatened to her equilibrium.

His jaw tightened but he remained motionless, not pursuing her, giving her the space she needed.

'I still think they're different, Bella.' That tired, rough edge to his voice returned. 'This murder is premeditated, cold, calculated. The other... Well, almost anyone has the capacity to lose themselves in that sort of immediate rage, when something they care about is threatened.'

'Could you?' she challenged him. Although she held his gaze, daring him to answer truthfully, fear of his answer almost choked her. Could he? Could he ever lose the control, the discipline, he'd shown over the past two days? Become just like the others who had beaten Dan Chalmers to death?

He stood silent so long he might have been a statue, except no statue had eyes that clouded.

'I don't know, Bella. I hope not. I haven't yet.'

A siren sounding on the main road gave her an excuse to turn away from him, brush away the tears that pressed against her eyes. She'd wanted honesty and she'd got it, but she'd also wanted him to deny the possibility outright. If a man as principled, as emotionally strong, as Alec might still succumb to that darkness, then she had every reason to be afraid.

The afternoon dragged by, a hundred tasks demanding Alec's attention. He'd reluctantly agreed to Isabelle's request to stay at the Gillespie place to work with the forensic team, and had left Kris and Adam there with strict instructions regarding her protection. Yet not having her in his sight unsettled him, and he kept glancing at his watch, impatiently counting the time to when they might be expected back at the hall.

In the meantime, Jeanie Menotti confirmed that the publican he knew of in Sydney was Gillespie's son, and he contacted his team down there and asked them to notify the man of his father's death and ascertain whether he might have been involved. He filed the necessary initial reports, called the coroner's office, allocated Steve Fraser to start another round of enquiries in the town, argued – again – with his superiors for more officers, and won the small concession of an additional half-dozen uniformed staff and two more detectives. Not enough, but a start.

And wherever he went in the hall, Finn paced a few steps behind, his toenails clicking softly against the wooden floor, his dark eyes watching.

'She'll be back soon, Finn,' he finally assured the dog – or was it himself? 'There are plenty of people to look after her out there.'

The sound of vehicles pulling in on the gravel outside the hall instantly drew his eyes towards the open double doors. Not Bella, damn it. The television network logo on the side of one of the vehicles didn't do a whole lot to improve his mood. They'd been lucky to get this far without the media swarming – probably due to Dungirri's isolation. Each of the networks only had a single crew to cover a huge region. If one of them had decided the story was worth sending a crew out for, there'd likely be others arriving soon, as well as newspaper and radio journalists.

He sent two uniformed officers up to the Wilsons' home to keep the media away from them, although he could barely spare the staff. With officers out at the Gillespie place, some working with Fraser on his interviews, and others searching with the SES, he had no one left at the hall other than a couple of civilian staff.

A media liaison officer from Dubbo had arrived earlier in the day, and he called her over.

'They've arrived, Alison,' he told her. 'Tell them I'll hold a media conference at…' he glanced at his watch, '…four-fifteen.'

The young woman nodded. 'Good timing. If other crews are on their way, they'll probably arrive by then, and there'll be enough time for stories to make the evening news.'

'We'll need the next media release ready to go by four,' he reminded her.

He wouldn't go out of his way to pander to the media's demands, but there was a chance that a member of the public might have information that would help them find Tanya, and the media's role could be important in publicising the case.

A woman in the neat attire of a television reporter knocked on the open door and peered in, and Alison went to her before she came inside, pulling the doors closed behind her to keep prying eyes – and cameras – out.

Unfortunately, it also kept out the small amount of breeze that had made the heat in the hall almost bearable.

Alec found the computer support technician outside in the police mobile van that housed the network connections and satellite dish. 'Phone around and see if you can beg, borrow or buy some fans, will you? I'll sign a requisition if you need it.'

The technician went in search of the local phone book, and Alec returned to his desk, wishing all his problems were as easily resolved. Finn took up position close by, head resting on his paws, but his ears upright, alert, eyes not wavering from him.

Alec briefly considered using the radio to check everything was okay at the Gillespie place, but decided against it for the moment. He had to let them do their work, and processing the scene for forensic evidence would take time.

The press conference had just begun on the steps of the hall when Bella and Kris finally arrived back. They skirted past the small throng of journalists, camera and sound operators, heading towards the rear door of the hall. As they went by Alec caught Isabelle's eye. She shook her head slightly, her face pale and grave. No encouraging news then.

'DCI Goddard, can you confirm that a man's body has been found, and that one of your officers was attacked? Are these crimes connected with Tanya's abduction?'

The most assertive of the journalists facing him had obviously been doing her homework, talking to people in town, watching the comings and goings of the police team.

Behind the journalists, a small crowd of locals had gathered, and they watched him closely too. They'd have seen the police vehicles going out along the Birraga road, and while the coroner's car wouldn't have travelled through town, someone might well have seen it. It didn't take much in a small community to put two and two together.

He confirmed both incidents but gave little else away. Fully aware that the abductor would likely watch the evening news bulletins – he could even be in the crowd before him – he purposely kept what he'd announced so far to a bare minimum. *Let the bastard wonder how much they really knew.*

He scanned the gathering, and continued. 'We urge members of the public who might have any information about Tanya's disappearance to please contact us here at the operations centre, or to phone Crime Stoppers.'

He thanked the reporters and returned inside, the bright sunshine contrasting with the duller light indoors so that it took a moment for his eyes to adjust before he found Isabelle. She sat on a chair, Finn on his hind legs half in her lap, trying to lick her face.

'What news?' he asked.

'Forensics have just about finished,' she answered. 'They'll call in here before they take what they have back to Inverell. They can do some analysis there, but most of it will have to go to the lab in Sydney, of course. Not that they're holding out a lot of hope of anything significant. The rifle is probably Gillespie's – the make matches the registration record. And the deputy coroner has been given clearance for the body to be taken for the autopsy.'

Which would have to be done in Sydney as well, Alec knew, meaning at least an additional day's delay in getting reports. In the meantime, Tanya was still missing, going through who knew what hell, and a murderer was loose in Dungirri, with Bella in his sights. Forensic evidence might help them make a conviction, but they wouldn't have the results in time to find the killer. That relied on the logic, process and instinct of detective work. And they desperately needed some sort of break, some lead, soon to fend off the looming, nightmare prospect of failure.

The hall door swung open and Steve Fraser strode in and straight up to them, his face as dark as Alec's mood.

'We've got another problem,' he announced. 'Joe Ward has disappeared.'

SIXTEEN

Isabelle pushed Finn down and rose to her feet, despite her shaking legs. Her instant thought that Joe's disappearance was bad news, not a breakthrough, was mirrored in the flash of bleakness on Alec's face, an instant before he resumed his professional mask.

'Ward went on a delivery run this morning,' Steve explained. 'It was supposed to be only an hour, and he hasn't been seen since. His daughter, Melinda, said he was acting strange, nervous, and she's out of her mind with worry.' Steve glanced around the group and added, 'She also said he went out late last night, didn't come back till around dawn. And his rifle is missing.'

'He was very uneasy yesterday when we interviewed him too,' Alec observed. 'Kris? Isabelle? What are your thoughts? Abductor or victim?'

'He's always been nervous around me,' Isabelle admitted. She'd not mentioned why earlier, but now the truth needed to be told, for her hunch leaned towards victim, not abductor. 'There was an incident years back, when I was fourteen or so, and I had to knee him. I never told anyone about it, but I think he was always afraid I would, that they might take Melinda from him.'

'He assaulted you?' Alec growled, and in the midst of all this madness, that masculine concern for her touched a place deep inside and warmed her even as she denied inwardly that it mattered.

'A minor drunken grope. Nothing I couldn't handle, even back then.'

Her dismissal of the incident as unimportant did little to reduce Alec's frown.

'He wasn't too fond of your father, though, Bella,' Kris commented thoughtfully. 'I overheard him carrying on in the pub one day about how your dad ridiculed him by putting him in one of his books.'

Isabelle stared at her. 'Joe Ward? In a book?' She did a quick mental scan through her father's writing, and shook her head. 'I can't see how he got that idea. I can't think of any character at all like Joe.'

'Some people can read all sorts of twisted things into the most innocent situation.'

Alec's quiet comment wasn't accusatory, but Isabelle noticed Steve's suddenly flushed face. Yes, *he'd* read twisted things in

Dan Chalmers' innocent behaviour. But he hadn't been the only one to do so.

She exhaled slowly. No sense going over old history. Steve had learned, regretted his mistakes, as did others. Holding on to the past would help no one, especially not Tanya.

Was she overlooking something obvious? Could Joe be the person who'd taken Tanya? She'd dismissed his unease in his store yesterday because he'd always been uneasy with her since that indiscretion years ago. And in the discussion with Jeanie and Kris, they'd discounted Joe because he didn't have the smarts to come up with a complex plot. A basic, straightforward thinker, that was Joe.

Surely the person who played such cold games with the police wouldn't show nerves in their presence? That person would be smug, laughing at them, at least inside.

The sudden recollection of her attacker's cold snigger threw her back into reliving those moments when she'd struggled for her life, and she shut her eyes against the memory, drew in a long breath because she *could*.

'Isabelle? What is it?'

Alec's voice anchored her to the present, kept the remembered sensations from drowning her as she searched for the clue she felt *had* to be there.

Then she found it, a drop of clarity in the midst of all the fear, and she opened her eyes to meet Alec's.

'It wasn't Joe on the veranda last night. I'm sure of that.'

'Why?'

'He's shorter than me – he's only five four or so. And the person who attacked me was definitely taller. I remember his breath on the top of my head.'

She was safe, there in the hall with the three of them and Finn, yet the recollection of that malicious ruffle of air on her hair brought a shudder to her body that even wrapping her arms around herself couldn't restrain. And then a second realisation crystallised, so sharp and cold it tore away her breath for a long moment.

'If…' She forced herself to say the words with a level of objectivity. 'If he really wanted me dead, why didn't he use a knife or gun at the hotel? Either would have been quicker, more effective.'

She would *not* dwell on the thought of a knife plunging into her back, or slicing across her throat, yet despite her determination and the heat in the room, her body trembled even more and she turned away, trying to hide it.

'You think it's just part of the game? Trying to scare you?' The rasp came from Alec.

'Yes. Cat and mouse, only I'm not the damned cat.'

To her consternation, her eyes filled with tears. A tissue box sat on the edge of a desk nearby and she retreated to it, keeping her back to them while she blew her nose and wiped her eyes. But of course they'd all seen, and Kris put a reassuring hand on her shoulder when she returned, while Steve muttered, 'We'll get the son of a bitch, Bella.'

Alec's intense stillness dragged her attention from Steve and Kris. Anger blazed from the blue fire of his eyes and his hands gripped white on the edge of the desk, a stark contrast to his usual self-control. Something powerful affected him, she thought, dazed by the raw heat of his reaction. Something akin to her own gut-wrenching response, just a few hours ago, when the snake had threatened his life. His fury could not be ascribed to some professional concern, the need to notch up another arrest, to succeed. Nor to 'liking' or 'respect' or any other of the safe words she'd used in her mind earlier to explain the inexplicable. She couldn't just pack this crazy and illogical and hopeless and frightening *thing* in a box, nice and simple, label it, close the lid, tuck it away on a mental shelf and forget about it.

Sometime, somehow, she would have to deal with it. Face her own paralysing fear of being vulnerable, the certain knowledge of not being *whole* enough, of not having enough left in her to trust or give to another.

To allow herself to feel for Alec anything more than she felt for others – Kris, Steve, Jeanie, even Beth – would be to plunge into a chasm of emotion that she no longer had the strength to endure.

Afternoon dragged into evening, evening to night, and the unspoken urgency to end the nightmare, to find Tanya, to make Bella safe, drove Alec on.

Fear spread, plague-like, with the news of Gillespie's death and Ward's disappearance, infecting the town. The unspoken question – who would be next? – hung in every pair of shadowed eyes as Alec and Isabelle went door to door, trying to wrest any ideas, thoughts, *evidence* that might point them towards answers.

But no one knew anything of substance.

Darkness settled over the town. The wind had dropped, and the dry air, although still hot, had cooled a little from the blistering heat of the afternoon.

Gravel crunching underfoot, Alec walked with Bella past the silent school, and along the road towards the hotel. Across the road, the Truck Stop Cafe was closed, and Jeanie's house behind it equally dark. They'd spoken with her an hour or so ago, at Melinda Ward's, where she was keeping the distressed young woman company.

Lights shone in the front bar of the hotel, and a murmuring of voices drifted through the wide open windows. Inside, Alec could see more than a dozen people, mostly men, seated at the bar, at tables, and playing pool.

Bella paused in the shadows under a large tree.

'We should go in and talk with them. Joe's a regular, so he'll have mates in there. And maybe we can find out who's been buying single-malt scotch.'

He didn't miss the reluctance in her voice, or forget that the mob that had set on her and Chalmers had originated at the hotel bar. 'You don't have to do it, Bella. I'll take you up to the hall first then go in myself.'

He wanted her back somewhere safe. This last half-hour, as dusk had deepened to night, he'd been inceasingly uneasy, but she'd insisted on finishing the door-knock.

'No. I know most of them,' she said.

She squared her shoulders, stepped out of the shadows. He held the door open and let her in before him. The low rumble of conversation took a slow slide to a halt as the drinkers turned to see the newcomers.

Alec scanned the room as they walked to the bar. On a stool at one end of the bar, an older man nursed an almost-empty schooner, alone. A group of SES volunteers, still in various forms of uniform, sat near the pool table at the end of the room – four men and two women, with another two guys playing a half-hearted game of pool. Alec didn't recognise any of them and figured they might be from the out-of-town crew.

Of the eight men loosely grouped around a couple of adjoining tables, he did know a few faces: Mark Strelitz, Darren Oldham, a middle-aged man by the name of Barrett whose first name he'd forgotten, and one of Barrett's sons.

The publican, a man in his late sixties, Alec guessed, emerged from out the back, walking with a heavy limp. His manner stiffened when he saw them. He greeted Isabelle by name, nodded to Alec. 'How can I help you?'

'Would you like a drink, Isabelle?' Alec asked, adding, 'My shout,' when she frowned and slipped her hand into her pocket. She wasn't carrying a bag and he doubted she had much money on her.

She accepted his offer without protest. 'Thanks. I'll have a mineral water, please, Stan.'

She came across calm enough, and Stan's body language

relaxed marginally as he reached for glasses and poured their drinks.

'Bad business last night,' he commented. 'We don't usually bother with locking up much other than the booze, but I will tonight. I'll get you a key for the main door.'

'You don't live on the premises?' Alec asked, keeping his tone remarkably polite given his anger. How could anyone, in the twenty-first century, not bother locking up? Maybe things were different out here in the bush, but Bella had almost died because of it.

'We're a couple of doors down.' Stan gestured to his leg. 'I need a new flaming knee. Can't do the stairs any more. There's a night bell through to the house, though. And I could get my lad,' he waved a hand towards the local group, 'to bunk down in the back bar tonight if you want the extra security.'

'That would be a good idea,' Alec agreed. Assuming Stan's son wasn't a killer, he added to himself. He'd have to check what they had on him later.

Mark came across to them. 'Are you having a quiet drink away from it all, or still working?'

'Working,' Isabelle answered before Alec could. 'Do you mind if we join your group for a chat?'

Mark pulled over a couple more chairs for them and made the introductions. Composed but far from relaxed, Isabelle sat next to Mark, drew a notebook and pen from her pocket and laid them on the table beside her drink, making it clear that this was business, not social.

She knew them all, and, across the table from her, Alec studied them, seeking something, anything, in their responses that might provide a clue or a lead.

Stan's son, Dave, was in his mid-twenties, worked out on the gas fields in outback South Australia, and had only arrived back in town that afternoon for a visit – which cleared him from involvement and eased Alec's concerns about his presence in the hotel overnight.

Karl Sauer, of similar age to Dave and obviously good mates with him, wore an SES T-shirt, with the top of his orange overalls undone and rolled around his waist. Both men treated Isabelle with an easy respect.

Of the three who were her contemporaries – Mark, Darren and Paul Barrett – Alec could detect no particular nervousness or discomfort, beyond the expected worry about the situation facing the town.

Likewise with the three older men – Jim Barrett, Frank Williams and Tom Trevelyn. Jim was slightly wary, but given he'd been interviewed earlier in the day with his son, and neither of them had an alibi for the time of Tanya's disappearance, this wasn't a surprise.

If any of them had attacked Isabelle, either last year or last night, then Alec doubted they would have looked her in the eye as easily as they did. Yet seeing Isabelle there, surrounded by men, heightened his own uneasiness.

Pen in hand, she asked the group about Joe – his movements over the past few days, his mood, where he might have gone. Well aware he was the outsider, Alec stayed quiet.

'We've been going over it ourselves, Bella, and we can't come up with anything,' Jim said. 'He's a mate of ours. Tonight's our weekly cards night. He should be here, with Frank and Tom and me.' He took an unsteady sip of his beer, wiped his mouth with the back of his hand. 'Jesus, Bella, I can't believe he's done anything wrong. Not with Gillespie, and definitely not with Ryan's girl.'

'He knows what it is to lose a kid. He wouldn't do that to his worst enemy, let alone a friend,' Frank added. 'He thinks the world of Ryan.'

'Yeah. I was here on Tuesday when he heard the kid was missing,' Karl said. 'He got really cut up about it. Kinda frantic, you know? And then he left.'

'What if Joe thought…' Paul stopped abruptly.

'Go on, Paul.' Isabelle's tone was quiet, but firm.

Paul hesitated, clearly uncomfortable, and Mark chimed in, 'If you have any ideas, for God's sake tell her, Paul.'

'If he thought Gillespie had done it…could he have gone after him?'

The sudden silence thick enough to cut, Jim and Frank glared at him, while the others looked anywhere but at Isabelle.

Paul flushed, anger rising. 'Shit, I'm just saying what we're all wondering. But I don't frigging know.'

'Gillespie was in Joe's store yesterday morning,' Darren said slowly. 'I saw him go in as I was driving past.'

'No. Not Joe.' Tom jerked his head up, his denial edged with desperation. 'He wouldn't. He was a wreck for months last year after Chalmers…'

His words died, panic twisting his face, as Jim hissed, 'Fuck, Tom, shut it.'

Isabelle paled, her eyes wide, her fingers clenched in a death grip on her pen. Alec shifted his chair back, ready to go to her, get her out of there.

'He doesn't mean Joe was there,' Frank corrected quickly. 'I'm sure he wasn't. But what happened scared Joe, Bella. It scared all of us,' he added with a painful, gruff honesty.

Alec didn't breathe as Isabelle held Frank's gaze. Then she nodded mutely and closed her notebook. He wanted to go to her, but Mark was there already, his hand on the back of her chair in quiet empathy. So Alec drew the attention of the rest of them away from her by standing and speaking with deliberate formality.

'We have a number of leads that we're pursuing in relation to each of these crimes. If you think of anything else, please contact us immediately. In the meantime, given the circumstances, I recommend a high level of personal caution for everyone.'

'You think Gillespie was murdered.' Paul's statement edged towards accusation.

'We've not yet determined the cause and circumstances of his death,' Alec said. 'But, yes, we are considering murder as a possibility.'

He left the rest unsaid, but it hung in the air around them – that Joe could be the perpetrator or a victim, and none of them could be sure of that until they found him.

Paul shoved back his chair. 'I'm going home. I've got a wife and kids to worry about.' He jerked his head towards the old man alone at the bar. 'You'll take Mick, will you, Dad?'

Jim nodded. 'I'll see that he gets home safely.'

The group broke up. As Alec collected the hotel's front door key from Stan at the bar, Jim helped his brother off the bar stool, Tom and Frank left, and the two young guys and Darren drifted over to join the SES group.

Isabelle waited with Mark just outside, and Alec walked up beside her. 'How are you doing?' he asked.

She gave a tiny shrug and a wan smile. 'I'm okay.'

'I'll go up to the hall with you,' Mark offered.

With Isabelle between them, they walked the two blocks along the silent street. The uneasiness still wore at Alec and he quickened the pace, anxious to get her inside again, wishing for once that she'd brought Finn with her for added protection. Despite her strength and stoicism, she seemed smaller and more vulnerable than ever.

They'd found out little more this evening, other than the fact that Joe had seen Gillespie yesterday morning. This case was going bad fast, and if they didn't get some kind of break soon... Alec didn't dare think about the possibilities.

SEVENTEEN

The team back at the hall had found Joe's truck, abandoned on a track deep in the bush, with no signs of foul play, but also no signs of Joe.

'His tracks went into the bush, but it was too dark to follow. I can go out again at first light,' Adam offered.

Alec agreed. 'You'd better get a little sleep first, though. In fact, everyone go and get some rest. We can't do much more tonight. We'll meet here again at six in the morning.'

He didn't miss the relief flickering on faces overly fatigued by the past two long days. His responsibility weighed heavily; he had to ensure they didn't wear themselves into zombies in their dedication.

'Who'll watch the hall?' Steve asked.

'I will,' Alec replied. 'The extra officers should arrive about midnight. I'll brief them when they get here. Can you take Isabelle –'

'I'm staying,' she interrupted. 'I need to check through the people who were at Birraga High when I was there.'

Even though he knew it was selfish of him, Alec didn't protest. Steve opened his mouth to say something, but shut it again quickly when Isabelle glared at him, and he left with the others without argument.

'Has the Education Department sent the class lists already?' Alec asked as Isabelle headed to her desk, his voice echoing in the emptiness of the hall.

'No. It'll take a while to get them from the archives in Sydney. But I asked the school to send the old year books from the library, for the five years either side of my age group. Not quite as complete as the official records, but it's a start.'

She picked up one of the booklets from a pile on her desk and passed it to him.

'Photos of each student in Year Twelve, and class photos of the others. Maybe the pictures will jog my memory even more than the names. All the parents are around the same age as me. I don't know of any link the Tomasis in Jerran Creek, Kasey's parents, have with Dungirri or Birraga, but the others... Well, if it isn't random, maybe the connection is in these somewhere.'

He nodded, flicking through the pages. In the Year Ten class photo – her last year at Birraga High, he guessed, before she and her father had moved away – her sixteen-year-old face stared at him from decades ago. A Mona Lisa smile played on her lips, yet those same solemn, grey eyes looked out beyond the camera as though she could see right into the future, to him. Which was entirely too fanciful for a man who prided himself on common sense, yet the disconcerting sensation itched between his shoulders.

He scanned the others in the group. Forty-plus kids in her year, all those youthful faces full of life and hope and promise.

He recognised Darren Oldham, gangling and skinny, even his hair spiking out. Mark Strelitz, neat without being nerdy, his trademark open smile hinting at the public life to come. Paul Barrett, his school tie crooked. And Ryan Wilson, topping the others by a head and already with the broad physique that must have given him an advantage on the rugby field.

'Jessica's parents – the Sutherlands – were they in your year?'

She stepped beside him, looked over his arm at the page, and her nearness kicked his pulse into overdrive. Halted it when she reached to point at the photo and her forearm brushed his. He dragged his attention back to the page in front of him.

'That's Sara, in the front row,' she said. 'And there's Mitch, next to Ryan.'

The two boys wore huge grins as though they'd just shared some ribald teenage joke. They both looked so incredibly young. Young and innocent, even with that impish glint in their eyes. Neither of them had the edge, the hardness, that he'd seen too often in kids he'd apprehended on city streets.

But he'd seen the shattering disillusionment in Ryan's face yesterday, and wherever Mitch and Sara had gone after leaving Dungirri, he knew they sure as hell wouldn't be smiling.

Bella took a sharp breath beside him, almost a wince.

'Five of them are already dead,' she said. 'Barb Russell – she died of cancer. Paula was killed in a car accident, just after finishing school. Mick, the alcoholic at the bar tonight, is her father. Robbie and Pete were killed in a railway crossing smash. And Ben…' She stopped, swallowed heavily. 'Ben was Mitch's cousin. Kris told me that he drank weed poison last year, a couple of weeks after Jess…' Her voice trailed away.

Weed poison? Alec almost retched. Why, with all the other suicide options available, had the man chosen one so awful? It suggested either a strong sense of guilt or a very disturbed mind. If he'd been in the mob that killed Chalmers, both were possible.

'Five out of forty-five in just nineteen years,' Bella remarked with an unsettling quietness. 'We'd never have believed it back then.'

'Teenagers tend to believe they're immortal.'

'Yes.' Her deep, tired sigh held infinite sadness. She closed her eyes for just a moment then lifted her head again. 'I'd better get working. Before it becomes six.'

'I can have a police helicopter fly in within an hour to take you to a safe house down south.'

Please, please agree to it, he urged silently, hopelessly, but she shook her head as he'd known she would. Of course she would stay, until they found Tanya or until there was no hope left. He could order her to go, but she'd more than likely refuse, and he understood her need to be here. Every cop had at least one case like this in their life, one that mattered beyond all the others. This was Bella's, and she would see it through to the end.

And he had no choice but to see it through with her, no matter where it led them.

'I'll make some coffee,' he offered, the inadequacy of the only thing he could do for her right now raising his anger at the situation further.

By the time he returned from the kitchen a few minutes later with two mugs, she was deeply immersed in her work. Her hair, freed from its knot, tumbled about her face and the desire to touch those waves tingled in his fingers.

Instead, he placed the mug on her desk and crossed to his own. Work, that was what he needed to do. Solve this sickening crime before anyone else got hurt. *Find Tanya, and keep Bella safe.*

The mental exercise of jotting down all the occurrences of the case on a large piece of paper, colour-coding their similarities and links, analysing their significance, kept him busy for some time and clarified in his own mind that Bella's analogy of a cat toying with a mouse fitted the circumstances. But there came a point in every cat and mouse game when the cat tired of playing and sank its teeth into the mouse's neck.

From Kasey's abduction in Jerran Creek to now, each case demonstrated an increase in risk, an increase in daring.

Whoever had taken Tanya was confident enough to have escalated his activities, altered his strategy beyond abducting the child. And this person had to be some sort of sociopath, without even a flicker of compassion or feeling for others. Remorseless.

His cell phone ringing, suddenly loud in the silent hall, startled them both. Petric, his offsider in Sydney, the display told him.

While he took the call, Bella rose, collected their empty coffee mugs and went down to the kitchen. Finn stretched languorously before padding along behind her.

Petric's news was exactly what Alec expected: he'd checked out Morgan Gillespie, and the man had a cast-iron alibi for the last few days. He hadn't murdered his father.

Alec finished the call and dropped the phone back on the desk on top of the mind-map he'd scrawled. The sound of a running tap, Bella's voice, soft and indistinct, talking to Finn, drifted out to him. The thought of everything they could lose made him drop his head into his hands, exhausted by the constant tension. He'd worked some tough cases in his time – plenty of them – but he'd never felt this tired, this vulnerable, this doubtful before. So much at stake, and so few leads, so little to go on, even two days in.

Every sound from the kitchen vibrated in his awareness. A scrape of plastic on the floor. Finn's slurps. The squeak of a cupboard door. The soft clink of a glass. Bella might be out of his direct line of sight, but it only served to accentuate his acute awareness of her.

He pushed back his chair. He needed to tell her that Morgan Gillespie was in the clear, that her judgment hadn't been wrong. He needed to reassure himself that she was all right, that she was holding up to the incredible pressure on them.

Who the hell was he trying to fool?

He needed *her*.

Isabelle stood in front of the kitchen window, looking out, but the blackness of the night outside turned the glass into a mirror. So she saw Alec come into the kitchen, pausing just behind her.

Their reflections hung in the glass, all else indistinct around them, and she couldn't draw her gaze away from the image of his eyes, watching her image, watching her. Her heart beat faster, and every nerve responded to his presence as automatically as the hand of a compass swinging to north.

Magnetic attraction. Even as the words formed in her thoughts, she understood that it went far deeper than just physical desirability.

Gorgeous men that other women raved about had barely stirred her in the past, so that she'd sometimes wondered if there was something wrong with her, if maybe she really deserved the Ice Princess nickname her colleagues had given her. Now here was proof that she didn't. Six foot plus of proof, in a man who had not only earned her respect, but who had melted away her reserve, her need for physical and emotional space, and woken parts of her that had slumbered for so long she hardly recognised them as herself.

Maybe later she'd be afraid again, but not just now, not when they shared the dark and the quiet of the late hour, alone, and whatever passed between them was private, just the two of them.

The image of him wasn't enough to satisfy her, and she turned slowly to face him, studying him as he studied her, their unsteady breathing and the soft whirring of the computers the only sounds in the hall.

He stayed the same considerate distance from her he'd kept all evening, all day, not crowding her, yet close enough for her to see the pulse fluttering in his neck, the reined-in but no less powerful need in his eyes.

It hadn't been her imagination then. In the same strange, unasked-for way that she cared about him, he cared about her. And whatever invisible link bound them together, it could be no light, easy thing for either of them.

Authenticity. The word slipped into her thoughts, stayed, and it fitted him, what she'd learned of him. He wasn't a man who dissembled, played any role other than himself. Perhaps that was where her trust of him stemmed from. He might not speak everything he thought – underneath his self-confident way with others, she sensed the private reserve in him – but he always spoke honestly.

Depth, authenticity, compassion. How could she not respond to those qualities? And how could she not respond to the fatigue that dulled the normally sharp energy of him? For two days straight, he'd kept track of everything, everyone, listening to opinions before making decisions, answering questions, anticipating needs, directing and leading and coor-dinating without faltering. And all with only an hour or two's sleep, at most.

The toll it took on him showed now in the bleak, exhausted need in his eyes. He'd stood beside her all day, ready to support her whenever she needed it. Yet who was there to give to him when he needed it, on dark nights like tonight when answers seemed so far away?

I can. The quiet conviction formed deep within her, sure and certain and right. She could not fail him now.

She reached out, laid her hand against his cheek, and his eyes widened, breath caught, at her voluntary touch.

'You're exhausted, Alec,' she murmured. 'You need to sleep.'

He closed his hand over hers, trapped it against the warm, rough texture of his skin, and she made no attempt to remove it. For all that the old lights in the hall spread a garish glow, the stillness of the night around them centred her and a strange kind of peace folded itself around her.

When he spoke, his voice was low, edged with a huskiness that wasn't just tiredness. 'That's the first time you've called me by my name.'

No use trying to deny that, she recognised, surprised that he'd noticed what she'd scarcely been aware of herself. Yes, she'd used his name to introduce him to others – but not to acknowledge him directly.

There'd been no accusation in his observation, but she couldn't mistake the implicit message. He'd noticed. *It mattered to him.*

'I think… I haven't wanted you to be…real.'

Yet he was real, there in front of her, undeniably real, and her fear of becoming vulnerable to him seemed too distant to heed. He seemed to understand her stumbling words and nodded. With his other hand he caressed her face, lightly and tenderly.

With a half-sigh, half-groan, he pressed a kiss into the palm he still held.

Her breathing too erratic to speak, she took the step that bridged the distance between them, the step that could plunge her, ultimately, back into darkness. But the intense heat in his eyes held her, and the exquisite caresses of his fingers on her cheek, and the kiss they began together, equal.

They touched, tasted, touched again. Gentle, that first intimacy, gentle enough to be safe, easy to break away if she'd wanted to. But breaking away was the last thing she wanted.

He wove his fingers into her hair, held her face captive while he explored it with his mouth, dusting kisses along her jaw, her cheekbone, over her eyelids. The prickles of his jaw rasped lightly against her skin, and she inhaled, tasted, hints of salt and sweat and coffee as she kissed the pulse in his neck, found his lips and halted their wandering by deepening the kiss, indulging in the incredible, sensual delight of him.

Soft and unhurried, he slid his arms around her, drew her to him, and the distance between them became nothing at all. And she didn't wonder at her trust in him, for how could this beauty and passion be frightening? Later there might be a time for sadness and fear, but not now. And she'd deal with later...later.

Desire and hunger and need for more of him sizzled through every nerve and muscle and vein, consuming all else.

She moulded her body to his, and revelled in the shape of him, his powerful masculine energy against her, hips and legs and bodies pressed close, hot and burning and craving even more.

He muttered her name against her mouth, and gentleness melted in the heat of possession, his hands claiming her body, his mouth claiming hers.

The woman she didn't quite recognise as herself met his every demand and gave back just as much. When his roaming hands slid under her top and marked her skin with their touch, she arched into him, wanting.

He caressed her back, her waist, sliding around to cover the flatness of her stomach, and the small part of her brain still capable of thought marvelled at the incredible sensuality of such simple touch.

Then he curved his hand over her breast, circling his palm ever so slightly against her hardened nipple, and a tidal wave of need and hunger claimed all her senses.

Trailing kisses down her face, the nape of her neck, he worked his way down, her hands holding his head and guiding him while her body quivered in anticipation and her pulse performed a crazy, halting dance.

And then somewhere in the rushing of blood in her head, she heard a sound that didn't belong. A low, insistent, threatening growl, carving into her awareness, into Alec's awareness, shattering the magic isolation around the two of them. Finn.

The dog stood on his hind legs beside them, his front paws on the counter, and he growled again, ears twitching, the hair on his neck upright.

Alec swore and jerked away from her, paced to the other side of the small room, leaving her suddenly cold and alone and confused, and, just for an instant, hating her dog.

Finn dropped to the floor, sat on his haunches beside her leg, but she couldn't look at him. Not when she couldn't draw a decent breath. Not when her entire body burned with such a powerful craving. Not when all she wanted was for time to reverse itself back a minute and take a different tangent.

Alec leaned his head against the far wall, fists rammed into his pockets, the muscles in his neck working with the struggle for control.

'Oh, Bella, I'm sorry. I shouldn't have done that.'

He blamed himself and she couldn't allow that to happen. Hell, she'd just about been on her knees, begging him. She managed to find a cache of common sense and clarity.

'Why not?' she asked. 'And don't try any bullshit about senior rank.'

He grimaced. 'Yeah, that too.'

She'd made it worse. Darn the man for his conscience. 'Alec, *we* kissed each other. Maybe it was wrong, or unwise, or stupid, or just plain crazy. But not for any reasons in a police policy, okay?'

For long, long seconds he stared at her, a furnace of emotion in his gaze, a potent mix of pain and longing and sorrow and need that resonated with the searing, aching hurt in her own heart and the clamouring of her unsated body.

'Maybe you're right, Bella,' he said at last, the words rasping across the stillness. 'But there are other reasons why I shouldn't have kissed you.'

Exhaustion etched on his face, he slid down the wall, sat on the floor and rested his arms on his knees. Her own legs still trembling, she perched on the edge of the counter, a metre or so from him. Even that distance did little to reduce the magnetism that tugged at her, the craving to cross the gap to him. Resolute, she kept the space between them, because if she touched him now, all the reasons *she* shouldn't have kissed *him* might be overwhelmed again by the powerful physical attraction that had just swamped her sanity.

Yet, despite the physical distance, she felt closer to him than she had to anyone in a long time. She'd be honest and open with him, just as he would with her. They'd gone way past the point of pretending that nothing existed between them. Even if nothing *should* exist between them.

And because he looked so ragged, she took the initiative and spoke first.

'Alec, I feel something for you. I'm not sure what it is. But I can't... I don't trust myself enough...'

The words tangled. How could she tell him how it was? How she'd lost...

'I lost all I was,' she said.

He nodded, comprehending what she hardly understood herself. His intentness on her encouraged her to continue.

'All the underlying certainties, the things I valued most – I lost them. And I don't know if...if I'll ever get that back, get myself back. Even if we find Tanya safe... I don't know myself any more. I only know that there's not enough of me left, to involve myself with anyone else.'

'You'll find your way again, Bella.' The deep conviction in his voice burrowed in and warmed the cold places inside her where doubt and mistrust had taken root. 'You had to deal with more than any person should be asked to. But you have an inner strength that has brought you through what would have broken many others.'

She wanted to believe him, except they weren't through this yet, and the fear of what the next days might bring drowned the brief, fragile image of a future.

'Bella, if I were an accountant or a lawyer or anything other than a detective, I'd do my best to convince you of it. I'd ask you out on dates, to dinner, concerts, whatever. But I'm a detective, and I work with the scum of the earth, and I can't risk...'

He let his head fall back against the wall, closed his eyes briefly, and there was a silence before he spoke again.

'Do you remember Eddie Jones?'

She recalled the name from long-ago media reports. 'The Sydney drug boss?'

'Yes. Drugs and other rackets.' He paused, and his Adam's apple bobbed as he swallowed. 'Jones and his cronies kidnapped my partner's wife. Said they'd kill her if Rick didn't hand over some crucial evidence we'd found against Jones.'

He shut his eyes again, his voice, harsh and uneven, coming straight from a private hell.

'They raped her, Bella – all of them. They had no intention of letting either of them live. When Rick arrived to hand over the evidence, they killed her, right there in front of him. Then they shot him. He was bleeding to death when I found him. Holding on to Shani, crying. She...' His voice cracked, but he continued on. 'She was pregnant with their first child. They'd asked me to be the baby's godfather.'

Horror scalded her throat and his sorrow twisted tightly around her heart. Alec carried his own ghosts, just as she did. Except he hadn't run away.

'Jones...he's in prison now, isn't he?'

'Yes. I arrested him a couple of months later.' Alec said it without pride or pleasure. 'But he's got plenty of associates still out there, and they all have more than enough reason to hate my guts.' His eyes sought hers, intense, pleading. 'Bella, do you understand what these people are like? If they discovered that I cared about anyone, then they'd have no hesitation – Jones himself would take immense pleasure – in destroying me by destroying her.'

And there it all was, laid out before her – the deepest, private layers of him. The man buried beneath the professional, self-reliant, detective. The man who would deny himself everything to keep others safe.

Aching pain – his, her own, she couldn't have untangled them – ripped across her heart.

She shivered. How could she be so cold in the middle of summer?

His hands gripped together on his knees, so tense the lines of veins distorted his skin. Hands that only minutes ago had caressed her, woken her desire with gentleness, and with possession, fuelled it to fiery need. Her skin still carried the memory, a fever-heat under the chill of loss.

'I can't ever be anything to you, Bella.' His quiet words offered no solace. 'That's why I shouldn't have kissed you.'

But we did. A fact, an experience, a *knowing* that would not be erased or forgotten. And while logically she accepted the reasons – hers as well as his – a desperate reluctance to let that kiss slide into the past warred with logic, and the cacophony of contradictory thoughts choked her.

The rumble of an engine, the intrusive sweep of headlights through the window and across the room dragged them back to the world outside the kitchen. The extra officers arriving.

Alec grimaced and swore under his breath.

'Duty calls.' The reluctance in his voice echoed the way he slowly pushed himself up from the floor. Of course he wouldn't ignore his responsibilities. First and foremost a dedicated cop.

'Yes.' Her mouth felt dry and she wet her lips. So much to say, and now no time to say it. 'Lousy timing.'

'It always is.'

Yet he hesitated at the door, his face grey and drawn. One hand reached towards her, but before she could take it he dropped it again.

'I'm so sorry, Bella.' Not an apology this time, but an expression loaded with regret, and finality.

'I'm sorry too,' she whispered.

Finn followed him as far as the door, then sat on guard in the doorway, watching as Alec greeted the new arrivals.

She should move too. Go out there and join them, pretend that nothing had happened and assist Alec in the briefing as though they were merely colleagues. *Act a lie.*

The blunt accusation of her conscience caught her unawares. *Not a lie*, she argued with herself. They had their reasons – good reasons – to call a halt to anything further. Except that right now those reasons seemed to be losing their potency, and the fact that both her body and her emotions disagreed with her intellect just added to the paralysing confusion.

The only thing clear in her mind was that she should be heading out there to do her job.

Weary, she pushed herself off the counter and patted Finn on the head as she passed him. 'Come on, boy. We've still got work to do.'

EIGHTEEN

With the arrival of more officers, Alec threw himself into the introductions and briefings, the familiar role of detective almost a relief compared with the unfamiliar and terrifying role of...of whatever he wasn't to Bella. Almost. Her face haunted him and, despite all his resolve, he could no more put the recollection of the taste and feel of her from his mind than he could cease breathing. Even in his exhaustion his body responded whenever he looked at her, and his heart – hell, his heart constricted with physical pain.

She'd understood, accepted what he'd told her without any argument, without trying to talk him out of it, or belittling the fear for her safety that kept him from her.

He'd thought, for a moment, that it was because she didn't care that much. Until he'd caught her unguarded gaze, intense with a woman's hunger, shadowed with sorrow, and he'd had to force himself not to shout out in anger and frustration and grief.

'We'll look after things here, sir, if you want to go and get some rest,' one of the new arrivals said, and Alec stared at him for a moment, too tired and distracted to even remember the guy's name.

'Thanks, Phil.' Isabelle covered for his vagueness. 'We'll all be starting again at 6 am.'

They walked to the hotel without a word, and for once Alec was almost glad of Finn's presence between them. Bella stared straight ahead into the night, locked in her own thoughts, her own pain, as beautiful and as distant as the stars overhead.

Tension twisted around his spine and, despite the exhaustion dragging him down, his imagination replayed their kiss endlessly, tormenting him with the impossibility of any fulfilment. And underneath his civilised, responsible shell, the raw male in him raged with envy at those who had known the closeness to Bella that he was denied. He was jealous of Mark Strelitz and that teenage kiss in the darkness. He was jealous of Steve Fraser and the everyday intimacies he'd shared with Bella. Hell, he was even jealous of her damn dog.

The hotel was quiet. In the back bar, Dave and Karl sat on camp beds, talking softly; they waved as Alec and Isabelle walked through the foyer. Upstairs there were only the small sounds of people sleeping: soft snoring and creaking ancient bedsprings.

Alec unlocked the door to Bella's room, checked inside before allowing her and Finn in, then retreated to the doorway. She flicked on the bedside light, and for an instant before she stepped away from it, it shone through the fine white cotton of her shirt, silhouetting her body in a hazy, sensual halo.

'I'll wake Steve – get him to stay with you,' he muttered, his voice low more because of the rock in his throat than out of consideration for others sleeping nearby.

'Steve?' She spun around to face him, frowning. 'Why on earth...?'

'I can't, Bella,' he confessed, despair begging for her understanding. 'I can't stay here, so close to you, and sleep. Not after...'

Her eyes, silver in the lamplight, burned into his, and everything in him went still while that intense, honest regard held him trapped.

'Do you want to go?' The huskiness edging her question set his pulse leaping again in a mad, insane hope.

A faint flush of colour rose on her cheeks, yet she waited for his answer without looking away.

'Want?' he repeated slowly. 'No, I don't *want* to go.'

Now she did look away, down at Finn's lead in her hands as she neatly folded it in four with her fingers. She drew in a slow breath and raised her eyes to his again with quiet courage.

'Then don't.'

Alec stilled, and for a long moment there were only small sounds – a moth tapping against the window, Finn snuffling at his toes, and Isabelle's own heartbeat pulsing in her head.

She knew that the very aspects of him that she admired and respected held him back now – his sense of duty, his fear for her, his capacity for self-denial. So she had to be strong enough to do this, to give him reason to accept what they both needed now, while the world around was quiet and it was just the two of them.

'Stay with me.'

She dropped Finn's lead on the nightstand and took a step closer to Alec, willing him to understand, to allow himself to *be* himself this once.

'There's hours before dawn, and neither of us is likely to sleep, and… I don't want to be alone. I don't want to think. I don't want to feel afraid…just for a while.'

She reached a hand towards him and, after a moment's hesitation, he took it, wrapping his larger hand around hers, trapping it against his chest where the irregular rhythm of his heartbeat reverberated into her palm.

Yet still he held on to his control, the tension in him radiating like bushfire heat.

'We have reasons, Bella…'

'Reasons for another time, not for tonight. We're alone, and…and we need this. *I* need this. I want to stop fighting everything I feel, just for a while. I need…'

She paused, scrambling for words she didn't have. She just knew with gut-deep certainty that if she never knew him, she'd never know herself, never be able to find the courage to deal with what might come after dawn, never be able to put the pieces back together and find peace.

'There's already too much lost,' she said at last. 'I need a light in the darkness, Alec.'

'Bella.' His voice shook, and he drew her into his arms, wrapped his warmth around her, and for long, long moments they simply held each other.

She closed her eyes, let herself absorb the closeness, the gift of being together. The sensual awareness of male heat and strength and the fit of her body against his, the physical desire rising with every breath of him, every heartbeat echoing hers.

His lips brushed against her forehead, and he pulled back just far enough to cup her face with his hands, his fingers in her hair, his thumbs brushing her cheekbones, her temples, the simple tenderness melting her bones and her heart.

'I want you more than I knew anyone could, Bella. But I have to go back to Sydney when this is over.' His eyes – honest, open to her, letting her see right into his soul – never left hers. 'Last night, when I thought you were...' He swallowed, unable to say the word. 'I couldn't bear it if anything happened to you, Bella.'

She understood his meaning. No matter if everything turned out all right – if they found Tanya in the morning, returned her to her parents, and arrested the perpetrator – she would still lose him.

The knowledge of it fuelled her determination, the fierce

need to know him totally, before it was too late, demolishing any remaining reserve or hesitation.

'Shhh. I know. But...don't think about it. I want to forget it all for a while. Just let it be you and me and here and now.'

'I wish –'

Almost unable to bear the sorrow in his eyes, she drew his face down to hers and silenced him with a kiss. 'No promises, no regrets,' she whispered against his mouth. 'Now is all that matters.'

He slid his hands down around her, drawing her against his body once more. 'You matter. To me. Don't ever doubt it.'

She shaped her body to his, her mouth to his. She wanted to savour every second, every taste, every simple, intricate, lingering, hungry touch and kiss and caress. Sheer, wondrous *aliveness* overwhelmed conscious thought, filled every sense. So much feeling, focused so intensely, that she could easily lose herself in it...

Until some tiny shred of awareness not totally absorbed in Alec registered a small sound that wasn't hers. A whimper. A canine whimper.

She broke the kiss, shaking and disoriented by the intrusion, not sure whether to laugh or cry at Finn's soulful, pleading face, and suddenly half-afraid that Alec might distance himself again, as he had last time. But he kept her firmly in the circle of his arms and his breathless murmur against her forehead held the softest of chuckles. 'Poor Finn.'

Relief made her light-headed and from somewhere in her spinning mind she dragged enough words to be coherent.

'I'll put him outside on the lead. So that you don't end up with his teeth around your throat.'

'Good idea.' Alec brushed his lips against her forehead. 'But I'll take him out,' he said, the quiet words a sombre reminder of the danger that still lurked.

She nodded and watched from inside as he crouched beside the dog on the darkened veranda, fastened the lead around the railing; heard his low tones as he spoke quietly and patted him for a few moments.

His gentle care for Finn, despite the dog's over-protectiveness, moved her, adding to the jumble of strong emotions overloading her senses. So many men wore their strength as a weapon. Not Alec. His strength was at the core of him, the essence of him, so that he was strong enough to be gentle. Strong enough to be vulnerable. Strong enough to admit to need, to take as well as to give, to accept and respect strength in others.

And in a moment of sudden clarity she understood that she'd asked him to stay not out of fear, but because of her own strength, because the attraction between them was powerful and positive and *right*, and because somehow – she didn't try to understand how or why – he'd made her whole again.

And now she *could* give of herself, could live in this moment and accept the gift of this one chance without fear or hesitation.

He rose to his feet in one fluid, powerful movement that stole her breath, and so she focused her wavering concentration on unbuckling her holster, taking out the Glock and laying it on the bedside table.

The door latch clicked, and she turned back to see Alec standing there, fire and light and need blazing in his eyes.

Her breathing faltered again.

He crossed the metre or so between them, lay his own pistol beside hers, then the wallet from his back pocket. He reached for her and, with hands on her waist, drew her against him, hips and thighs together, the intimacy making obvious his arousal and heightening her own, and she curled her fingers into his shirt and pulled him closer still.

His eyes searched hers. 'You're sure, Bella?'

'Yes.'

And she was. Tonight – now – was all they had. A short time stolen from the reality of the outside world, for just the two of them.

Under her fingers, his heartbeat pounded. She slid a shirt button open, then another, found his heated skin and pressed her hands against him.

How could touching a woman, kissing her, change a man so irrevocably? Here in the lamplight, with Bella's fingers burning trails on his skin, the sensual heat of her body under his hands, and their kisses overwhelming his senses, he knew he had no experience to prepare him for making love with her. Technique and knowledge were meaningless faced with a woman who'd wrapped around his heart so totally that he no longer knew where she ended and he began.

He wanted to strip his emotions naked and let her into the heart of him, the long-lost places he hardly knew himself. He wanted – *needed* – to pack a lifetime of intimacy and knowing into these few, short miracle hours.

Capturing her face in his hands again, he kissed her mouth, her cheeks, ran the tip of his tongue along her eyelashes, and she made a small, desperate sound of desire as she chased his mouth with hers, her fingertips lighting every nerve on the skin of his shoulders as he shrugged out of his shirt.

That slow smile curved her mouth again, pleasure and female appreciation lighting her eyes. Even as her touch nearly drove him to madness, he delighted in this side of her, the ease between them, and her trust in him, to drop her guard so completely. But if he didn't distract her wandering hands, he'd burst into flames way too soon.

He ran his hands over her lithe, firm body, down her arms, around her hips, up her waist to skim, tantalisingly, along the softness of her breasts.

His fingers on the first button of her shirt fumbled as he suddenly remembered doing the same thing when she'd been shot.

'Hey, I thought you could do that with one hand,' she teased softly, but it was gentle teasing, as though she could read his face.

He had to force his voice to work. 'Only when it doesn't mean anything.'

Candid grey eyes held his as she closed her hands over his and dealt with the buttons, letting the shirt fall open and off her shoulders on to the floor.

For a moment, all he could do was stand and stare, torn by a raft of conflicting emotions. For while there was part of him that noticed – *feasted on* – the soft curve of her breasts framed in white lace, the sight of the small bandage on her shoulder intersecting the surgical scars and the bruise above her collarbone slammed him back into reality.

He'd lay down his life for her, but the hard truth that he could never guarantee her safety sat heavily on him. Twice in just forty-eight hours – with him only metres away – death had almost claimed her. So now – whether it was selfish or not – he felt only a desperate determination to give her so much pleasure, to love her so thoroughly, so completely, that she'd never forget him.

Although how the hell he'd get through the rest of his life without her, he had no clue.

He traced a finger along the line of lace and soft flesh, watching her pupils darken, her lips part, and then he followed his finger with his mouth, holding back the roar of desire in his head with the single driving thought: *Give Bella pleasure*.

Skin against skin, mouth against skin, he found the places that made her tremble, touched and explored and discovered her body, echoed her gasps of passion with the pleasure her hands and mouth gave him.

He reached to turn off the lamp, eased the last of their clothes away in the muted light from the veranda, and almost forgot how to breathe when she stood before him, naked and beautiful and giving.

His Bella. The tumult of pure male emotion was simultaneously tender and fierce. He'd kill for her. Die for her. Do whatever it took to cherish and protect her.

Protect. The word and the need pierced through the hot haze of his brain. While he gathered her back to his skin again, kissed her devastatingly slowly and traced the sensual curve of her spine with one hand, his other hand felt for and found the condom in his wallet.

And then they were both kneeling on the bed, and those knowing, passionate eyes – far past teasing – held his while she rolled the condom on to him, and it was everything he could do to stop the hot haze from melting his mind completely.

Give Bella pleasure.

Determined not to bring back nightmare memories by looming over her, he eased down to lie on his side, and as she came to lie beside him he slipped his arm under the curve of her waist to draw her closer still, breast to chest, hips all but joined, legs and feet twining to seek total contact.

While the physical hunger raged in his body, clamouring for release, the even stronger soul-hunger needed this – lying together in perfect intimacy, sharing touches, caresses, kisses in the deepest of trust.

Bella understood without need for words. Time slowed, was lost in the passion-dark honesty of her beautiful eyes, and their tender, deliberately delicate brushes of mouth and hands and skin on heated skin.

For a thousand heartbeats they floated there together, suspended on the brink, until the need and passion built inexorably to an intensity beyond resistance.

'Now, Alec,' she pleaded, in shallow, urgent gasps. 'With me. Part of me.'

'Always,' he vowed on a fervent whisper, finally surrendering to lose himself within her, tightening his arms around her still more, as if he could meld their bodies together. As she took him in, moved with him, arched back in ecstatic abandon, the bliss of being with her erased conscious thought and there was only the two of them, and the unbearable pleasure and the driving need and the fiery tension, building and tightening and craving completion.

And he didn't know if it was his own cry or hers that he smothered with a final, desperate kiss as he fell with her over the edge.

NINETEEN

She woke in the first pale daylight, curled against him, her head nestled into his shoulder. The slow rhythm of his breathing and the warmth of him beside her reassured her in the momentary disorientation of first waking. Even in sleep, his arm kept her close.

A few quiet sounds drifted in. A muted electronic beep, a door squeaking, hushed voices in the corridor. Each sound of their colleagues stirring a signal that her time alone with Alec had only minutes left.

The strength she'd found last night faltered. *I'm not ready yet,* she wanted to protest. Not ready to let go, to face that emptiness. Not ready to deal with the day, however it might unfold.

A surge of fear rose, black and choking. If they didn't find Tanya… The thought terrified her. Everything that might define a future for any of them – herself, Alec, Beth and Ryan, Kris and the rest of the town – depended on finding the little girl. Without that, there could be nothing.

And for the first time in a year – maybe even longer than that – there were things that she wanted. Tanya safely returned to her parents, of course, and justice, and order. But beyond those, she wanted a life for herself. One that didn't revolve entirely around duty.

Her eyes burned, and she closed them again, trying to concentrate on absorbing the brief *now*, the myriad sensations of closeness, the soft touch of bare skin under the sheet. Alec's breathing changed, and his arm tightened around her as he nuzzled into her hair. She raised her head, met him with wordless, tender kisses, desperately stealing the last few quiet moments of being together.

Footsteps padded along the veranda, paused just outside the door, and they broke the kiss, both of them tensing, alert for danger.

'Hey, Finn boy.' The metallic jingle of a dog collar and Finn's excited huffs accompanied Steve's voice, and he tapped on the door, calling softly, 'Shall I take him for a quick run for you, Bella?'

She exhaled a sigh of relief that it was only Steve and not anyone else. And that he hadn't just barged in to discover her with Alec. This had to stay private, just between the two of them, too fragile and too precious to expose to the gossip and assumptions of others.

'Thanks, Steve,' she called back, forcing her voice to some level of normalcy. 'That would be great.'

Alec silently caressed her face while they listened to the footsteps fade away down the veranda.

'We should get up,' Isabelle murmured, the demands of duty, of responsibility to Tanya, fighting with her sorrow.

'Yes.' Yet he made no move, only continued his exquisitely light touch, brushing his fingers across every feature of her face, studying her with a focused intensity, as if committing every sensation to memory. 'Bella, I –'

She halted him with a finger against his lips. 'Shhh. Don't say anything. We both know.'

He cupped her face in his hands, caught her mouth in a gentle, lingering kiss of longing and farewell. And then it ended, and she rolled away from him lest her eyes betray her grief, groped for her robe and tugged it around herself. The bedsprings released as he stood and he began to pull on his clothes.

He left her under the guard of one of the female officers to shower and dress. The water dribbling from the ancient shower head seemed a sacrilege, washing away her body's remembrance of Alec, diluting the memories and sensations and the precious beauty that she might never capture again.

But Tanya had to come first.

She walked up to the hall flanked by Finn and two officers. The first peach-gold rays of sunlight edged into the pale silver dawn, the soft early light bathing the town in a gentle glow. The cool freshness before the sunlight baked the earth seemed to hold promise and hope. *Please*, she prayed to any deity listening, *please let us find her today.*

The blissful aromas of baking and coffee assailed her as soon as she entered the hall. Real coffee, not the revolting instant gunk they'd endured for the past two days. Even just the delicious smell of it was enough to jolt another brain cell or two awake.

Jeanie Menotti bustled around in the kitchen, setting out breakfast makings on the counter, pouring coffee from a large pot into waiting mugs. A half-dozen bleary-eyed officers had already been served, and they clutched their mugs as though they contained the elixir of life.

At a desk halfway down the hall, Alec leaned over a large map with Adam and Steve. His white shirt contrasted with the dark blue of the police overalls the other two wore in preparation for the search for Joe Ward. He looked up, as if he'd felt her gaze, and his tired smile didn't quite disguise the relief in his eyes.

Adam said something, and he returned his attention to the map, and she suddenly became aware of Steve studying her with a grave expression that suggested he was putting two and two together. But he just nodded, once, with a small, wistful smile, and then he too turned back to the map.

'You need to have breakfast, Bella.' Jeanie called her over and thrust a mug into her hand. 'It's all ready. Raisin toast or muesli?'

'Toast, thanks.' Grateful for the distraction, some small

part of her brain suggested that toast would use a whole lot less energy to chew than muesli.

Jeanie handed her a plate piled with thick slices of hot, buttered toast. Home-baked by the look of it. The aroma of fruit and spices blended with the rich coffee scent and jump-started her appetite. Not enough to do justice to the pile of toast, though.

'I can't eat all this.'

Jeanie waved a hand towards Alec. 'Share it with Alec. He hasn't eaten anything yet. Does he take his coffee black?'

'Yes,' Isabelle managed through a thick throat. Had Jeanie, too, guessed what had happened? But Jeanie merely poured another mug of coffee and handed it across, her attention already shifted to Finn.

'You have your breakfast. I'll feed the dog,' she offered.

Balancing the plate of toast on top of one of the mugs, Isabelle made her way across the room to the three men. Steve stepped to one side as she joined them, making room for her next to Alec, and the considerate gesture touched her. Because, despite the irrationality of it, the small solace of standing close to Alec was far better than *not* being close to him.

'Eat,' she told Alec, straining to keep her voice light. 'Jeanie's orders. And saints outrank DCIs.'

'Of course they do. Thanks.'

He shifted the plate to the desk, and his fingers brushed against hers as he took the coffee mug. A brief touch, but enough to bring every single moment of their lovemaking flashing through her memory.

She avoided his eyes and steamrolled *those* thoughts to a halt.

'There's plenty of toast. Help yourself, guys.'

'Thanks, but we've eaten already,' Adam answered. He tapped the map with his finger. 'Bella, do you know this area? This is where we found Joe's truck. But it's right in one of the more isolated parts of the forest and I can't think of anywhere in the area he might have been going to.'

She took a sip of her coffee as she studied the detailed survey map, trying to visualise the topographical lines and markings as landscape, searching among memories of times travelling with her father for anything familiar. The area lay deep in the scrub, south-east of town, where the flat land rose to ancient, rugged hills.

'This map must be relatively new. Years ago, before this part became a nature reserve, there used to be remnants of an old track through here.' She drew a line on the map with her finger, several kilometres into the bush from where Joe's truck was found. 'There was a farm there once, but it got burnt out sixty, seventy years back and there's nothing left now. Dad and I went camping out there a few times. There's a spring – about there, I think – and this part of the creek is in a deep gully and there's usually some water. It was around here that we came across old Charlie – he'd been living out there in a bark hut and surviving on bush tucker for years.'

'The man your father based a story on?' Alec asked. 'Could he still be alive?'

Dreams and whispers... Only two nights ago they'd shared that, under the stars. It seemed a lifetime ago.

She wet her dry throat with another sip of coffee. 'I'd be very surprised if he's still around. He seemed old to me then, and that would have been twenty-five years ago. He was already in the army when the Second World War began, so he'd have to be well into his eighties at the very least by now – if he's not long gone.'

'Some of the local elders spoke about an old hermit in the scrub years back,' Adam mentioned. 'I haven't heard of anything recent, but we'll check out the area anyway.'

'Would his hut be there still? Could Joe – or someone else – be using it?'

Alec's mind was moving in a similar direction to Isabelle's.

She shrugged. 'Who knows? But those sort of bark huts are very easy to build. Anyone who knows how could put one up just about anywhere in the scrub, and unless you knew where to look, you'd never find it. That spring is the only water for miles around, though. If someone is living in the area, or if Tanya's being hidden there, they're not going to be too far from it.'

Alec blew out a frustrated sigh. 'Hundreds of thousands of hectares – talk about a needle in a bloody haystack. Okay, guys, head up there and see if you can find Ward, and then search the area near the spring. If you find anything – anything at all – call it in straightaway.'

Isabelle waited until the two men had gathered up the map and headed towards boxes of equipment stacked in a corner, and then she looked directly at Alec.

'I'm going with them,' she said quietly.

More than just professional concern flashed in his eyes, and she hated defying him but she'd argue blue murder on this if she had to.

'I'm just as safe out there as here,' she added, before he could voice his objection. 'And I'm not going to sit around uselessly when I'm the one who knows that area better than anyone else here.'

A muscle flickered in the tightness of his cheek, and she saw instinct and fear warring with the rational reasons she'd given. Fear for *her*. After several moments he nodded with obvious reluctance.

'Did you bring uniform overalls? If not, get Kris to find you some. I want you indistinguishable from everyone else. And ask someone to get mine from the hotel.'

'You're going too?' The thought gave her more comfort than she wanted to admit.

'Yes.' Shielded from others' view by their bodies, he closed his hand lightly over hers as he handed her the hotel key. A feather touch, a small, silent connection that acknowledged everything that had passed between them in the night. 'I don't want to let you out of my sight until I know you're safe,' he said quietly, low enough to be audible only to her.

The independent, capable side of her that might have insisted she didn't need protecting didn't stand much chance against the honesty that not only did she need it, she felt safer for it.

But neither had a chance to say anything, because he was all DCI again, frowning and worried, and people were moving around them, and Finn trotted up to her, licking his lips from his breakfast and butting her hand for a pat.

'Is Finn trained to follow a scent?' Alec asked.

'Only if you want to find every kangaroo and rabbit in the scrub,' she confessed. 'He got a head injury before he finished his training that affected his concentration – which is why I ended up with him. I'll leave him here when we go out.'

Alec nodded, his thoughts obviously shifting on elsewhere. 'I've got a couple of calls to make before we go. Can you get together whatever I'll need?'

Isabelle sent a junior officer to the hotel, and then sought out Kris, who lent her her own overalls. Isabelle changed in the station, buckling the heavy equipment belt around her waist, checking her Glock before she slipped it into the holster. Relying on thoroughness and concentration to maintain a veneer of calm over the tension, she gathered up equipment from the station storeroom – water, sunscreen, evidence bags, toolkit, radio, GPS receiver, first aid kits, extra ammunition – and packed two backpacks.

She emerged from the station building and found Steve outside, stowing a high-powered rifle into a case in the back of one of the police vehicles. Uneasiness crawled up her spine.

'I hope you won't need to use that,' she said.

Steve turned from the vehicle, grim and subdued. 'So do I. But there's no knowing what we'll find out there, or whether Ward is a threat or not. I don't plan on taking any chances out in the scrub miles from anywhere.'

The quietly spoken words emphasised the changes in him. Even just a year ago, he'd have been buzzing with adrenaline at the challenge, his eagerness close to the edge of recklessness. A devil-may-care action hero on a constant overdose of energy and testosterone. Now...well, now she was looking at a man knowingly going into danger without that high, an action more courageous than his previous enthusiasm. Yet his stony-faced determination amplified, rather than alleviated, her own worry, and she almost wished for his old, irritating self. At least it would have been a distraction from her own sense of trepidation.

She swung the two backpacks into the car, checking over with Steve that they had all they might need. They'd both done enough bush searches over the years for the procedure to be routine, but they'd mostly been for missing tourists or bushwalkers, not cases where they weren't sure whether they were searching for murderer, accomplice or victim.

When they'd finished checking and packing the gear, Steve paused, glanced around. They were alone outside, voices from the hall an indistinct background murmur. He stuffed his hands in his pockets, dug in the gravel with the heel of his boot.

'Bella, about you and Goddard... I just wanted to tell you, I'm pleased for you. He's a good bloke.'

She felt heat flush her cheeks. 'He's not...we're not...'

A kookaburra started chortling on a nearby power pole, and there was a flicker of the old, teasing Steve as he chuckled softly with the bird. 'You locked the dog out last night, Bella.'

And Steve had taken Finn for a run before anyone else had seen the dog outside. She watched the kookaburra, its exuberant early morning laughter a drastic contrast to her own emotional turmoil.

'It's not going anywhere,' she said quietly. The immense emptiness of that one certainty threatened to break her control, and she kept her face averted to hide the stinging in her eyes. 'So please don't discuss it with the others.'

'I won't,' he said, and for once she trusted his assurance. He touched her shoulder lightly. 'Look, Bella, I know this is a lousy time and all, but hang in there, okay? I always figured when you finally fell, you'd fall hard, and although there's not a man on this earth I think is really good enough for you, Goddard might come close.'

'It's not that easy,' she murmured, brushing away an errant tear that might have been for herself, or might have been for him and his surprisingly generous, caring words.

A couple of officers emerged from the hall and Steve stepped away from her and swung the car door shut. 'You never did take the easy path, Bella. But you've never been one to give up easily either.'

Although his words warmed her a little, they made no inroads on the doubt deep inside. She hadn't given up on Jess either, or Dan, and they were both dead.

She walked back up the steps to the hall, her boots feeling heavy. On the porch she paused, willing herself the strength to go on, to go out in the vast forest and search for a man she'd known since childhood, who could be a murderer or a victim.

The honour roll to the side of the door caught a low shaft of early sunlight. Every Australian town had its war memorial – some a statue, some a rotunda, some a fountain or a clock tower. And some a memorial hall like Dungirri's. For all the worn appearance of the rest of the town, someone had retouched the gilt lettering of the honour roll recently, and cleaned away the cobwebs and dust.

So many of the names were familiar to her. Harry Fletcher, Beth's great-grandfather, killed at Gallipoli in 1915. Her own great-uncles, killed in the next war, one in France, another on the notorious Burma Railway. Ward, Barrett, Oldham, Russell, Dingley – names from families who'd been in the district for generations and served abroad from the Boer War to Vietnam.

Beneath the honour roll, a separate plaque commemorated a volunteer bush-fire crew who had perished in their tanker while battling a blaze in the forest thirty years before. Among the seven names were those of Jeanie's husband and her two brothers. Yet, despite her tragedy, Jeanie had served the town unstintingly in every crisis since then, an unshaking, steady presence, doing whatever needed to be done for as long as it needed doing.

Isabelle set her shoulders straight, took in a long breath, pushed the door open and walked in.

TWENTY

Alec had learned over the years to trust the gut instinct that said things were about to go pear-shaped. It screamed at him now, as they made their way through the thick scrub, and he constantly scanned the area around them, every sense alert.

Isabelle walked a few metres ahead of him with Adam, the two of them studying the ground and the landscape, occasionally talking in low voices. He let them do their job without interruption; he and Fraser keeping watch over them while they concentrated on their task.

Each time his eyes skimmed past her, he had to fight the desire to let it linger. But his awareness of her never wavered.

Out here in the wilderness, she seemed totally at ease, moving lightly and instinctively through the bush as though she belonged. Natural. *Elemental*. He could almost believe some ancient goddess or earth spirit travelled in her soul.

And he'd made love with this courageous, beautiful woman. *Made love.* For once the words meant something. He loved her, was bound to her in ways he could neither define nor deny. It was as simple as that.

And just as simple that he had to walk away from her when they finished in Dungirri. So there was only this time with her – and for Tanya's sake, he had to hope it was short. A day, maybe. A single day to be with her, to store up memories to last for ever.

One more reason not to let her out of his sight.

After a half-hour or so of rough hiking, they paused to drink a few mouthfuls of the water they each carried. Although still early in the day, the dry, burning heat sucked the moisture from skin as quickly as the body perspired, making dehydration a threat to take seriously.

Bella sat on a fallen tree trunk and Alec joined her, glad of the few still moments to be near her. Adam wandered a short distance away, still studying the land. Steve busied himself retying his boot laces, although whether he really needed to do so or whether it was just a way to give them some privacy, Alec couldn't tell. The man had been uncharacteristically quiet ever since they'd set out, the arrogance he'd shown in disparaging Indigenous tracking skills just two days ago nowhere in evidence now.

'Any idea where Ward's headed?' Alec asked Bella.

His sense of direction was all screwed up out here amongst the trees. Give him a city street and he'd have had no trouble at all; but here the damn trees closed in on him, obscuring the horizon and distant landmarks. Sure, he could pull out the GPS and get an exact location reading and compare it to the map, but somehow the logic of the scientific measurements seemed alien to the actual experience of being small and insignificant, deep in the bush.

'Travelling straight towards the gully,' Bella answered quietly. 'And…well, he doesn't seem to be thinking clearly. If he was, he'd have taken the easiest ways. But he's just scrambled through the bush, heading in a straight line. And he didn't stop, at least not between the truck and here.'

They both watched as Adam suddenly crouched, intent on something amongst the dried leaves and twigs that littered the earth, a good twenty metres or more from them.

'Someone else's tracks,' he called. 'They're from yesterday too. Somebody followed Joe, or Joe followed him.'

Alec moved closer to Bella, his hand resting on the Glock at his hip.

Bella screwed the lid back on her water bottle and tucked it into her backpack. 'Let's keep moving.'

They kept close together, Adam and Steve in front, Alec protecting Bella from behind.

Unease made them move at a brisk pace, despite the heat and the rough going. Alec kept scanning all around them, but he saw and heard nothing that seemed out of place. Insects buzzed high in the canopy, feeding on the eucalypt flowers, small birds flew away from them into the trees, and twice snakes slithered away from their path. And all the time the parching wind blew through the branches and leaves, an ominous accompaniment to the crunching of their boots on the dry forest floor.

A shadow passed over them and Alec glanced up to the sky.

'We've got company,' he commented, and when the others paused and looked back he nodded up at the huge bird circling on an updraught. 'Is that a wedge-tailed eagle?'

'Yes,' Bella replied, and as they watched it soared downwards until they lost sight of it behind the trees ahead of them. Seconds later, they heard the distant raucous wailing of a flock of birds.

'Crows,' Adam said. 'The wedgie's laying claim to their carrion.'

'Let's hope it's an old 'roo,' Steve added darkly.

Ten minutes later, the eagle ascended into the sky again as they approached a small natural clearing.

Slumped near a tree, what was left of the birds' meal wore the torn remains of a blue shirt and dusty blue jeans.

From the moment she'd heard the crows' haunting cries, Isabelle had suspected what they'd find. But the forewarning didn't prepare her for the reality, or for the despair that cried inside her. She'd seen worse – far worse – but the dreadfulness of *this*, added to everything else in the past few days, undermined the strained composure she'd been relying on. She wavered on her feet at the edge of the clearing, the world spinning and blood pounding in her head.

Alec stepped closer to her and slipped his hand under her elbow.

'I used to babysit Melinda for Joe and Mary when they went out sometimes,' she said, and she knew it was illogical but somehow she had to see Joe, whole, in her mind. 'He might not have been the world's greatest man, but...he didn't deserve this.'

'No one does,' Alec said, and the grave sincerity of his tone helped her slide a veneer of determination over the unexpected grief.

Steve stood a short distance away, his face a haggard white. Adam, his expression harder than she'd ever seen it, approached the body, stepping with care to preserve evidence.

'Shot in the head,' he said after a few moments. 'His rifle's here beside him. There are dog tracks in the sand too.'

Alec crouched beside Adam, sombre respect as well as professional scrutiny in the way he studied the body, as if he, too, saw the man, Joe, and not the nightmare corpse.

'Any sign of someone else?' he asked.

Adam shrugged. 'Hard to tell. Not after the dogs anyway.'

'You don't think he just came here to kill himself?' Steve said, but it was a question, not a challenge.

'He drove for fifty kilometres through the bush,' Alec answered, considering the question. 'Then walked for an hour over rough ground to get as far as this. If all he was looking for was an isolated place to commit suicide, then I doubt he'd have come so far, or in a straight line.'

A puff of breeze ruffled the sweat-damp strands of hair at the back of Isabelle's neck and she rubbed at the suddenly chill spot with her hand. She agreed with Alec's assessment, and that meant Joe's killer could still be out here, hiding amongst the trees, watching them.

They were an hour from their vehicle, and even if they called for backup, it would take almost two hours to arrive. Wary, she scanned the edges of the clearing, conscious of their vulnerability.

'We need to check out the area,' she said. 'Joe came here for a purpose, and we need to know what that was.'

Alec nodded, his mouth a tense line. 'I'll call the forensic crew in, and get an extra team out here as well.'

He reached for his radio, but all they heard in response to his call was a scratchy hiss.

'We're probably too low for the signal,' Adam said. 'Coverage is patchy around here. It'll probably work up on that ridge over there.'

He pointed to a ridge just visible amongst the trees to the east, a short distance away. The shape of a rocky outcrop on the slope struck Isabelle as familiar, and she turned once right around, slowy surveying the clearing.

'Bella? What is it?' Alec's question seemed to come from a long way away.

'This is where we camped, Dad and I. Right here, in this clearing. We rode in, from the old track to the south.'

That was why she hadn't recognised it straightaway. The different approach, and the changes over the years. Several of the grand old eucalypts had died, and the faster-growing native cypresses had crowded out the young eucalypts, shifting the balance, shrinking the clearing. But in her mind she

could see it all again: the huge starry sky at night, the silhou-
ettes of her father and their visitor by the small campfire,
the light playing on the old man's snow-white hair. The wispy
scents of smoke, billy tea and her father's pipe; the low rumble
of the men's voices, the soft whinnies of the horses
tethered nearby.

Everything had been so *right* then, so safe, and now
everything had changed. Flies were swarming around Joe's
body, and it wasn't safe at all.

'Old Charlie…' She turned to Alec. She had to concentrate on what needed saying instead of throwing up or
screaming, or both. 'His hut was nearby. And the gully and
the spring are just the other side of that ridge. But he can't…
he couldn't be…'

She paused, shook her head to clear the smothering dread.
She *had* to think clearly.

'It's got to be unlikely that a man in his eighties or nineties
could be responsible for everything.'

'But not impossible.' Alec quietly spoke the truth of it.
'Do you remember which direction the hut is?'

'It was at the base of the rise, over that way. Four hundred,
maybe five hundred metres from here, I think.' She turned
back to face Alec. 'We have to go there. All of us.'

Behind his frown, she saw him quickly considering the
possibilities, coming to the same conclusion she had. Safety
in numbers. Four of them together made better odds against
whatever they faced than separated pairs.

'Yes,' he agreed. He reached for the Glock at his hip. 'Weapons out, everyone, and keep close. Steve, we'll lead. Adam, you cover the rear and...' His expression became hard, all DCI with no room for argument. '... protect Isabelle at all costs. That's a direct order.'

They walked in silence, save for her occasional brief directions to Alec, until they reached another clearing, smaller than the first. In the dappled shade of a circle of native cypresses, where Charlie's hut had once been, there now stood an old-style shepherd's watchbox, a small construction of saplings and bark, just large enough for a man to sit in or lie down in, its floor half a metre off the ground.

Nerves on edge, she registered it in a single glance, noted the small door swinging open, a solid metal latch on the outside.

But she didn't have time to consider the implications of that before she saw what lay on the ground in front of the hut.

A greyish, weathered skull, its wide gap-toothed jaw seeming to grin, sat on top of a blanket-covered hump – a hump the size of a child's body, the thin brown blanket shaping the curve of a small back.

The world spun around her and she was back in that other paddock, staring at Jess's body, but she was here too, and she couldn't run from either of them, couldn't move, couldn't cry out, could hardly even breathe through the cold, burning agony ripping through her.

TWENTY-ONE

They'd frozen, the three of them. If it was like a hundred knives to his guts, Alec thought, then what must it be for them? Nobody should ever experience this once, let alone twice.

Bella's eyes were dark with a torment beyond bearing, and he cursed himself, hated himself, for his stupidity in bringing her here.

He pushed Steve towards her. 'Take Bella away. I'll go and...' He couldn't finish the sentence. He would just do what had to be done.

Steve stepped across to Bella, put his arm around her shoulder, tried to turn her away from the sight, but she didn't move or respond, just stared with those wild, grief-stricken eyes.

She needed to know. Hell, they all needed to know.

The image of Bella's distress burned in Alec's own vision so that it took him a moment, as he knelt beside the blanket, to notice that the shape beneath wasn't quite what he expected. But the flies buzzing near a hole in the cloth foretold grim tidings, and although the sun wasn't high enough to cut through the shade of the trees, the smell of death was unmistakable.

He made his fingers grip the blanket and, with a leaden arm, he lifted the edge back carefully, steeling himself to deal with the sight of a young, smooth limb...or worse.

The leg he saw was covered in brown fur, definitely not human. Two legs, long tail, powerful hindquarters.

'It's not her.' His voice came out so rough he hardly recognised it. He looked up from the dead animal and spoke directly across the distance to them. 'It's not Tanya. It's a wallaby. Or a 'roo.'

Hell, he didn't really know the difference and they probably all did, but it didn't matter a damn because it wasn't Tanya.

Bella swayed, and Steve caught her, tugged her into him. He turned his face away from Alec but not before the sunlight glinted on his wet cheeks.

Adam turned on his heel and walked off into the bush.

Alec didn't call out to stop him. They'd discovered what they were meant to find, had been dragged through the emotional wringer just as their opponent intended. His gut told him the bastard would let them contemplate their failure for a while before striking again.

He wanted to be with Bella, but she didn't need to feel the fury raging in him, the violence of his anger at the murderer doing this, and at himself for failing. Failing Tanya, and Isabelle, and everyone. So he stayed where he knelt, and lifted the blanket off more of the animal, careful not to disturb the skull, focused on his duty to ensure there was nothing dangerous or more disturbing before the others came near.

The animal's glassy eyes stared vacantly ahead, above a hole high in its chest.

He heard a footstep crunch on dry leaves, and Bella crouched beside him. Right beside him, so their shoulders touched, and she closed her hand over his. The simple act of closeness was unexpectedly comforting, as though she understood what it had cost him to look beneath the blanket. He tightened his fingers round hers, grateful for her presence, awed again by her strength in thinking of him after such a shock.

'It's a juvenile kangaroo,' she said. 'Maybe only a few hours dead.'

'And one clean shot to kill it. I suppose that's not remarkable out here.'

'No. Kangaroos are regularly culled by landholders. Especially during a drought like this, when there's not enough feed for stock. They're not hard targets, and a lot of people around here will have some experience shooting them or other feral animals.'

No easy answers there, just as Alec expected. He indicated the human skull with his free hand, keeping his other clasped with Bella's, as much for himself as for her. 'The skull has wisdom teeth, so it's an adult. Probably male, given that jaw shape and brow. Charlie, do you think? Was he missing his front teeth?'

She frowned, considering it. 'I don't remember, but who knows? I was only a kid. I don't even think I could recognise him from a facial reconstruction. And I have no idea of his surname, so tracking him down will be hard, unless someone else in town knew him too.'

'Well, the skull's quite old by the looks of it, so he's probably been gone a long time, whoever he was.'

'Yes. Possibly even a couple of decades, depending on where it's been. So not a top priority for us right now.'

She sighed, and there was a brief pressure on his hand before she loosed her fingers. Rising to her feet, she nodded across to where Steve studied the hut. 'We need to see if there's anything there.'

'Have you ever seen a hut like this before, Bella?' Steve asked as they approached.

'In the Birraga Folk Museum,' she answered wryly. 'There's a replica there. They used them a century or so ago, when there were enough employees on stations to have shepherds out watching the sheep.'

Alec looked over the empty structure. Over two metres long, maybe a metre deep, and about a metre and a half high. He could have sat in it, protected from the sun or the rain, and a smaller man could easily lie down in it. Or a child.

'The only lock on this one is on the outside,' Bella said quietly. She pointed to the sapling ends framing the small doorway. 'And the timber is quite recently cut – maybe a few weeks or so.'

Alec leaned in through the doorway, took a moment to let his eyes adjust to the dulled light inside. It was empty, as he'd expected…except for a dark blue hair ribbon he almost missed seeing, curled on the rough sawn floor right in the corner.

He reached into his pack for an evidence bag, and brought the ribbon out into the sunlight as Adam rejoined them.

'She was here,' he said. He hadn't needed the ribbon to know that. None of them had. What other purpose could there have been for a newly built shepherd's hut in the middle of nowhere?

'He took her out on horseback early this morning,' Adam said, his voice as flat with bitterness and failure as Alec felt. 'There's a small corral nearby where the horse has been kept for at least a few days. I found the child's footprints.'

Steve cursed. 'We should have come last night.'

The same thought hammered in Alec's head. *What if they had?* Was it *his* fault for not ordering the continued search for Ward last night?

'We wouldn't have known where Joe was going.' Bella's logic broke into his doubt. 'And we'd have made easy targets blundering about in the dark, exhausted. Plus we'd never have found this place.'

She was probably right. And 'what ifs' wouldn't get them anywhere anyway. He hauled his attention to the here and now. 'How much of a start has he got on us, Adam?'

'A couple of hours. More than enough time, on horseback, to get to a track where he could have a vehicle waiting.'

Alec swallowed back the frustration. Just *two hours* they'd missed Tanya by.

'Is there any point trying to follow him?'

Adam thrust his hands into his pockets and shook his head. 'He could be anywhere. We're hours behind him, and on foot.'

Alec surveyed the three of them. They were over an hour from their vehicle with unreliable radio reception. Despite their fitness, the fatigue of the scorching heat and constant stress showed in the dark shadows under Bella's eyes, the tense edginess of Steve and Adam, the way their shoulders bowed under the weight of their packs.

They would walk on, no matter how tired, but he wasn't prepared to risk his officers without decent backup.

'Right, we're going back to the vehicle. I'll call in the forensic team, give them the coordinates of Joe's body and here. We'll probably meet them on the way in.'

'We're giving up?' Steve's protest fell short of his usual passion.

'No, we're going back to Dungirri to process all the new information we have.'

That might have been a slight stretch of reality, but Alec figured they'd all need motivation to make the hour-long trek back to the road.

'Tanya's still alive,' Bella said, as though she could read his mind. 'And we need to go through Joe's connections now we know it isn't him.'

Her voice trembled on the last, and she turned her head away from them, her hand shielding her face as she adjusted her hat. Alec hoped to hell that no more people she knew would be eliminated as suspects by turning up murdered.

He reached for his water bottle, wet his dry throat with a mouthful of liquid while he sought an optimistic perspective to bolster their morale.

'The perpetrator can't be working to a well-structured plan any more,' he said. 'He might still be a step ahead of us, but he's making it up as he goes along.'

'So there's more chance he'll make a mistake, get careless in his arrogance,' Bella said.

'Yes.'

But neither of them mentioned the other possibility: that an over-confident, careless killer was unpredictable, and far more dangerous than a careful one.

Two hours later, back at the hall, Isabelle stared at the names scrawled in loose groups on the whiteboard. People without alibis. People with any sort of prior conviction. People seen on the Birraga road. Too many names, yet the answer was there, somewhere. It had to be. If only she could make the links, the connections.

With her mental focus still on the board, she absently pushed some folders further along her desk so that she could sit on the edge of it, almost leaping out of her skin when a pile of year books fell to the floor with a loud slap.

She picked up the scattered magazines; one had fallen open and she flicked through it again. Last night she'd been concentrating on the photographs of the students. Now she glanced at some of the articles and reports, the poetry and artwork. The double-page spread of photos of the graduating students were mostly familiar faces – this book was from the year her contemporaries had finished high school. Each of them looked a little more grown up than when she'd left, confident and eager to step out into the world.

With bittersweet nostalgia, she flicked past those middle pages and on to the sport reports, intending just a few seconds more before she closed the book.

Until the name 'Tomasi' leapt out from the words.

She read the report through, the pages shaking in her hands. Birraga High's senior rugby team had played Murren High School in the north-west district grand final that year.

In the last minutes, Birraga was leading the closely fought game by a single point. Seconds before the siren, Murren's Len Tomasi had scored a try, winning the game for Murren.

Len Tomasi. Kasey's father. Murren wasn't far from Jerran Creek – it was probably the nearest town with a high school.

She stared at the photo of the team. They were all there: Ryan and Mitch, Mark, Paul Barrett and his younger brother Sean, Darren, the inseparable Robbie and Pete, Ben. All in their rugby jerseys, sponsored by Ward's Rural Supplies. To the side of the team stood the coach, Jim Barrett.

Dungirri had always been rugby-mad, its contribution to the district's adult and junior teams a source of immense pride. And Len Tomasi had stolen a grand final victory from them.

It couldn't just be a coincidence. Maybe the name, the match itself, had been forgotten by most of them over the years – eighteen-year-old boys weren't big on remembering details. Isabelle wasn't surprised that no one had made the slim connection between the Tomasis and Dungirri.

But chances were someone had. Someone connected with the team, who'd maybe recognised Len in Jerran Creek and decided on him for a first target.

She turned back to the whiteboard again, blocked out everything but the names. Just the names, in black and blue and green pen, colours changed each time the well-used pens drained out. People without alibis: half a dozen names, including Paul and Jim. People with a prior conviction: Sean, on top of the list. People on the Birraga road: Delphi, Joe, the library van, Darren – the green pen fading away on the last, hanging on only long enough to complete the name in a pale, fuzzy green. Like Darren himself, she thought. When they were kids, he'd been a bit of a hanger-on, never quite part of the crowd, always on the edge. She'd been a little the same herself, except Darren had wanted to belong while it hadn't worried her.

Darren had wanted to belong . . . He'd told jokes that weren't very funny, bragged about how his dad had won the wood-chopping championship in Sydney, and talked incessantly about his intention to join one of the intelligence agencies.

More often than not, the kids around her age had just ignored his annoying ways, ignored him, not actively excluding him, but not including him either...

Hammers pounded in her head, pounding in the truth that had been so easy to overlook because Darren himself was so easy to overlook. The jigsaw pieces kept clattering into place, everything fitting together into a dark, terrifying picture.

TWENTY-TWO

'Alec!' Her throat was so tight it came out as a croak, but he heard, and so did Finn, and in an instant they were both there beside her.

'Bella? What is it?'

Without taking her eyes from that single name on the board, she said, low enough that others nearby couldn't hear, 'I know who has Tanya.'

A heartbeat passed in silence. 'You're certain?'

She tore her gaze from the blurry green name to meet his, suddenly needing the anchor of him in the face of the horror unfolding in her understanding.

'Yes. It all fits. Everything *fits*.'

'Come into the kitchen.'

His hand under her elbow, he steered her away from the general activity in the hall towards the relative privacy of the kitchen, where they could discuss it first, without twenty other officers around. As they passed Steve and the two local officers, Alec nodded to them to join them.

They were all watching her – Alec, Kris, Adam and Steve – waiting for her to speak, and Isabelle thrust still-shaky hands into the pockets of her trousers and leaned against the bench for support. She had to pull herself together, keep controlled, keep functioning.

'It's Darren Oldham,' she said.

'*Darren?*' Kris stared at her, eyes wide.

'Yes.'

Alec didn't seem to react. He considered her statement, wary, *careful*. 'There are witnesses – people saw him at the depot. And he has an alibi for when you were shot.'

He didn't disbelieve her; he just needed the evidence, as she would do in his place. She had to put all the tumbling pieces of realisation into some sort of coherence – for him and the others.

'Nobody was close enough to see into his truck.' Her words rushed together with the urgency to make them understand. 'He probably had Tanya in there the whole time, either in the cab or the lockbox on the back, right in front of everyone's noses. And as for the shooting, we've assumed that it was the abductor – but that could have been someone else.'

Steve swore, but Alec just nodded, his expression guarded and controlled. He let her continue without interruption.

'Because of his work, Darren's always coming and going, driving around the back roads, inspecting paddocks, managing weeds in the scrub, so no one thinks anything of it. He'd know this whole region – the forest, and all the properties right across to Birraga – like the back of his hand. And his house is just across the road from here – he's had a ring-side view of all our activity.'

Hell, she couldn't explain everything in slow words, with all the hundreds of images and thoughts that whirled in her mind. She'd naively thought that the blind, black nightmare would end when they worked out the identity of the murderer. Instead, all the dark despair she'd struggled against since Jess's death crashed back down around her.

Darren Oldham had Tanya. Darren Oldham had, twice already, held a gun to a small girl's head and pulled the trigger.

She'd known him since they were children, had travelled on the school bus with him to Birraga every day for years. And these past few days she'd talked with the man several times, had looked into his eyes and never once seen even a hint of it. The hard truth was that she'd scarcely even given him a passing thought, just as she'd hardly noticed him all the years of her childhood.

God, she'd thought him *harmless*.

'He's manipulated everyone,' she said, struggling to keep the bile from rising in her throat. 'He's used, played on, the fact that people ignore him, to make his actions invisible. He's been laughing at us all, the whole damn time.'

Right up until that moment, Alec had still hoped that, despite everything, it would turn out to be someone from out of town. Or at least someone on the fringe, not woven into the fabric of the community. The implications of this – hell, he didn't want to think about them. Oldham had been there all along, right in front of them, subtly misdirecting them by playing the role of the concerned citizen.

Then Alec recognised belatedly that he *had* experienced an inkling, when the man had asked Bella out for a drink – except he'd put it down to uneasiness because of his personal feelings for her.

He knew Bella was right. But he was in charge of this case and thoroughness and procedure mattered. He needed more than gut instinct and possibilities to authorise an arrest.

'Shit. Shit. Shit!' Kris broke the uneasy silence, kicking at a chair so hard that it scraped along the floor and toppled with a crash. 'I've lived across the road from the bastard for years.' She stomped across to the chair, jerked it upright, and dropped down on it, head in her hands.

Adam stared out the window, his face flushed with anger; Steve leaned against the fridge, methodically shredding a piece of paper between tense fingers, his head low.

And Bella... Bella looked like a ghost. Not for her an outburst like Kris's; she'd hold it all inside, buried deep. Another betrayal. Another person from her childhood shattering the fragile faith in humanity she'd been gradually rebuilding these past few days.

As for himself, he couldn't risk stopping to analyse how *he* felt about it all. Being emotional didn't come into the job description. Others relied on him for leadership, and he had to focus on facts and actions and lock away all his personal feelings lest they rip his self-control to shreds.

'Kris, do you agree with Isabelle?' he asked.

The sergeant raised her head. 'Yeah. I've been looking for a mad psychopath, but to have done all this he's got to be cold and controlled. And Darren – well, he's friendly enough, but there's always been something missing – as though he's learnt to be social rather than doing it naturally. I'd always just thought him a bit of a dork. But dorks usually have some sort of warmth to them, and Darren doesn't. He just never makes real connections with people.'

'His home life wasn't great growing up,' Bella said. 'His father walked out on them when Darren was fairly young, and Mrs Oldham was always a bit strange, very distant. I don't know if she ever had any proper psych assessment. Doctor Russell was the only doctor here and he was one of the old all-women-are-neurotic kind.'

Alec stayed silent, letting them talk, allowing the information they needed to build the profile to flow without interruption. Tension pulsed in the room, all of them too aware of the significance of the discussion, all of them silently preparing themselves for the confrontation that would have to come soon. When they were sure.

Adam half-turned from the window, joining in the conversation but with regular glances out – keeping an unobtrusive watch on Oldham's house, Alec assumed, and silently approved the young constable's forethought.

'Darren told me that he had to leave the army because his mother came down with some form of dementia and he had to look after her,' Adam said. 'He reckoned he would have got into the commando unit if he hadn't had to leave.'

'Mrs Oldham died a couple of months before Kasey was abducted in Jerran Creek,' Kris added.

'He often goes away at weekends, camping and bush-walking, so he says. He could easily have gone to Jerran Creek.' Adam grimaced, shaking his head. 'He even started talking to me once in the pub about bush survival skills – as if I didn't know anything. I didn't stick around long to listen.'

Alec heard it all, each piece another layer to a profile that was making alarming sense. A psychologist would probably have long medical words for it, but his street-sense for people, built up over years of dealing with violent criminals, didn't need a formal diagnosis. The disconnectedness that Kris had spoken of, the thwarted commando ambition, the bush skills, all rang every mental alarm bell, loud and long. He joined the discussion.

'Okay, so we know he's got opportunity and the army training and bush skills to carry this off. But we don't have a motive and we don't have hard evidence. We're going to raid his house very shortly and I want some idea of what makes him tick before we do.'

Silent until now, Steve slammed a kick into a cupboard door and burst out angrily, 'He's a fucking psycho. What sort of *motive* can there be for shooting small girls?'

'He thinks there's one,' Bella contradicted him, but she did it quietly, with no sign of the irritation she'd once shown towards him. 'There'll be a reason for it in his mind, although the logic may seem screwed to us.'

'Revenge of some type?' Kris asked.

Alec shook his head. 'I doubt it. Revenge is too emotional. This is more intellectual, proving that he's superior to us. But why those particular targets, I don't know. Any thoughts, Bella?'

'The three couples – they're all around the same age, and all local achievers, active and respected in the community,' she said after a moment. 'According to the case notes, the Tomasis owned the Jerran Creek pub, were turning it into an outback tourist attraction. Mitch and Sara both did environmental science at uni and then came back here and set up an agri-consulting business, working with landholders in the region. Ryan was something of a local star for a while. He won a State title in boxing when he was only nineteen, but he gave it up a year or two later and settled back in the area. Both he and Beth were active in the Rural Fire Service until his accident, Beth in the communications group, and Ryan ran a lot of the regional training courses.'

'And you're a decorated police officer.' Steve's temper had reduced to a simmer, but his words rammed home the chilling reminder that Bella, too, was still a target.

'Yes. I'm sure it was Darren on the veranda the other night – he was the right height and build. But he could be targeting me because…' She paused, nipping at her lip again.

'Because why?' Alec asked.

'Maybe because I had the one thing he always wanted – a father. Darren was seven or eight when his father left. Mr Oldham was the national wood-chopping champion for several years and Darren used to boast about him. But alcohol got the better of him.'

'And you had a father who stayed around, one you could be proud of,' Alec said.

'Yes.'

The simple word held an echo of sadness, a hint of the grief she must have felt at losing him. By all accounts, Patrick O'Connell had been a man to respect, to mourn. If Darren Oldham was capable of enough emotion for envy, then Isabelle's relationship with her father would surely have earned it.

Adam, still standing near the window, tensed. 'He's there. I just saw movement in the front bedroom.'

Crunch time. They still didn't have hard evidence, but Alec couldn't risk waiting to gather it. He had strong reason to believe a child was in grave danger; it was enough to justify a raid.

Instinctively he switched mental gears, running through a checklist for the operation.

'Right, we're going to raid the place and bring him in. But we need to coordinate it so we get a full team in there without giving him any warning. He's likely to be armed, and if he's got Tanya in there he'll use her any way he can. I also don't want any risk of bullets flying and hitting locals.'

'Roadblocks?' Kris queried. 'I can put a couple of constables ready at each end of the main street to put up blocks the minute we move in.'

'Do it. Adam, gather up all the protective vests we have, and tell everyone we're having a briefing in five minutes and I want them ready for action. Steve, get your rifle ready. I'd rather have a whole team of sharp-shooters for this sort of op, but today you'll have to be it.' He paused, hauled in a deep breath before he spoke the order he always hated giving. 'If Oldham uses Tanya, or anyone else, as a hostage, and you can get a clear shot, then do it.'

His face draining of colour, Steve nodded, and followed Kris and Adam out.

Everything seemed suddenly quiet, now that there was only he and Bella and Finn in the room. The calm before the storm.

Pale but composed, Bella poured some more water into Finn's bowl, and crouched beside him while he drank, lovingly massaging his neck. As if...

Oh, God, as if it were a farewell.

'Bella...' The gut-deep premonitions he'd barely managed to overrule for the last half-hour now slammed hard against his ribs, crushing his breathing.

She looked up from the dog, too calm.

'I'm going too.' A statement, not a request.

A snaking, coiling dread wound ice through every vein.

He should order her to stay, send her to man a roadblock or, damn it, have her making cups of tea for the Wilsons – anything but let her go in on the front line of this raid.

He should, but he couldn't. This was her battle even more than his. Her nightmare, her challenge.

And he owed Tanya every officer he could get – especially his best.

'Yes,' he agreed, against every ounce of his instinct. 'But you'll go with me.'

At least with her beside him, he might have a chance of protecting her. He might have a chance, as long as he could see her, of keeping all his focus on the job and keeping all his officers, and Tanya, alive.

They might well be walking straight into hell, and the only thing he knew for certain about the outcome was that Darren Oldham wasn't the kind of man who would meekly surrender.

Alec left nothing to chance. Under pretence of examining something in the creek, Kris had a team of half a dozen officers around behind Oldham's house, standing by to go in at the rear, and to search the garage and garden shed, the moment the raid was launched. Junior constables with less experience were placed ready to block the roads.

The rest were gathered just inside the door of the memorial hall, geared to surround the house the moment Alec gave the word. Beside him, Kevlar vest bulking her slight frame, Bella drew in long, slow breaths, and in those last moments he matched his breathing to hers, as if that small ritual of connection might somehow keep her safe.

Finn, tied up to a desk, whimpered.

Alec checked his watch, counted three more breaths with Bella, and then spoke into his radio and gave the order to move.

They burst through the doors and down the steps, straight across the road for Oldham's front door, the others fanning out to surround the house.

Alec kicked open the front door, the central passageway ahead of him clear, the first two doors on either side open. He quickly scanned the main bedroom while Bella checked the living room. Both empty, save for old furniture.

The next door stood closed, and he motioned to Bella to follow him in.

He heard the splinter of the rear door giving as Kris entered the house at the same time he kicked open the door before him and burst into the room, gun ready, Bella at his back.

A banner hung from the ceiling in the centre of the room, with five words painted in large, red lettering: 'Tick, tock, tick, tock, kaboom.'

The smell of fuel hit his nostrils at the same moment the words registered.

'Bomb!' he roared. 'Get out! Everyone *out*!'

Behind him, Bella spun on her feet and sprinted for the door. Adrenaline gave him extra speed and he caught up to her in a few paces, lifting her bodily and hurtling out of the house, protecting her back with his body against whatever was to come.

The explosive force caught them on the front steps, throwing them forward onto the dry grass of the lawn. As they hit the ground, he curled around her, using his body as a shield while debris spewed from the house and landed around them.

The roar of flames, timbers breaking and falling, people running and shouting, all pounded along with the drumming in his head. Something small and burning fell on the ground in front of them, setting what the drought had left of the lawn alight, and he knew they were still in danger lying there.

Bella moved under him, and he struggled to his knees, still trying to protect her. Strong hands – Steve's – hauled them to their feet, and together they stumbled across the lawn to the road, Bella between them.

'Are the others out?' Alec demanded through a burning throat. A single glance had told him that Bella, although shaken, was all right. Yet he kept his arm around her, needing the assurance of her warmth, her breathing, to believe the miracle of their escape.

'We're fine,' Kris announced breathlessly as she and her team ran up to join them. 'Is Tanya in there?'

'I don't know,' Alec rasped, the deep dread that Oldham had rigged the house and left the child to die rising as a terrifying possibility.

'I'll go in.' Steve didn't wait for a response.

Alec squeezed Bella's waist once, briefly, then let go and followed Steve across the yard, back into the house.

Fear and shock froze Isabelle where she stood. She stared at Alec's back as he strode away, the upper arm of his overalls shredded by flying debris where he'd caught some of the blast, blood running dark amongst the tatters. Before she could think clearly enough to comprehend that horror, the two men were making their way into the house, through the remains of the living room window. The other side of the house was a blazing hell.

She held her hand against her mouth to restrain her cry. The deafening wail of the fire alarm burst from further down the road, the decades-old method of calling the volunteers of the fire brigade and alerting the town. It would be some minutes at least before they'd be there.

Kris shook her shoulder. 'Fire extinguishers – there are two in the hall. I'll get the one in the station.'

The words jolted Isabelle into action. She raced across to the hall, another officer close behind her, and went straight to the extinguisher hooked on the wall in the kitchen. She handed it to the constable.

'Go. I'll get the backstage one.'

Her shoes pounded on the wooden floor as she ran the length of the hall. She vaguely registered that Finn lay still beside her desk, not stirring despite her steps, but panic and worry for Alec and Steve inside the burning house overrode her concern and she didn't stop.

She yanked open the door beside the stage, reaching for the light switch as she went into the dimness of the wings.

It didn't work.

She groped her way along the wall, feeling for the extinguisher she'd seen there earlier. Uncertain in the darkness, she paused, hoping her eyes would adjust to the shadows. Above the pounding of her own heart, she heard another slight sound – the soft footfall of someone treading very carefully.

The click of a safety catch.

A hand clamped over her mouth, stifling her cry, the point of a pistol pressing into her temple.

'Well, well, Isabelle,' Darren Oldham said in her ear. 'I can't believe how easy you made this. It must be my lucky day.'

TWENTY-THREE

In a nightmare of smoke and heat and spreading flames, Alec and Steve groped their way through the two east rooms, and into the kitchen and bathroom, without finding any evidence of the child. Steve was about to plunge into the inferno where the bomb had gone off when Alec grabbed the back of his shirt and dragged him back.

'There's not a chance,' he yelled above the roar of the flames, although the reality of saying it, of giving up hope, sickened him.

If Tanya had been in that second bedroom, she'd be dead already, and exposure to the intense heat and flames would kill anyone who tried to go in.

The ceiling above them exploded into flames, and together they made a dash out of the house. Kris emerged from the smoke to cover their exit with a blast from a fire extinguisher.

A safe distance from the house, on the edge of the road, Steve collapsed to his knees, hacking and coughing. Alec stood beside him, trying to gasp a decent breath, while people milled around them. Too many faces, too many voices, and not the one he most needed to see.

He found Kris, grabbed her by the arm. 'Bella?' he croaked. 'Where's Bella?'

Kris scanned the group, glanced over at those still fighting the fire with whatever hoses and buckets they'd found. 'She was here...she went for an extinguisher. Maybe she's around the back. I'll go look.'

He followed her round the garage at the side of the house, now well alight. Neighbours and police worked together in a desperate attempt to stop the flames spreading into the trees along the creek bank, and from there to the tinder-dry forest. They both called Bella's name, asked if anyone had seen her.

'She wouldn't have gone in, would she?' Kris asked.

'I didn't see her.' Surely he'd have seen her, even in that smoke. *Known* she was there.

'Neither did I. In fact, I didn't see her come back at all,' Kris said.

Alec bolted across the road, dodging the fire truck as it halted, and burst through the doors into the hall. Empty, save for Finn lying still. Too still.

'Bella!'

The back door of the hall was open, creaking in the breeze, and beyond it there was nothing but the trees along the creek and the empty paddock behind the police residence stretching to the swimming hole.

He heard a rush of footsteps and Adam eased past him, out the door. 'My car's gone. I park it behind the station, in the shade of those trees.'

Yes, Alec remembered seeing it – a restored mid-'70s blue sedan, the type of inexpensive car popular with young guys who liked to do their own mechanical work. If Adam parked it there every day, Oldham would have known it was there, would have counted on it.

'Did anyone see the vehicle go? Anyone?'

He barked the question, but everyone shook their heads. Of course not. They'd all been too busy fighting the fire, dealing with Oldham's very effective diversion.

A diversion that had given him the opportunity to take Bella.

Terror rose in him, gripping, choking, the darkness almost smothering the rational self he relied on, and he gritted his teeth to restrain a howl of denial and anger.

Movement on the side road beyond the police residence caught his eye and he swung around, but it was Beth, not Bella, running down the road. She saw them, and veered across towards them, and Alec pushed past the other officers and strode to meet her, knowing he had to somehow deal with her – deal with everything – even though half his soul and all his heart screamed at him to find Bella.

'What's happening?' Brown eyes, wide and wild, stared at him, close to the edge of panic. 'The fire... Why are you out *here*?'

'Beth, come inside.'

He took her arm, signalled to Kris to join them, and she quickly opened the door to her own house and ushered them inside.

With hands he barely managed to steady, Alec pulled out a chair from the kitchen table and made Beth sit down. He sat too and took her hand. *Do your job. Focus on Beth just now.*

'Beth, we believe that Darren Oldham abducted Tanya.'

'Darren? *Darren?* Oh, my God. He drove past our house just a few minutes ago, in Adam's car.' Incredulity turned to stark-eyed horror. 'But his house... Tanya – is she in there?'

She was on her feet already, three steps towards the door, before Alec caught her gently by the arms, stepped in front of her.

'No, Beth, she's not there. We're sure she's not there.'

God forgive him the lie, because he wasn't sure at all, but if she was, there was nothing anyone could do until the flames died and the fire investigators came, and maybe he could at least spare Beth the agony of those hours of not knowing.

'Then where is she?' she cried against his chest.

'I...' The words froze in his throat, his strength collapsing. *I don't know. I don't know where either of them are.*

'What is it? Tell me!'

'Darren's taken Bella too,' Kris answered for him.

He pressed Beth into Kris's hold and walked blindly out of the house, towards the trees at the creek, dragging in shuddering breaths, and it had to be the smoke making his eyes water and his throat and lungs so painful, because he was a DCI and didn't cry and he hadn't cried since his father's death, long ago.

He whirled around and smashed his fist into a tree, the physical pain a faint shadow of the agony ripping through his mind and soul, taking him apart, piece by piece.

He slumped against the tree, bowed his head, and drew on every ounce of his eighteen years' experience as a cop and all his self-discipline to gain some control over the convulsions of his throat.

In the distance, he heard a series of shouts, and the crash as Oldham's house collapsed.

Footsteps crunched on the dried leaves behind him.

'Are you okay?' Adam asked quietly.

'No,' he answered. No, he wasn't okay. He might never be *okay* again.

He straightened, turned to face the young officer who, in the course of all they'd been through these past few days, had proven his dedication – and his capacity for friendship – over and over. 'But I'll manage.'

Adam nodded, his dark eyes reflecting only concern and no trace of judgment. 'Good. We need you. She needs you.' They both knew which 'she' he meant. 'Oldham made her get in the boot of the car. That's as far as her footprints go. We found her vest and her gun belt in a corner. Without the handcuffs.'

The image of her, cuffed and trapped in the small space, without the defensive weapons on the uniform belt, was only bearable for one reason.

'She's still alive. Taking her is another twist in the game.'

'That's what I thought.' Adam indicated Alec's shoulder. 'Your arm's hurt. Come in and get it seen to.'

In all the turmoil, he hadn't noticed the pain in his arm or the blood on his sleeve, but now he became aware of the physical ache.

When he strode back into the hall, several dozen pale, drawn faces stared at him, shocked and uncomprehending. Not just police officers, but townspeople too, who'd come running in response to the fire and had now heard all the news. And Finn, lifting a groggy head under Steve's coaxing.

Drawing on every fraction of internal strength he could find, Alec launched immediately into allocating tasks, giving directions, forcing them – and himself – out of the mind-numbing shock into any action that might help. Steve and Adam he sent to coordinate roadblocks on all the district roads; Jeanie to take Beth home and stay with her and Ryan; Kris to contact any criminal psychologist she could find for suggestions as to Oldham's next move.

Delphi's old truck skidded up in a spray of gravel, and after she'd sworn vigorously and publicly at him for losing Bella, he agreed with everything she said and requested that she take Finn to the vet in Birraga. When Mark Strelitz appeared, he asked the politician to organise a meeting of all the locals he could gather – anyone who might know Oldham or anything about his background, and where he might have gone.

He just kept going, directing and coordinating, not letting himself stop for a moment because he knew if he did, he'd crack. He didn't even stop for the ambulance officer to examine his arm, phoning Sydney to set up an aerial search while the medic washed and taped the wound.

If he stopped, he'd never find Tanya and Bella.

It was half an hour before he went near his desk. He was reaching across the keyboard for a pen when he noticed a large envelope propped against the monitor. An envelope that hadn't been there before the raid on Oldham's house.

Heartbeat thundering, he pulled gloves on, ran his finger under the tab to open it, and slid out a CD case and a large photograph.

A dark, grainy, home-printed but nonetheless entirely recognisable photo of himself and Bella, kissing in the kitchen. They were oblivious to Finn, paws on the bench, looking straight at the photographer.

The noise in the room faded to a distant hum as he stood and stared, anger and dread streaming together.

Oldham had been watching. Oldham had photographed them, and left the photograph as some sort of message.

Alec sat on the edge of the desk, carefully placed the photo face down on the envelope, and turned the CD case over in unsteady hands. No writing, just a disk inside.

'Alec? What's that?'

It took him a moment to register Kris's voice.

'I…' Intuition told him he didn't want to put the CD in his computer in the middle of a crowded room. Or show her the photograph in public view. 'Your office. Now.'

She keyed in the security code and opened up the station and her office, and he handed her the photograph as he crossed to the computer on her desk.

'Holy shit. I mean, that he was watching. When…?'

'Last night.'

The CD whirred in the drive and a directory window opened, indicating a single audio file. Feeling for all the world like a condemned man stepping onto the gallows, he clicked on the file.

But instead of Oldham's voice, as he'd expected, it was his own that sounded through the computer's speaker, and every nightmare he'd ever had paled into nothing compared to the living nightmare closing around him now.

'*They raped her, Bella – all of them. They had no intention of letting either of them live… Bella, do you understand what these people are like? If they discovered that I cared about anyone, then they'd have no hesitation – Jones himself would take immense pleasure – in destroying me by destroying her.*'

TWENTY-FOUR

Curled and cramped in the boot, Isabelle tried to brace herself against the constant rough jolting. Darren was taking dirt roads and taking them fast. With her hands cuffed in front of her, she had limited options for movement. He'd made sure the cuffs had locked in place after he'd ordered her to put them on. And with his gun at her head, she'd had little choice.

He swung around another corner, the back of the car fish-tailing in the dirt, ramming her head against the wheel well.

A right turn this time. She pictured on her mental map where they might be. The north firebreak road, perhaps. He'd slowed, the road too rough to tear along.

She wriggled around as best she could, searching with her hands for anything she might use as a weapon. She might just have a chance when he opened up to let her out.

Nothing. Adam, unusually for a guy of his age out here, hadn't left a bag of useful tools in the back of his car. They might be in the back seat, but that did her no good. Maybe she could find a tyre iron, or part of the jack – if she could find the compartment they were stored in.

She ran her fingers over the frame – no joins in the metal, no handy places to store the jack. Must be underneath her then, with the spare tyre. Damn.

She peeled back the mat as far as she could, squeezing herself into the corner, and found the tyre compartment cover – but not any sort of latch to open it. She squirmed around to the opposite side with difficulty, and managed to jerk up the cover a little. Something gave with a crunch and the cover lifted a couple of inches then stopped. She thrust her hands underneath as far as she could, groping around in the well for anything metal and small enough to tug through the gap. Her wrists and forearms scraped hard and painfully against the cover's edge and her contorted body screamed in cramped discomfort, but she finally closed her fingers around a length of metal and manoeuvred it out, letting the cover fall back when her hands were free.

The scrapes on her arms stung and she felt drips of blood running down them, but she had a weapon in her hands – the wheel-nut wrench. Now all she needed was the opportunity to use it.

The car slowed, made a left turn, and bounced down what must have been little more than a rough track, jarring her with every pothole as she shifted into a position she could attack from.

What tracks went left off the north fire trail? She racked her brain to try to estimate time and distances and make the mental map less fuzzy. The entry to the old cutters' camp ruins? The SES had searched there already, one of the first places they'd looked. And the ruins weren't far in from the fire trail – surely they'd already travelled further than that?

The car stopped finally, at her guess a couple of kilometres past where the camp would be, which meant she'd got the track wrong, because that track didn't go into the scrub that far. Maybe there was an old logging track in the area she'd forgotten about – or a new one since she'd left.

She heard the car door slam and braced herself, hands gripping the wrench, ready to strike out the moment she saw daylight and Darren.

But his footsteps on the ground faded away.

It had been hot before, but now the car was stationary the heat built quickly from hot to stifling.

Oh, God – he'd left her in the car in the blazing summer sun, and that gave her maybe ten or fifteen minutes, if she was lucky, before she lost consciousness and suffocated in the heat. And she'd lose the ability to think clearly and move quickly within minutes.

Already feeling faint, she scrambled to a corner, desperately feeling with her fingertips over the metal moulding, hoping to find a panel giving access to the rear lights. If she could punch out a light, there might be just enough air from outside...

Nothing. If there was a panel, she couldn't find it.

Almost panicking, she tried jamming the handle of the wrench as hard as she could into the tiny gap around the lock, praying for enough room to lever it open. Again and again she tried, but the space was too small, the round metal handle too bulky to fit.

The effort exhausted her, and she dropped her head to the floor, wishing she could feel a breeze, knowing hopelessly that within a few minutes the stifling temperature in the car would render her unconscious.

Sucking in slow, hot breaths, she used the rough end of the wrench to scratch a map on the frame, not able to see in the darkness whether it actually made any mark, but finishing it anyway with her best guess as to where she was. If Darren dumped her body here and took the car, he'd probably ditch it somewhere and the police might find it and see her scratchings.

If. Might. An incredibly long shot, but it was better than just lying here and dying.

When she heard a small, distressed sob, she thought for a moment it was her own. Except her mouth was too dry to make that kind of sound. She lifted her head and strained to listen through the drumming dizziness.

Another little sob, nearby.

A car door opening, and then the pop of the latch on the boot.

She groped for the wrench, but she could hardly even close her hands around it, let alone lift or swing it.

Sunlight flooded the space, blinding her.

Another sob sounded, and she opened her eyes enough to see the silhouette of a small child move into her line of sight.

Tanya. Alive. And she herself was still alive, and that meant, despite everything, there might still be a chance.

'Don't move suddenly or try anything stupid, Isabelle.' Darren's voice drifted to her from some distance away. 'You see, Tanya's carrying some C4 explosive for me, all primed and ready to go, and I've got the remote control in my hand.'

Fighting the dizziness, Isabelle raised herself to her knees. Tanya stood by the car, still wearing the blue T-shirt and checked school skirt she'd been abducted in, but fastened to the front of her T-shirt with gaffer tape around her body was a chunk of what certainly looked like C4, wrapped in thick clear plastic, and a detonator.

Darren stood five metres away. He pointed the device in his hand towards Tanya, elaborately mimed pressing a button, and grinned.

Tanya looked uncertainly between the two of them, not quite understanding but scared and shaking anyway.

Isabelle understood all too well.

No way could she cross that distance and disarm him before he detonated the C4. Even if she weren't reeling from heatstroke and dehydration. And there was no way she could remove the explosive quickly, or even just the detonator, as long as Darren held the control. One wrong move from her or Tanya – and she herself would be dead.

Which meant Isabelle's only choice was to wait, and watch for Darren to slip up and give her an opportunity.

She climbed out of the car slowly and carefully so as not to lose her balance. Cuffed hands on the tow bar to steady herself, she knelt beside Tanya. The girl didn't appear to be physically injured in any way, but her dusty face showed many tear tracks and she shivered despite the sun's heat. They'd found traces of strong sedatives in Jess; perhaps Darren had drugged Tanya too.

'Hello, Tanya.' She forced her voice to be light. 'I'm Isa –' The thought of the way Darren used her full name so derisively brought a wave of distaste. 'I'm Bella,' she said, and the name for herself that her old friends – and Alec – used felt right. 'We met a few times, when you were little. Your mother and I were best friends when we were children.'

'Aunt Bella?' Tanya whispered.

'Yes, that's me.'

She should have made more effort to visit Beth and her family over the years, and then Tanya would have recognised her, not just her name. But at least it seemed that the small packages she sent Beth's girls each Christmas had registered with the child, so that she trusted her.

She brushed a lock of blonde hair back from the girl's face. 'I promised your mum and dad I'd look after you.'

'Very touching,' Darren mocked. 'Such a nice little fairytale. Now walk.'

'Which way?'

Other than the track they'd travelled on – which went no further – she could see nothing but bush.

He pointed with the remote control. 'Just keep walking north until I tell you to stop.'

'I need some water. The car was too hot.'

'There's a creek a little way in. You can drink from that.'

Although it was awkward with the handcuffs, she took Tanya's hand and kept the girl close to her as they walked into the forest. The trees were mostly native cypresses, adding weight to her guess that they were in the north-west part of the forest, thirty kilometres or more from Dungirri, and nowhere near any other settlements or major roads.

Her legs heavy and head spinning, she let her feet drag slightly every now and then, hoping it would leave a clear trail for someone to follow. Darren couldn't have noticed, for he said nothing.

After fifteen minutes they reached a small creek, not much more than a trickle amongst the rocks, but it flowed and seemed clear. Isabelle went straight to it, scooped up handfuls of water and gulped them down, and encouraged Tanya to do the same. Bending over the creek again for more water, her back to Darren and shielding his view, she unclipped her watch and left it on a rock just above the water.

Tanya, dazed and exhausted, sat on the ground and stared, unseeing, into the creek. Isabelle left her there, and advanced a few steps towards where Darren leaned against a tree some distance away. She'd only gone a couple of metres when he held up his hand with the remote control and motioned her to stop.

'Are you going to kill us now?' she asked in a low voice.

'Pressing this button would be quite easy, wouldn't it?' he said, as carelessly as if he were discussing the weather. 'And I'll do it if you do anything stupid, believe me. However, I'd prefer the alternative I have planned for you. You'll end up just as dead, but it'll be so much more interesting. They'll be running around looking for you, but they won't find you. Your detective chief inspector will be devastated when he eventually has to admit that he's failed.'

Isabelle closed her eyes to quell the wave of despair. She'd last seen Alec heading back into the burning house, had no idea if he was still alive, or killed or injured in the flames. And if he was alive, then her disappearance would have been discovered by now and she could only imagine what he'd be putting himself through.

'Why are you doing this?' she asked.

'Because I can. Although it's almost too easy, really. I thought you might make it more of a challenge, but you're the same as the rest of them.'

She made a last plea. 'Let Tanya go, and you can do whatever you want with me.'

Darren's condescending smile scared her more than his hand waving the remote control. 'But I can do anything I like with you now, Isabelle. I could rape you, torture you, make you scream for mercy.'

'Is that what you're planning?' For all that she was trying to keep herself calm, she could barely even whisper the words.

'You'll find out soon enough. Start walking again – follow the creek east.'

The going became a little rougher, and she had to help Tanya over rocks and fallen logs. The child was tiring, and so was she. The few mouthfuls of water hadn't been enough to make any significant difference to her hydration. She contemplated refusing to go further, pretending to faint, but she doubted that Darren would fall for that ruse and come near enough to be disarmed. More likely he'd just use the pistol in his belt and shoot her on the spot, and then continue with whatever he planned for Tanya. And now that she'd found the girl, she wasn't going to leave her alone with Darren again.

The creek led them to a small hill, not much more than a rise, and Darren ordered them a short way up the side.

'The mine entrance is above you. There's a torch just inside. Go in and keep going.'

Mine entrance? Isabelle scanned in front of her, almost missing it. The timbers framing the entrance were ancient, and almost hidden by forest undergrowth. Whoever had dug the mine had done it many decades ago, and then it must have been forgotten, for she'd never heard of it. The old prospectors she'd met over the years had never spoken of anything of value in the forest.

The shaft was dug horizontally into the rise and she had to crouch to make her way inside. She groped for the torch and flicked it on, the weak beam revealing more old timber framework and a tunnel sloping downwards. With her hands restrained, she couldn't hold both the torch and Tanya's hand and keep her balance in the bent-over position she had to maintain.

'You take the torch, Tanya, and show us the way. I'll stay right here beside you.'

They'd only gone a short way in when a strong beam of light from behind them danced along the walls. Darren, with a better torch he must have hidden outside somewhere.

'Keep moving, Isabelle,' he ordered.

'Are you going to blow us up in here?' she asked.

'No. I'm going to blow the entrance once you're chained deep inside. You're not going to die for, oh, maybe a week or more.'

His words gave her a flicker of hope, although it struggled for survival in the reality of their plight. Better to avoid being trapped here at all than believe in the miracle of being rescued.

But the mine shaft was long and straight, and, caught in the beam of his spotlight, Isabelle couldn't hold back in the darkness to ambush him. She had no choice but to stumble forward with Tanya, deeper into their probable grave. The dark, dry air closed around her, and she struggled to keep the claustrophobia at bay and to encourage Tanya with small words.

Eventually they came to a slightly larger space, tall enough for Isabelle to stand up in, perhaps six metres square and over two metres high. She stood straight, stretching the muscles strained by the crouching walk, fully aware that if Darren gave her an opportunity she would have only an instant to respond to it.

But Darren stopped metres behind them, crouching in the narrow tunnel.

'Tanya, keep walking,' he instructed. 'If I see your light stop before I tell you to, I'll shoot Isabelle. Do you understand me?'

The child whimpered, threw a terrified glance at Isabelle, and then stumbled on, frightened sobs hiccuping from her.

'Isabelle, there's a chain on the post in that corner, with an open padlock. Loop the chain around the cuffs and lock it with the padlock, then lie down flat on the ground on your stomach with your hands out. Do anything stupid and I blow up the kid.'

'You'll die too,' she challenged.

He laughed. 'No, I won't. I did advanced explosives training in the army and I've calculated the amount of explosive she's wearing. She'd bring down the back of the mine, but not this far. My great-grandfather built this part very solidly, as a hiding place in case the Japanese invaded during the war.'

She did as he instructed, although in a last-ditch hope she didn't quite push the large padlock all the way in. As she lay down in the dirt, Tanya's small beam of light bobbed in the distance.

His footsteps came closer, and again she braced herself to take any chance he gave her. But he dropped to his knees right on her back, pushing her face into the dirt and knocking the wind from her. With all his weight on top of her, she couldn't move to dislodge him, let alone disarm him. He checked the padlock with one hand, clicked it properly closed.

'Stupid, Isabelle,' he said casually, and slammed the butt of his torch into the side of her head.

Pain exploded and she heard herself cry out, the sound at the same time distant and yet throbbing against her skull. She twisted to press her head against her arm, trying to ease it. She felt his weight move from her, but could do nothing.

'Tanya!' he called. 'Come back now. And hurry.'

Shafts of agony lancing her head, Isabelle moved gingerly to sit up, the chain tugging uncomfortably on the handcuffs and limiting her range of movement. Darren stood two metres from her – out of reach. She crawled closer to the post, so she could sit with her back against the wall and watch him, but in reality she knew she could do nothing.

When Tanya returned, he cut the package of explosive from the terrified child with a knife, took off her T-shirt, and then pushed her none too gently towards Isabelle.

'You can keep the torch,' he said. 'Make sure the kid doesn't follow me. I've already wired the front section of the tunnel and I'll let it off as soon as I'm out.'

He shone his spotlight directly into her eyes, the brightness making her flinch in pain.

'If they could all see you now, Isabelle. The clever detective, all chained up. But they'll be too busy chasing red herrings to find you here. I'll send them a postcard from Spain in a few weeks to tell them where your bodies are.'

TWENTY-FIVE

Alec had always thought that when a person went numb with fear, they no longer felt anything.

The shell of him kept working, because he needed it to. His brain kept thinking, analysing, deciding, directing, and his body obeyed all its commands and worked at maximum efficiency. But the rest of him – the core of him – was locked, frozen and icy. Not numb-frozen, but ice-crystals-tearing-him-apart frozen.

And the time kept ticking away, every minute reducing their chances of finding Oldham. It took time to get roadblocks in place – maybe more time than Oldham needed to leave the area. And he could have used any one of a hundred narrow dirt tracks that crisscrossed the forest.

With such a huge area and so few officers, Alec could hardly send them out in pairs, without backup close by, to search for a killer. The best hope lay in aerial surveillance, but it would take time for the plane to get in the air and fly up from Sydney.

So they waited for news, on edge, the tension and helplessness wearing away at all of them. To keep them busy – himself included – he gave orders to gather whatever information they could about Oldham.

After an hour, Kris and Steve met with him at his desk to combine notes.

'We've found three listening devices – one in the kitchen, two in the main room,' Steve reported. 'All along, he knew what we were doing before we did it. High-quality devices, according to the techies. You can't buy that sort of stuff anywhere in the district, so chances are he bought it over the internet. I'm chasing up credit card details to see what else he might have and from where, but that will take a while.'

'Good. What else?'

'I spoke with one of the neighbours, Nell Sauer,' Kris said. 'She said that Mrs Oldham had bad nerves and was taking Valium. Mrs Sauer got a prescription filled for her in Birraga one day, just a few days before she died. Valium is a brand name for diazepam, the drug found in Jess and Kasey's bodies.'

Alec frowned. 'But that's over three years ago. What's the shelf life on it?'

'I phoned the pharmacist and asked. In the right conditions, quite long apparently. Five years or more.'

'So looks like Oldham had easy access to sedatives. Any idea on his weaponry?'

'He has a .22 rifle registered,' Kris answered. 'Nothing else on the official system.'

'He may have more than that,' Steve interjected. 'I called in a favour from a contact of mine at ASIO, asked him to find out if Oldham had ever come up on their radar.'

Alec wondered briefly what Steve had done to earn a favour from the secretive intelligence agency. 'And?'

'Oldham's not specifically been noticed, but the explosion sure has them interested. There may be no connection with Oldham at all, but apparently a twenty-five kilogram barrel of C4 explosive went missing from a mining company lockup west of Jerran Creek about ten months ago.'

'Twenty-five *kilograms*?' Alec said. If Oldham had that much C4…hell, the link with Jerran Creek was hardly likely to be coincidental.

Kris sat down hard on a chair, her hand against her mouth. 'That's enough to blow Dungirri halfway to Birraga.'

'*If* that's what Oldham rigged his house with, then he's still got plenty left.' Alec ransacked his memory for long ago training about explosives. 'The house would have taken at most a kilo – probably much less than that. It was the accelerant and the fire that did most of the damage.'

'ASIO is sending an agent up,' Steve added. 'They may be able to trace it through the chemical marking.'

Alec's mobile phone rang and he snatched it up. The police air service, notifying him that the plane would be delayed due to mechanical problems.

He finished the call and let the phone drop on the desk, frustration and despair pounding in his head.

'Bad news?' Kris asked.

'No aerial coverage for at least another hour. Christ, I can't stand this useless waiting. We need to be *out* there.'

'When we know where to be, we will be.' She reached across and picked up his phone, dialled a number briskly. 'Birraga Air Charter, please... Harry? Kris Matthews from Dungirri here. We've got an emergency. Can you get a plane in the air over the Dungirri scrub right away? Yes, we're after a stolen blue Kingswood sedan, went north on Scrub Road an hour ago. Could be anywhere now, but I'm betting he's still somewhere in the scrub. Just radio us immediately if you spot it – and keep away from it, Harry. Thanks. I owe you one.'

She handed the phone back to Alec. 'He'll be in the air in ten minutes. We'll worry about the paperwork later. Let's just hope Darren's not halfway to the Queensland border already.'

The rush of relief overrode Alec's professional conscience. There were a dozen official channels they should have gone through before sending up a civilian plane to find a killer. But none would have got action as quickly as Kris's local knowledge and the pragmatic ways of isolated communities used to doing things for themselves.

He drummed his fingers against the desk, his mind still racing. 'There's got to be a good chance he's stayed in the area. He sees himself as a sort of game master. He intended to take Bella – otherwise why would he have left the recording? But he couldn't have counted on being able to take her when he did. That was an unexpected opportunity. And I don't think that the explosion was meant to be the final move in the game. I'm guessing he's got something else planned, some sort of confrontation. And if that's the case, it'll be somewhere he knows well, where he feels in control.'

'There's a thousand square kilometres of bloody bush that he knows well,' Kris interjected, frustration lacing her words.

'And if he has twenty-five kilos of C4 – that could give him one hell of a lot of control,' Steve added.

And a literally explosive final confrontation.

Alec saw the same thought in both their expressions, although, like him, neither of them dared to put the fear into words.

If it came to the worst…No, he'd just have to hope that it wouldn't. That they'd find Oldham before he had a chance to put anything like that into play.

Within twenty minutes the radio crackled and the charter pilot reported a sighting of the stolen vehicle.

'Heading south from Riley's Corner,' Alec announced to the room, striding to the map on the wall. 'What's out there, folks?'

Adam pointed to the place on the map immediately, on the east side of the scrub. 'It's an old logging track that ends at Cave Hill. The hill is actually a sandstone bluff riddled with small caves. Some of the caves are important to the local Murris, and they're not stable because the sandstone is easily damaged, so they're not marked on any of the tourist maps.'

'I had a local SES unit and some of the elders search there yesterday,' Kris said, adding bitterly, 'But Darren was in that team.'

Caves. Hiding places. And Oldham had seen to it that he was there when they were searched.

'Get all available vehicles and officers to meet there. Adam, warn the elders we may have to search the whole place. They can send a couple of their people if they wish, as long as they stay at a distance until it's safe.'

Safe? A cold-blooded murderer, two hostages, a cave-riddled hill, and possibly a barrelful of plastic explosive?

Oh, yes – about as safe as walking into an erupting volcano.

He took the four-wheel-drive police vehicle, with Kris as a guide, and sped along the bush tracks, the others following behind. The intense concentration required to drive that fast only barely stopped him thinking of what might be happening – could have happened already – to Tanya and Bella.

The rough track ended at the base of the steep bluff of Cave Hill, and he pulled to a sharp halt near where Oldham's vehicle stood in the blazing sunshine. Instantly, a bullet fired from the hillside slammed into the car and another shattered the windscreen. He and Kris dived for cover behind the car.

Within minutes, half a dozen vehicles and a dozen or so officers took up defensive positions in the rough ground at the base of the hill, but Oldham had the advantage of height and cover.

Centuries of wind and water had carved myriad twisted holes and caves in the sandstone bluff, and Oldham held them off from the mouth of a cave about halfway up the slope, protected by an outcrop of rock.

Kris opened the back of the vehicle and hauled out a crowbar. Alec took it from her and bolted across to the abandoned car. Keeping low as bullets smashed through the windows above him, he wrestled the boot of the car open, not daring to think what he might find. But the space was empty.

He sprinted over to where the others crouched behind a vehicle, the last few metres a dive while bullets shot into the dust around him.

'There's a rock ledge not far above where he is,' Steve told him. 'I may be able to get a shot at him from there, especially if he tries using Bella or the kid as a shield. But I'll need someone to cover me while I get up there.'

Alec risked another quick glance. To get around to the side of the slope, out of Oldham's view, Steve would need to cross twenty metres or more of open space, climb the hill through sparse tree cover, and then make his way down over rocks to the ledge.

A bullet zinged above his head as he ducked down, and smashed into a tree. Adam, who'd been talking with the Aboriginal elders further back, made the dash across to join them.

'There's apparently a sort of tunnel that leads into the back of that cave,' Adam told them. 'Worn by water, and long and narrow.'

'Can you show me where?' Alec asked. 'If I can get up behind him...'

Adam shook his head. 'You're too broad in the shoulders, you'd never make it through. It will have to be Kris and me. It's not a sacred place – they wouldn't have told me about it if it was – but the elders only want people they know and trust to go there.'

'How long is this tunnel?' Kris asked, and only the slight hitch in her breath gave any hint of her apprehension.

'About thirty metres – crawl space the whole way. We'll have to get to the top of the hill first, on the north side. One of the elders will show us where the entrance is.'

Alec quickly weighed up the issues and risks. There was no time for pointless wishing that they had more options: there weren't any that didn't involve risking officers.

'I'll create a diversion by heading up the front of the slope and draw his fire,' he said. 'Steve, get into position to make a run across that clear ground. Adam and Kris, you'll have cover for the first part. I'll aim to keep him busy and not looking your way for the rest. If Tanya and Bella are in the back of that cave, get them up the tunnel to safety if you can.'

He glanced around the three of them, fully aware of the dangers they were going into. 'Those aren't orders. If any of you don't want to do this, say so now.'

Steve lifted his rifle, his face hard and determined. 'You're not the only one who'll do whatever it takes.'

Within a minute, they were all in place and ready, with the other officers instructed to provide covering fire as soon as Alec gave the order.

Alec crouched behind a vehicle in the middle of the pack and eyed the rock partway up the hill he'd be aiming for. Fifty metres of rough, steeply sloping ground.

He took a long, slow breath.

Then he gave the signal, a barrage of shots rang out, and he launched himself across the unprotected space.

After interminable seconds in the open, he skidded in behind the rock, ten metres below the cave entrance that Oldham sheltered in.

Keep him talking. Keep him distracted. Steve, Kris and Adam needed time to get into position.

'Put the weapon down, Oldham,' he called out, 'and give yourself up. You're in a no-win situation here.'

'Oh, so brave, Goddard. And so stupid. You don't seriously think you can arrest me, do you?'

Emphasising his words, a bullet smashed against the rock, drilling out a chunk of the sandstone.

'Where are Tanya and Bella?'

'They're tucked up nice and safe, somewhere you won't find them.'

Tucked up nice and safe... The words gave him no hint if they were alive or not. But they did suggest that they were together – somewhere other than with Oldham.

Surely, if they were with him, he'd be using one of them as a hostage?

'If you cooperate, and tell us where they are, the court might be more lenient,' Alec said, edging around in the protection of the rock. He could see Steve crawling towards the rock ledge above the cave.

The sound of Oldham's snort carried clearly across the distance. 'You're suffering from delusions, Goddard. You won't arrest me, I won't go to court, and you won't find Isabelle and the kid.'

'What have you done with them?'

'They're both alive. For now. Although your girlfriend was in a bit of a bad way when I left her. I told her I'd send you a postcard from Spain in a few weeks, so you can find their bodies then. Then I thought, Spain's a bit ho-hum really, so maybe I'll go to South America instead. Or perhaps I'll go and train Al-Qaeda troops in Afghanistan. That would be quite entertaining, don't you think?'

And Alec understood in that moment how a crowd of ordinary people had torn a man apart, because, God help him, the desire to do just that to the jeering, taunting Oldham raged in him and it would have been so easy to let go and give in to it.

He clung to reason, and the revelation that Tanya and Bella were both alive and not there with Oldham.

He could see Steve moving into place, crawling on his stomach to avoid Oldham's awareness. Only a minute or so longer – but Kris and Adam had further to go, and an awkward tunnel to get through.

'Sounds like you've got it all planned,' Alec said, with a casual evenness he was far from feeling. 'How are you going to get out of the country?'

'Oh, a backpacker came through town a while back who happened to look rather like me. So I relieved him of his identity, his money and his life.'

'You killed him?' Hell, how many bodies had this man left in his wake?

'He was an idiot Brit. It wasn't hard to arrange an… *accident*. And you lot are so inept you haven't even found him, despite all your searching.'

He laughed, the sound crawling like a nest of cockroaches along Alec's spine.

Don't respond to his taunts.

'Why did you kill Gillespie and Ward?'

'Gillespie got it into his mad head that you lot would come after him, so he tried to shoot Isabelle in the hall. But the crazy bastard can't even aim straight any more. I didn't want him stuffing up my plans, so I dealt with him. Ward saw too much, and, dumb as he was, he got suspicious. I gave him a choice – shoot himself or I'd shoot the kid. The old fool pissed himself before he pulled the trigger.'

'Ward found where you'd hidden her.'

Disgust burned Alec's throat, but he had to keep the man talking, keep his attention away from where Steve was climbing down to the ledge – in full view if Oldham turned that way.

'Pure fluke,' Oldham remarked. 'Ward couldn't find his way out of a paper bag.'

A stone clattered down the hillside from Steve's direction, loud in the stillness. Alec burst out from behind his cover to draw Oldham's attention away from the noise, but in the same moment, Oldham spun around and fired towards Steve. He shouted in pain and fell down on the ledge, out of view.

Standing in the open, unprotected but for his vest, Alec faced Oldham, his Glock drawn and pointing at the man, finger poised to shoot.

'Put your weapon down, Oldham. It's over.'

He fully expected a bullet to slam into him at any moment. Oldham pointed his pistol at him, smirking, uncaring – a twisted man to whom winning was everything.

'It *is* over, Darren.' Kris's cool voice came from further inside the cave, out of Alec's sight. 'There's no way out.'

Oldham glanced her way, not quite able to hide his surprise.

Good. He obviously hadn't expected that. Alec took several steady paces towards him.

Oldham let his arm fall, the pistol dangling from his fingers at his side, but instead of surrendering he began to laugh, a long, rolling eruption of disdainful amusement.

'Oh, you think you've won, Goddard, but you haven't. You won't find them. You'll search for weeks and weeks, but you'll never find your girlfriend. And Isabelle will have plenty of time to understand what a failure she is, as she watches the kid die. So, you see, you still lose and I win, after all.'

And quick as a snake striking, still smirking, he whipped the pistol up to his temple and squeezed the trigger.

Two gunshots thundered in Alec's ears, a split second apart, as he leapt to stop Oldham.

The man fell in a spray of blood, his pistol flying from his hand, clattering to the cave floor some feet away as he crumpled to the ground.

Dead.

Maybe it was the gunshots still reverberating in his head, or his own heartbeat pounding, but Alec had a strange sense of nightmarish unreality as he knelt by the man and automatically checked for a pulse. There was none, of course, only Oldham's vacant eyes staring and his mouth still open in a twisted, triumphant grin.

'Shit! Did I...?' Steve's voice came from the ledge above as Kris and Adam joined Alec by the corpse.

'No. You hit his arm. But he'd already pulled the trigger.' Alec looked up at Steve, the sight of the detective's grey face bringing reality back into sharp focus and ratcheting up his concern. 'Are you all right?'

'Uhh...well, there's a frigging bullet hole in my thigh that might need more than a band-aid.'

Alec swore. 'Get an ambulance here,' he called down to the officers below. 'And bring up a first aid kit. Now.'

Adam was already clambering up the rocks to Steve, but Kris's hand on his arm stopped Alec from following.

'Adam and the others will see to him,' she said quietly.

'What's wrong?'

'There's no sign of Bella or Tanya back there.' She didn't quite succeed in keeping her voice steady. 'But there's a stack of C4. Looks like he was starting to lay it out, but he didn't have time to finish. It's nowhere near twenty-five kilos though. And...' She stopped, exhaled a breath that might almost have edged into a sob.

'Tell me,' he ordered, although from her expression he sure as hell didn't want to hear it. Oldham's taunt echoed again in his thoughts: *You still lose and I win, after all.*

'There's a T-shirt,' Kris said. 'It looks like Tanya's. And... and a bra. With blood on it.'

When Alec stared down at the cotton lace bra splattered with red – the bra he'd slid from Bella's shoulders just last night – the man he'd always thought himself to be died inside him. All that was left was a fierce, pain-ravaged animal, and he knew the answer to the question Bella had asked him outside Gillespie's shack.

Yes, he was capable of losing himself in rage and committing murder. If Darren Oldham hadn't already been dead, he would have killed him there and then.

TWENTY-SIX

Isabelle wasn't sure which would be worse: the dim glow of the torch continuing to illuminate their prison, or the total, oppressive darkness that would surround them if – *when* – she turned the failing light off.

She'd used the torch's beam to check the chain holding her, but it was wrapped around the thick post several times and impossible to remove. She'd tried picking the padlock with a sliver of wood she'd torn from the post, but that too was unsuccessful. It wasn't as though being able to remove the chain would make any difference; they were still trapped deep underground, and even if she could get to the blocked part of the shaft, she had no tools to start clearing it. Nothing to help her tunnel through the hundreds of tonnes of dirt and rock that had fallen along a good length of the mine shaft. From the sounds of the explosion and the falling rock,

Darren had known exactly what he was doing with the explosive. She and Tanya had been showered with dirt, but their part of the mine had held.

The light dimmed to a pinpoint, and Tanya crawled closer, right onto her lap. Bella looped her arms around the girl, holding her close, murmuring soothing words as she turned off the failing light.

Tanya cuddled into her, face pressed against her shoulder. 'Are we going to die?' The small, brave whisper asked the question she'd dreaded.

'No, honey, we're not going to die.' She made the words as confident as she could, as if they might pierce the darkness.

'How will we get out?'

'We're going to be rescued. Did you know that there's a whole team of police searching for us? As well as all the people in town?'

'But how will they find us?'

'They'll work it out. I left some clues and some tracks for them to follow.'

She wanted to believe it herself. Wanted desperately to believe that any moment there'd be voices and light and they'd climb out of this grave into the sunshine and Alec would be alive and the whole nightmare would be over.

But she'd seen far too much over the years to be convinced. Life mostly didn't work out the way it did on TV. The good guys didn't always win. The rescuers didn't always make it in time. People disappeared without ever being found.

Adam would have to be in the right area to find their tracks. Or someone would have to know about the mine and remember its location – highly unlikely, since no one had remembered it through two abduction investigations.

'I want my mum and dad,' Tanya whispered.

'Yes, I know, sweetheart.' *I want Alec.* The longing just to see him, to know whether he'd walked out of that fire alive, almost undermined her composure and she struggled to keep her voice calm and reassuring. 'Close your eyes and try and sleep. It will make the time pass faster.'

Tanya wriggled into a more comfortable position, still snuggled in close. Maybe reassured, or maybe still affected by whatever drugs Darren had given her, within a few minutes her breathing slowed as she drifted into sleep.

Whatever the outcome, she had to look after Tanya. Even if she couldn't save her, she'd damn well make sure the kid didn't die scared and lonely.

How long would it take for them to die? She tried to think logically. Dehydration probably, before starvation. How long did people survive buried in earthquake ruins? Five days? Maybe a week? If they weren't already dehydrated to start with…

She suppressed a shudder. However long it took, she had to last longer than Tanya and spare her the nightmare of being alone in the dark. She'd hold her and reassure her and keep her brave and believing in rescue, just as Beth would do, right up until her last breath. And if their bodies were ever found, they'd be together, and Beth and Ryan would have the tiny solace of knowing that she'd looked after their little girl as much as she could. *As though she was my own daughter...*

She hugged the child closer and stared out into the black nothingness, not daring to close her eyes. With the head injury and the dehydration, she couldn't risk letting herself sleep.

The smothering darkness closed in around her, echoing with Darren's malevolence, and she felt the edge of panic beckoning. Her breath started coming in short gasps, and she bit her lip, hard, to choke back sobs.

I don't want to die, she cried out in her head. *Not like this.*

Oh, God, she was going to lose it. Her heart raced, painfully fast, and she drew her knees up, wanting just to curl up and scream and scream...

Tanya whimpered, pushed in her sleep against her legs, and the movement jerked Bella to the realisation that she'd been squeezing the girl too tightly. That she'd almost let terror overwhelm her responsibility to Tanya.

She pushed down the rising panic by forcing herself to slow her breathing, to think rationally. He *wanted* her to be alone and scared and to lose her sanity in hysteria and despair.

She could not give in to his evil. For Tanya's sake, for her own sake, she had to deny any thought that might erode her determination to stay strong.

Breathe. Believe. Don't let him win.

And so she sat there in the timeless black void, holding Tanya despite the discomfort in her back and legs, murmuring soothing words when the girl cried and whimpered in her sleep, and she brought every good thought, all the positive things she could remember, to the forefront of her mind.

Her father, holding her after her mother died, just as she now held Tanya. *We'll make it through, little one,* he'd promised her. She whispered the same words to Tanya, and made herself keep breathing deeply, steadily, the memory of her father's quiet courage bolstering her own.

She didn't for a moment believe in ghosts, but here in the silent darkness she could recall his face more clearly than at any time since he'd died.

Other memories floated to the surface of her thoughts, and she let them come. Her mother's laughter, and her love and warmth. Jeanie's affection and guidance during her teenage years. Delphi's down-to-earth loyalty.

Mark and Beth and Ryan and all the others who'd been part of her childhood. Steve and Kris and Adam. Friends who knew her, accepted her, cared about her.

The knowledge of their friendship curled around her, warmed her. They cared, and she'd pushed them away this past year. She'd pushed them away because she hadn't wanted to be reminded of it all – Jess and Dan Chalmers, and her own failure to save both of them.

Yet they'd understood, had respected her need to be alone. And they all, in their own way, had kept contact with her. Beth's chatty, optimistic emails. Kris's regular phone calls and her visits. Mark's offer to help with any legal issues. Even Steve had sent get well cards, and a basket of flowers when she'd left the hospital.

Bob Barrington had insisted on watching over her, his initial sense of responsibility transforming to an almost paternal concern. He'd brought her home from hospital, made sure she could manage, driven up from Sydney every week to take her to physio appointments before her smashed shoulder was healed enough to drive. And, worried by her isolation, he'd brought her Finn for company.

Finn, lying so still on the floor of the hall.

If Darren had poisoned him...

No, thinking that way would only weaken her resolve. He'd just been sleeping, surely, maybe drugged a little. He'd be up and around in no time, begging for pats from anyone who'd give them to him.

And then there was Alec.

She leaned her cheek against Tanya's hair. While there was breath in his body, Alec would search for them, holding true to the promise he'd made Beth and Ryan. Because that was the sort of man he was, honour and integrity woven into the core of him, and his promise had not been lightly made.

She blocked out the memory of him heading back into the fire, refusing to acknowledge the possibility of him dead or badly burnt. No, she would imagine him out there searching for them. He'd be leading, coordinating, keeping everyone working together as a team, following up every clue.

She strained to hear any sound, but there was only Tanya's breathing, and her own, in the darkness.

'They'll come, Tanya,' she whispered to the girl. 'They're good people, strong people, and they won't give up. And neither will I.'

They were all there, the entire town, crowded into the front and back bars of the pub, spilling out into the courtyard at the back. Men and women in SES uniforms, Rotary aprons and CWA aprons; stockmen and graziers and retired loggers and the women who worked alongside them; teenagers and kids. Delphi and the Wilsons at a table in the courtyard with Mark Strelitz and Jeanie.

Everyone stilled and turned to Alec as he pushed through the gate into the courtyard. All of them hushed and solemn and waiting for news.

Except Finn, sitting beside Delphi, who leapt to his feet and began to bark, straining at the leash that held him.

Alec made his way straight to the table with the Wilsons and Delphi, focusing just on that group. Ryan held his youngest daughter on his lap, his other arm round Beth and the middle girl. Delphi, her back ramrod straight, shoulders rigid, clasped her hands tightly on the table in front of her.

Mark gave up his seat for him, and Alec slid into it with a nod of acknowledgment, vaguely aware of the exhaustion dragging at his body as the adrenaline that had kept him going drained away.

'We haven't found them yet.' He answered the most pressing unspoken question first. 'They weren't there in the caves. But we're sure – I'm positive – that they're still alive.'

Everyone let out a collective breath, and Beth buried her face in her husband's chest, her shoulders shaking.

'Darren?' Jeanie asked.

'He's...dead. He shot himself.'

The image of Oldham laughing, swinging the gun up to his head, danced again in his mind and bile burned in his throat. Hate had a taste, he'd discovered in the last hour, and it was hot and bitter and ugly.

'And the ambulance?' Mark, this time. Nobody else seemed capable of speaking.

'Detective Fraser was shot in the leg. He'll be okay.'

Ripples of murmuring flowed behind him as the news spread in respectful whispers, but he kept his focus on this group. They needed him the most.

A tear dropped on the table from Delphi's cheek, and something about that small drop of moisture doused some of the raging fury in him. Delphi, alone in the world but for Bella, crying in fear for the niece who shared the same pride and determination, the same reserve. She needed his humanity, not wasted energy on hate and anger. Alec reached across and closed his hand over her gnarled fingers, and although he meant the gesture as support for her, the simple contact was strangely strengthening.

'They're alive,' he repeated, as much for her as for himself. 'It was part of Oldham's game, but he can't hurt them now. All we have to do is find them.'

'Tell us how to help, what you need,' Mark said.

What did he need? How could he get all these people to usefully help? He forced himself to think. Some of them had lived here all their lives, had families going back generations – as had Oldham.

He pushed himself to his feet, made his way to a table just outside the back bar where most of the people could see him, and stepped up to stand on top of it.

The murmurs died away and the entire crowd turned to him, hushed and expectant. Ordinary people. People who'd been through too much this past year. People who now had to deal with the knowledge that one of their own had put them through it.

'Darren Oldham is dead,' he announced, making his voice strong, projecting it to the back of the crowd. 'But we believe that Tanya and Isabelle are alive, and that Oldham has hidden them somewhere. You all know that there are hundreds of thousands of hectares of bush out there, and we don't have the time or resources to search the whole area. So we need your help to work out where Oldham might have taken them.'

He took a breath then ploughed on. Unorthodox this approach might be, but any small clue could help them find Tanya and Bella.

'I want you all to go back over your knowledge of Oldham. Talk together in groups – that will help prompt your memories. Think about things he's done, places you've seen him, areas he knows well, people he hung around with, places or happenings that might have been significant to him or his family. Anything that you remember could be important.

Mark and Jeanie, can you find and distribute paper and pens so people can write down what they come up with?'

The young politician and the elderly woman nodded, both understanding he was asking more of them than just arranging paper. The townsfolk knew them, trusted them, and they would move amongst the crowd, encouraging, facilitating, gently prodding and prompting and teasing out as much information as could be gained.

'Please…' His voice failed, and he bowed his head for a moment, Oldham's taunts nagging in his mind. *They're both alive. For now.* How the hell long was 'for now'? He looked back to the community in front of him and, although he couldn't make eye contact with every individual, he tried to get as many as he could. 'We may not have much time. Please remember everything you can.'

He left them in the capable hands of Mark and Jeanie, and walked back up to the hall, the burning, icy numbness taking over his body again while his mind whirred, frantically searching for answers that didn't exist.

He didn't know where Bella was, and, unless he found some clue soon, she could die. And he didn't know what Oldham had done to her… He blacked out that train of thought. If he let his imagination go there, he'd lose his sanity.

Most of the small gaggle of journalists were busy talking on their cell phones or doing pieces to camera based on the brief statement he'd given them before going to the pub, and he went past them without stopping.

Inside, his eyes took a moment to adjust to the duller light after the glaring sunshine. And his mind took another moment to register that the older man waiting at the interview table was Bob Barrington.

Bob sprang to his feet, crossed to him in a couple of steps. Alec's father's best mate; Alec's honorary uncle, mentor, one-time commander and colleague.

'Christ, Alec, you look like hell.'

'Yes.' He didn't doubt it. All the definitions of hell he'd ever heard had nothing on how he felt now. 'What...? Why...?'

'I won't get in your way, lad. But I was going mad just staying at home, listening to the news. I left this morning, didn't hear about Bella until I got here. It's true then?' Eyes desperate for a denial searched his. 'She's missing as well?'

Bob cares for Bella too. He'd always been a tough commander, expecting the best, but with a strong sense of responsibility for the officers who worked with him. The same sense of responsibility that had made him keep a watch over his dead mate's family all these years. And, after the case last year, Bob had watched over Bella as well.

Alec nodded, and saw the pain cross the other man's face. 'Yes. I think they're together. I hope they're together.' He explained briefly all that had happened.

'It's my fault we didn't get Oldham last year,' Bob said. 'If we'd worked it out then –'

Alec cut him off. 'None of us could work it out, except

Bella. The man was like a chameleon. And now she's paying the damn price.'

'I'll keep out of your way, but if there's anything I can do...' It was almost a plea, the man begging to be useful rather than just stand by helplessly. Another person needing him to take charge, to be strong.

Alec strode to his desk, retrieved a pile of papers and handed them to Bob. The man's skills and extensive police experience wouldn't have disappeared with retirement, even if his confidence had drained away.

'Read through the old case notes. Check every mention of Oldham – his statement, sightings, whatever. He saw this whole thing as a contest of wits, so he may have dropped some clue, counting on us to miss it. And review everything Bella was looking into, in case she was getting close to something.'

Out of the window, Alec saw Adam towing Oldham's car – no, his own car – on a trailer behind one of the police vehicles. Alec was out the door and beside the vehicle before Adam had finished parking.

'Kris is staying out there until the coroner's officer arrives,' Adam said, as he got out of the car. 'But I brought the car in so we could go over it. Unless you want to wait for Forensics?'

'We can't wait that long.'

'That's what I thought.' Adam began to undo the chains holding the vehicle on the trailer. 'I already checked the speedo, and I reckon he's put about a hundred kilometres on the clock.'

Which scarcely narrowed the search area at all, Alec calculated quickly.

As soon as the car was on the ground, Alec opened the boot. A vision of Bella trapped inside the cramped space overlaid itself on his real vision for a moment and he gripped the edge of the car, fighting the surge of fury.

He forced himself to focus. The wrench. The displaced mat over the spare tyre space. No, she hadn't panicked; she'd done what she could.

The sun had moved too low to shine directly inside, and he found a torch in the police vehicle so that he could see more clearly.

He swung the beam of light around the confined space, examining every surface. His hand holding the light shook when he found the traces of blood on the edge of the tyre cover – but if it hadn't shaken, he might not have caught sight of the scratches, barely visible on the metal moulding. A flicker of hope ignited within him.

'Can you find me a pencil?' he asked Adam. 'And some light paper?'

Adam procured them from the office within minutes, and Alec leaned into the car, lightly shading the paper with the pencil over the scratches to make an impression of them.

They both studied the paper. A series of lines, some joined but others not.

'I can't make out any words,' Adam said.

'It's not words,' Alec mused, working it through aloud. 'The lines are mostly straight – no curves. It's a map.'

He sprinted inside to compare it to the maps they had, adrenaline beginning to pump again now that they had a clue to go on. He yanked open a map of the forest, spread it out on a table.

'If north on Scrub Road is the starting point, this right turn could be Geary's Road,' he traced the line with his finger, 'or this track here.'

'That's the north firebreak track,' Adam said.

Alec scanned the map, fitting all the pieces together. 'If he travelled around a hundred kilometres and ended up here,' he pointed to Cave Hill, 'then I'm guessing the firebreak track is the right one. Which could make this line Cutter's Track, or whatever this road here is.'

'Cutter's Track leads to the old loggers' camp site. There's nothing left there but a water tank and a few timber footings from the old huts. The other track – it's not much at all now. Used to be a firebreak years ago, to protect the logging camp.'

The door swung open and Mark strode in, heading straight for them.

'What did they remember?' Alec demanded.

'Darren's grandfather apparently had a mine, sixty or more years ago,' Mark answered. 'He never found anything, but he spent a lot of time up there in his youth, convinced that he would. No one's quite sure where the mine was, but old Snowy Fullerton thinks it might have been in the north of the scrub. He remembers seeing Oldham Senior up in that area a few times, although he lived here in town.'

'That's *got* to be it.' An old mine – it had to be the sort of place Darren would hide his captives in.

'Ryan's on the phone to the Council archivist now,' Mark added, 'trying to find out who held land up there then, and exactly which block it might have been.'

'Did someone mention Cutter's Track?' Bob asked, coming across from the desk he'd been working at. 'The SES searched the section east of there last year, but they had to stop because a bushfire started in the area. Oldham was the one who reported the fire and warned them about it.'

And he damn well probably lit it himself. Oh, yeah, hindsight was wonderful, Alec thought bitterly.

Certainty settled in his gut and stayed there as he fired orders. Cutter's Track ran for about five kilometres, according to the map. The old fire trail – well, no telling now how much of that was passable. They'd narrowed down the search area from hundreds of square kilometres to tens of them. What they might find – if they found anything at all – he wouldn't pause to contemplate.

TWENTY-SEVEN

Just as the sunset faded and dusky twilight descended, they found signs of a car having turned around at the end of the old fire trail. Alec scanned the thick bushland surrounding them, cursing the disappearing light, desperate for any sign, any clue. A sliver of moon hung in the west just above the treetops. Soon it would be gone and there would be only starlight – and starlight could not penetrate the forest shadows.

'Darren's brushed this whole area,' Adam said, crouching by a leafy branch at the side of the track, covered in red dust. 'Finding their tracks – which way they went from here – will be damned hard in the dark. Assuming they were here at all.'

'They were here,' Alec replied. 'He wouldn't have swept the tracks away otherwise.'

'If we get strong spotlights…'

'Finn.' Alec spoke over Adam as the solution formed in his mind. 'Finn's our best chance. Bella said he's not a great scent dog, but he'll probably follow hers.'

He phoned back to Dungirri, and Mark drove out with Finn. Alec had the back door of the car open and was grabbing Finn's lead as soon as Mark pulled up. Finn leapt from the vehicle, peered around and sniffed, and within seconds he yelped and tried to run into the bush, pulling hard on the lead Alec held.

'Do you think it's Bella?' Adam asked, handing him a powerful torch from the police vehicle.

Alec watched the dog for a moment. Finn stared intently into the bush, whining and quivering as he leaned hard on the lead. 'Yes. There must be a lot of scents around here – kangaroos, rabbits, possums. But he seems to be intent on just one. Okay, boy, let's go.'

The dog dashed into the bush, nose to the ground, and Alec had to keep a firm grip on the lead as he followed behind, Mark and Adam beside him, their three spotlights dancing eerily amongst the shadows of the forest.

Finn wasn't the only one who strained to sprint, but the darkness and the rough ground slowed them to a careful pace. And the whole way, Alec repeated over and over in his mind, as if she could hear, *Hang on, Bella. We're coming.*

At a small creek, the dog stopped, sniffing around near the water. Alec shone the light over the area. Where Finn stood, a medley of footprints, animal and human, blurred indistinctly in the sand. But beside a rock he caught sight of three clear shoe prints – two about the size of Bella's boots, the third smaller.

'It's definitely them.'

The relief almost made him light-headed. He dropped to a kneel, flicked the torchlight around the rocks, and it glittered on something in a gap. He recognised the slim gold band instantly. Bella's watch.

He knew he should probably use an evidence bag, but Darren Oldham was dead and would never face court, so he picked it up in his bare hands, the metal band warm against his fingers. He could almost fool himself that it was Bella's warmth, rather than the heat of the day's sun stored in the rocks and the metal. He tucked it into the top pocket of his overalls, where it rested just below his heart.

'Good boy,' he said to Finn, rubbing the dog's ears. 'Now, find Bella.'

But the budding sense of hope evaporated when they confronted the tumble of fresh earth and broken timbers that scarred the hillside. Finn whined and scratched at the ground while Alec stared, fear freezing him for a long moment. He had no doubt that Bella and Tanya were somewhere in the mine. And although he wasn't a religious man, he prayed that they were somewhere behind those tonnes of dirt and rock, not under them.

They're still alive . . . for now. But that had been hours ago.

A burning anger took him, fuelled by the fear. Anger and sheer bloody determination not to give in to Darren Oldham's will.

He saw a flat piece of timber amongst the rubble and dropped to his knees and began scraping away loose dirt with it, even while he gave orders to the other two.

'Get the SES here. And lights, a generator, digging equipment. There's a mine rescue team at Newcastle – get Barrington to get on to the authorities and arrange for them to fly in. And I want ambulances and paramedics here.'

He heard Adam relaying instructions into his radio, and nodded in acknowledgment when the constable said he'd go and meet the others at the track and guide them in, but he didn't stop working at moving the dirt. The SES, the equipment, the lights – it would all take time to get here. And it would be hours, at the very least, before the mine rescue team came. Time that Bella and Tanya might not have.

Mark set to work beside him, pulling out broken pieces of timber with his bare hands and piling them to one side.

'You shouldn't be doing this,' Alec objected, for form's sake. 'It could be dangerous, and you're not police or SES.'

The politician grunted disagreement as he shifted another spar of timber. 'I love Beth like a sister. Maybe more. So I'll do anything to get Tanya back to her. And I spent a lot of my youth with my grandfather mining opals up at Lightning Ridge, so I've dug a hell of a lot more mine shafts than you have.'

The SES arrived eventually, with gloves and shovels and lights and other equipment, and there was activity that he was dimly aware of, but Alec focused on the rock and earth and timber in front of him as he and Finn dug their way deeper into the hillside. Just behind him, Mark gave directions to nameless voices about timber props and hanging working lights, and others widened the narrow tunnel that Alec dug, clearing away earth and rocks and debris and making it safer.

Hours passed, but he couldn't have said how many. He'd taken his watch off, buttoned it into his pocket with Bella's. He had dirt in his hair, his mouth, his eyes, even inside the gloves he wore. The knees of his overalls were worn through from kneeling and crawling on rocks and earth. Someone handed him a couple of muesli bars and a bottle of water, and he gulped them down, then requested a water bowl for Finn. Worried about the dog's paws, he tried to have someone take Finn away for a check, but the dog yowled so loudly they gave up on the idea. It seemed that Finn, too, cared only about reaching Bella and Tanya.

They'd worked a long way in when Finn yelped and began digging even more furiously, sending dirt flying and whining in excitement.

Alec hardly dared to hope. For hours he'd carried the dread that any moment he might see a hand, a foot, a face, cold and lifeless, in the earth.

Finn broke into what seemed to be a looser patch, an air hole perhaps, and his whines turned to frantic yelps.

And then he wriggled through the hole and disappeared from sight.

Alec scrambled to the hole and lay flat on his stomach, pointing the torch through, but he'd have to dig around several large rocks before anyone bigger than the dog could pass through.

Finn's barking now sounded from a distance, and Alec strained to hear any other sounds.

'Bella!' he shouted at the top of his lungs, then held his breath, listening intently.

Above Finn's barking, and the pounding of his own pulse, he heard a faint voice.

'Here...'

Bella's voice. A wild surge of pure relief overwhelmed him and he let his head fall onto his arm, heaving in a shuddering gasp.

Then he forced his head up again and shouted into the narrow hole, 'And Tanya?'

'She's here too. She's okay.'

'They're alive,' he called back to Mark, and he didn't care that his voice was so rough with emotion it cracked. 'Tell Beth and Ryan and Delphi that they're both alive.'

He needed to see her, not just hear her. See her and touch her and hold her before he could believe this nightmare over. But he couldn't make out anything but tunnel walls from this angle. He thrust the torch into the hole as far as he could reach.

'Can you see the torch, Bella? Just come to the light.'

'Tanya's coming. I... I can't.'

His euphoria dulled in an instant. 'Are you hurt?'

'No. I'm chained...' Her voice faded for a moment. 'Need boltcutters... or handcuff keys.'

'We'll get them, Bella. It won't be long now.'

He barked orders behind him, but stayed where he was. No way would he move any further from her. Within a few moments he heard small, shuffling footsteps, not far away.

'Is that you, Tanya? My name's Alec. Put your hands through the hole where the light is, and I'll get you out of there.'

He pulled her through the gap as gently as he could, relieved to see that, other than dirt and tears, she seemed uninjured. Mark was there behind him to wrap her in a blanket and cradle her on his lap.

'Hi, little mate,' Mark said, smiling at the girl through tears he didn't try to hide. 'How about we go see your mum and dad, hey?'

Someone else came in to take Mark's place as he carried the child out, and Alec began to dig again, scraping the base of the hole deeper while others braced the rocks with timber.

He pushed himself through the moment it was large enough, scrambling along the low tunnel in a crouching run. Anger and fear, relief and joy all tore at his heart when he finally caught Bella and Finn in the torchlight.

Blood matted her hair on one side of her head, smears of dirt dragged across her face, the chain weighed down her hands, yet she smiled at him.

That smile, with all its courage and beauty and strength, undid him, eroded the worn-thin, desperate control he'd held on to for so long. He fell on his knees beside her, wrapped her in his arms and held her tightly, rocking her, burying his face in her hair.

She didn't want to move. Wanted just to be held, to not think, to let go of fear and be secure. Tanya was safe; Alec was alive, with her, and he'd brought light to the dungeon. Everything else could wait for a few more moments.

Alec held her tightly, and when he finally spoke his desperate, choked words tore at her heart. 'Oh, God, Bella. I'm sorry. I'm so sorry he hurt you. It's my fault. He wouldn't have if I hadn't –'

She lifted her face from his shoulder and, even in the deflected light from the torch, could see the raw pain in his eyes.

'Alec, I'm okay. Other than a whack on the head and a few scrapes and bruises, he didn't hurt me.'

'He didn't...?'

In the unsaid words she glimpsed the mental torture Darren must have put him through.

She cupped his face with her hands, despite the drag of the cuffs on her wrists, and let him see the truth in her eyes. 'Whatever he's told you, it didn't happen.'

He closed his eyes, sucked in a ragged breath. She leaned her forehead against his, giving him time to regain his equilibrium.

He almost lost it again when he unlocked the cuffs and saw the bloodied chafing on her wrists.

'Hey, it's all right,' she insisted, marshalling a crooked grin. 'Just get me out of this damned hole.'

Her legs gave way when she tried to stand, and he supported her, half-carrying her, as they stumbled along the tunnel, Finn prancing impatiently ahead of them.

They scrambled into a wider space, and hands reached to help her, but she kept a grip on Alec and he picked her up in his arms, carrying her the last distance out of the mine.

A cheer sounded and cameras flashed when they emerged, and people crowded around, smiling, touching her on the arm, murmuring their relief.

Many, many people. Dungirri people. Faces she knew, bleary-eyed with exhaustion but familiar. People who must have been working for hours through the dark night to find her and Tanya. People who had struggled with hard times and desperate circumstances, yet who cared enough to keep going, keep hoping, despite the odds.

Her people.

Her eyes blurred, she croaked her thanks again and again.

Beyond the searchlights she could see the first rays of sunlight glowing through the trees. Morning. Already. Which meant she'd been in that hole for . . . too long to bear remembering.

Medics brought a stretcher and Alec set her down on it. She tried to keep hold of his hand but had to let go while the paramedics fussed over her. Journalists with cameras crowded in and he ordered them to give her space, so then the media turned their focus on him. He was still answering their questions – and holding on to Finn's collar – when the paramedics and a couple of SES guys lifted the stretcher and started back towards the track.

'Please...'

'We're taking you to an ambulance, Detective. You just lie still and we'll have you out of here in a few jiffs.'

They carried her through the bush to the track, where two ambulances waited with lights flashing blue and red, and Beth and Ryan held their daughter, and Delphi gripped her hand painfully tight and cried on Kris's shoulder.

They all tended to her, making her comfortable, preparing her for the ride to the hospital. All the while she watched for Alec, but he didn't come.

TWENTY-EIGHT

'We're here, mate. This is the hospital.'

The man's voice invaded his dream and Alec jerked awake, disoriented. The mine shaft... Bella's body, bleeding like Shani...

No. He shook his head to clear the image as the patrol car slowed and turned into a car park, the low buildings beyond shining light into the gathering dusk. Birraga hospital. Hell, he must have dropped off as soon as they'd left Dungirri.

'Sorry I haven't been much company,' he said to the constable who'd given him a lift. Damn, he couldn't even remember the man's name, couldn't read his name tag in the dull light.

'No worries, mate. I figured you needed a bit of shut-eye. The last few days have been pretty tough.'

'Yes,' Alec agreed out of courtesy. 'Tough' didn't even begin to cover it. He opened the door, forced his tired, aching body into cooperation. 'Thanks for the ride.'

'Are you planning to stay in town for the night?'

Was he? Alec had to stop and think. He'd got through all the reports and the Internal Affairs questioning about Oldham's death; had finally made it into Birraga to see Bella, thanks to Kris arranging this ride for him, and he hadn't thought any further than that.

'Yes, I guess so. There's a pub somewhere, I suppose?'

'Three. The Imperial has the better food, the Federation's better for accommodation, and avoid the Royal.'

'Thanks.'

He closed the door, stepped up on to the footpath, and the constable drove off. He stood in front of the entrance to the hospital, willing himself to go in. To see Bella one last time. To say goodbye.

'Alec.'

Her voice came from his left, and he turned his head, half-expecting that he'd imagined it. But there she stood, two metres away, wearing casual cotton trousers and a T-shirt, her hair loose around her face, a small bag at her feet. Alive and whole and well and so beautiful she stole his breath.

'Bella! Shouldn't you be...?'

'I've checked out. All the X-rays and scans are clear, they gave me plenty of fluid this morning, and my blood work's fine, so when the doctor came this evening she said I could go if I wanted to.' She smiled wryly. 'Hospitals aren't my favourite places. Twelve hours of being poked and prodded is enough. I phoned Kris, and she said you were already on your way in.'

'Oh.' He stared at her, stupidly trying to get his brain to process all of that, and keeping his distance because if he touched her now he'd never be able to let her go. 'Are you really okay?'

She wasn't, he thought. In the light spilling from the hospital foyer he could see the dark lines under her eyes, the small pieces of sticking plaster on the cut on her forehead, the bruising around it. How could they have let her out of hospital? How could she be okay, after everything she'd been through?

As if she'd read his mind, she closed the distance between them; but the fingers she lightly laid on his arm burned his skin and he had to concentrate on her words to comprehend them.

'Alec, I'm fine. Other than a headache, I'm better than I've been for a while. And…knowing that it's over, that he won't harm anyone again…there's a kind of peace in that that I didn't have before.'

Peace. Would he ever have that again? She was only inches from him, the scent of soap and light perfume and her mixing with a nearby honeysuckle, taunting him, and he had to stuff his fists in his jeans pockets so he wouldn't touch her.

She didn't miss his unsubtle rejection, and stepped back from him, uncertainty flickering in her eyes. Hell, he'd hurt her, even though the last thing in the world he wanted was to cause her pain.

'Bella, I . . .' *I came to say goodbye.* The words jumbled in his head, tangled with all the things he wanted to tell her, the hurt in her eyes ripping his emotions to shreds.

The hospital door squeaked as someone swung it open, and he turned on his heel, walked away from the light and the intrusion, and into the shadowed garden beside the building. The sweet honeysuckle perfume enveloped him, but he didn't need a physical sense to know that Bella had followed him.

He stared out beyond the garden, to the silhouetted line of eucalypts that must mark the river, judging by the chorus of frogs.

'I promised to protect you.' His voice grated in the softness of the evening air. 'And I couldn't.'

'Don't, Alec.' A brief butterfly-touch on his arm reassured him of her presence behind him, that he hadn't driven her away. 'Don't hold yourself responsible for everything. You can't blame yourself for what Darren chose to do.'

'Can't I? When we found –' He did turn to her then, so she could see what he was, the anger and ugliness inside him. 'I would have killed him, Bella. I've never felt more like ripping a man apart.'

'But you wouldn't have.'

'You can't know that,' he argued. 'Hell, *I* don't know that.'

'Yes, you do. Kris told me that you walked away from his body. You didn't kick it, fire your gun into his head, lose your control at all. You made yourself walk away.'

He wanted to believe her, but the rage still smouldered, the taste of it hot and harsh in his mouth, fuelled by the fear he would never be rid of.

'Christ, when I think of what he did...what he could have done to you...'

Her fingers clasped his wrist, sought his hand, and, after a moment of uselessly fighting his conscience, he slid his fist from his pocket, *needing* that contact, gripped her fingers although his hand was bruised and aching.

'I'll be fine,' she repeated. 'Tanya's safe, and home with her parents. Even Steve is already flirting with the doctor. You're the one I'm worried about. You need to sleep.'

'Sleep?' His hollow laugh physically hurt. 'I fell asleep coming in just now, and I dreamed I was digging in that damned tunnel. Digging and digging, but when I found you...it was your grave. Yours and Shani's.' He shuddered, the horror of it knifing his guts, because it was too close to being real. 'I can't do that again, Bella. All those hours of not knowing...' He swallowed, then surged on. 'I came to say goodbye.'

'No.'

The flash of fire in her eyes seared his conscience, still determined to do the right thing, and eased the pain in his heart, which desperately wanted some reason not to walk away.

'Not yet,' she said. 'Not tonight. Not when you're exhausted beyond reason and I'm almost the same.'

She lifted their clasped hands, pressed her mouth against his fingers. 'Alec, both of us – we need to find a bed, hold each other while we sleep. We *need* that tonight. If you dream again, I'll be there. If I see you walking into that burning house for the thousandth time, you'll be there for me. Tomorrow we can talk. When we're rested and can think clearly again.'

He was too tired to argue, too tired even to come up with a reason to argue, because as soon as she planted the idea, the craving to sleep with her in his arms, to let go of worry and hold her safe again, overwhelmed any other concerns. She was right: tonight he needed that more than he needed anything else.

Sleep. And Bella. For one more night.

And maybe tomorrow he'd have strength enough to leave her.

Bella breathed more easily when Alec gave up struggling against his demons and nodded his agreement. She picked up the small bag of necessaries that Kris had brought in for her and, with her other hand still in his, led him across the car park, away from the brighter lights that marked the centre of the small town.

'Where?' he asked, clearly confused. 'The hotels are in town – one of them's supposed to be okay.'

'The caravan park has new cabins, down by the river,' she explained. She'd asked the hospital clerk for a recommendation when she'd signed out. 'They're quieter, more private than the hotels. It's just down the road.'

The night was warm, the air dry, the stars bright in the huge sky above them. Neither of them spoke, but she kept hold of his hand, kept him close, as they walked.

The woman in the park office recognised them – Bella had been surprised by the number of times the footage of the rescue had played on the TV news programs during the day – but she must have sensed their fatigue because, other than a heart-felt 'thank you', she signed them in without any chatter.

The cabin she gave them was at the edge of the park, surrounded by trees, secluded and peaceful. A security light lit up on the veranda as they approached, and as Alec unlocked the door Bella saw how stiff his hands were, bruised and raw from digging in the mine shaft, and how he could barely keep his eyes open.

While she'd spent the day in hospital, resting between tests and visitors, he'd still been carrying the weight of responsibility, with no time or privacy to deal with all the trauma the past days had brought him. Kris had told her this afternoon, in a stark tone, all that had occurred at Cave Hill, and all that had followed as they'd searched into the night. Then, because armed officers had been present when Darren died, making it a death in custody, Internal Affairs had arrived and begun a rigorous investigation, interviewing them all multiple times. Throughout, Alec had taken responsibility for the officers under his command and insisted on thorough procedure.

'The man's a walking zombie,' Kris had said, 'but he's still doing his duty.'

Maybe not a zombie, Bella thought as they entered the cabin, *but definitely an exhausted, wounded warrior.* And despite having had some sleep during the day, she wasn't a whole lot better off herself.

She glanced around the cabin – new, relatively spacious, comfortable, with a bedroom and bathroom off the living area. The queen bed was already made up, and she steered him towards it with a hand on his arm, and pulled back the light covers.

'Bed,' she ordered. 'Kick off your boots and jeans. I'll just get a glass of water and be there in a moment.'

By the time she'd swallowed a headache tablet and carried a glass of water in, he was in jocks and T-shirt, flat on his back on the sheet, as if he'd simply lain down and fallen asleep. But he opened heavy-lidded eyes as she unbuttoned the trousers Kris had lent her and shucked them off, and rolled over to wrap her in his arms when she lay down beside him.

He held her tightly, exhaling on a sigh as she put her arm around him and cuddled in close. She let her eyes close, her head resting against his shoulder, felt his lips against the unbruised side of her face.

'Definitely medicinal,' she murmured.

His mellow sound of agreement didn't make it to a full word. Already his breathing was slowing, the tension of his body relaxing.

She breathed with him, long and slow. The nightmare was over, and tomorrow would be a new beginning. There'd be time then to be with Alec, to talk, to explore, to follow their feelings.

She let herself drift to sleep on that thought.

Tomorrow came with a loud electronic tune that dragged Bella from deep sleep into daylight. Alec groaned, disentangled one arm from her and reached for his mobile phone on the nightstand.

It took him only a second to wake fully. It took Bella less than two seconds to understand that something was terribly wrong.

Then he was standing up, serious and duty-focused, reaching for his jeans with his free hand.

She didn't want to interpret the glance he gave her before he strode out to the living area, didn't want to hear the quick, sharp questions he shot to his caller. She rolled out of bed, went into the bathroom to splash her face with water and give him a few moment's privacy for his call.

'I'm in Birraga but my gear's in Dungirri,' he was saying when she emerged. 'Can you get me transport from the Birraga station back there? Yes, I'll be there in ten minutes.'

He flicked the phone off and began to tuck his T-shirt into his jeans without looking at her.

'Bad news?'

He did look up then, and he might have been all DCI but there was pain with it, and a harrowing grief.

'Two officers...' He stopped, shook his head as if to clear it, and went on with stark facts. 'Killed by a car bomb this morning. I'm to head up the task force. The helicopter's already on its way to Dungirri for me.'

Sorrow gripped her heart – for Alec, stoically bearing a new burden, for the dead officers, for herself. In a few minutes he'd be gone, and she'd be left alone, unable to help him.

'Did you know the officers?'

'Yes.'

He ran his hand through his hair and turned away, went back into the bedroom and sat on the bed to put on his boots. She followed, stood in the doorway.

'They worked with me years ago,' he said, and his voice was hard and bleak as he rapidly tied his laces. 'Their evidence was critical in convicting Kevin Jones. Another witness went missing two days ago. And Jones was released from prison last month.'

She didn't need her detective experience to understand the significance of that. 'Kevin Jones? Any relation to Eddie?'

He raised his eyes to hers and stood slowly, tucking his phone and wallet into his jeans as he spoke. 'His younger brother. More vicious even than Eddie. He took over Eddie's organisation and expanded it.'

He paused for a ragged, steadying breath, the grief in his eyes far more than that of an officer for his colleagues. 'I have to go, Bella.'

Everything stilled. He stood there, so close yet an abyss away, and his tortured words from last night echoed unspoken in the air between them. *I can't do that again, Bella... I came to say goodbye.*

She nodded silently, unable to speak, and moved out of his way, determined not to make this any harder for him. She'd let him go now to do his job, to be the man and police officer he'd always be. But no way in hell was she letting him walk away for ever.

'I'll call Bob Barrington, get him to come and get you and drive you home.' His voice cracked, and he walked past her, without touching her, to the door.

'Alec.'

He stopped, the door half-opened, his hand clenched white on the handle, his head rigidly facing forward.

She swallowed to make her throat work. 'Don't let them win.'

She watched him go, striding through the caravan park, shoulders parade-ground stiff.

When he was out of sight, she closed the door, leaned against it, wiped away the tears that filled her eyes.

Maybe it wasn't the best start to a new beginning, but she was alive and mostly whole, Tanya was safe, Darren would harm no one else, and Alec cared for her as much as she did for him.

It might take some time – heck, after the intensity of the past few days, they could all use some healing time – but she already knew in her heart that she wouldn't let the Oldhams and Joneses of the world deprive them of the things that mattered most.

TWENTY-NINE

Six weeks later

Alec dropped down into his chair in the deserted office, fatigue taking over now that the stress and concentration of the past few weeks was finally over. As of this morning, Kevin Jones was back behind bars – along with seven others, including two corrupt officers who'd been conspiring with him.

After a protracted, exhausting case, Alec had had to tell a barrage of television cameras this afternoon that two officers the public should have been able to trust were involved in organised crime.

He'd sent his team home straight after the initial debrief. They'd all been dazed with exhaustion after too many long nights of surveillance and undercover operations. But he'd had to stay, to make a full report to his superiors, to face the media on behalf of the police service.

Now he could go home too, but the overloaded in-tray glared at him after weeks of neglect, and dealing with it almost seemed preferable to facing his empty apartment.

It wasn't the sleep he didn't want – hell, he'd had so little lately that he'd be out like a light within a micro-second of lying down. It was the waking up he hated. Every time he snatched a few hours of sleep, whether in the back of a surveillance van, in his bed or at his desk, waking brought only the cold reality of being alone, his body and spirit craving Bella.

Just two nights with her had made him an addict.

He glanced at his watch – five o'clock – and then had to look again to check what day of the week it was. Friday. He flicked open his desk diary and thumbed through the last few weeks to see what he'd missed. Routine meetings, a dental appointment, a charity function he might have foregone anyway. On today's page he'd scribbled 'Sam – b'day' and in a different pen at a later date had added '5.30' and underlined it heavily.

Family dinner, he remembered with an effort. His sister, Jill, still invited him to every family occasion, although he'd missed far more than he'd attended. He thought back, trying to remember her kids' ages, which birthday Sam was up to, and caught himself doing it by remembering which major case he'd been working when they'd been born. He grimaced. That sure made him a far better workaholic than an uncle.

He glanced at his watch again. If the Friday night traffic wasn't too bad, he'd probably make it to Jill's place almost on time. She was going to be impressed. Or die of shock.

Sam and Emma mightn't even recognise him, and the baby certainly wouldn't. But after these last weeks, he needed some level of normalcy for a while. Needed the reminder of why he did what he did: that there were good, ordinary people in the world who laughed and loved and treated each other decently and didn't have warehouses full of drugs and guns and corrupt cops on their payroll who'd arrange a murder for a thirty-thousand-dollar bonus.

He shut down his computer and headed to the car park, the wall of humid summer heat hitting him as he emerged from the air-conditioning. A cloying, suffocating heat, unlike the dry heat of Dungirri.

He didn't kid himself. Yes, he needed an evening at Jill's. But he was also going because Bob would be there and, more than sleep and rest, he needed to hear from Bob about Bella.

In the organised chaos at Jill's, while the kids played on the lawn, his mother and sister put salads together in the kitchen, and his brother-in-law, Terry, prepared the barbecue, Bob handed him a beer and sat beside him on the back step.

Straight out, without any preamble, he said, 'I had lunch with Bella a couple of days ago.'

Alec took a long sip of the cold, refreshing beer, wondering what was going on in the man's mind. He pretended a nonchalance he didn't feel and asked mildly, 'How is she?'

'Good. Very well. More at peace with herself, at last, and happier than she's been for a long time.' Underneath the light-hearted exterior his sharp eyes watched Alec closely. 'Are you going to see her this weekend?'

'No.' The single word cost a lot of effort to say.

Bob stared at him. 'Why not? Surely you don't have to work?'

Alec heaved a sigh, almost wished he hadn't come. 'I'm not going to see her again. So could we just leave it, please?'

'Not until you tell me whether this is because you don't care or because you do.'

Anger at Bob's interference burned briefly but he was too tired to maintain it. 'Yes, I care,' he admitted. 'But today I've just put Kevin Jones away for the second time, and he cursed me and mine the whole way to Long Bay jail.'

'You're thinking of Shani Webber,' Bob said quietly.

'Shani, Rick, my mother. Christ, Bob, I lead a unit that specialises in particularly violent homicides. That's not exactly conducive to happily-ever-afters. The divorce rate in the unit's sky high, and for the few whose relationships haven't cracked under the pressure there's always the risk that one day a bullet or a knife or an explosion will end it all.'

'It doesn't happen that way to everyone.'

'No, but the worry sucks people dry. I saw that with my mother. When the superintendent came to the door that night, she knew before he'd even said a word. She just crumpled on the doorstep. You think I want to do that, or worse, to Bella?'

'Your parents loved each other deeply and had fourteen very happy years together. Do you honestly think your mother would have swapped that for a longer time with a lesser man?'

Alec didn't answer, couldn't answer. Couldn't find his way through it to make any sense.

Bob must have figured he'd said enough. They sat in silence for a while. Alec took another slow mouthful of beer. It didn't make anything any clearer.

Bob spoke again eventually, shifting the subject. 'I had lunch with Bruce Fraser today. Your name came up in conversation.'

Alec raised a wary eyebrow. Assistant Commissioner Bruce Fraser, one of Bob's former colleagues and in charge of personnel for the police service. And Steve Fraser's father.

Bob threw him a sideways look. 'Seems they're having a bit of trouble filling positions at superintendent level lately. And now Ron Harrison from up the north coast has been put on indefinite sick leave and they're looking around for someone to act in his place. There's been a few problems up there and they need someone thorough, with credibility and good leadership skills. I suggested you.'

Alec took a few moments to absorb that. 'Thanks for the vote of confidence. But they'll want someone with more general policing experience, I'm sure. I've been out of that for years.'

'Don't sell yourself short, Alec. You have an excellent reputation for liaison with all branches. You've earned a lot of respect across the service for your role on the various review committees and the internal investigations you've been on. Your investigative and people management skills are just what that command needs right now.'

Alec frowned, bits of news he'd heard coming back to him. 'Isn't that where two detectives have been charged over an ecstasy supply ring? And the superintendent stuffed up the handling of sexual harassment complaints?'

'Amongst other things.' Bob grinned at him. 'At least you won't be bored up there in the sticks. Fraser's going to call you first thing Monday for a chat. If I was a betting man, I'd say it's yours if you want it. I know you can do a damn fine job cleaning up after Harrison's incompetence. He won't be coming back, of course, so there'll be a permanent vacancy eventually.'

Yours if you want it . . . Bob's words echoed in his head all through the lively family meal. Did he want it? Did he want to give up active investigative work for a management role? Sure, he'd taken on more and more management tasks as he'd risen up the ranks – he was no stranger to juggling significant resources and determining short and longer-term priorities for a large team – but did he want that on a full-time basis? He was meant to be a detective; ever since high school, all the way through basic police training and the obligatory time spent as a general duties cop, he'd known exactly where he was heading.

After the meal, he found himself again sitting on the back step, looking after his youngest niece, Chloe, while Sam and Emma had a last game of bucking broncos with their father and Bob before bedtime, and the words still chased round and round in his head: *Yours if you want it.*

The terraced backyard was cooler than the house, with the evening breeze relieving the dense humidity and bringing with it the sweet scent of a neighbour's honeysuckle – and a hundred memories of Bella.

Chloe sat contentedly on his lap, snuggled into the crook of his arm. In addition to the honeysuckle, baby smells assailed his nostrils – soap, milk, talcum powder. He rested his cheek for a moment against the downy softness of Chloe's hair, the painful yearning in his chest a lump of rock he had no idea how to dissolve.

His mother came and sat beside him. 'Do you want me to take Chloe?' she offered.

He tightened his arm around the child imperceptibly, strangely reluctant to let her go. 'No, she's fine.'

'You're quiet tonight.'

'Hmmm.'

'Is it the woman you rescued? Bella?'

Her perceptiveness caught him off-guard. 'How did you know?'

'I saw it on the news when you brought her out of the mine. I knew that you'd been hurting more than any person should.'

'That obvious, was I?' he said quietly.

'Only to me, and I guessed, I didn't know for sure. Bob's mentioned her a few times, as well. But next time you and Bob have a private chat, don't do it under an open window.'

'Oh.'

He didn't know what to say, couldn't remember the last time he'd shared anything private with his mother. With anyone...other than Bella. He stared out at Terry and Bob and the kids, engrossed in their game, Terry prancing like a wild horse with Sam clinging on, and Emma hanging on Bob's back, hooting with laughter every time he bucked.

'Jill and I used to play with Dad like that.'

He didn't realise he'd said it aloud, until she answered, 'I remember.'

She linked her arm in his and, after a few moments, said softly, 'Alec, I was just sixteen when I met him. Nineteen when I married him, and you were conceived. When he died... I had no experience of life without him to fall back on. I was still young, and all my adult life he'd been there. It took me a long, long time to learn to cope alone.'

She paused, faced him, and he noticed, maybe for the first time, that her eyes were no longer sad and lost, but gentler, wiser, and he wondered when that had happened, what he'd missed in his absorption with his work.

'Your Bella,' she continued, 'she's a grown woman, Alec. Strong, capable and experienced. Stronger than I was. Trust her to know what's right for her.'

Trust Bella. The memory of that last agonised morning broke from the wall he'd locked it behind and played through his head. She'd understood, stepped aside and let him go. Let him walk away to do the work he had to do.

But she hadn't said goodbye. She'd just said, *Don't let them win.*

The lump of rock in his chest cracked through, crumbled into smaller stones, and he sucked in a long, sweet breath of honeysuckle-scented air.

Her hands clasped around the pottery mug, Bella sipped the hot herbal tea and stared out the window into the night. The full moon bathed the muted shapes of the valley below the house and the hills beyond with a soft light, and in the garden a possum and her youngling wandered across the grass, unafraid.

In the moon-shadows among the trees a boobook owl called, the gentle two-note cadence peaceful in the semi-darkness.

She would miss this place when she left.

The leaving would be soon, although to where she didn't yet know. In the past six weeks she'd found her emotional strength again, had regained a balance long missing from her life. She could sleep, most nights, without nightmares, and she'd proved to herself she could go amongst crowds – even in the centre of Sydney at peak hour – without panic crushing her breath.

In the long, quiet hours, surrounded by the bushland and memories of her father's faith in her, she'd decided on her way forward – a way to bring together and make meaning of the various strands of her life, to contribute to the future. Her research proposal was drafted, and initial discussions with two universities about PhD studies were positive, so that she had only to decide which one to apply to – a university in Sydney, or the one further north, with academics already leading the field in research into rural crime and policing, but which was a long way from Sydney...and from Alec.

She took another sip of the soothing tea. On the TV news just now he'd looked drawn and weary, the gravel in his voice betraying the depth of disquiet underneath the stoicism. Absorbed all evening in her research proposal, she'd only caught the late news bulletin tonight – too late to call him, although the urge to pick up the phone tugged at her anyway.

Finn padded into the kitchen, slurped at the water in his bowl and then leaned against her leg. She dug her fingers into the thick, soft fur and kneaded his neck.

'What do you think, Finn boy? Do you reckon he's thinking about us right now?'

Finn tensed, ears pricking up, and a moment later she heard it too – the rumble of a car engine. A sweep of light flashed over the glass of the window as the vehicle swung in to park in front of the house.

Her instant wariness – the reality of being alone in the bush but for Finn – evaporated the moment she recognised the car.

A silver sedan, just as he'd driven last time.

With his normal excitement for any visitor, Finn raced to the door, whining and butting his nose against it, and she tried to hold on to his collar to stop him dashing out as she opened it. She didn't succeed.

When Finn saw the man at the foot of the veranda steps, he jerked out of her hold and leapt down to greet him. Although he refrained from jumping up and licking his face

– she'd been working on his training – his exuberant prancing almost knocked Alec off-balance.

Leaning against the doorframe, Bella watched Alec crouch beside the dog and rub his ears. Waves of emotion rose and engulfed her heart. Relief, delight, excitement. Joy and gratitude that she was here and whole and able to give again. Pride – in him, in herself, in what they'd already achieved, individually and together.

Love.

The word slipped naturally into her thoughts, without argument or doubt.

Alec gave Finn a last pat and rose to his feet. In the light from the house she could see the uncertainty behind the smile in his eyes, and the depths of seriousness that would always linger, not let him take anything for granted. And she accepted that they'd always be there, just as they were with her, because both of them had walked through too many dark places to ever take happiness lightly.

He stepped up the first few steps and paused.

'I probably shouldn't have come so late, but… I wanted to see you, Bella.'

She smiled, uncaring that tears of joy welled, and held out her hand to him. 'I'm very glad you're here.'

His fingers closed warm and firm around hers, and she led him inside.

ACKNOWLEDGMENTS

No book is written in a vacuum, especially not a first book. I am indebted to many people who have supported me and this novel on the journey to publication.

The Romance Writers of Australia and the Romance Writers of America offer their members incredible resources, and wonderful camaraderie, at conferences and online, and I have benefited from being a part of these amazing groups. I was deeply honoured to be a finalist in Romance Writers of America's prestigious Golden Heart Award in 2007, but I was even more touched by the warmth and generosity of the members of both associations, who made winning the award such a special experience.

My particular group of online writing friends who congregate in the BatCave and the Belfry have joked, commiserated and cheered with me through all the ups and downs of the writing life. Their wit, humour and friendship have brightened my day, every day for five years.

My agent, Clare Forster, publisher, Bernadette Foley, and all of the team at Hachette Livre Australia have been a dream to work with. I am incredibly grateful to them for having such faith in the book, and for turning a manuscript into a polished, visually beautiful, published novel.

Gemma Gallagher generously gave of her time to meet with me, and then to read the entire manuscript. Her advice on police procedure and police life in remote communities has been invaluable, and is sincerely appreciated. Any errors and literary licence are my own responsibility.

My parents, my sisters, and all the family have been unstinting in their encouragement of my dreams, and enthusiastic and practical in their support; reading manuscripts, brainstorming scenes, and gently kicking my proverbial butt when I needed it.

Gordon has patiently put up with my distracted writer's brain, brought me chocolate fudge when I've been glued to the computer for hours, and brought home French Champagne to celebrate each success on the way. Real love is not only in the big things, but in those small, everyday gifts of sharing and caring. I am truly a fortunate woman.

INTRODUCING

DARK COUNTRY

ALSO BY BRONWYN PARRY

COMING SOON FROM PIATKUS

ONE

He shouldn't have come back. Gil's hands tightened on the steering wheel as he approached the bend in the road where everything had fallen apart, half a lifetime ago.

For an instant he considered slamming on the brakes and turning around, getting the hell out of the area, driving through the night and the rain to get back to Sydney and far, far away from his past. He should have taken it as a bad sign when the direct route to Dungirri was closed due to flooding, and he'd had to take the long detour, looping an extra two hours' drive through Birraga to come into Dungirri from the west, passing the place where one set of nightmares had ended, and another begun.

The tall gum trees bordered the road, ghostly white trunks catching the headlights, twisted branches like fingers reaching out as menacingly as the memories.

He gritted his teeth. Memories couldn't affect him now. He wouldn't let them affect him. He'd just go to Dungirri, do what he'd come to do, and leave again.

He took the bend slower, cautiously, exhaling pent-up breath when the road proved clear. No kangaroos this time. In the shadows just off the road, he could barely see the eerie shape of a particular huge tree, but his mind's eye still filled with the vivid image of another time, when it had stood with a vehicle wrapped around it, the drooping branches scraping over the roof and the flashing lights of emergency vehicles surreal in the once-peaceful darkness. His gut clenched tight, and the recollection of the sharp, nauseating scents of blood, petrol, eucalyptus and alcohol came to him again, as though the mix was permanently scarred into his nostrils.

He stared ahead, determined to keep his brain as focused on the road as his eyes. Twenty kilometres to go. Fifteen minutes at most, as long as the rain didn't get heavier again.

The shadow of Ghost Hill rose to his left, as ethereal in the lightning and rain as its name, and the road curved around to nestle into its base. As he came out onto a straighter stretch, a vehicle on the side of the road began to flash blue and red lights. He glanced down at the speedometer and swore. Just his damned luck – seven kilometres over the speed limit, and the Dungirri cops were ready with a special welcoming party, just for him. If he'd needed any confirmation that coming back was one hell of a mistake, he'd just got it.

The cop, swathed in reflective wet weather gear, stood in the middle of the road with a torch and signalled him to pull over. He wound down the window but kept his eyes forward, schooling himself not to respond to the triumphant look on the old sergeant's face when he recognised him.

He jerked his head around when a definitely female voice said, 'Sorry to pull you over, Sir. I was hoping it was one of the locals. Were you by any chance planning to stop in Dungirri?'

'Yes,' he replied slowly, searching for the sarcasm in her voice. After flicking the light quickly around the interior, she turned the torch sideways, so that it didn't shine in his face, yet provided some light for both of them. Under the dripping brim of her hat he caught a glimpse of lively blue eyes and a few wisps of red hair around her face. Not a face he knew, which, given he'd been away so long, shouldn't have surprised him.

'Oh, good. Would you mind doing me a favour? Could you get someone to phone my constable and tell him the patrol car's bogged out here? Just ask anyone – they all know him.'

He stared at her, trying to make sense of her unexpected request. 'You can use my mobile, if you like.'

She grinned – an open, friendly grin that he wasn't used to seeing on police. 'If it works out here then your phone company performs miracles. It's a notorious dead spot – the hill's between us and the towers, and blocks the phone and the police radio, which is why I flagged you down.'

He glanced at his phone in its holder on the dashboard. Sure enough, no signal.

'I could give you a lift into town.' Hell, had those words come from his mouth? He'd avoided police as much as possible all his life, and for good reason.

She smiled again, shook her head. 'Thanks, but I'll be fine. If you could just make sure the message gets to Adam – Constable Donahue – I'll wait here until he comes.'

Despite the perfectly reasonable logic, her refusal gouged across the old scars that he realised now were still so raw. Yeah, well, what did you expect, his inner voice taunted him.

'No offence intended,' she added quickly, as if he'd frowned.

Something about the way she grinned at him, like an equal, kicked logic back in again. No sane woman would get into a car with a strange man, miles from anywhere. He knew he looked like someone you definitely didn't want to meet in a dark alley, and he'd been in enough dark alleys in his life to know he lived up to that impression. In his black T-shirt and well-worn leather jacket, he certainly didn't fit the image of safe, respectable citizen – more like the type that most cops itched to arrest, without bothering to ask questions first.

He understood, accepted, her refusal, yet the idea of leaving her here, alone in the dark and out of radio contact, didn't sit comfortably on his conscience.

'Maybe I could help you get your car out?'

'Thanks for the offer, but it'll need the four-wheel drive and the winch. It's in a ditch, and the entire road shoulder is axle-deep in mud.' She gave a rueful shake of her head. 'You'd think that after ten years out in the bush I wouldn't be stupid enough to swerve to avoid a kangaroo on a wet night, but I did. At least I didn't hit a tree.'

He had just enough presence of mind to turn his head away before he betrayed his shock. The parallels brought the other memories crowding back, so intense they stopped the breath in his throat.

Yeah, coming back to Dungirri had definitely been a bad idea.

Kris caught the instant of bleakness in his shadowed eyes before he jerked his gaze away. So, the granite-faced man was human, after all.

Already off-kilter from the shock of running off the road, the thought of waiting out here in the rain another hour or so longer didn't appeal. She didn't dare sit in the patrol car – maybe it was stupid, but she couldn't help the feeling that the car was on the verge of tipping over onto its side in the mud. So, stand alone in the darkness and rain on jelly legs for fifty minutes or more, or risk going in a car with a guy who made James Dean look like an angel?

A flash of lightning almost overhead heralded a smashing of thunder that had her ducking her head instinctively. Just her luck that the long drought was being interrupted with a thunderstorm on the one night she'd skidded the car into a ditch.

The man yanked the keys out of the ignition and thrust them at her through the window.

'Take my car. I'll wait here till you get back.'

Maybe the thunder had befuddled her brain, because she couldn't for a moment work out what he meant, but realisation came as he opened the door and got out of the car.

In the torchlight he looked tall and dark and potentially dangerous, six-foot of muscle, with an unsmiling face that had seen more than a fist or two over the years. Even a knife, if she read the scar on the side of his cheek right. Eyes dark in more than just colour met hers, and his scowl suggested one hell of a bad mood.

Not a man to mess with, and sure as heck not the average guardian angel.

Yet, in some bizarre way, she trusted him. He stood several non-threatening feet from her, shoulders hunched against the rain, water already dripping from his black hair onto his leather jacket.

'I can't do that.'

'Yeah, well I'm not going to leave a woman out here alone without radio or phone, cop or no cop. So take my damn car.'

Light exploded nearby, with an instantaneous crash of thunder so loud it jarred every bone and muscle in her body and pounded her eardrums. A tree a hundred metres down the road flared a brief light before being doused by the rain.

'You all right?' He reached a hand out, touched her on the arm. At least she wasn't the only one shaking. That lot of lightning had been way too close for comfort.

She gave a nervous laugh. 'I will be, when my heart starts again. Okay, you can give me a lift into town. I don't plan on becoming a human lightning rod. Have you got room in the back for a couple of boxes? The senior sergeant at Birraga will kill me if the new computer gets drowned in mud.'

The two computer boxes were on the near side of the patrol car, held in place by less precious boxes of stationery, so she didn't have to wade into the muddy ditch to retrieve them. The guy took the heavier one from her, stowed it in the empty boot of his car while she brought the smaller box.

Wherever he was going, he was travelling light, her observant cop eye noticed as she slid off her wet jacket, shook it out and folded it so it wouldn't drip water everywhere. A slightly battered kit bag lay on the back seat, a laptop case on the floor, and that was it. No maps, no fast food containers, no CDs, no general bits and pieces that might accumulate on a trip or in daily use. Probably seven or eight years old, the car was clean – not sparkling rental-car clean, more not-used-often-at-all sort of clean.

She scrambled into the passenger seat, out of the rain, putting her jacket onto the floor beside her. He shucked off his leather jacket, too, before he got in, tossing it over onto the back seat. He wasn't fussy about a bit of water on his seat, then.

'Thank you, Mr...?

The interior light was still on, and she saw something dark flicker in his eyes.

'Just call me Gil.'

Oh, yes, she knew an evasion when she saw it. So why would a man offer her his car and then not give a surname? He could have just driven off when she'd first asked him to contact Adam, and she probably wouldn't have even taken his registration number.

'Thanks... Gil.' She emphasised his name enough to let him know she hadn't missed the evasion. 'I'm Kris Matthews.'

He pulled his door shut properly, and the interior light flicked off so that she could no longer see him clearly. Only a profile silhouette, stark and sharp.

'Buckle up, Sergeant Matthews,' was all he said in response to her introduction, and he clicked his own seatbelt into its clasp before he turned the key in the ignition.

So, Mr Cool and Distant had recognised the sergeant's stripes on her uniform shirt after she'd taken her raincoat off. Sharp of him. And Mr Cool and Distant wasn't overly fond of police, it seemed, for all that he'd offered to wait in the rain while she took his car.

Too bad for him. He was heading into her town, and these days she was pretty damn protective of it.

'You're not from around here?' she asked.

He put the car into gear, pulled out on to the road before he answered. 'Not any more.'

One of those who'd left over the years, then. Dungirri had been bleeding population for decades, dying the slow death of many rural communities. Tragedies in the past two years had torn it apart further, and on bad days Kris had her doubts it would ever recover. On good days, she hoped the recently formed Dungirri Progress Association might have some success in rebuilding the community. Good days didn't happen too often.

'Have you come back for the ball on Saturday?'

An eyebrow rose. 'The ball?'

'The Dungirri Spring Ball.'

No, he'd obviously not heard of it, and come to think of it, she really couldn't imagine this man in the Memorial Hall, mixing with Dungirri's citizens. It would be like throwing a panther in with a cage full of chickens.

'No. I'm just here to see someone on…business.'

He didn't explain further – another evasion. He'd lived in these parts, knew that everyone knew everyone else, but he mentioned no names, gave no hint of his business, as a local would have.

Not a good sign.

They came out of the shadow of Ghost Hill, and within two minutes his mobile phone bleeped in its holder. Perhaps mindful of her beside him, he grabbed the headset draped on the phone with one hand and slid it on before punching the answer button.

'What's up, Liam?' He listened for a moment. 'Fuck.' Definitely bad news, by the harshness of the word and the way his jaw clenched tight. Another pause. 'She's all right?' A gruff note touched his voice, a hint of real concern.

She tried not to watch him, to give him a semblance of privacy, but in the silence as he listened, she saw out of the corner of her eye his fingers gripping tight on the steering wheel, and although he didn't stop driving, he slowed a little.

'Look, take Deb away with you for a few days' break, okay?' he said. 'To that eco-lodge she was raving about, or somewhere like that. Tell her it's a surprise bonus from me for the two of you. Charge everything to the business account.' Another pause, and his tone hardened again. 'I've already dealt with Marci. You look after Deb. Might be best if you get her away from there tonight. I'll call you tomorrow.'

He ended the call, muttering another curse under his breath as he dragged the earpiece off.

'Bad news?' she enquired. She couldn't pretend she hadn't heard his side of the conversation.

She counted to four before he eventually said, 'One of my employees was attacked by an intruder at her home.'

She had the distinct impression that, while that might be the truth, it wasn't the whole truth.

'Is she hurt?'

'Only shaken. She has a black belt in karate.'

'So the attacker came off worst?'

In the dim light from the dashboard she saw the corner of his mouth twitch, for just an instant. 'Yeah. Something like that.' But his mouth firmed again straight away, and he stared ahead, tapping a finger on the steering wheel, his expression tense and shuttered.

And, although she wondered, she didn't ask why a man would send two of his staff away for an all-expenses-paid break just because one of them was shaken up. Or what sort of business he ran, that was profitable enough to give generous bonuses and brought him back to Dungirri for a meeting. Or what the rest of the bad news was that made his mood even darker than it had been when she'd met him on the road.

She didn't ask because she suddenly had a strong suspicion that she might not like the answers.

She let her head fall back on the headrest, closed her eyes in weariness. They were almost at Dungirri, and if the guy had dastardly intentions towards her he would have acted on them by now. Her trust that he'd get her there safely seemed well enough placed.

But then again, that proved nothing. She'd been neighbours with a murderer for years and never twigged. Just-call-me-Gil could be a dark angel straight from Hell, for all that she felt safe, just now.

If he planned on staying around, she'd have to damn well ask those questions, and find out, one way or another.

She just hoped he didn't plan on staying around. 'Safe' wasn't a word that was likely to stick to him, long term, and Dungirri had had more than its share of visits from Hell already.

Gil silently ran through every single swear word he knew, and made up a few more when they ran out.

There had to be something about this damned road, because the last time he'd been on it, his plans for a new life had been smashed to smithereens, and now, tonight – almost eighteen years later, and the first day of what was supposed to have been another new start – Liam's news had brought that all crashing down.

Damn Vincenzo Russo for getting himself shot twice in the chest last night. It was lousy frigging timing for Vince's personal security to fail him, as far as Gil was concerned. With Vince on life support, his son Tony would waste no time in moving to take control of the Russo family operations – and Tony had neither reason nor inclination to honour the agreement that had kept Vince out of Gil's affairs for years. Gil's plans of being long gone from Sydney by the time Tony eventually took over had just been screwed, well and truly.

The sergeant had gone quiet, stopped her questions. With her head back, eyes closed, a hint of vulnerability underlay the confident cop persona she'd shown earlier. Wayward curls of rich red hair framed her face, and a few wet ends curled against the pale skin of her neck, just above her shirt collar. For some reason, that sight gave him a sharp, hot kick in the guts.

He turned his gaze back to the road. Oh, yeah, lusting after a *cop*, in Dungirri, of all places – that truly made the definition of stupidity.

Christ, he hadn't even given her his surname, because even if she hadn't heard of him, she'd have made the connection between his name and that of his old man, and those blue eyes would have turned cold, lumping him with the same label as his mad bastard of a father.

And if the locals had told her about him, or if she'd heard the other end of that phone call…well, she'd sure be doubting the wisdom of getting into a car with him.

And what did it all matter, anyway? In just a few minutes he'd drop her off at the cop station, and he'd never see her and her lively blue eyes again. He'd go and call on Jeanie, do what he'd come to do, and then he'd leave Dungirri forever, get back on the road and try to sort out the god-awful mess his life had just become, before Tony Russo took his vendetta out on people who didn't deserve it, like Liam and Deb.

The dim lights of Dungirri appeared in the darkness, and he shifted down a gear as he came to the first scattered houses. Another landslide of bad memories tumbled out thick and fast from the dark places in his mind, catching him unawares, jumbling on top of his current worries and making his gut coil tight.

Damn his memories. Damn this town. Damn that stupid conviction that he'd had to come back here, finish once and for all with his past before he moved on. Dungirri held nothing for him but bitterness and nightmares.

As he drove into town and along the deserted, mostly dark main street, a line from something he'd once read suddenly appeared in his mind like some premonition and drummed again and again in his head: *The wheel has come full circle; I am here.*

Well, he might be here, but he wouldn't be for long.

The old police station hadn't changed much. A new keypad security system, a phone link to connect straight through to Birraga for when the local cops were out, and a coat of paint were about the only differences Gil could discern on the outside. When the sergeant opened up the station and he carried the larger of the computer boxes in for her, he saw that the wooden 1950s chairs in the small reception area had been replaced by 1970s orange plastic chairs.

So much for progress.

She pushed open the door to the interview room. 'In here, thanks, Gil. I have to make space in the office first before I set it up in there.'

Hell, it would have to be the interview room. Definitely a place he had no desire to linger. He slid the box onto the table in the small room, made for the door again without letting himself check if it was the same wooden table he'd had his face smashed into.

On the veranda, he sucked in a breath of fresh, damp air.

'Are you staying at the hotel?' the sergeant asked him. 'Can I shout you a drink, later, to thank you for your help?'

He turned round to her, and the light from the porch illuminated her in the doorway. Not a classically beautiful face, yet attractive in her own way, and small lines around her eyes revealed that under the aura of relaxed competence she carried tension and concerns. Well, if she'd been in town longer than a year or so, she'd have had more than enough stress and worry. Two abducted kids and several murders couldn't have been easy for any cop to deal with, let alone one who seemed to have a whole lot more soul than the old sergeant had ever had.

Kris Matthews, he recalled. A woman with a name and a history, not just 'the sergeant' as he'd called her in his mind – since there could be no point in thinking about her as a real person.

'I'm not staying,' he told her.

She stepped out, directly under the light, so that it glinted in the red-gold of her hair, but cast her face into shadow.

'Oh. Well, thank you for the lift. I do appreciate it. And drive safely, wherever you're going.'

He raised a hand in acknowledgement, took the three steps down from the porch in one pace, and strode to his car.

He drove back down the main street, past the empty shops and the few businesses still struggling to survive, past the council depot, the pub, and pulled into the empty parking area of the Truck Stop Café. It was only eight o'clock, and lights spilled from the café, but other than a couple of teenage kids laughing at the counter, he could see no one inside. Jeanie might well be in the kitchen, or in the residence upstairs.

He pushed the door open, and both kids watched him enter. The girl, maybe sixteen or so, wore a blue 'Truck Stop' apron over her jeans and T-shirt, the fabric of the apron stretching over an obviously pregnant belly. The lad, sweeping up behind the till, might have been a year or two older. So, Jeanie was still giving employment to Dungirri's youth.

The girl smiled. 'Hi, there. I'm afraid the kitchen's closed, if you were after a meal, but I can still do coffees and there's pies and sausage rolls left.'

The mention of food made his gut do an uneasy somersault. It had been a while since he'd eaten, but his appetite had disappeared somewhere on the road to Dungirri.

'No, that's okay. I was looking for Jeanie Menotti, actually. Is she around?'

'I'm sorry, she's out tonight. There's a meeting to finalise the ball arrangements. She won't be back until late.'

Of course – the damn ball the sergeant had mentioned. As incongruous as a ball in Dungirri sounded, if there was going to be one, then Jeanie would be involved in running it.

It just put one hell of a spanner in his plans to be out of here tonight. For a brief moment, he contemplated leaving an envelope for her with these kids, but he ditched that idea straight away. Jeanie would be more than hurt if he went without seeing her, and Jeanie, of all people, didn't deserve that sort of shoddy treatment.

'What time does she open in the morning, these days?' he asked the kids.

'Six-thirty. I'm opening up for her tomorrow, but she'll be around not long after that,' the girl answered, and something about the way she smiled struck him with a vague sense of familiarity. Probably the daughter of someone he'd once known – although, in his day, Dungirri kids hadn't worn multiple studs in their ears and nose. A touch of the city, out here in the outback.

'Thanks. I'll call in tomorrow, then.'

Out in his car again, he thumped the steering wheel in frustration. He'd be spending the night in Dungirri. He could sleep in the car, out on one of the tracks that spider-webbed through the scrub east of town…no, not a good idea. All day in the car had been more than enough for a tall body more used to standing than sitting, and he had the return journey to make tomorrow.

He reversed out, swung around to park in the side street beside the hotel, away from the half-dozen other vehicles parked randomly out the front.

Harsh weather and neglect had worn away at the century-old hotel. The timberwork cried out for a coat of paint, and the wrought-iron railings around the upstairs veranda were more rust-coloured than anything else. The 'For Sale' sign tied crookedly to a post had faded in the weather, too, adding another forlorn voice to the visible tale of lost glory.

He yanked his bag and his laptop out of the back and went in through the side door, avoiding the front bar. The back bar was dark and empty, as was the office. He tapped on the servery window into the front bar, keeping out of the line of sight of the customers. He had no desire to meet up with any familiar faces from his past.

A young bloke in his early twenties in a work shirt and

jeans finished pulling a beer and strolled over to him. Not anyone he knew.

'Have you got a room for the night?' Gil asked.

'Sure, mate.' He reached into a drawer, passed a key and a registration book across the counter. 'Room three, upstairs. Just sign here. You wanna pay in the morning, or fix it up now?'

Gil paid cash, signed the book with an unreadable scrawl the guy didn't bother looking at, and headed up the stairs. The room was basic, as he'd expected, relatively clean but with tired, ancient furnishings that had seen a few decades of use already.

He dropped his bag on the floor, lay flat on his back on the bed and stared up at the old pressed-metal ceiling. A few creaking springs warned him that it wouldn't be the most comfortable of nights. He'd coped with far worse.

Staring at the ceiling only let his brain wander to places he didn't want to contemplate, and his body clock wouldn't be ready for sleep until at least his usual time of two or three in the morning. He swung his legs back over the edge of the bed again, hauled out his laptop and set it up on the small, scratched wooden table in the corner, draping the cord over the bed to get to the single power point. The room had no phone line or wireless network – the twenty-first century hadn't made it to Dungirri, yet, it seemed – but after a moment's hesitation, Gil plugged the laptop into his mobile phone and connected to his account. It wasn't as though he had to worry about the expense, after all.

For an hour he worked, tidying up the loose ends of the business he'd just sold, checking and sending email, making payments to creditors, transferring funds between accounts. And all the time, the half of his brain that wasn't dealing with facts and figures tussled with other questions – like who the hell might have had the balls and the opportunity to shoot Vince, and what the response of his various rivals would be.

Maybe Tony would be too caught up in fighting for power to pursue his long-desired vengeance.

Gil dismissed that hope as quickly as he thought of it. Tony would view getting even with him as a sign of his new authority, and a message to anyone who might stand in his way.

Somewhere around nine-thirty, the single light bulb in the room pinged and went out. A light still burned outside on the veranda – just his bulb blowing then, not a loss of power.

Reluctantly, he headed downstairs to ask for a replacement. In the corridor behind the bar, an older guy swung out of the gents' just as Gil passed, almost knocking him with the door.

The bloke turned around to apologise, and Gil stifled a groan as they recognised each other. His bad luck was still holding strong. Of all the people in Dungirri to come face to face with.

The man's face whitened. 'You...' He seemed to struggle for control, pain and rage contorting his face, and lost it. He raised a fist, took a step toward Gil and roared, 'You murdering bastard.'